LIBERTY
EPIC OF SHADOWS
Revised Edition

The Libertad 1640

L. A. Espriux

Song of Xeantee Aconee

His star wondrous appears in heaven bright
Shadows awake from ancient sleep
Prince Aconee borne upon wings of night
Frogs congregate children at his feet
Peace made in Valley Xeantee

Face in a canyon grins sepulcher white
Place Fallen Eagle makes his nest
And walks still an Indian spirit blind of sight
His soul stripped naked without rest
Bones forgotten in Valley Xeantee

Blood weeping at first morning light
Recalling sin of the father's shame
Summer flies consume his flesh into twilight
The beaver proclaims treachery of his name
Violence remembered in Valley Xeantee

Xeantee Aconee where fountains meet
Frogs singing his chorus tonight
Souls rise from graves buried deep
Legions resurrected into hoary flight
Days restored in Valley Xeantee

Translated by: Jeremiah Wake

Author's Note:

Many authors and critics have asked me why I chose to name my book **Liberty Epic of Shadows**. My response has always been because it can be classified no other way. I, therefore, challenge the reader to question what is meaning of an epic. There are two potential responses to this query dependent upon reference. The academic assessment is that an epic conforms to a literary construction of grandiose genealogy usually expanded through elaborate historical context. The second is that it stems from classical origin, thus metaphorically transcending contemporary society by measure of the ongoing human experience. This book fits both these conditions, exceeding the mechanics of what it means to be within present value. **Liberty Epic of Shadows** describes concept of necessity distorted through consumption of desire. It discerns difference between spirit and religion, between knowledge and indoctrination, and between truth and convenience. Most of all **Liberty Epic of Shadows** unmasks the irrefutable shadow of mortal fear: time and the inevitable meaning of time being the greatest of all fear. We remain conditioned to believe in quantum reality of a lie. This lie perpetrated through actions and desires not truly our own, but cultivated by a mind trapped within a collapsing singularity. It is this mind that makes mankind enemies in the name of mankind. A mind that hungers for blood of human sacrifice, distorts proportionate measure of practical need, and promises love in the name of passion. An insatiable appetite that can never be satisfied, it makes all believe that emptiness of its hunger the only definition of necessity. This book promises to take you on an adventure through passage of time and possibility, beginning from an arbitrary point, and expanding into all directions, touching principalities past, present, and future. Grounded in a history we think to know, it scratches away veneer of heroic adulation, while at the same time piecing together puzzle of a past of conjectured potential. The characters are real within context of the stage set, each snared in mortal conflict; each forced to make an ultimate choice with eternal consequence. But some are chosen from the beginning, whose destiny not according to design of this world. Liberty Epic of Shadows is a story pieced together and retold by the character Jeremiah Wake, a simple educated man who just wanted to know. What he ultimately learns is astonishing even to him. Every writer harbors one story, which excels above all others. **Liberty Epic of Shadows** is that expression. Soul of the author unveiled.

L. A. Espriux

Acknowledgement to the Book Illustrators
Special Thanks to the creativity of the Artists

Front Cover Design and Original Artwork in Acrylic
By Cendi Baugus

Back Cover Design and Original Artwork
By Jean Hamby Baugus

1st Illustration The Libertad 1640
By Bonnie Blackmon Guirguis

2st Illustration Temples of the Gods
By Cendi Baugus

3rd Illustration *Final Voyage*
By Cendi Baugus

4rd Illustration Tahmoh and the Angeni-Cuauhtemoc
By Bonnie Blackmon Guirguis

5th Illustration Until the King Shall Come
By Bonnie Blackmon Guirguis

6th Illustration Revelations Begin
By Bonnie Blackmon Guirguis

7th Illustration *Seeds of Eden*
By Bonnie Blackmon Guirguis

8th Illustration Kingdom Restored
By Bonnie Blackmon Guirguis

9th Illustration *Lost Liberty*
By Cendi Baugus

10th Illustration The Past Remembered
By Bonnie Blackmon Guirguis

Table of Contents

TEMPLES OF GODS

BOOK 3 *UNTIL THE KING SHALL COME*

BOOK 4 *REVELATIONS BEGIN*

BOOK 5 *SEEDS FROM EDEN*

.

BOOK 6 *PRINCE OF FROGS*

BOOK 7 *PROMISE OF THE HEREAFTER*

BOOK 8 *THE PAST REMEMBERED*

L. A. Espriux

Temples of Gods

The Prologue

Cities of El Dorado

Two shadows slither alone glistening walls of a siliceous passage gutted into the limestone *Cenote* before drowning of a world that once was. They descend as shades into the serpentine labyrinth guided by struggling flame of a lighted torch feeble against pressing darkness. There is no turning back now.

Faint pulse of a malignant presence resonates below. Something neither alive nor dead entombed deep in the heart of this oppressive place. It has a name no one dares speak. Trapped body of an immortal appeased only by blood of human sacrifice that flows along ziggurat steps of the nearby city, representing apex of a rival civilization discovered at end of the earth.

They call this particular architecture *Pyramid of the Sun*, a geometry constructed by gods of antiquity, old as the ancient tombs of Egypt awaiting zodiac rebirth. In this pleasure dome is another promise of glittering riches enshrined to Mammon soon to fully awake.

The two emissaries from vast extremes of the world only eye each other apprehensively. Neither trusts the other, both prepared for more bloodletting. Was it so long ago that the illusion of friendship melded hopes of these two men from different societies? Once they spoke together as men desiring friendship. They happily share banquets of exotic fruits and fowl prepared exclusively for the King's table. Together they toast a lasting federation and drink from the same crystal cup oblations of wine originating from a region the Spaniard calls *Raventos Codornia*. All before knowledge of this place-- the time for words now long passed!

King Montezuma had welcomed this man of marvelous appearance with such gifts that should have satisfied the desire of any deity. Would a stranger have known the ancient scrolls so well, or the expectant longing in a King's soul? Could one born of mortal vision have conjured so perfectly the timely arrival of this grandiose presence adorned in shining armor and seated anthropomorphically upon a white beast never before seen?

The Emperor of Tenochtitlan remembers well the day this Spaniard arrives with his legions on steps of the grand ziggurat city. *Indeed, how can he ever forget!* In beginning, they call his name *Quetzalcoatl*, which from ancient dialect means, "*Feathered Serpent.*" How readily they accept this returning god with expectant adoration, as children might admire the return of a long departed father. How prophetically true *Quetzalcoatl* fulfills meaning of his name.

King Montezuma had envisioned future security and peace for his people through this alliance. Time of peace ended, as now the ninth king of a once great Mesoamerican empire and all of *Mexica,* unwilling hostages to the unpredictable whims of this foreigner with eyes of a devil! His only desire the lust for gold and silver buried within the vault of this cursed treasure house. His only true devotion pledged to an even viler evil seated upon throne of a distant principality from across the vast water whose time has come.

An already fragile alliance with the kingdom's neighbors grows weaker, fueled by rumor that an unknown pestilence has begun to spread in diver's places. Now hated by even his most loyal citizens, Montezuma stands isolated, alone against the armored presence of this driven soul.

Forced against his will to bring the Conquistador into the most hallowed shrine, the king has committed the worse kind of sacrilege. This place feared by even powerful Shamans, a temple sacred, constructed by ancient gods. No sacrifice can save them now-- no earthly force greater than the determined zeal of this man and his armored army. Awake in a nightmare, the final aristocratic monarch of Tenochtitlan considers too late the imminent jeopardy he and his citizens now face. If only wealth of the gods they want, then pray let these men of strange customs have it all and be gone! Do these Spaniards not know to what principality the gold really belongs? Do they not know the vengeance that will follow, as hounds chasing the scent of fresh blood?

They enter a gaping hall that travels along the interior base of this clandestine structure guarded by statues of frog-like creatures wearing animal masks with twisted faces. Perhaps the Shaman would have led the way into a gauntlet of demonic channels laced with deadly booby traps. The king provided knowledge of only one access. Besides-- this Conquistador is a shrewd one, able to sense subterfuge, charmed with the instinct of destiny! Would some other way make any difference?

Arriving at a dead-end, Montezuma apprehensively reaches his hand into a camouflaged recess and pulls the concealed lever hidden inside the crevice. The adjacent wall pivots slowly inward, a bone-grinding grate of rock against rock, triggering precision sequences of weights and counter weights of carefully designed mechanisms within the structure.

Floor of a pit ignites instantly with mounds of burning bullion and silver ingots, encrusted with glowing embers of precious stones speckled at the base of two brazen pillars smelted from "*tumbaga*," a composition of copper and gold. Ascending grandiose and straddling these pillars stands a gigantic effigy with twisted demonic face.

"En nombre del padre!" Cries the Conquistador astonished.

By some ingenious arrangement of polished mirrors, sunlight reflects through quartz windows placed at the temple peak of this ancient pyramid. Treasures of the earth scattered everywhere just for the taking, representing mere pretty ornaments to these South American societies.

The man from across the ocean raises his hands against the consuming brilliance. Never in his dreams could he have imagined any presence more magnificent! It is his soul reborn, magnified by the spirit of this place. His birthright at last discovered-- promise of an earthly estate his for the taking! Now Cortez knows why they call this location *The City of Gold. Legends of El Dorado true after all!*

Removing his glistening helmet and filling the cast overflowing with fiery embers, the one called *Quetzalcoatl* ascends over the subjugated sovereign as shadow of a dark angel etched in consuming light.

This moment the last bloodline ruler of the Aztec Empire understands fully name and intent of this harbinger commissioned by foreign invasion. Now that it is too late, a king of foolish dreams comprehends future fate of his doomed kingdom. He submissively bows his head and weeps, a man defeated. In his heart, Emperor Montezuma knows the pit of Pandora opened at last, unleashing bound legions within.

Here marks beginning of bloodlust, a rebellion destined to run course, as it has run before, leeching once again into the feverous soul of humanity. In months to come even streets of Tenochtitlan City will run red with blood of tired resistance. The priests slaughtered first, along with hosts of terrible protectorates slain by fire-sticks that spit smoke and death. Then begins the pillage of a culture destined to ruin.

According to legend, the first *Mexica* settlers to arrive on the swampy inlet call this Aztec valley *Anahuac*, a word meaning *'surrounded by water.'* Upon witnessing the sign of an eagle perched upon a cactus, they receive divine instruction from one of their patron gods, named *Huitzilopochtli,* to establish residence upon the soggy inlet isles of Lake *Texcoco.* In a nearby valley to the northeast are ruins of an ancient civilization the Aztec call *Teotihuacan.* Here intact foundations of two great pyramids rise out of the jungle referred to as, *The Sun* and *The Moon,* believed built by the gods with special celestial alignment to the mountain of Cerro Gordo and the cosmos beyond.

After establishment of a forced treaty with the neighboring city-states of the *Texcocans* and *Tacubans*, the Aztecs remain secure in the belief of immunity from foreign invasion. Through many centuries, they flourish prosperously, serving the capricious whims of their bloodthirsty deities, thinking themselves center of the universe. Never could they have imagined a peril of such magnitude against their rooted principality. Never has a force of such military superiority come against them, as the one invited openly into their grandest city. This peaceful metropolis is first to fall of many once great civilizations on the *New World* continent.

Systematic invasion of the Americas begins thirty years earlier in the summer of 1492 when Italian explorer, Christopher Columbus, sets sail from the coast of Spain with three ships to cross the great expanse of unmapped ocean in quest for fabled riches of the West Indies. That same summer Queen Isabella the First, and Ferdinand the Second, issue the Alhambra Decree, forcing all practicing Jews out of their joint kingdoms. The Basque registered *Santa Maria,* along with two smaller ships, named *La Pinta* and *La Nina* bravely navigate uncharted seas manned by poorer citizens, fortune hunters, and some now without a country. They land on an island in the Caribbean; christened Hispaniola-- *but here Columbus finds no gold.*

After this fruitless expedition, future explorers learn from the indigenous populations about vast resources of wealth on the nearby isles. King Ferdinand of Spain commands the treasures extracted and transported back at any cost. First Santo Domingo, followed by Cuba, as both surrender their catches of gold and silver. Mapping out the chain of landmasses spread upon the turquoise ocean, like inviting breadcrumbs, dedicated seekers of wealth unearth even greater buried riches hidden on Puerto Rico and Jamaica. As compensation, these island populations enslaved or murdered. Then in the year of 1518, *Juan de Grijava* arrives, exploring the North American territory known as Tabasco, populated by natives identified as Chontales. These Spaniards are astonished that the local inhabitants serve them on utensils made of gold, a plentiful substance considered of little value. This sparks renewed interest for the potential resources of this unexplored region. King Charles V now sits upon throne of the empire, decreeing commitment of greater investment to know more about the potential assets of these distant realms.

A year later, in the fall of 1519, the Conquistador *Don Hernan Cortes de Monroy y Pizarro Altamirano* arrives on steps of the ziggurat capitol of Tenochtitlan City. Welcomed peacefully in the beginning by a naive king, this encounter marks the flashpoint of a war lasting three years that will precipitate assimilation of a culture with more than a thousand years of independent history. Made aware of vast storehouses containing refined gold and silver hidden in a valley the local Aztec king calls *Teotihuacán*, Cortes forces the reluctant sovereign to take him there. Here he finds an abandoned boulevard appropriately called *Avenue of the Dead*, leading to the steps of two Mesoamerican pyramids reported to be earthly habitation of the gods.

Driven by ambitious decree, Cortes determines to claim this venerable kingdom, made weak through decadence, in name of the Spanish Empire with the goal of adding citizenry. Joined by men of similar nature, conquest of the Aztec Empire begins. This New World Continent now the envy of eyes perched upon pinnacle of another earthly kingdom across the vast sea set to run course.

After sustaining heavy losses during months of bloody resistance, the proud Conquistador regroups to *Pontonchan*, secures the Tabasco Harbor, and orders burning of his own ships, so that none might find opportunity to retreat. From here, he declares open war on the *Texcoco* and *Tlaxcalteca* people, forcing a subjugated alliance that splits fragile peace of the unified Aztec Empire. By the end of 1520, the imported European disease of Small Pox decimates more than fifty percent of the indigenous population respecting no treaties. Receiving reinforcements from the motherland, along with a conscripted contingency of 100,000 Tlaxcalan warriors, the Spanish land armada follows their leader on an aggressive offensive to take the capitol city, with Cortes declaring victory in late summer of 1521.

A society devastated by war and pestilence, as few as twenty percent of the original population remains, once estimated to be six million inhabitants dispersed throughout 500 states. By now, King Montezuma dead, slain by his own citizens, the monarchy of Tenochtitlan City consumed by rebellion, many now exhausted from burying their dead. After the capture and arrest of the last Mexica Emperor, Cuauhtemoc, blood relative of Montezuma II, the once great sovereign empire bows in final defeat. Military leader Hernan Cortes declares himself first Governor of New Spain, renaming the metropolis Mexico City.

The Aztec Empire represents the premier collapse of the great Mesoamerican societies that succumb to momentum of European colonial invasion, inspired by righteous determination to dominate and unify the world.

Cortes is only the first of many Conquistadors to follow golden veins that bleed freely from three kingdoms known as El Dorado. Cutting ever deeper into the jungles, military campaigns spearhead the Isthmus with merciless precision. These first emissaries bare no flags of truce--

their only desire for peace in the gold! North, and then south again, they pierce into rainforests hiding clandestine citadels, where the rain and mosquitoes never cease. They burn city after city, slaughtering the indigenous populations— their reason no longer human, but possessed by zealous desire, changed wicked by love of this new continent's promise of earthly riches. Judged marauders from another quarter of the world, they fulfill in measure every apocalyptic prophecy, littering streets with human carnage, and engorging rivers with human blood. These harbingers of greed stop at nothing, until every ounce of treasure runs into the bellies of their ballasted ships commissioned from another part of the globe.

Pushing into the Yucatan, they search for riches belonging to the Mayans. These armored conquerors arrive in fleets of strong seafaring Galleons built to transport armies of invasion. They return to mother Spain laden with the pillaged wealth of many fallen principalities. Sea armadas sail from Guatemala to Panama, establishing the safe harbor of Portobello, conquering and pillaging all in their path. Through thick jungles laced with infected malaria pools, they push ever deeper into the southern frontier of this new unexplored continent. Here they find a flourishing civilization, home to the mighty Incas, whose name mean *"Children of the Sun."* This rich empire extends a thousand miles south of the equator, ending at the ruins of Machu Picchu, a city mysteriously abandoned on slopes of the Andes in Peru.

By messenger dispatch sent back to the unified hub of the world, they confirm inconceivable riches harbored in grand metropolises rising magnificently out of surrounding jungles, or perched on stepped plateaus. These *Soldiers of Fortune,* driven by personal ambition and greed, strike deep into the naval of the world, until gouging into the capital city heart of Cuzco. They commit crimes of genocide, ravaging diver's places without conscience. They desecrate temples, trample diver's dwellings, and subdue resistance of even the most terrific Shaman-led armies. All this they do in the name of a new world vision to accomplish God's will on earth, unconscious that the soul of a man not justified by the measure of wealth clutched in mortal hand. Nor that interpretation of scripted history justified by greed of carnal appetite.

Soon even the proud Incas fall to superior armored forces wielding double-edged swords forged in steel and long lances with points of sharpened iron. Neither the enchanted frog people in the Brazilian rainforests, nor the many conjured dark forces east of the Great River, are able to resist the fierceness of these foreign invaders. In time, all people of the New World continents forced to bow down in defeat to the Hispanic Monarchy. All made to pay tributes of gold and silver to their new sovereign, as have the subjugated Aztecs and the Mayans to the north. The many Inca idols melted into bricks of bright bullion, minted into coins, and loaded into hulls of strong seafaring ships arriving daily from across the seas.

The wealth of these conquered nations transported across the world and funneled into the coiffures of a growing European Confederation for more than a century. Joined by the Portuguese and the French, mighty Spain will eventually become protectorate of the revived *Holy Roman Empire* ruled by the Catholic House of Hapsburg, providing ships and wealth to this insatiable new world order intent upon establishing an earthly vision of God's kingdom. These Kings of Hapsburgs reach into all corners of the globe, assimilating every society from Africa to the Indies. The chimera of their presence overshadows borders beyond, as approaching smoke of raging fire consuming stubble. Through these ashes spreads the phoenix wings of Renaissance that has already begun to overshadow the world with another kind of blindness.

Even during turbulent transitions of history and alliances, riches from the new Americas continue to flow through the centuries into the bulging bellies of masterfully constructed Spanish Transport Armadas. Men inspired by cruel agendas volunteer on missions of exploration in search of answers to obscure legends shrouded in these malaria-infested jungles. Some begin to turn their dark imaginations into quest for even greater treasures. Fabled magic fountains that promise eternal youth, for power in animal masks, special shields, and enchanted weapons to make one so armed invincible. Things conjured through evil incantations, mighty demon-possessed creatures endowed with extraordinary force. Even these seekers of the occult compelled by even darker desires, as they fill their bosoms with shining souvenirs forged from the earth of these invaded lands.

Gold– *the legendary Pieces of Eight–* brightly minted new coins, embossed with the imperial insignia of the richest monarchy on earth. Treasures gathered from storehouses, spilling along the grand slopes of some of the world's highest mountains, and into deep sunless valleys. Dark places where the Amazon, the Negro, and the Tocantins flow. Caravans of wealth transported through sunless rainforest jungles, and emptied into insatiable bellies of waiting armadas. Grand galleons– strong workhorses of the seas-- ships that anchor daily in safe harbors loaded with missionaries, new architectures, and disease unknown to the New World populations. They return to motherlands of the Empire loaded beyond capacity with human cargo, precious stones, and silver. Still the greatest treasure held in these hulls shipments of sealed caskets bulging with freshly smelted gold doubloons bearing the stamp of an imperial crest representing the mammon of this world. His greed streams irresistibly through time, as a canker worm in florescent pools. His promised reward is an illusion of excess that consumes mortal souls, like moths drawn into flames of perdition.

In each generation emissaries of light sewn together with shades, and mingled with blood of progressive philosophies. Many sent nameless and without reputation into darkest shadows of this world, proclaiming testament of greater witness, than blinding glitter of acquisitions calculated through a measure of quantum value.

L. A. Espriux

BOOK ONE

Final Voyage

CHAPTER 1

Captain Belasko

The year 1640, Hapsburg Spain now entered into its twilight, battle weary from nearly thirty years of conflict, made decadent by glut of pillaged treasures stolen for more than a century.

The Imperial Army already destined to suffer a crippling defeat by the French at the Battle of Rocroi. King Philip IV, heir to the throne before his time, lives lavishly, pursuing dilettantish whims, lacking awareness of this critical crucible in history. The once great spirit of the revived New Roman Empire slips daily into decline, spending less money to build ships and to finance armies. Spain has recently suffered its greatest loss through conspiracy of nature and maneuver of better strategy by the English fleet off the French coast of Grapevines. The near decimation of the most powerful naval Armada of the world leads ultimately to forfeiture of dominance in the long held Straits of Gibraltar. Even before signing the Treaty of the Pyrenees at the end of the Thirty Years War, Portugal will break its allegiance to neighboring Spain, allowing the Basques to the north more autonomy, and thus eventually shake free the yoke of conscription.

The Basque-built Libertad is a seaworthy vessel, top of the line Galleon, her captain a man of reputation, with seasoned experience and jaded principles. It is just another routine voyage. Just another crossing of wilderness ocean separating world continents, a vessel commissioned to replenish the coffers of a complacent empire.

This stoic vessel bearing insignia of a Spanish Crest departs the port of Veracruz and skirts along the northern coast of Brazil loaded with the usual hold of minted gold coins and silver bullion. Docking at Portuguese harbor of Port Seguro, renowned for exotic pleasures and slave trade, something special added to the manifest. A thing almost human held fast by links of unbreakable chains. Reports state that the savage demon-possessed Shaman captured near the mouth of the Xingu River to the north, reputed to be direct descendant of a local royal family. He is a terrible monster in the Captain's mind, a caged beast standing nearly seven feet tall with a misshapen face and eyes of a dangerous animal.

"Such evil merchandise should not be transported to the civilized world!" Captain Belasko breathes to himself.

He is only the appointed master of this vessel, a commissioned officer with an assigned task. Therefore, he orders the caged creature stowed in the ship's hold along with rest of the other cargo. By now the new Americas taken for granted, thought of only as an endless resource of free flowing wealth to fund European appetite for war, lavish estates, and things curious. No longer satisfied with mere riches, the new Spanish elite have become preoccupied with mysticism; collectors of artifacts and creatures embodied with fabled black magic.

Jacob Belasko, last Captain of the fated ship Libertad, stares into zenith of the horizon, as mast of a dark angel into the gulf of time. His visage a burnt canvass after what seems a lifetime forgotten to the elements. Only the face of a stranger reflects back, someone once he might have known, now trapped in a clouded windowpane on his poop deck. An image of hard countenance etched with deep wrinkles that blend into the rigging of his ship. Was it that long ago he stood on the shores of dry land at foothills of the Pyrenees? How long has it been since he kissed the breast of a woman or touched the heads of children? How long ago since he saw the house built by his father, or visited the graves of his parents? All gone now— too long for him to remember, and forever long ago-- all only shadows now; all glimpsed in a vision, as birds scattered in the wind at sunset, slipping into a darkened horizon never witnessed again.

His wife no longer his wife, but married to another. His younger brother's children now grown with wives and children of their own– and he, Jacob, only a figment in their minds, the lost legend of a distant uncle and absent brother to their father, just vaguely remembered.

Jacob Belasko born and nurtured at the feet of the grand Pyrenees near varnished shores fed by sullen wind off the Mediterranean. Here his heart still beats with longing to see again the highest peak of Pico de Aneto. He longs for the day when his true compatriots will be their own masters again. Sired from linage of a proud seafaring people that once freely circumvented the globe in search of whale and schools of elusive cod, he feels in his blood the currents swirled around the keel of his ship. His earliest ancestors the first Europeans to bring back evidence proving existence of this New World. Long before Columbus commissioned three Basque ships to navigate a way to the East Indies, Basque seamen already in possession of maps drafted with the coast of Hispaniola.

Jacob can trace his bloodline back to the once great Roman Empire-- a time even before this-- the Basque language known then only as *Euskara*. A dialect that endured the rein of the great Emperor Charlemagne, lasted beyond the graves of the terrible Ottoman slaughter, and mingled in bloody vengeance through gallant Crusades to restore Holy Jerusalem. These people of the Catalans and their language continue to survive through many violent storms of history, resistant to changing tides of world politics dictated by empires. The Basque soul continues to survive slaughter of nations against nations, remaining resolute even now in ruthless face of spreading colonialism. Through laws and edicts-- kingdoms of good and of evil–

always faithful remains the integrity of the Basque heart in the solid fortress of the grand Pyrenees, never conquered, and without the need to conquer.

In Jacob Belasko's flesh courses spirit of a nation distinct from the dust of ever shifting principalities. So many things forgotten, so many things no longer present-- all as shadows of past and future suspended on distant ocean horizons.

At this junction in history, all of Europe forced to bow before the banner of the Hapsburgs, a worldly kingdom made sick by insatiable appetite. All nations of the earth subjected to the same idol of material excess. Even the once proud houses of free Catalan sequestered and made subservient by the lash of this conquering overlord, constrained in the harness of a weakening self-indulgent empire already destined to eventual failure through capriciousness of gluttony.

In this generation, Jacob Belasko has known no other freedom, except in dream. In this present, he lives to the wind of burning salt in his eyes and the tides of many seas in his veins. However, in the fortress of his heart, he submits to no flag and to no foreign sovereign. His true allegiance given to him by his father bearing silent witness of a treaty signed at the ancient oak tree of Guernika Arbola, where the Basque and the Castile once met in peace to establish the *First Laws*. Here endures memory of the Basque heart. The Basque soul made immutable in time, which no principality able to subdue.

Even the thought of home seems but a distant dream, too long ago to remember. As is often the case with brothers, he and his younger sibling rarely agree on anything, growing more separate through the years. Nor was his father, when still alive, particularly religious in the ways of imposed Catholicism, his personal convictions often appearing more secular to world affairs. As for Jacob, he has become a man solitary, lacking faith. A displaced soul doomed to wander the oceans of the world, finding no rest, and no place to call home.

Here on the deck of his ship, he stands master of the only destiny that means anything. In the stoicism of his heart Jacob Belasko, a Captain of the seas, preserves the statutes of greater tradition passed down from father to son through countless generations. At least, this is what he believes through grand nature of his pride.

From his mothers lips whispers of another genesis, not recorded through vines of present estate. A history disguised as bedtime stories read to Jacob and his brother when they were very young. The first story she reads is about creation of everything from nothing, and then destruction by a flood that swallows all dry land. Only one man named Noah, and his family, spared from drowning, preserved in the belly of a grand boat called an Ark, along with many animals.

Over time, these stories change more personal, becoming what his mother calls memories of a people that begin with a nomadic sheepherder named Abraham, to whom God speaks in a dream, commanding him to depart civilization and enter by faith into wilderness. His second born he will name Isaac, a child of promise conceived by Abraham and his wife, Sarah, in old age. From Isaac Jacob conceived, later named Israel, meaning *"one who prevails with God."* Through Israel are born the twelve patriarchs, which will become heads of the twelve tribes of Israel, as recorded in the *Old Testament Bible* used by the church.

After a sojourn of 400 years in Goshen of Egypt, another man named Moses born, raised an Egyptian, who will establish statute of the Jewish religion by delivery of austere commandments. This Moses will lead the Israelites through wilderness for 40 years by the strong hand of God to the borders of a divinely *Promised Land*.

Jacob remembers to this day a painting made by his father on a piece of sail canvass depicting a severe presence with fierce eyes, parting a sea of turbulent waves with wooden staff in hand. His father produced this by commission of the local Priest. Artistic ability was just one of his father's many talents.

"A man must learn all that he can in this world if he is to succeed," he repeats often to his two sons. "And no job too great or too small, as long as you put your heart into it."

Yet to Jacob's young imagination, stories read by his mother mythically more enticing. She fills the minds of Jacob and his brother with visions based on images often changing into events terrifying: tales describing righteous battles fought by angels, fierce warlords judged by stronger warlords, and miraculous deliverance against forces of overwhelming odds. Legend of a man named Samson, who slew an army of a thousand Philistines with jawbone of an ass. Images of violent insurrections, war campaigns, and promise of Messiah to come-- all conjured from an anomalous black book that always she kept near. A history about Judges and Prophets, and one particular chronicle of a simple Sheppard boy that one day reins as king.

Jacob always most admired the life of David. Often he would close his eyes and imagine him bringing down a mighty warrior giant with a single pebble. This man revered a great ruler, founder of a fabled city named Holy Jerusalem. He remembers the pain David suffers as he mourns contritely the tragic loss of Absalom, his first-born son. His last son Solomon destined to build the first temple and rule with reputation as wisest man on earth. Jacob hears often in his mind the voice of his mother reading from this book night after night, until her two children no longer interested. All changed now to legends past in Jacob's cosmopolitan mind-- all just *Psalms and Fairy Tales* read to young children before bedtime.

She stops reading to her two children when they become older. Perhaps because she knows now they prefer more the company of a man and the things of the world he has to teach.

Now Jacob embraces the palpable experience of his father, considering this closer to the earth he knows and understands. Past downed memories of great houses in the Catalans; ancient crossings of vast oceans by sturdily built ships in search of elusive whales and rich fishing banks near the ice sheets in straits of northern coastlines. He teaches his sons laws and history going back a thousand years, when the Basque served no foreign invader. He instructs them on how to hunt game and effective fighting techniques. More importantly, Jacob's father teaches that the fortitude of a man rests in his own hands and the integrity of will.

Jacob is still a teenager when his father dies because of an unfortunate accident. Rend by an Ox on his forty-fifth birthday while attempting to extricate one of the beast's hoof from an invisible crevice, when ordered to plow a field annexed by a despotic sovereign. Even the land of his nativity no longer his own, all now belonging to ruling authorities of the *de jure separate of Lower Navarre*. The church said it because he decided to work on the Sabbath. Jacob believes otherwise, resenting the imperial laws that made his father a hired sharecropper of his own land.

It is the last night before Jacob departs for Bilbao to board a Spanish ship headed to South Africa, as a newly commissioned Seaman First Class. He and his mother have communicated little since the death of her husband. Not that he loves her less, only their two worlds seem so different now that he is a man. Just as twilight begins to descend, she invites him secretly to her room with an urgent message.

"Jacob, do you remember when once I read to you and your brother from the Bible each night before you slept?"

"Yes," Jacob replies, uncertain why his mother brings this up now.

"I wanted you to know that there is more to this world than knowledge and religion." She then pauses, and takes a deep sigh. "I wanted to tell you and your brother, but never time seemed right. The parents of your father took me in and raised me as one of their own. When I blossomed into a woman, the elder son wanted me to be his wife. I accepted because he was a good man, and with a faithful heart-- a heart not unlike your heart. We were happy together. The greater happiness fulfilled when I gave birth to you and then to your brother. But you especially, Jacob, must hear the truth."

"Hear what truth?"

"I am a Jew, last daughter to a Rabbi father. He could trace our ancestry back to the House of David, and even beyond. Always he insisted my older sister and I learn how to read from a book called the TANAKH. In this preserved testament, the most important history ever recorded-- a history proclaiming existence to the God of creation. My father studied always these pages, sitting every day at the kitchen table, bobbing back and forth. It was his desire that all his children learn Hebrew. He felt it important that we remember and understand meaning of traditions passed down through many generations."

"A Jew--" Jacob trembles slightly, stunned by this revelation.

Although he did not fully comprehend the meaning, the label of a Jew in these days, or any other, represents something not desirable. Expression of Anti-Semitism never openly witnessed in their village, as in other places, but always it seethes below the surface. The only history in Jacob's awareness of the past being the Jewish Diaspora in the reign of Queen Isabella of Spain on the eve of Columbus' voyage of discovery across the vast oceans in search of a shorter passage to the West Indies. At this time, all the Jews expelled from Spain, forced to find refuge in other lands. His mother tells him that their ancestors some of the lucky ones, migrating into the high pastures of the Catalans to survive as Sephardic sheepherders, many forgetting the roots of their genesis, or else choosing to hide their real identity. This exodus happened five generations in the past; and still discrimination remains against those who openly profess their Jewish ancestry.

Until just now, Jacob has never considered what being a Jew might mean in present society. All he knows is that his father is Basque, which makes him Basque. Judea and Jerusalem represent unverifiable places of religious enchantment-- only figments in his mother's mind. The reality being that today the Biblical land of Israel no longer exists, if ever it existed at all.

"It is because the grandfather you never knew a Rabbi that those marauders came to our house by night and burned it to the ground. Every one perished, and only I survived because my older sister pushed me into the vegetable cellar. I listened to the violence-- to the screams of murder, the heat and the smoke-- these are my last memories before losing consciousness. When next I open my eyes my family and my home are all gone."

Now Jacob understands why his mother never truly happy, understands why always something sad and faraway in her eyes. She had carried this survivor's burden secretly all her life, hiding the truth of her linage even from a husband of almost twenty-five years. So why must she feel the need to share it with her eldest son on the eve before Jacob's departure?

"That was a long time ago. No one else needs to find out," Jacob consoles.

"It does matter, my son, and you need to listen to what I have to say now. I never told your father or your younger brother because for them it is of less importance. Your brother is more like your father; but you, Jacob, most like your grandfather."

Pausing here, she reaches under her bed, retrieves a small coffer, and opens the lid. From within she retrieves a tattered parchment scroll written in letters of a language Jacob has never seen before now.

"These are scriptures from the Book of Isaiah, a mighty prophet of God," she says, her eyes transfixed, as though another presence in the room.

She then turns and looks deeply into the eyes of her son. No longer tender visage of his mother-- no longer familiar-- but as a soul transfigured, reflecting from eternity.

"While you were still in the womb, the angel of the lord appeared in a dream, proclaiming my first-born child will be special, and that I am to give him another name in accordance to the promise of scripture. Rising up early the next morning, I begin reading these few passages taken from the Book of Isaiah. My eyes fasten immediately on the verse that reads, *"Therefore the Lord himself will give you a sign: behold a virgin will be with child and bear a son, and she will call his name Emmanuel."* I named you Jacob, after your grandfather, and Emmanuel, which in Hebrew means *'God is with us'."*

Again his mother pauses, takes a deep breath, tears of joy welling in her faded eyes. In this moment, she appears lovelier than Jacob can ever remember. No longer just his mother, but a woman filled with dreams and so many disappointments-- a woman, whose life not always easy-- this woman his mother. She calls him Emmanuel in her heart and her soul in anticipation of something better. He is Jacob Emmanuel Belasko, name given to him by his mother, a name to brand him unwillingly a Jew always, without completely understanding why.

"The moment I looked upon your face, I knew you chosen by God for a special purpose. You are, my son, living testament of Messiah, whose days not numbered upon the earth of men. Written in that book I read nightly to you and your brother are not just stories, as you think! All things have happened already! In course of time, the meaning will become clear! Look into the heart of your soul and see that part, which lives within me. There will come a day you will know that all I say to you now, Emmanuel, is truth of your destiny! I have kept this secret from you until now, because only now is the time right. You are a seed of Adam by will of the father, but within dwells hope of greater promise. Believe not only in the legacy of your earthly heritage, for you also have a heavenly destiny. Keep these words of the prophet secret in your heart always and submit to salvation as a presence of hope for those the Lord will deliver by your hand. Where God leads you, remember that you stand not alone, but in company of mighty angels. Never forget you are born a son of David, the blessed offspring of Messiah."

"Who is this Messiah," Jacob demands stubbornly.

"He has come already, and you will know his meaning through measure of love, and not by will of the father's determined pride."

"Then I will know him if one day sent by your God." Jacob replies superficially.

"There is something else my son," she says, firmly taking his arm. "Even though your brother already engaged to a girl here in our village, I have been instructed by the Spirit that this be given to you."

Her other hand then reaches again into the coffer, producing what at first glance appears to be a charred turquoise-colored pendant bearing effigy of a beetle set within a frame of melted copper and brass.

"This is from another history long ago. Father gave it to my mother when they married." She says, placing the damaged ornament firmly into the palm of Jacob's strong hand. "It is the only thing that survived the fire… the only thing left of our forgotten heritage."

Jacob feels a jolt travel up his arm and into his chest, but resists the influence. He will keep this enigmatic heirloom, choosing to remain ignorant of its potential meaning. He is, after all, a young seaman commissioned by will of the grandest navy in the world and with many dreams to explore. What possible meaning in the past could be greater than promise of this present?

Jacob takes the parchment scroll and the pendant, kisses his mother goodbye, never to see her again. After receiving news of her death, Jacob will study often shape of the unusual speckled greenish-blue insect carved from stone and the scroll written in an unknown foreign language. He cannot help but wonder if the two somehow connected. Nevertheless, Jacob Belasko finds little consolation in the revelation of his Jewish heritage-- a heritage of which he wants no part!

These many years later, he begins to feel the full weight of his bones, feeling the heaviness of centuries bearing suddenly down upon his mortal presence. His father's family name in the Old Basque tongue is a derivative of the meaning '*a lone crow*'. A name well suited to this hour of his countenance and present position in the scheme of worldly affairs. He commands only half a crew because of cutbacks to the navy-- mostly Spaniards-- all able-bodied seamen-- all serfs of the once great Spanish Empire. All subject to him, Captain Belasko, master of the seafaring Galleon Libertad. Nothing else in heaven or on earth matters! He knows the principality grows weaker daily. Soon the ruling Hapsburgs will lose their powerful grip on regions along many fragile borders. Only a matter of time now until the rein slips from hands of the monarchy. However, in this moment, all constellations of the civilized world made to orbit the shadow of a self-indulgent kingdom doomed to fall beneath the weight of its own excess.

Jacob determines this to be his last voyage. Once this expedition over he plans to go home and rediscover the land of his nativity. He grows tired of transporting merchandise and flesh, longs for peaceful days and nights in the fulfillment of his own desire. Yes-- he feels worn out-- spent to the core-- his flesh a fading garment fluttering in a stiff ocean breeze! He is no longer that young man with gallant dreams and grand promises to keep. With the passage of each night, a face more skeletal peers back at him from twilight, an image only darkly familiar with eyes almost once he knew.

This moment, he sees in the reflection a man named Jacob Belasko, Captain of a proud ship belonging to the world's greatest naval fleet. His assigned position made to serve as commander of a Top-of-the-Line Spanish Galleon laden with the King's treasure on a return voyage home. This visage of solitary presence committed only to duty of greater calling.

It is this captain stands unwavering on deck of his ship. A steadfast silhouette etched against the stars, as presence of the Great Pyrenees, which endures rain and wind throughout the ages. Yet within the stoic resolve, whispers the soul of another remembered from days past. One he fears already dead and forgotten. Surrounded by constellation of a southern night sky, his singular purpose is to navigate secret passages traversed by seafaring generations since earliest memory. For as long as he is Captain, the Libertad and the souls of all she holds belong to his charge.

CHAPTER 2

Ship Log of the Libertad

The Libertad harbors briefly in La Florida and here boards fifteen unusual Indians: three men and twelve women. According to the manifest, this small matriarchal delegation of Native Americans has requisitioned audience with the Sovereign of Spain requesting repatriation to another region. Only these fifteen souls survived destruction of their village by a local disaster. They bear little characteristic to North American Indians Belasko has seen over the past decade since his appointment as Captain of the Libertad. Almost they remind him of the Norse people around Scandinavia encountered on an earlier voyage through the northern straits. Yet, they are also variant-- a mixture of genetics not displeasing-- only different.

As this vagabond company crosses timidly the extended gangplank, one of the women arouses his attention, with eyes as a topaz sky seen in spring off the coast of Iceland, and hair with streaks of auburn red burning in the morning light. More than just her eyes and hair, but something alluring about her entire demur, which makes him think about his mother. This as far as the man of austere discipline will allow himself to imagine. She is, after all, just another passenger-- he the Captain of this ship. These are rules of the maritime. Laws he has taken personal oath to preserve and legislation he must live by. Without further reflection, Jacob allows this woman of unique character to pass, dutifully registered as any other cargo on the listed inventory.

Accompanying the party is a Franciscan Friar named Miguel, acting as their official representative. After the interview, he plans to retire to his home in Portugal. Captain Belasko studies the details of the manifest with detachment. He has transported Indians and Friars before. The cargo makes little difference. Something about this Friar makes him uncomfortable, something for which there is no particular reason. Maybe the way their eyes lock on the day this older man steps aboard the Libertad, eyes deep and unflinching that do not waver upon contact. Is this a true man of God, or just another crafty zealot in sheep's clothing? Belasko has met all types. Yes, he determines in himself to keep an eye on this one.

A hundred nautical miles off the coast of Bermuda, the spectral hand of a storm reaches out and snatches the Libertad, dragging her over mountains of waves and into dreadful deep troughs of dark diluvium valleys rarely witnessed by living men. The strong Basque built Galleon resists definitely the goliath elements; Captain Belasko stationed at the helm resolutely determined. Above the roar of wind and waves thunder of his voice snapping orders. In minds of all, he is vision of weathered Prometheus grasping firmly the wheel, etched indelible in streams of violent lightning. He knows particularly well the danger of having so heavy a cargo-- knows that the slightest shift in the load might gut the belly, spilling all their lives into the deep. When there seems no end to the stalemate, the sea suddenly relaxes its death grip on the floundering vessel. The waves changed calm…too calm, the air breathless and pressingly hot. Off in the distance shivering sheaths of splintered sky pulse beneath canopy of ominous dark clouds dancing into zenith of a receding horizon.

Here lifelessness, the waters changed to oil, void of current or even wind to fill the sail. The Spanish galleon, Libertad, now stranded and left for dead in a sea of rotting vines.

"These be waters of the damned," spits Luis-Fernando, First Mate of the Libertad. "We have been cursed, Captain."

Luis-Fernando has heard tales of such a sea. A sea without wind and with little current, a legendary tangle of ships wandering treacherously slow through the Atlantic called Sargasso. Even the name conjures up the worst kind of image, nightmare of all seafaring men to imagine this Hades of crawling weeds thick with rotting bodies grinding together; becoming a mesh of sharp splinters made from broken masts and crushed hulls. A graveyard of ill-faded vessels swallowed down throats of tempests and spat out into this rotting death in life realm. Here even the air oppressive with odor of decay. In his heart, he believes there is a reason to their present predicament– believes the Captain somehow responsible!

Long sweltering day changes into hot breathless night with only the dry creaking of the stressed hull indicating motion of time. They continue to drift ever deeper into the thick black-green swill; until finally, on the evening of the second day, the Libertad ceases to move at all, now trapped in a pane of stained glass stretching into a crimson sky.

On the morning of the third day, Captain Belasko orders the skiff lowered and manned by the Second Mate, along with six strong able bodies, to begin rolling by shifts. Ever so slowly, the heavy Galleon begins to inch forward again. At the twelfth hour the rudder locks, her keel stuck fast in a knot of underwater vines. The Libertad imprisoned by links of an unbreakable chain from deep below.

One of the oarsmen dives down to inspect the situation, never to resurface. Next morning, the Second Mate, a stout middle-aged man born in the Netherlands, defiantly volunteers to venture into the depths. Moments later, he rises to the surface screaming in pain, a garland of poisonous coral snakes coiled around his neck.

"What did you see down there?" Luis-Fernando demands unceremoniously, glaring angrily into the dying man's eyes.

"We are snared in tentacles of an evil hand!" The seaman cries deliriously. "This ship and crew will never see the coast of Spain again!"

Captain Balasko orders the Friar brought on deck to say last rites and to make supplication for all souls aboard. The situation hopeless, all they can do now is pray for a miracle. In his heart, Jacob does not believe in miracles, but he will pray for one all the same.

Miguel has not laid eyes upon the shores of his native Portugal since many years. He longs for the pleasant breeze sent from the mountains of Serra da Estrela during the wine season, the currents dipping into the rich fertile Douro Valley where he grew up. Another lifetime ago, he lived peaceably in his father's home content to tend the vineyard passed from father to son since many generations. That was before an appointed governor of Imperial Spain took the vineyard as his own, forcing young Miguel and his father to labor for wages. Even then Miguel content to remain, until one faithful day the Holy Spirit courses through his mortal being, calling him away to a service more pressing, than attendance to the needs of already cultivated gardens.

He wonders how fares the child of his only sister, a boy much like himself before detaching from worldly affection and embracing a vow of fellowship. That boy fully grown now, blessed with a pretty wife, sons, and daughters of his own. Miguel wonders if he might still find peace at the *Monastery of Santa Mario de Pombeiro*; wonders if the birds of summer continue to flock to the garden behind the main chapel. Would he even recognize his home after so many years; and would it still be home in his heart?

Miguel's eyes fasten on those of the Captain as he passes. Here is an austere man, whose mortal soul grounded in the keel of his ship. He sees this also that first day upon boarding the Libertad. He does not judge or condemn this man's mortal position. Captain Belasko snared in a web of greater design, like all men dedicated to an earthly purpose. Yet, there is something about this Captain of the seas that stirs his spirit.

In contrast Miguel is a simple man; a man touched by a divine calling at an early age, chosen to separate himself from the cares of humanity. He joins an ascetic order to fulfill a longing in his soul. In truth, he does not believe in many of the self-righteous decrees accepted by church authority; nor does he believe in the many worldly interpretations of doctrine to justify the politics of greed. Therefore, Miguel seeks permission to transport the living gospel he knows to a people of different custom and different understanding, believing them a special congregation. Miguel is acutely aware that he is their prophet sent by the hand of God for a purpose he has yet to learn, a bearer of *Good News* to preach salvation in the face of *Animalism*, and to break through the shroud of obscure ritual mediated by Shamans through superstitious conjuring.

Therefore, this man of humble position, quickened by the Holy Spirit, comes in company of many missionaries to preach the gospel of deliverance and measured meaning in the worship of what these people on distant continent call their Great Spirit. This Great Spirit without name being the same creator of heaven and earth, father of all lights, revealed in the fullness of time to a world deceived, corrupted by desires of many fallen principalities and policies of ritual designed to conceal the testimony of truth most evident. Miguel has grown less religious in the face of present political dogmatism, but his faith revived greater than ever before.

As a boy of only seventeen, Christ first appeared to him in a vision instructing him on what he must do. Since that day, he believes wholeheartedly in the power of love and faith, capable of reconstructing every matrix. In this present, he is only a servant made to serve.

Now, after more than half a century Miguel feels the need to return to his native soil, the land of his father and of his father's father, at least one last time. He considers also that perhaps this no longer his destiny to fulfill.

Miguel looks up into the burning firmament of the sky and beseeches the Lord of heaven and earth to have mercy on the crew and passengers of this fated ship. Already the unfortunate sailor has succumbed to deadly poison coursing through his veins. Miguel can see contortions of fear in faces of the remaining crew, a fear of the unknown, the apprehension all living things feel when standing at the threshold of oblivion. Only then can a man grasp the truest meaning in being alive, only then might a man really question the authorship of his existence. Only Captain Belasko stands resolute in the face of peril, his penetrating stare transfixed upon some distant place in the flaming horizon.

After a moment of silence, the skiff raised and secured. Ceremoniously, the corpse wrapped in sail-canvass and swallowed into the belly of purgatory with setting of the sun. It goes against the principals of all to abandon even a dead man in this damned region. Now the only thing left to do is to wait and to pray.

The atmosphere grows more brazen with each passing hour, the waters as the stench of death. Each evening, those deadly sea snakes slither boldly on the smooth oily surface like colorful strands of Medusa hair untangled from the depths below. Jacob can just make out her cruel visage, as she tugs with determined purpose the snared hull of the overloaded Galleon changed to stone. But this is his ship! He just as determined to escape her gapping lair!

Each night lightning scatters upon an ember horizon, shuddering evidence of a storm in progress– *but not here.* Somewhere a stiff ocean breeze moves across taunt surface of a deep turquoise sea— *but not here.* Except for an occasional albatross, no other living thing ventures from the sky above or from the depths below. Sebastian, a young sailor on his first voyage, sits near the spar of the bow sharing a bottle of Port with the First Mate and two other sailors. They all knew the Second Mate well. Therefore, they drink to his memory. Whispering, they grumble about the Basque Captain of this ship, agreeing with the First Mate that somehow he should have foreseen these events. Not because they really believe him responsible, only this excuse provides them with someone to blame.

Luis-Fernando never particularly liked Captain Belasko– *never cared much for the Basque*! Even more personal-- he does not like the man! This is their second voyage together and to take orders from one he considers inferior turns in the First Mate's gut. Luis-Fernando feels he should have been promoted and by now given his own ship. Not just the presence of this foreigner he dislikes, but the entire institution of authority represented through his appointment. Therefore, the disgruntled First Mate of the Libertad drinks in the presence of men with similar natures in order to relieve at least a little of the bitter poison seething below the surface.

Just before noon of the fourth day, Captain Belasko commands half their cargo of gold and silver dumped overboard. If there is any change, then he intends to be ready. This deliberate waste becomes more than the crew can bear. With Luis-Fernando at the lead, they threaten a mutiny, ganging together at the foot of the Poop Deck. Belasko stands unflinching, his two elegant pistols drawn. These weapons once belonging to his father, smelted from elements mined at foot of the Pyrenees.

"No, Captain–you are mad!" The First Mate cries. "The empire will have all our heads– and yours in particular!"

"I am Captain of this ship– and my orders will be carried out without question!" Leaping down on the main deck, he stares fiercely into Luis-Fernando's small beady eyes. "Are you going to perform your duty First Mate?"

Belasko knows Luis-Fernando is a coward, and nape of the serpent's hood. The First Mate hangs his head and looks away.

"Do as the Captain has ordered and waste half the King's treasure into gut of this hell."

From inside his cabin, Belasko can hear their murmurs of discontent throughout the day. These Spaniards consider it unnatural to throw minted gold and silver into the unfathomed depths of the sea. Nevertheless, this moment they will do his bidding. His orders now the only thing left for them to perform, even if those orders contrary to personal conviction. By evening the waterline of the 500-ton Galleon rises by twenty feet. She will be ready in the event that a good wind blows.

Rumor begins circulating among the crew that it is because of presence of the chained demon locked in the cargo hold this curse has come upon them. Several of the men draw lots and would have broken down the door were it not for intervention by Friar Miguel. Although small in stature and meek in spirit, he positions himself between the chamber threshold and mob of angry men. Looking older than his years, because of poor nourishment and bouts of malaria, Miguel's faith is emboldened in the face of these men's fear.

"You must refrain from this murder," pleads the friar calmly, barring the way. "Be not as this heathen held captive here, ready to shed blood out of superstition. If there be some hope for this man's soul, then let God decide!"

"God has already decided! This evil must be cast from among us!" Implacably growls Luis-Fernando.

The Friar fearlessly turns to the First Mate entrusted with the key, looking steadfast into the other man's frightened eyes.

"Open this door and let me through. If I should come out of my own accord, then it is because Angel of the Lord has performed a miracle. If not... then do as you will."

Armed only with his Latin Bible, Miguel enters alone to face the monster. He has never seen a real embodied demon before now. He believes from passages found in the scriptures that such phenomenon exists; but in this life little expected to come face to face with such a spirit. Here stands a creature like no other. The eyes those of a fierce Jaguar, shot through with blood, eyes that follow his every move. Crouched as a mountain, scarred with cut and burn marks by a lifetime of self-mutilation, his fierce eyes watch intently the smaller man's every move. He has a face broad from cheekbone to cheekbone, void of distinct feature. A countenance only vaguely human, and with flared nostrils that stink of decay. His head pushed down slightly, cocks to one side because of a hump on his back from a badly healed collarbone broken by the weight of some heavy presence when he was only a child.

Before changed into this monster from South America, the monster once a young boy born to a prominent family living in the region called Jurana, Brazil, along the Xingu River. According to local custom, it became the duty of his parents to sacrifice the child to serve as high priest to a capriciously cruel local god named Sinaa, later becoming this ferocious demon-possessed creature with strength of twenty men.

Only those unique individuals born with special intuitions receive the appointed position of this kind of Shaman, a guardian over an ancient evil treasure dedicated to the possessions of bloodthirsty gods. This particular prodigy one of the strongest ever captured in the rainforest of deeper jungle.

According to official reports, it takes an army of fit soldiers to subdue him. Those sent on this terrible mission claim he had power to change hanging vines into poisonous snakes and to cause burning hail to rain from heaven. Spawns of inhuman warriors resembling frogs leap out of shadows to his defense, slaughtering many. Those Spanish soldiers that survive testify that these unusual beings emit haunting battle cries sounding strangely like singing: a macabre chorus slithering out of shades in a nightmare they will take to their graves.

There is no doubt in Miguel's mind that all these accounts true. Just as Moses had stood with a raised staff before Pharaoh and his dark magicians, so he must stand now. As in the days of the prophet Daniel, delivered from the mouths of hungry lions, so shall this deliverance be according to God's will. The friar prays for strength, prays to be an instrument of the Holy Spirit. Armed by this faith alone, Miguel faces the demon.

The creature jumps up, rising to a height of nearly seven feet. The heavy chains binding both arms strain against the force, and seem weak elements compared to the enormity of his strength. Miguel first removes the pewter cross that always he wears around his neck, holding his worn Bible in the other hand. The Friar steps boldly toward the creature, raises the cross and begins to adjure the demon, charging that it depart in the name and blood of the resurrected Christ.

This only agitates the native even more. He begins to pant, growling as he pulls at the chains with increased fervor. Miguel steps even closer, until the brimstone stench of the creature's hot breath nauseating, feeling on his face like the very fires of hell. He reaches up, touches the protruding brown brow, and again adjures the demon. The Shaman screams in fitful agony, collapsing lifeless to the floor of his cage.

A breathless pause in eternity, silence, followed by groans from deep within the ship. The dead man opens his eyes and leaps suddenly up with tears streaming along his disfigured face. He then begins singing in a most beautiful language, a heavenly chorus Friar Miguel has heard often through course of his spiritual life.

"Aconee–" the man cries, reaching up into heaven with his hands open wide, "Aconee!"

Miguel understands only a little of the dialect spoken by the local tribes of the southern continent prior to the arrival of the Spanish and Portuguese. He wonders within himself what the word Aconee could mean. Is it the true name of this man, or perhaps the place of his nativity? Miguel baptizes his new brother in the name of the Father, the Son, and the Holy Spirit, humbly sprinkling his misshapen head with water, embracing the one named Aconee, as a new brother reborn by the same grace of salvation.

"Brother Aconee, we have much work to accomplish." He says, placing his hands on the mountain of this weeping man's shoulder.

To those outside there appears a flash of light from the cell within, then a blood-curdling screech, which makes their knees weak. The First Mate rushes in, his ax poised over his head, the fearful crew cowered behind him. All are witness to a most extraordinary sight. The restraining chains have fallen away of their own accord, the terrible monster imported from the jungles of South America knelling as a child peaceful at the friar's feet.

"The merciful Lord has delivered this man from demonic torment and the bondage of sin," Miguel affirms, placing his hands on the shoulders of the sobbing giant. "Know that every hair on his head is now precious. No physical harm shall befall him."

A sudden shudder shivers through the timbers of the vessel, followed by a cracking noise that vibrates along the keel. The Libertad is in motion. All hands rush on deck, apprehensive to the meaning of this unexpected change of events.

"Come Aconee, let us go up together to witness another miracle performed by the Lord this day!"

The eastern sky now changed to cobalt blue, a chimera boiling out of the deep. Giant Neptune stands menacingly above the distant horizon wielding a fiery pitchfork. Captain Belasko appears instantly at his post, snapping orders to raise sail and steer course of the wind. The waves continue building with intensity, ripping the Sargasso in twain, damaging the rudder gears in the process. Navigation will be difficult, but at least the Libertad free at last. Captain Belasko grabs hold of the wheel, aided by a young strong sailor named Sebastian. He reminds Jacob of himself once upon a time-- a time when he thought to tame the very elements in nature. Together they will steer the Libertad through hell's gate if need be.

Spat from purgatory and clinched in jaws of another storm, the sturdy Galleon fights valiantly to stay in front of the violent elements. For a day and a night, an irresistible southwest wind drives the Libertad blindly without a course through shroud of thick twilight, neither light of day, nor dark of night. Then the wind changes abruptly, howling from the north, the crippled vessel now forced to follow along an uncertain tact. On eve of the third day, the tempest begins somewhat to subside, the waves less fierce,

"Land spotted leeward!" Voice of young Sebastian cries out.

Captain Belasko decides to make for a narrow channel to port in the hope of finding harbor from this raging tempest. Giving orders to raise all sails, he commits the Galleon to this exploit. Captain Belasko and Sebastian hold steady the wooden rudder arm, struggling to maintain a steady tact. Several hundred yards from shore, the Libertad grounds fast, stranding upon the shoal of quicksand. The forward mast snaps in two, signifying the back breaking with an agonizing shudder.

Now fearing the worst, the Libertad crew begins a planed mutiny by frantically lowering the skiff, determined to abandon ship. Already they have agreed to leave behind the Indian delegation, the Friar, and the Shaman. Instinctively, Captain Belasko bars their way, his two pistols cocked and ready. After a tense standoff, he lowers his weapons, silently allowing the frightened mutineers to pass. He knows the Libertad dead. He could easily have chosen to depart with these men, only constrained by bond of a greater vow. He has sworn a maritime oath shared by every sea captain, never to abandon ship for as long as another living soul remains aboard his vessel.

As it turns out, the First Mate and two other sailors, one being the impressionable young Sebastian, have conspired together to salvage each a bag of gold coins; thereby missing the planned exodus. They call out belligerently to the overloaded skiff, as it appears and disappears between swelling troughs, altogether vanishing, swallowed into a fold of sea and mist.

"Captain, you must allow the Indian delegation on deck," Miguel implores. "There are men and women, and it is God's divine will that all be spared."

"Do as you will," Jacob says despondently. "They are no closer to land below deck or above. Allow them to prepare as they see fit. They are no prisoners of mine. There is but one God over land and sea, and but one Captain over the Libertad. I will perish with no innocent blood to stain my conscience. By the morrow we may all circle together with angels of the deep."

"Take heart, Captain Belasko, power of the Lord I serve is able to still even storms of the sea. I believe it his will that we shall not perish-- not your remaining crew, nor those people in the hold of this ship."

"Yes, get them all above decks." Then looking up at the disfigured giant at the friar's side, Belasko adds, "Even this silent creature may be appointed our task master on the day of reckoning."

The timbers of the Libertad continue to strain against violent crushes of wave after wave rolling over the poop deck. Still the well-designed Galleon manages to resist splintering into pieces, thanks in greater part to the lightened load. On this last eve Miguel and his new companion spring into the cargo hold of the lowest deck and begin urging the frightened passengers to seek refuge by following them outside. The women, cold and shivering, huddle together because of more than a foot of water that has begun to seep through the cracked hull. The three men, only adolescents, leap forward prepared to attack. Upon seeing terrible presence of the Shaman looming behind the Missionary Priest, they hesitate.

"Fear not my children, we are here to help you," Miguel tries to explain, learning only a few fragmented words of their unique language during the early weeks of first contact. "We must all take strength of one another. For the Lord has delivered the soul that you see standing behind me now from the firry jaws of hell. Surely, he did not save this man just to die. And if by faith one be delivered, then through belief in the same power shall all be delivered!"

One of the Indian women hastily begins to translate, encouraging her frightened clan to follow the Friar and South American to the upper deck. Her name is Amadahy, the appointed spokesperson for the group because of her knowledge of spoken Spanish. It is Amadahy, who has interceded on behalf of the delegation since arriving at the Fort of La Florida.

"Shelecheyanu," she says to her clansmen.

"Shelecheyanu," each repeats.

A consensus of agreement reached, as they become immediately more at ease, passing sheepishly between this fearful giant from another continent and the kind Friar they trust.

Miguel has heard this spoken word, *Shelecheyanu,* often during his months of association with these people, without fully comprehending the meaning. A definition, he has yet to learn.

Emerging into openness, the party faces conditions all too familiar. They witness a vortex of churning waves and cold pelting ocean spray, conditions remembered the night the great storm pounced upon their village. Great walls of crashing water dredged from the deep, washing away all that they knew. Only these few boys and several women left to tell the tale. Only these few survivors remain out of a village population of more than three hundred souls.

Finding shelter near the poop deck and persuaded by the man of God to consume nourishment, they eat a last supper in preparation of what is to come. The giant from South America looms over the congregation as a guardian spirit that still makes them feel apprehensive. Nevertheless, they trust the Friar, who continues to stand with them through many perils, and in the judgment of their appointed representative, Amadahy.

Miguel next goes to the Captain determined to convince him and his few remaining crewmembers to do the same.

"Captain Belasko, I have had a vision that every remaining soul aboard this fated vessel shall surely be delivered tomorrow. But it is necessary that you and your men take food this night in order to be saved."

This night Jacob Belasko feels mortal to the core, as much broken as his ship. He is just a man now, a man with many thoughts, but with so little faith. Always he has believed in powers he can see, in mastery of experience and wind on the open sea. He has heard how this Friar cast out the demon. Now sees with his own eyes the changed creature, no longer that terrible fiend from South American brought aboard his ship. Such a miracle is beyond his understanding. Yet here evidence of that miracle, a monster changed benevolent standing in the flesh. Therefore, the practical Captain of the sea accepts this phenomenon without further question, just as he accepts the chain in command, and just as he accepts the winds favorable or contrary.

Therefore, in accordance to the Friar's instructions, Captain Belasko gathers his few remaining men and commands them to eat a last meal of dried fish. If tomorrow comes at all, the morning will be dawn of the last day or necessity for living strength.

As predicted, a particularly violent surge sweeps over the poop deck at early light, crushing the stern of the Libertad, a splintering crackling noise that rips through the doomed vessel. The strong maiden of the sea finally gives up the ghost and begins breaking apart, sending a stream of debris composed of dismembered timbers racing toward the shore. Miguel poised near the sinking bow, raises his hands toward heaven, commanding all to grab hold of anything that will float. The water, less tumultuous now, pushes toward shore, streaming in the direction of a beach north of the channel opening.

The South American embraces pieces of the shattered hull and begins kicking mechanically toward the shore with three weaker folk clinging tightly to his broad shoulders. The Friar secures three empty vegetable crates, shared by the female interpreter and another woman at his side, with arms of a teenage boy clutched around his neck. The First Mate and the two crewmen have prepared empty wine barrels on the preceding night, sealing their bags of gold coins inside, and use these as buoys of escape.

The Captain is last to abandon ship. Securing a few of his ship's logs, along with the scroll of the Prophet Isaiah given to him by his mother, he wraps these in a watertight satchel, respectfully makes the solemn sign of a Basque seaman in honor of a proud ship once under his command.

This done in accordance to maritime tradition, Jacob Belasko launches into the swift tide, grasping a slab of floating wood once half of the captain's dining table.

CHAPTER 3

Xeantee Aconee

As promised by Friar Miguel, all twenty-one souls stand on dry land accounted. They build a fire and consume the few provisions thoughtfully brought by the Indian women. Later they scour the shore, finding enough tack and dried sardines to last a month. It takes a day and a night for the Libertad to altogether breakup. A few ribs protrude above the sweep of waves, until finally even these vanish, buried in the quicksand. For many centuries to come, violent storm surges will mysteriously wash Spanish gold doubloons on this stretch of Carolina shoreline. However, no treasure hunter will ever find remains of the registered Spanish Galleon Libertad, lying only a few meters below the surface on an ever-shifting shoal.

The Indians boarded at La Florida remain in the beginning cautious of the grotesquely scared giant from another continent, refusing to venture too near. They have heard about the terrible inarticulate monster locked in the hold of the ship. Also heard how the Missionary Priest cast out the demon. That giant creature now gentle and with a presence of peace exemplified by the humble Friar that has volunteered to be their mediator. Now they believe without doubt in the power of Friar Miguel's God, believing also in the potential of many miracles. Nevertheless, they choose to maintain a discreet distance from this man of strange appearance. One who neither speaks, nor approaches near the person of any, always hovering in shadow of the meek Friar.

Captain Belasko appoints himself leader of the expedition. A leadership no one wishes to challenge-- not even the contentious Luis-Fernando. On morning of the third day, he decides the safer course is to explore inland. Navigation through dangerous swamp mazes between clumps of Cyprus islands proves to be greater challenge than expected. Every step proves tedious, adding to the torment are swarms of mosquitoes, particularly relentless this time of year.

Prior to sunset on evening of the nautical fifth moon, Amadahy steps into quicksand, miring immediately waist-deep in the suctioning black mud while picking wild berries. Without hesitation, the South American leaps several feet across a shallow depression, lands on a partially submerged tree trunk, managing to balance on just one leg. By now, the terrified woman has sunk to her neck, gasping desperately to keep her mouth and nose out of the stagnant waters. With one mighty hand, Aconee lifts her bodily to safety just in time.

The woman clings limply to his mighty arm, weeping and crying something repeatedly in her native tongue.

"Xeantee– Xeantee *Shelecheyanu*!"

The savior gently raises her to dry land. His brow furrowed, his eyes flashing, as almost his lips purse into a smile. To the saved woman, his countenance changed to that of a wood spirit wondrously benevolent,

"Aconee," he says, reaching toward heaven.

"Xeantee Aconee," she answers back.

Touching his grotesque brow against her smooth forehead, the South American mumbles something particularly strange in an unknown language. This moment, she witnesses in his face way of future passage clear and forever.

"Xeantee Aconee Shelecheyanu," again cries the woman.

"*Shelecheyanu Xeantee Aconee*!" He proclaims, shaking his head in acceptance.

As if on cue, choruses of frogs begin singing from invisible crevices. A shaft of pure light breaks through the swamp canopy, settling on the one now proclaimed *Shelecheyanu Xeantee Aconee.*

It is nature's mantle of coronation draping his head and shoulders with last embers of the setting sun. The event stunningly majestic to all: name and presence of Xeantee Aconee elevated immortal and coroneted by nature to defy natural reason. Even Miguel cannot help astonishment upon witnessing the sovereign will of the phenomenon. A man delivered from demonic possession, now changed regal challenging greatness of any earthly principality. He stands undisputed monarch of this place, a son of man crowned ruler in strange realm of light and shadow.

After this extraordinary event, the Indians begin reverently referring to the South American in the simple superlative, Xeantee, which roughly translates to mean one *"Born of Water and Spirit."* The conjunction is actually more of a declaration, used nominative as the subject of a verb, as well as being descriptive of some higher meaning to convey physical salvation, depending on context. The elevated sense of Xeantee, when used as a proper noun, changes to mean *"Prince of the Water People,"* but in the diminutive form, it can also connote simply *"the frog."* However, expression of the word, when spoken with dialectical stress on each vowel, the original connotation seems altogether to change, becoming reflective of some higher meaning altogether transcendent to physicality.

Friar Miguel devotes all the linguistic and cultural knowledge gained during his several years of library study preparing for missionary work to understand better the unusual dialect of this oral tradition. He has begun to comprehend at least some of the derivatives of meaning. For example, the word *Shelecheyanu* appears in many contexts, seemingly untranslatable through applied congregation. In the beginning, Miguel thinks it nothing more than a greeting, the meaning *"hello,"* or *"goodbye."* However, the more he examines the descriptive context of this unique spoken language, Miguel becomes convinced the etymology of these people associative to greater elevation of meaning that unearths the very root of this people's genesis and spiritual belief system. The word *Shelecheyanu,* when used alone, means blessing or acceptance, or more accurately submission to purpose of greater design. This can be as common as stating thankfulness to a dispatched animal for daily sustenance, or reverent farewell to a dead loved one. The meaning in fact changes little with the use, embodying belief that all things made to fulfill a purpose, as well as acceptance of that purpose. There is no consensus necessary, no doctrine of rational judgment, nor injection of personal emotion. Something either is, or is not, and when used within context of other words, it creates a transient elevation of meaning, expressing a concept that Miguel can only describe as attributions of faith.

In the case of *Xeantee,* add the word *Shelecheyanu,* and one derives an expression altogether lacking any particular locality of reference. Within this context, *Xeantee Shelecheyanu* can also refer to an appointed presence, or guardian sent at a crucial apex in time and space. Through exercise of personal choice, *Xeantee Shelecheyanu* becomes dividing edge of amplified directive, dissimilating the living matrix of revitalized potential from condition of collapsing disassociation. Through one acceptance is an ever-expanding heavenly existence without end. Through the other, one becomes part of a fading nether region inhabited by warring deities of pagan origin imploding into oblivion.

Unlike the early cultures of ancient Mesopotamia Miguel has studied, *Xeantee Shelecheyanu* expresses a condition of absolution, especially when used in the superlative form. Through this meaning, it becomes a spiritual transfiguration of every atom constructed in the past, present, and future, expanding from the smallest of things into escalation of a vast cyclic universe destined eventually to end. In other words, *Xeantee Shelecheyanu* changes to a transcendent meaning, becoming the Messiah poised at a cosmic focal point connoting both end and beginning of everything.

Miguel has learned other things about this distinct culture recorded by a people transplanted from the northern continent. They share many of the historical markers thought exclusive to societies surrounding regions modern civilization calls the Fertile Crescent. For example, they sincerely believe in a Genesis story based on oral tradition that is very similar to the Torah version inscribed by the hand of Moses just over twenty centuries ago in the region of Mount Sinai. They further describe a universal flood that happened in the distant past, wiping-out all life, except for the family of a few survivors and certain animals saved in a floating lodge. They even accept freely the meaning of personal salvation through testimony of one sent by the Great Spirit to restore all things. It perplexes Friar Miguel how they could know all these things without having a written language or proper religious instruction.

One evening after the dramatic rescue of the Indian woman Amadahy, Miguel receives further insight into these mysteries while sitting around the campfire with Aconee and the three young Indian men. One in the group produces a smooth white rock from his pouch and places it center of the congregation. Then tapping on it, he points to the South American.

"Shelecheyanu Xeantee," he proclaims.

He next puts the fingers of his two hands together creating the sign of a triangle. Reverently raising the sign skyward, he then points to a constellation of stars framed within geometric context of the three lines.

"Shelecheyanu Xeantee," he says again, moving slowly his hands around the congregation, while maintaining sign of the triangle.

"Xeantee Shelecheyanu," the other two Indians chime in unison, imitating the sign of a triangle with joined fingers of their two hands.

Aconee's brow wrinkles perplexedly, his face rippling with shadows. After some moments of reflection, he grins garishly, his eyes sparkling with sudden revelation. He then takes the white rock in the palm of his hand and presses it against the chest of a surprised Indian boy nearest him. Next, he points to the reflective pewter cross that always the Friar keeps around his neck.

"Aconee," he says, gazing deeply into the young wide-open eyes. *"Aconee Xeantee!"* Then placing one hand of the other man over his own heart, the South American again quietly articulates, *"Aconee Xeantee."*

"*Xeantee Aconee*," the three Indians say, and begin to repeat the name reverently over and over, each nodding his heads in respectful agreement.

Although Miguel does not fully comprehend the significance, he feels an unspoken bond of agreement has happened between these Indians from Florida and this strange South American. He is now the *Xeantee Aconee*, a chieftain of unique position, one sent to them in the fullness of season by the Great Spirit. In time, they will respectfully refer to him in the familiar only as the "*Aconee*."

Miguel convinces the Captain that it to the advantage of their expedition to allow the one called *Aconee* to take point, since his experience of jungle swamp greater than their own. Jacob is of a practical mind, therefore easily agrees with soundness of this reasoning. Without the Libertad, he feels useless and without definition, a man like any man, a man far from the strong mountains of his progeny— a man once upon a time the proud Captain of a once proud ship.

Truth is that he as much lost in this vast wetland as any of them, tormented by mosquitoes, uncertain of each next step. Not even the maps contained in his few remaining ship logs provide him much bearing. Nor do positions of these stars point him in any familiar direction. Perhaps the experience of this creature in ways of jungle swamp terrains a serving instrument raised-up by Miguel's God to lead the few survivors to a place of security.

Aconee proves worthy of his appointment. He makes a heavy trident with three spearheads from a long freshly cut branch of a living tree. Burning the hewn tips in fire, he uses this as a probe to determine the depth of innocent looking pools. He is able to sense bog pits just by smell, instinctively knowing the safe passage. He feels without actually seeing; knows by instinct the underlying dangers that lurk within every shadow. On the eve of the twelfth day after the shipwreck, they arrive on an island of solid ground, flourishing with plant and animal life. A land that receives a pleasant breeze from the north, not too humid, not too hot, neither is it cold.

Aconee stops and raises his hands in thanksgiving. Here is the place he has been searching for, a place of refuge to serve the needs of his new brethren. Surrounded in a grove of trees, they discover a solitary white boulder razed flat on one side and with a shallow natural depression making a bowl on the surface. Here Aconee and Miguel kneel down together, bow their heads, and give prayer of thanksgiving. The Indian woman saved from drowning several days earlier, reverently knees down, smells and tastes of the black earth, then raises her hands to the sky.

"*Shelecheyanu,*" she announces to her clansmen. "*Xeantee Aconee* has led us safely to this foundation rock of our rest and our new home!"

After the majority female council meeting, they set about clearing the area and building makeshift shelters. The young men make tools for hunting, while the women cultivate places in the sun to establish lattices for gardens. Upon the instructions of Miguel, they had wisely taken seeds from the cargo hold of the Libertad, along with foodstuff on the final eve before abandoning the ship. Now the reason made clear, as though Miguel knew all along what was to come, seeing this place as part of his vision. By faith, they had left the familiar shores of their land, passed through valleys surrounded by shadows of certain death, and led to this land of rich promise by the guiding insight of their new leader, *Xeantee Aconee*. Here at last they are home. And here these Indians declare constitution to remain.

CHAPTER 4

Measure of Shelecheyanu

Miguel's desire to embark on a journey around the world is primarily to act as a representative to the small congregation of refugees from the northern coast of the rich Florida peninsula. They are very dissimilar to the other Indians he has made contact with during his experience living in the New World of North America. Though many of their domestic customs consistent to the ways of other native indigenous peoples, they appear physiologically very different. Instead of being dark, they have fair skin, some with blue and green eyes. A few speak some words of Spanish, which aids in establishing communication. Miguel also discerns that their vocabulary infused with an archaic root mixture of Scandinavian words, a language he studied in the early years before leaving seminary training. They call themselves descendants of the *Dragon Folk*. The matron of the group, a middle-aged woman with reddish-brown hair named Amadahy, is able to speak Spanish more affluently than the rest. This makes her their appointed translator. Through hand signs and broken words, she manages to relate the tragic events leading up to their exodus, describing in some detail a terrible storm that nearly wipes out their distinct cultural heritage.

Amadahy also shares with Miguel another distant historical linage that traces back long before Columbus set foot on the isle of Hispaniola. The woman claims her people originally from a place called Vineland, so named by the Norsemen that first arrived in dragon ships and created temporary settlements along the northern coasts. Some choose to stay and take for themselves wives, eventually becoming breakaway settlements. For six generations, these families of strange customs coexist in peace with the "*Skraelingar*," or local tribal populations. Then war breaks out with an unprovoked attack by another Indian group arriving from the west, killing all of the men above a certain age, but sparing some of the women and their children. Those that did, themselves became outcast, forced to live separate in exile.

All would have perished before winter were it not for the timely arrival of a Basque whaling expedition, taking the several outcast refugees aboard their two vessels with plans to relocate this surviving remnant further south. However, the sturdy ships blown many days off course into the open straits, before being able to navigate again nearer the shores. Luckily, both vessels endure the hostile elements of nature. These men of noble character safely deposit their human cargo near a southern inlet. Amadahy's great grandmother and great grandfather listed among these new settlers.

Now, three generations later tragedy has pounced once more. Again, only a remnant survives. Only these fifteen souls escape the natural catastrophe of a devastating hurricane that plows into the coast months earlier and altogether decimates their village. No longer feeling secure, the council consisting of a female majority makes decision to embark on an exodus to the southern settlement hoping for a new life.

Miguel pensively remembers that storm, the vicious destruction gouging even into the settlement of La Florida. He remembers the day a matriarchal group appear on steps of the La Florida Mission hungry and exhausted. Miguel dutifully attends to their many needs and agrees to intermediate on their behalf to the local government authorities. Surely a location can be allotted for this small displaced band, most of whom young.

However, the colony of New Spain, first founded by the explorer Ponce De Leon, refuses citizenry. Even the Priesthood reluctant to get involved, turning their backs on the Friar's often intercession. Therefore, Miguel invokes the legal right of citizenry to make their case heard before the Royal Counsel of Spain. Taking leave of his position, the Friar secures passage for them and himself to the hub of the world on the next departing cargo vessel.

Amadahy has already surpassed the flower of youth, never married, never in love. She learns to speak some the foreign dialects, as did most of the Indians within proximity to European settlements along trade routes. A few French and English fur trappers stop occasionally at her village. For as long as she can remember, it is the Spanish, who come most often, bearing gifts and ready to make a deal. Because Amadahy has an exceptional ear for sound, she becomes the natural choice as trade translator once she is old enough.

The young girl proves gifted in other ways as well. Born with instinct and intuition beyond her years, she often feels things before they happen. Like the time her older brother almost dives into the jaws of a waiting Alligator, but prevented because Amadahy persistently forewarns him. The near fatal event later revealed when a full-grown Buck ventures too near the water's edge and dragged suddenly into the stagnant deep by the waiting reptile.

Without realizing it, she later sees the destruction that befalls her village in a dream many days before the wicked hurricane rises out of the sea. No one believes her, not even her only brother, not her parents, or the village counsel. Then the storm strikes while everyone sleeps. All perished in one night– her family-- her friends-- and all worldly presence erased from existence. The history of an entire tribe washed away, leaving only these vagabond wandering refugees of a people again forgotten.

Amadahy likes Friar Miguel, feeling within this simple humble man a surpassing peace savored with compassion. It is not just his kindness toward them, but the sincerity of meaning that speaks loudest. Although Amadahy understands only a little of the meaning in his words during those early weeks at the Mission, she feels the certainty of his conviction. After hearing about the miraculous conversion of the terrible Shaman from another continent of the vast world, she believes his words more than just the ideals of a man. The day Aconee saves her from the bog pit she understands completely. This moment Amadahy knows– not just in words– but true power of the Holy Spirit. It is no mere man that lifts her bodily from the grasp of certain death. He is the authority of one of Miguel's angels sent to deliver her in body and soul– *revelation of Xeantee Aconee!*

This moment melancholy of despair flees from her. Amadahy's spirit instantly revived. This hope not just for her alone, but hope for all the remaining tribe. By instruction of Friar Miguel, they had set out across the great sea to make a petition to the sovereign of the world for a new territory. Through passage of unpredictable events and by mystery known only to the ways of *Shelecheyanu*, sign of deliverance at last! The Xeantee Aconee, sent to them by will of the Great Spirit to guide them to this place. A place they will establish as a new beginning.

There is also the man with eyes of destiny inspiring desire of something else, his presence since the beginning, like body of approaching wind sent to disturb the still water of her mortal position.

Jacob has known other women since his divorce. None touches him deeper than his flesh, none that moves him to want more than pleasure found in the fleeting moment. This Indian woman saved from the bog pit is quiet and unassuming, crowned by long burning hair that cascades softly along her shoulders, and with deep river-green eyes and just a tint of blue. Nor is she like other Indians he has seen-- *like no one he has ever met*!

Jacob remembers particularly well that day the South American lifts her effortlessly out of the quicksand. No one else could have known where to stand. No ordinary man could have moved so quickly. Jacob had been admiring the woman since beginning the long trek through this swamp... his thoughts of her even long before that. She possesses a quality that reminds him of his mother-- not in physical appearance-- but in the way of feeling. So much about his mother that remains in mystery, so much of her past lost to his comprehension.

Yet the connection he feels with this Indian woman runs every day deeper, dredging up dreams and feelings he thought drowned long ago. He had known less attraction for his wife of many years. He blames himself that she left him for another man during one of his long voyages. He knew it inevitable: all things inevitable to men that spend their lives at sea. Maybe this is the true reason he married her in the first place. He knew that because he loved her less, he would feel less the sharpness of the pain when eventually she betrays him. Yes-- there is something about the woman that is different! Yes– this is it! Instinctively he knows that within Amadahy harbors a seed of life to revive the spent core of his being. A seed he did not even know existed.

"The Friar tells me your name is Amadahy," Jacob ventures

"Yes, it is a name that was in the beginning. It means *"Soul of Water."*

"*Soul of Water*," Jacob repeats gazing deeply into her eyes.

Jacob likes both the sound and the meaning, but finds the name Amadahy difficult to say. He likes the way she smiles shyly when he tries to pronounce the native name. He likes the brightness in her eyes that remind him of the Northern Lights seen off the coast of Labrador, the tone of her voice, which sounds like wind whispered through passages of his childhood memories where he grew up.

Since the beginning, Amadahy always respectfully addresses him as Captain Belasko. Now Jacob wishes to share a truth with this woman of unique value, he has never shared with anyone else.

"The name given to me by my mother is Emmanuel," he confesses softly. "Now I am just a man, no longer Captain of the Spanish Navy, no longer just Jacob, but a man in the presence of a lovely woman."

There is that shy pleasant smile again. A smile that lifts his heart from the siren depths of brazen skies without dimension, singing a lullaby of perpetual days and nights funneled into the solitary zenith of this present. Here is refreshment so desperately needed by his estranged soul.

"Your name is the promise of *Shelecheyanu,*" she says, her gaze deeply disturbing.

"What does *Shelecheyanu* mean?"

"*Shelecheyanu* means everything, my Emmanuel. *Shelecheyanu* is evidence of all things, even things not seen with eyes or touched by hands. It is like your name. Jacob is the beginning, Emmanuel promise fulfilled". She reaches out and touches his furrowed brow. "*Shelecheyanu* cannot be found through reason, but by what Friar Miguel calls *'faith'.*"

"Miguel is a man of religion. I am just a man in the eyes of a lovely woman."

"You are my Emmanuel, and by you only am I "*Soul of Water.*"

Amadahy remembers well the first day boarding the Libertad, remarks the regal presence of the one called Captain Belasko intensely studying his cargo manifest. Then he looks up; their eyes meet. A passing glimpse only, a moment suspended in time. Over the next many days, she and her party remain below deck. Even with the heat, they refuse to venture outside, fearing the crew and calamity of another storm. Then fury of the elements returns, threatening final hope of their refuge. When all seems lost, the door bursts open.

Friar Miguel appears, accompanied by the terrible giant from South America, promising them salvation. She also remembers that last night seeing the Captain stand quietly and alone on his shattered Poop Deck armed with his pistols and a sword confidently hung along contour of his strong thigh. Always she imagines him alone.

It later concerns her that he refuses to abandon the breaking hull until certain all others departed. He is the last to leave and the last to arrive on shore, cold and shivering, but alive. In the days that follow, Amadahy will have some casual contact with the other three men from a distant continent. She feels altogether repulsed by the presence of the one named Luis-Fernando, addressed as First Mate by the Captain. It is not only his appearance that makes her uneasy; something in his eyes when he looks at her-- black and soulless-- as those of the waiting alligator that nearly snatched her brother away. She makes a point to avoid this one always.

In contrast, Amadahy has a certain fondness for the young seaman named Sebastian. He tells Amadahy that her name reminds him of his sister Amada, so he affectionately calls her this. She likes the name Amada, a name in Spanish so similar to her own. In her mind, Sebastian is as the brother she has lost, and likes the idea of being his sister. She likes the inquisitiveness of his youth, easily inspired by visions. Nevertheless, like Amadahy's own brother, he can often be too impulsive, easily led astray by dreams not altogether of his own design. This is the beauty and the danger she sees. It is obvious that Sebastian reveres his Captain, as a son might revere a father. Just as obvious, Captain Belasco thinks of this younger man with greater affection than just another sailor under his charge.

Since arriving here in this peaceful glade, Amadahy finds herself growing more curious about the Basque Captain. Not that he is particularly more handsome than the rest; but something in his presence that touches feelings inside of her not touched before. Something in the way he looks at her, which makes her feel warm, reminding Amadahy she is a woman. Yes-- she feels a woman made complete, fulfilled in the depth of this man's fathomless eyes. This is also new to her. He has asked she call him Emmanuel. This is a special name with special meaning, a name filled with light and with life. Therefore, Amadahy calls his name Emmanuel in waking and sleeping dream.

The mutual attraction between the Captain and the Indian woman Amadahy escapes no one's attention. In the weeks that follow their growing affection for each other evident, especially to the Friar. Miguel knows well the carnal end to such chemistry; but feels, also, that destiny is at play. He cannot imagine two people more suited for each other. It is though separated they are two halves of independent vessels self-fulfilled, needing the addition of nothing more. Together, they change hermetically whole, transcendent elements of spirit and soul reborn complete, complimenting each other as celestial bodies poised at perigee during emergence of a new heaven through ballet of balanced motion. To such natures, Miguel makes no judgment.

On fourth day of the sixth week after the wreck of the Libertad, Captain Belasko, his First Mate, and the two sailors meet privately with the Friar Miguel to discuss plans, since all not content to remain in this haven of rest. According to a surviving map in his incomplete ship's logs, there should be a European trading post further north. Even French and English fur trappers used to trading with the local Indian tribes will be accommodative to render safe passage for a profit of gold Doubloons.

Captain Belasko is satisfied to remain here, now that he has discovered the peace and companionship too long absent in his life. He wants none of the salvaged gold. Besides, his career as a Captain of the seas will end abruptly once testimony heard that he ordered dumping overboard of the King's treasure. Such waste considered inexcusable. There can be no greater transgression against the House of Hapsburg. He feels, nevertheless, compelled by sense of personal honor to ensure that his remaining crew, particularly the Friar and the young Sebastian, might find safe passage back to Europe. He will accompany them at least beyond the swamp country. From here, they will continue by the hand of providence. After much heated discussion, the First Mate and two sailors settle to split the gold evenly between them once they reach a commodious settlement. This journey planned to begin on the following fortnight after third cycle of the full moon.

CHAPTER 5

The Weight of Gold

Luis-Fernando is particularly motivated to return to civilization where money and resources mean something. He is a man driven by greed for as long as he can remember. To him this not perceived a negative attribute. It means to have enough when there is never enough. This is just way of the world. He had grown-up poor, a member of peasantry with three brothers and four sisters. Only one of those brothers still alive and he never knew what happened to any of his sisters after they were married off. Forced to fight and claw his way into social ranks, at last promoted a soldier of the Empire. Then one mistake that nearly cost his life. Unceremoniously demoted, he enlists in the Navy as a seaman, once again working his way through the ranks. He should have been captain of his own ship by now, except memories run deep. Luis-Fernando is better than this man he presently pays homage to-- better than any man aboard the Libertad! Now he has a second chance for the only thing that really matters to him. This time will be different.

Miguel has convinced Aconee to be guide through remainder of the swamp to threshold of solid ground. As with all men nearly at the end, he misses his native Portugal, hoping one day– *the Lord willing*– to return there and die. Instinctively Miguel has little trust in the company of two of these men. They are of a baser sort, whose only conscience, a voice in their belly. Nevertheless, his Christian faith provides him courage, surrendering to the ultimate will of God. Glad also that Captain Belasko has determined to join them.

After some debate, they prepare to depart before morning light at beginning of the first quarter of the moon.

All gather around the party in final prayer, hoping for the speedy return of their new leader. Miguel assures the people that Aconee will come back before end of the new moon. Each native desires to reach out and touch the one called the *"Frog Prince"*. He has taken on the character of a deliverer in their eyes, a representative of the Great Spirit sent to show them passage to this new land.

"*Xeantee Aconee!*" They say repeatedly as he passes among them.

Only Amadahy remains silent, her head bowed to the ground, unable even to look into the face of her Emmanuel. Why must he go-- especially now!

"I will come back," swears Jacob. "I owe it to these men to see they reach sure footing on a solid trail. Until then, they remain my responsibility. This promise made to my mother before I was born. To ignore the voice in my conscience would mean to abandon her faith in me."

"And what of your promise to me-- to the special vow made between us?"

"We are one, Amadahy; the cord that binds us made of such that no earthly force may break, and that no other destiny able to change. My lovely *Soul of Water* we remain bound immutably by greater will of what you call *Shelecheyanu*. This I believe with all my soul and body."

He then retrieves from pocket of his lapel an object that reflects eerily in the pale of waning moonlight. It reminds the Indian woman of something she has seen before, as though in a waking dream. Without knowing why, Amadahy immediately ascribes sacred meaning to carving of the strange, yet somehow familiar, effigy depicted on face of an amulet from distant continent.

"This was given me by my mother. At the time, I did not know why, only that she thought of it as something special. I place it in your care until my return."

"Yes, my Emmauel, we are and will always remain one body and one soul." Amahady wails, releasing herself into his beautiful spirit. "We are forever *Shelecheyanu*."

Jacob Emmanuel embraces Amadahy, kisses her passionately one last time, and is gone. The party vanished into foliage. Her newfound love disappeared in a wisp of morning twilight, leaving her apprehensive, a feeling as though some part of her gone and feared never to return.

Without understanding why this woman in love experiences emptiness not known before, as if a rib pulled from her body. Mostly she does not trust Luis-Fernando, yet believes he is no match against the man she loves. There is the young Sebastian, who will certainly always stand with his Captain. She is sure he would lay down his life for what is true, loyal to the end. Amahady prays the faith of Friar Miguel will watch over them all, believing his presence made of greater things not seen. This moment she submits to the providence of *Shelecheyanu*. And poised above every apprehension stands strong presence of the Xeantee Aconee!

The first day spent exploring the land mass. It turns out to be an island, shaped like a giant forearm that extends in length for a few miles, and less than two miles across. At one tip of this appendage is the way they came, at the other end bayous stretching into a lake littered with rotting cypress trunks. It is here that the first casualty occurs.

During a period of rest, one of the sailors wanders too near the water's edge. Sitting down on a clump of cypress moss, he opens his bag and begins handling the cherished gold doubloons, rubbing two coins in his fingers. Seeing what he thinks a smooth stick floating in the black water, he reaches out and seizes it. The stick changes instantly alive, whipping around, sharp fangs piercing the man's throat. Before anyone can do anything, the monster Water Moccasin slides away, disappearing into the stygian deep.

The astonished sailor stumbles forward, falling facedown into the lake. His corpse gone in an instant, devoured into a grave of quicksand. Even Aconee seems taken by surprise, a glint of remorse flashing deep in his eyes. Unobserved by anyone, a shiny gold *Piece of Eight* has slipped from the dead man's fingers, landing in the cleft of Cyprus root. Here an evil seed planted, prepared for some future soul to discover it.

"At least he had the good sense to put down the gold," the First Mate snarls to the young Sebastian sitting at his side. "Now there's that much more to divide between just the two of us."

Miguel has known such men before, men who never have enough, and who will never have enough. Within this man grows a cancer that has corrupted empires in the course of time. His eyes like dark pools, his complexion dirty and pot-marked, with a slice of a nose that curls down and to the left of his long face. His overall features unmask a cruel and traitorous ambition. He sees the sky without wonder, beholds only the surface tension of the great oceans, and comprehends so little during the fruitless hour of his passing. Luis-Fernando's imagination exists in the allure of future riches only, the present a place dry and empty in his mind. The young Sebastian sits at his side, as an unsuspecting lamb near quivering mouth of a hungry lion.

"All men are blind when it comes to worldly riches," Miguel remarks to Captain Belasko. "Ships laden with gold and treasure houses that spill at the feet of Mammon, and still his appetite unfilled. Shadows that cast shadows; and all made of shadow in the end."

Jacob says nothing. The Mate is after all right in his practical observation. Nevertheless, it bothers him that another man once under his command has perished without ceremony, without meaning or purpose. This is the problem with practicality. Rarely does it ever make sense. He wishes for the peace he sees in the Friar and the strange South American constantly at the other's side. Some part of him is glad for their abiding presence, and in this moment feels a little less restless. He longs to be back in the arms of Amadahy, his spirit restored by *Soul of Water*! He misses her already, misses to gaze into the tender azure calm of her eyes that provides refreshment to his parched soul.

He senses in these two men strong faith that adds glimmer of strength to Jacob's present resolve. But more, this practical captain of the seas hungers for the hope they share, both believing in something not seen, which elusively escapes the logic of his comprehension.

Now there are only two partners and three bags of gold, making it abundantly clear to Friar Miguel and faithful Aconee that all the gold in the world remains insufficient for the possession of at least one man in their party. A man, whose soul changed as dark as the stagnant water that has interred the man just perished. Therefore, they do the only thing left to do in mortal course. Bowing their heads, these men of God pray earnestly over the watery grave.

Early evening of the second day, Aconee discovers a narrow mote not more than fifteen feet wide that meanders slowly through thick underbrush and trees. With a single bound, he leaps to the other side, using his spear as a vaulting pole. Knelling on one knee, the South American touches the earth, as though feeling for a heartbeat. He next follows the bank downstream, until finding the standing corpse of a rotting tree dead at the edge of the pool. With a mighty shove, the body falls across the mote, providing access to the rest of the company.

They continue through thinning brush, hearing the distinctive audible sound of churning water that grows louder. Just before sunset, the foliage opens onto the rocky shoals of an engorged river rushing muddy-red because of early spring runoff. Here they pitch camp for the night.

Brother Miguel has not been feeling well. The next morning he awakens with a fever and is too weak to travel. He knows it to be return of his malaria, and that only time will tell. Aconee does what he can to comfort his companion. He builds a fire, supplying fresh water captured in the shallow of a dammed basin for the declining Friar to drink. Miguel can see in Aconee's misshapen countenance the vexation of his spirit.

The man from South America stands suddenly up and begins pacing the area, staring up at the wondrous canopy of stars, sweat gathering on the protruding hump of his crooked back. He begins to groan, breaking suddenly into song of a beautiful language, as when first baptized by the Holy Spirit.

Next morning Miguel has taken a turn for the worse. By now, too weak even to rise, preferring to remain lying down. Although the river dangerously high, Aconee explores along the banks for a way across. Discovering pattern of a potential access point, he leaps from rock to rock, landing on the other side. Captain Belasko and the First Mate follow precariously slow, leaving the young Sebastian to watch over the Friar.

It is Luis-Fernando first discovers the cave behind a small waterfall pouring into the river on that side. He has parted ways from Aconee and the Captain upon realization that the only way out of this canyon is a shear climb to the top, or else to wait until the turbulent waters subside. By animal instinct, or because of an imaginary voice that calls out to him, Luis-Fernando's eye catches the glint of something glimmering ever so faintly behind the curtain of shimmering water. Squeezing through a narrow crevice, he discovers an enclosed quartz chamber illuminated by light shinning from above that refracts through shards of semi-translucent crystalline rock protruding to the surface. Little struck by the wonder of this phenomenon, he determines by practical instinct that here a good place to stash the heavy bags of gold— at least for a little while. Aconee is standing outside when he exits the cave, the South American's countenance as judgment to Luis-Fernando's covetous soul.

That evening Captain Belasko and the two sailors camp some distance away from the sick Friar in order to get an early start exploring the narrow canyon hedged by an un-scalable sheer rock face. They hope farther down-river will perhaps be an accessible way to the top.

Aconee huddles beside his tended fire protectively near his sick brother, watching from a distance. The Captain and First Mate begin arguing heatedly, both gesturing in the direction of Aconee and Miguel. In frustration, Captain Belasko leaps angrily to his feet. Separating himself from the other two men, he beds down for the night at a neutral position between the two campfires.

Next morning Aconee rises early and catches three large river bass, using his bare hands. He then pierces them on each tip of his spear and cooks them over an open fire. As is the custom in his native jungle, he shares freely with the Captain, also offering portions to the two other men.

After the three set off exploring again, Aconee lifts the delirious Miguel in his arms and carries him across the river, navigating gracefully along a maze of stones he has mapped out in his mind. At the cave entrance, he puts the Friar down and points for him to squeeze through the narrow passage alone. This cavern will serve as a place of protection from the elements, at least until his sick companion revives in strength.

Miguel exhales astonished by what his eyes behold, the pewter cross around his neck seeming to burn intensely bright. As a young man, he and his brother explored together the fascinating grottoes near a village outside Batalha, yet never witness to a formation like this!

While visiting an abandoned mine in southern Spain, Miguel had opportunity to study unusual drawings depicting the lives and activities of men from an earlier time. He did not know what the records meant, only that they tell a story of events long before Spain and Portugal called countries.

He has heard of caverns located in the upper Pyrenees with large exposed crystallized formations similar to this— but never a cave of pure light! Earthly principalities that rise and fall by dictate of divine dispensation, only to vanish into dust. Yet, none of the places he has seen of read about compare to the geologic wonder he now beholds.

This unusual phenomenon, shaped as the inside of a pyramid, is in all appearance a preserved capsule or the burial chamber of a prepared tomb. It could even be the splinter of some magnificent star fallen from the heavens, landing here even before the great flood recorded in the story of Genesis. Impact of this extraterrestrial rock is so great that it cracks open like a glass eggshell, splitting at the base, with the top half remaining intact as an inverted cone. As far as he knows, there exist no records of anything like it. He cannot help but wonder if this is the bitter star of Worm Wood foretold to bring a plague upon the waters of the earth. This place intentionally reserved through the course of time, until Day of Judgment. One thing certain, a magnification of power exists here, emanating from a source indiscernible.

Were Miguel not sick, Aconee and Captain Belasko might have left immediately. This is as far as the South American guide will serve. They are now beyond the fringe of the swamp, the rest of the way left up to those that wish to continue. Toward evening, the three shipmates return from their expedition. Tensions remain high between the First Mate and the Captain, leaving the young Sebastian looking glum and introspective, exhausted of reason. He now fears his alliance to Luis-Fernando to be a mistake, uncertain of what to do next. He trusts the integrity of his Captain; now trusts less the First Mate. He wishes that

Captain Belasko might continue with them at least as far as a European settlement. Also knows this unlikely, since his Captain's thoughts are only for the lovely Indian woman, Amahady. He has begun to fear that his salvage partner a devil. Of his own accord, he never would have thought to take the gold treasure. Now that those coins in his hands, Sebastian wants to keep them, sharing every young man's vision of prosperity. With his mind, he follows the directions of the First Mate, but in his heart serves another man, both his Captain and his friend.

Although they have discovered a vertical vine-covered face of ascent, it is too steep a negotiation to carry anything more than the essentials, requiring a man use both hands and feet. Since there are no ropes, this means the bags of gold must remain behind. The two partners have agreed to stash the heavy bags of treasure in the cave presently occupied by the Friar and the South American. Luis Fernando is not the trusting sort. He especially does not trust the Shaman, certain still that the creature evil, thinking that he wants revenge; but mostly that he wants the gold stolen from his country. Like so many, this man of earthly appetite believes through greed in only things he can see and touch, believing thoughts of destitution the greatest of all fears.

Luis Fernando holds particular distain for his Basque Captain, thinking him a fool-- a man with foreign principal- - unmoved by natural desire. For this reason alone, Luis-Fernando trusts him even less. Nor does he like the idea that so many now know the hiding place for his salvaged gold, certain of what he would do in their place. As for the fate of his young shipmate, many things can happen to one without experience in the real world of men and their possessions.

"We need to find a way to take the bags of gold with us." Luis-Fernando says to Sebastian once they make a new camp on this side of the river.

"Maybe one of us should stay behind and guard it while the other goes to find a settlement. You go and I will stay here with the others."

Sebastian has begun to have second thoughts about journeying with this crazed lunatic. He no longer has any trust at all in the intentions of the First Mate. He is sure now without a doubt the other man's interest based solely on insatiable craving, believing him capable of anything. To look into Luis-Fernando's eyes is like looking into the eyes of a savage animal, unpredictable, lacking completely the restraints of human compassion. In fulfillment of worst prophecy, the First Mate unexpectedly whips out his gun and points the barrel at Sebastian's head.

"No– we stick together! Besides what good is gold to you here?"

Sebastian feels suddenly weak to his knees, realizing himself in the presence of no man, but a monster driven by more than mere survival or desire for wealth.

Morning of the third day Sebastian comes secretly to the campsite of Captain Belasko desiring to borrow one of his two elegant pistols for protection. In exchange, he offers to give a share of his own gold, expressing growing uneasiness concerning the First Mate. The night before Luis-Fernando had forced the younger man to swear a dead man's oath concerning the hidden location of the gold, while staring down the end of a loaded barrel. Even more troubling is the radical demeanor of the man. On occasions, he begins breathing threatening remarks to invisible presences, whispering all night that the South American witchdoctor watches their every move from the shadows.

"I think he means harm to us all," Sebastian pleads. "He is a mad man, Captain, and harbors a particular hatred against you and that thing from the jungles."

"You can keep your gold, Sebastian." Emanuel says, handing the younger man one of his two weapons. "Watch your back and also keep in mind to protect the Friar."

"Do you believe he will be able to travel with us anytime soon? I don't think the First Mate will wait much longer."

"I've seen this kind of sickness before. The Friar's fate will be determined in the next several hours. It remains in the hands of his God now if he should continue with us. As for Luis-Fernando, I will do everything in my power to see he does no harm to any here."

"And what about the South American-- do you think the First Mate right about him wanting to take back the gold?"

"If he wanted the gold, he would have taken it long before now and done away with us all. He is no longer that beast brought aboard the Libertad chained in irons. I cannot explain what happened to this man, only that he and the Friar now share knowledge of something else. Something peaceful that far exceeds the glittering weight of this world. Such men are rich and without need of earthly treasure. The one named Aconee is not the one you need to worry about."

This is the last conversation the Captain and Sebastian will have. During the afternoon, Jacob dozes into a nap and dreams Amahady at his side stroking delicately the wrinkled contour of his brow. A sudden wind begins to blow, becoming the embodied fury of a hurricane. He tries to speak, but his beloved cannot hear him. An evil shadow coils suddenly out of a dark abyss, forcing them apart. Amahady's visage becomes face of his mother, then transforms into a radiating brightness that consumes the darkness. Her presence no longer corporeal, but is a fervent burning passage. From within this corridor, he hears and comprehends meaning of a word clearly spoken, *"Shelecheyanu."*

The man awakens from his mortal dream shaken and confused. So disturbing the vision, this Captain of practical reason goes for a long walk following the banks of turning water to clear his logical mind of thoughts and visions difficult to understand.

Near evening, Jacob makes decision to visit the cave occupied by Miguel and Aconee. He carries with him the satchel containing ship logs of the Libertad and the cryptic parchment pages of the Torah. His decided excuse is to check on the wellbeing of the Friar, but deep down another reason even more compelling.

He remembers vividly the first day Miguel boarded his ship. He remarks most his eyes, as light reflecting light. Those eyes nearly translucent in the morning sun inspire Jacob's soul with possibility, and yet something about those eyes disturbing. Perhaps, this is why he feels always uncomfortable in his presence. His mother had told him often about the Messiah. He is uncertain if this is Christ of the New Testament Bible or promise of a Jewish Messiah only.

On this voyage, Emmanuel has witnessed a miracle, seeing the South American changed from a beast into something else. No longer grotesque in his mind, delivered from violent possession, now a man of peaceful presence. Jacob has heard from young Sebastian how the demon cast out by command of the humble Friar. He did not want to believe in demons, but here stands evidence in the flesh. This unsettling testimony of a miracle disturbs his practical mind, causing him to struggle these many weeks. Just as miraculous, Jacob believes that he has also found true love in the Indian woman named Amahady. Such love is rare on this earth! But more than even the love of a woman, this Basque sea Captain desires to find a truce of peace between the logic of his reason and hunger in his soul.

Upon entering the magnificent cave, Jacob Belasko struck by an aura of even greater being. The giant captured from the dark depths of the South American jungles kneels beside the bed of Friar Miguel praying in the spirit, gazing steadfast up and with tears streaming along the twisted contour of his face. Together they are more than the appearance of flesh and blood, but are the presence of Holy Angels.

"Come in my son. We have this day been praying for you– wrestled battles of many principalities on your behalf!" Miguel states boldly from his couch. "As written by the prophet Isaiah upon parchments given to you by your mother concerning the coming of Messiah, this is the hour of eternal salvation! Jesus of Nazareth, a son of David as are you, stands even now at the door of your heart. Let not the significance of this moment pass without making the most important acceptance designed in a pattern of eternal consequence! This moment has been prepared for you from beginning-- a time and place prepared for all mankind in course of mortal passage!"

Aconee reaches out his large brown hands and places them on the head of one named Jacob Belasko. Instantly an irresistible force jolts through his physical being, as he falls prostrate on the floor of the cave. He sees in a vision the transfigured countenance of one born as a son of man, pinned inextricably upon bough of a fiery apex in heaven, and then lifted into a void. His eyes changed to jewels of many suns, opening a rift into a sublime heaven of eternal magnitude. This man no longer constrained to a pattern of mortality. Nor is this image the inspiration of a dream!

"Yes Lord!"

A voice shouts acceptance, resonating through every fiber of his being. This voice, once his own voice, a proclamation added to the witness of many other voices shouted eternally, as filament of that singularity shoots up into heaven and circles down, a quickening spark purging his mortal soul. The searing flame consumes an inanimate corpse stretching into eternity. No longer his body-- no longer is his name just Jacob, made of elemental substance! No longer is he subject to the commandment of final death!

In an instant, he is born again through Emmanuel, joined by legions of angels prepared for a grand final battle-- a battle engaged since the beginning of creation! Now he knows something his soul has known all along. This is the faith he has hungered for and wished always to embrace. The faith he could never find through many trials of living.

And all the good he has tried to accomplish and tried to be. He knows now what his mother meant so long ago. The hour of this destiny carefully orchestrated since before he exited the womb. This moment he comprehends the power in being alive. The certainty of Messiah lifted above time divided by time, his anointing blood of sacrifice coursing freely through mortal history as a river of refreshment provided to the thirst of every generation. His own thirst quenched at last, Emmanuel Jacob Belasko rises from dust of the cavern floor inspired with new purpose.

"I now know Messiah of my mother's prayers!" He shouts again in revelation, tears streaming down his weathered face. "Thank you, my Lord! Before this moment, I knew not my brothers! But now we share a bond immutable."

He then kneels weeping and begins kissing feet of the South American.

"My dear brother, now I see. We are all chosen vessels. Remember me always in prayer!"

"Yes, Brother Emmanuel, we are all unbound and bound again by love of one sacrifice. In this love made forever free through the Lord of resurrection." The Friar manages weakly from his reclining position. "What consolation might a man receive were he to gain the wealth of all life's bounty and lose his soul? Or what golden weight of a man's soul might be measured in exchange? We each have a cross to bear, as our Lord bears his cross even now on the hill of Calvary! This is the hour of fulfillment to a greater constitution than imagined through illusion of present flesh and blood passage!"

Crack of pistol fire shatters the spiritual revival, echoing loudly through the crystal chamber. Time begins again. Aconee instantly exits through the narrow passage, his wide shoulders scraping the walls. Without saying another word, Captain Belasko places his remaining pistol at the Friar's side and follows the South American through the opening. Upon exiting the curtain of water, he witnesses what his heart hopes not to see. Young Sebastian lay dead on the ground, blood streaming from a deadly wound to his forehead. A second shot, and Aconee collapses in front of him.

The First Mate struggles anxiously to reload, all the while cursing, as he seemingly tries to fight off assault of an invisible presence.

Instantly, a serene calm overwhelms Emmanuel, revealing to his newborn soul a clockwork design in the heavenly constellations, as the zodiac of events slow to a pulse. Now he knows clearly his purpose, understands meaning of his name conceived through Jewish ancestry. It is also Jacob, who comprehends most the significance of his disturbing dream just a few hours earlier, ready now to submit in acceptance. Moreover, here is the destiny of his birth, the place in time he has seen before. This moment is his salvation made complete.

Luis-Fernando grows more agitated by the hour. He has not slept in two days, certain that all are conspiring to kill him and take his gold. In their place, he would do the same. It is just the nature of men! He just as determined not to give them the satisfaction!

He remarks that the young Sebastian now has one of Captain Belasko's pistols. Now he is certain the conspiracy real. He makes note that the Captain disappeared for hours without explanation, and later watches him enter into the cave where they keep watch over the Friar and his three bags of gold doubloons. Even a man of the church corruptible if the price right-- what on this earth can be more tempting than opportunity to steal a fortune in minted gold coins?

Sebastian is standing near the cave entrance when Luis-Fernando startles him from behind. He is thinking about his sister and all the beautiful corsets and dresses he will buy her upon his return to Spain. The days of spring are getting warmer, and already the water level has subsided by several inches. In another week or two, he and the First Mate will be able to follow the riverbed on foot with their bags of gold to reach the higher country. The sharp familiar click warns him that a loaded gun pointed in his direction.

"What is this?" He says, twisting around to face the demon.

"Where are your loyalties?"

"With you sir... and with the Captain," he manages weakly.

"You want the gold for yourself! You have made a pact with those in the cave. You have been planning for this since the beginning. That is why you took one of Captain Belasko's pistols– to murder me at a convenient time!"

"No sir–"

Before Sebastian can finish his sentence, Luis-Fernando fires his pistol striking him dead center of the forehead. Quickly reloading, he sees from the right corner of his eye a large shadow approaching. Spinning in that direction, he fires another shot. The South American giant crumbles to the ground, also bleeding from a head wound. As he struggles to reload again, Captain Belasko appears.

Never could he have imagined a man capable of moving so swiftly, tackling him to the ground. It is as if time moves in slow motion, Luis-Fernando bound by the judgment of an irresistible force. They stumble violently, falling together, and begin rolling onto the smooth white surface of an outcropping rock at the water's edge. The man of perdition cursing and foaming at the mouth gripped inescapably in the strong arms of this man of the Pyrenees.

He sees for an instant a resolute peace in his Captain's unwavering eyes, a peace that he can never know. Then they tumble together into the churning white water still locked together. Even then, Emmanuel will not release his hold. Not even after the two swept beneath the plate of a subterranean ledge and into abyss of a sinkhole. Jacob Emmanuel Belasko determined to restrain this devil here for all eternity.

The crystal chamber darkens slowly, fading like a star in the night sky as it burns slowly out. The two shots fired can only mean the worst. Yet, neither saint nor devil enters into the keep. Miguel feels altogether abandoned, left alone to face the encroaching shadows of evening.

In a dream of delirium, he wanders to the edge of the rushing river to stick his tongue into the cool water, quenching his feverous thirst. He manages to nibble the remaining salted provisions and perhaps he sleeps. Miguel awakens, no longer tired, no longer old. Now brightness fills the chamber, a noise of wind, his body light as air. Aconee kneels at his side, a ladle of cool water poised to his lips. He is no longer scarred and misshapen, but as the beauty of man with a countenance of purest gold.

"Brother, drink now," he says and gently kisses the friar's forehead.

Instantly lifted into a celestial stream, light surrounding, the garment of former things fallen away and passed into insignificance, he is reborn, now made of eternal substance, joined by angels surrounding a throne in heaven. He is as always Miguel imagines, his face shining bright as the sun! This man of God, free at last, takes his place in a chorus of halleluiahs to sing his name forever.

Aconee opens his eyes to a canopy of distant burning stars rippling through the Milky Way. The bullet has grazed his temple, feeling like the crush of a large river boulder shot through his skull. It reminds him of a time before he became a Shaman, swiped by the tail of a Crocodile, measuring more than twenty feet long, dashing his body against a tree. He survived the event without knowing why or how. He remembers face of his mother, a porch veranda with pink Flamingos standing in a garden pond, and breath of a tropical breeze marking approach of the wet season. The name given by his parents is Aconee, which means *"River that flows deep."*

This before sacrificed by fearful commandment to dictate of local superstition. Born humpbacked and less than perfect, Aconee appointed to serve as high priest to the cruel local water god, Uiara. Infected by many spirits, Aconee becomes the strongest and most possessed of all Shamans. He is able to make fire rain out of heaven and resurrect from water legions of frog warriors. Then men in impenetrable armor wielding weapons of steel and fire sticks capture living proof of a demon.

Aconee locked for a week and a day in belly of the deep. In this darkness, gnashing and wailing, sound of ocean waves dredged from the deep. His soul trapped in even deeper darkness. Then appears sudden grander of an archangel, holding lance of a flaming cross. It is the visage of one known always, an emissary sent to resurrect Aconee's incarcerated soul by commission of grander will.

Prior to losing consciousness, Aconee vaguely remembers Emmanuel racing past him and tackling the crazed Luis-Fernando to the earth. Together they roll-off an outcropping ledge and into the raging river. He must have passed out after this. Aconee knows from experience the many invisible dangers lurking in the depths of river currents. Knows it unlikely anyone might have survived. All the same, Aconee will scour the banks next morning, but as expected finds nothing.

Friar Miguel is also gone now. He died peacefully in his makeshift bed, resembling a child in repose. Bowing his head in reverent pray, Aconee says goodbye to his departed companion. He then begins to sing in the spirit, praising the

Lord of Lords for the deliverance of his messengers sent in mortal dispensation to fulfill a design of living testament predetermined in heaven through shadow of earthly passage. He has no doubt his two brothers alive, resurrected even now, forever in a kingdom without end. He knows also that in the course of time he must join them in presence of a better heaven and earth.

Aconee buries the young Sebastian on the opposite bank of the river where the earth fertile in a grove of wild flowers. He will leave Miguel undisturbed in the cave where he lies, also leaving the three bags of gold doubloons, along with the fine pistol belonging to Jacob Emmanuel Belasko, last captain of the Spanish Galleon Libertad. He will carry back with him the parchment scroll with spoken promise by the Prophet Isaiah. He will include the worn Latin Bible of Friar Miguel and the leather satchel containing Ship Logs of the Libertad. These he will keep together in the safety of his own tepee and pass them down to the son of Emmanuel when the time comes.

These artifacts will continue to hold reverence to the people of Aconee for many generations to come. Stacking several of the white river rocks to conceal the cave entrance, Aconee seals the crypt against mortal intrusion. On one of these rocks, he engraves the pictographs of his language, using a knife and a flint stone taken from the body of dead Sebastian.

Amahady weeps bitterly upon receiving news that her beloved is dead. At least she finds some peace in knowing that he died for a noble cause. She knows in her heart that her Emmanuel would not have chosen any other way. She does not fully understand the meaning of the spiritual events related to her by Aconee, at least not with her mind. Xeantee Aconee, after all, is not of this world! Nor can his heart be broken, as do the hearts of those born with natural affections. Nevertheless, she accepts these irrevocable events as *Shelecheyanu.* At least the name of Emmanuel

Belasko, last captain of the Spanish Galleon Libertad not forgotten; his fruit ordained to live-on through the water of her flesh.

Amahdy's first-born son she will name Qualetaga-Tahmoh, meaning *Angel of the Father*. Tahmoh will continue to preserve the ancient parchment scroll left by his father, and learn the pictograph language of Xeantee Aconee. In the fullness of time, he will receive from his mother the turquoise-blue amulet with effigy of a beetle carved in the face, never knowing its greater significance. This he will pass on to one of his children, as they will pass it on to one of their children. This repeated from generation to generation, until the meaning fulfilled.

In the procession of his days, Tahmoh will continue always to bear witness to benevolent sacrifice of his father. He will provide living testament of ritual meaning found in the sacred black book of Friar Miguel; importance of the parchment scroll written in a language no one able to understand; and genesis record of the Libertad ship logs proclaiming how the first Aconee got here. Most importantly, he instructs them never to forget the truest measure of *Shelecheyanu.*

Presence of the first Xeantee Aconee will remain among his new people for fifty moons before vanishing into the great swamp. He grows old and wise in time, learning their language, as they in turn master some of his engraved pictograph language. His name and position remembered in daily prayers of instruction. Always he is depicted a hunter providing daily sustenance to their needs.

As rite of passage to each generation, the coronate Tahmoh receives special instruction on how to reach banks of the Great River. Here he must leave continuing testament by chiseling a pictograph record on one of the white river rocks.

Xeantee Aconee is no monster in their minds, but a holy angel of the Great Spirit sent by *Shelecheyanu* always near.

He is an abiding presence of things living and not living, a testament of faith in what none can know through life and present reason alone. In beginning, the new tribe call themselves *The Children of Xeantee Aconee*, but in the course of time shortened only to *Tribe Aconee*.

These Aconee Indians will remain isolated and continue through many changes of the moon to flourish on this obscure marshland island located in a region later known only as Liberty Swamp. This is true record of the first seeds planted here.

Liberty Epic of Shadows

BOOK TWO

Tahmoh and Angeni-Cuauhtemoc

CHAPTER 6

Desertion of Adam Pixley

The infamous Waxhaw Massacre remains the historical turning point in the fight for freedom against Colonial rule. These permanent residents of the new America, no longer content to remain neutral, have taken up arms against Loyalist forces. Many have joined the patriot army after the rebellious Boston Tea Party, exacting terrible vengeance upon the predictable military tactics of the *Red Coat* occupation. The war for independence will rage on another three years, until the signing of the Paris Treaty between King George III, marking the eve of Great Britain's decline in reputation as a despotic world empire no longer able to subdue its citizenry. From the decay of another fallen principality rises up chimera of the new United States of America. As in all wars, many lost in action, whose fate remains forever unknown.

Adam Pixley finds himself a man without rank or position, a man alone and easy prey. It was not always this way. As recently as this morning, he marched a proud soldier on the Front Line of His Majesty's Imperial Army. Days earlier, he had participated in the slaughter of many at a junction near Lancaster, a battle where he personally ran-through two unarmed men. It is war, after all, and young Adam just following orders. Today he stands in formation with fifteen other soldiers scouting the borders of marshland, searching for any signs of a band of patriots led by the infamous Swamp Fox. The order received to split-up, with instructions to reunite further upstream. Just as they cross into the shadow of an outcropping rock named *Devil's Jaw* near the river mouth, a ghost militia strikes out of nowhere, band of ragged scarecrows wearing no uniform or insignia. They fight as savages and kill as savages. The bloody battle lasts less than ten minutes, but long enough for the massacre of his entire squad. Adam is one of the lucky ones. A musket ball grazes the left side of his temple knocking him unconscious. By the time he is lucid again, bodies in red coats lay everywhere. The officer in charge looks blankly into the sky, chocking slowly to death on his own blood.

In blind panic, Adam Pixley tosses aside his musket rifle, along with most of his gear, and escapes blindly into the nether region of the encroaching swampland. After what seems an eternity, he tumbles headlong into a mote, precariously saved by moldering branches leeched with hanging vines on a tree fallen from the opposite shore. Pulling himself free from the suction of black mud, he thinks to rest, except that he hears voices somewhere in the distance. Convinced his enemies still searching for him, he springs back to his feet, fleeing deeper into this perilous region.

When finally he stops to run, twilight of night begins to descend. Those earlier events seem shadows of a bad dream in his mind. He is now lost in a vast swamp. The shadows here represent something else, nightmare visions born out latent memories no longer remembered. Incandescent pools shimmer serendipitously, as lost treasures fleshed just beneath the surface. Adam knows from experience this promise an illusion. Just another lie reflected in oblivion of the deep. The truth is that the fist of night closes ever tighter around him, a skeletal hand of slithering mist made with tentacles of damp air.

Suddenly, everything swallowed into darkest night. Exhausted and nowhere to turn, Adam Pixley wishes only to sleep. Feeling a clump of solid earth at the base of a great Cyprus tree, he curls into a fetal position, succumbing instantly into dreamless slumber. Adam jerks suddenly

awake, aware of something cold brushing across his face.
He can just barely make out the prehistoric thing, slithering
mechanically into a body of blacker night. A horrific
screech from the upper branches of the tree just above his
head, a crunching noise nearby of soft bones being
devoured whole. Fully aroused in the terrible reality of his
nightmare, Adam will not know rest again.

The hours pass as the slow pulse of the universe fading
into the boundaries of this world at edge of what always he
imagines Hades to be. There seems no end to this
nightmare. He waits expectantly in the dark, alone, afraid
even to move. Then early morning twilight fades ever so
faintly into this nether region, changes slowly brighter,
imparting new flesh to the swamp interior.

The European is amazed how everything so different.
Things evil and ominous the night before transformed into
garlands of beautiful green archways opening into shrouded
cathedrals. Those passages that led into abysses of
purgatory now open gates into paradise. Spring has just
commenced, tiny buds dripping near the water's edge, soon
to explode into intoxicating flowers. The bright morning
sun climbs ever higher, winking through entangled
branches as a kind spirit sent to guide his way. The soldier
feels now more at ease, a sense of reassurance that he has
not known since the terrible events that have propelled him
here. Hungry, he decides to consume a portion of dried
military rations. Brushing away the mosquito scum, he
drinks his fill of swamp water.

Adam stands refreshed, ready to continue his odyssey.
Then a golden glint catches his eye. Something bright
wedged in a clef between two roots, something golden
embedded into the living wood. Upon closer examination,
Adam realizes it is a Spanish doubloon. Using his eating
utensil, he digs this trophy from the soft bark. The earthly
treasure glitters brightly in the morning, as new as the day
of its mint. Adam searches for others, but finds none. The

origin of its meaning is to remain presently clandestine, as enigmatic as circumstances that have propelled him to this forsaken realm. He places the coin into a pocket close to his heart. There will be time enough later to imagine its greater significance.

Adam Pixley walks more easy now, a gait light, as though he follows a known path. He imagines he is a boy again exploring the lower wetlands outside of his home near Nottingham. They also call that area a swamp, but it is nothing like this place. Here is perfected solemnity, except for the occasional call of a bird, a remote inconspicuous splash of a frog. Here distances expand with no foreseeable end, altogether lacking boundary. He hopes to be heading in a good direction-- any direction that leads out of this idyllic marsh and back into the world of men.

Time has no meaning in a swamp. Every direction looks the same, every tree like another. Judging by the position of the sun, it is already well past noon. The humidity sticks to his flesh like the membrane of a second skin. He would gladly have shed his red coat made of British wool were it not for clouds of mosquitoes that swarm furiously around him, attaching any exposed flesh. Adam does not know that he has become delirious, that the swamp water poison, and that the mosquitoes carry more than just a fiery itch.

Once more night descends, transfiguring all that is beautiful again into the grotesque. In his mind voices that condemn him as a deserter, others cursing him as an alien intruder lost in this no man's land. Adam covers his ears, curses back, begging the voices to stop! The garish slither of moon appears, slicing into twisted lattices overhead like a hoary demon watching him through web of a cage. If he might have seen himself through those eyes, then Adam Pixley surely would have known that he is mad. In this madness, Adam clearly witnesses things no mortal dare, except in the faded radiance of life, as one's soul descends into shadows of finality. A deluge of heavy splashes sound to the right of his position. Adam pivots in that direction, but sees nothing through the slithering haze. Another splash– this time behind him– then in front—something stands just beyond his vision! He feels the presence, more than seeing with his eyes. Then an accompaniment of grotesque croaks rise with the rising of the mist that resonates into the incoherent pattern of his madness. Suddenly all light vanishes into a cloak of night!

Frogs begin singing hysterically! It is a song out of purgatory, escalating ever more maddening, curdling in his gut! Adam feels panic as he has never felt before, a terror of things invisible approaching from every direction. He looks-- but can just barely discern their shape. Now every way the same-- as wraiths of escalating dread reach into the sanctuary of his mind. Voices and faces only vaguely remembered resurrected from grave of his conscience! Grabbing his hair, Adam begins to run blindly, screaming obscenities against the darkening void! He is a man forever alone-- lost in this terrible realm of shade! The swamp floor opens without warning. Adam Pixley devoured whole, swallowed into a bottomless pit for all eternity.

Strong tentacles drag him down with determined force. The more he struggles, the stronger they pull. Clutching anything near, he tries desperately to escape- all elements impotent to save him. The stygian water reaches his chin-- by now even hope gone! In final desperation, Adam cries- out to no one. Who is there to hear? Who will ever know this his final resting place? He tries futilely to hold his breath, the cold stagnant water pushing irresistibly into his nostrils, down his throat, causing him to choke involuntarily. Adam Pixley has arrived at the end of life, as do all men in their generation. His name forever exiled in purgatory of this place. Buried and forgotten in the vastness of time, without even memory of a prayer. A soldier of the British army vanished in a bog pit without hope or record of the event.

Liberty Epic of Shadows

It is hand of the almighty that grabs him, resurrecting the limp creature back among the living. The man from another world chokes, vomiting swamp mud, his eyes clouded by centuries old blindness. Rib of a quarter-moon begins to creep cautiously from behind a shroud. Half-life existence of this nether region restored. Only now does Adam Pixley see his savior at last! It is a man– no not a man-- but a creature. Yet it is more than man or creature, ascending above every shadow, draped with animal skins covering impressive shoulders. Black strands ooze along exposed knotted knees, supporting trunk of a body thick as Carolina Cyprus Trees, rising solidly out of the diluvium mist, and a large head shaped alarmingly amphibious. In one extended hand flash of a three-headed javelin speared with something prehistoric withering convulsively on the tip. The other mighty hand clutches Adam Pixley by the scruff of his neck, helpless as a kitten. Most striking is strangeness of the eyes that shine from the pitch mouth of a gaping cowl.

The creature speaks-- or at least Adam thinks this in his delirium-- a horrible croaking noise stabbing his mind with even greater apprehension. Chorus of frogs again sing, as once again the swamp changes, becoming vision of lost paradise. Adam Pixley closes his eyes, his exhausted mind sinking irresistibly into unconsciousness.

CHAPTER 7

Days of Fallen Eagle

Man from the outer world dressed in a red coat dreams terrible dream. His nightmares make him sweat feverishly and to curse madly. There are brief moments of lucidity when he imagines he is in the presence of someone else, imagines soft feminine hands stroking his brow, forcing something tasteless into his mouth. In distance, he thinks to hear the rhythmical beating of drums. Sees disembodied spirits in the air chanting a name that almost he knows. A distinctive rush of sweat and the fever breaks at last. Adam Pixley sleeps. His body of flesh finally at peace.

The sound of children playing nearby, the familiar bark of a dog, the melodic laughter of women rising and falling as a soothing brook-- the stranger from nowhere opens his eyes in presence of no one.

Adam Pixley is once again back in the living moment. He always thought of Indians as scouts only. Always he imagined them to be of the most vicious sort, blood thirsty, and not given to normal affections experienced by the civilized of this world. Taught that they are all heathen, he believes them more animal than human. Yet, it is obvious these natives have nurtured him back to health. Touch of a human hand had soothed his burning brow and tended him through despair. It is human compassion that cared for his comfort and human patience that guided his mind through those terrible shadows of delirium.

All watch silently as he staggers out of the tent, brightness stabbing his eyes. Adam always considered beautiful for a man, stands tall, his countenance naturally regal. The younger ones seem particularly curious. He is the first European to come into their village in present memory. Except for legends passed down from generation to generation, Adam Pixley is the only outsider these Indians have ever handled in the flesh.

Maybe because of the uniqueness of his stature, or the way light of morning sun reflects in his flaxen hair, he is special in their minds. Maybe the sheen of his pale skin, unblemished, except for a painful red wound slashed across his left temple from recent event of a bullet graze. Unafraid, children surround this stranger from beyond, their innocent eyes looking up at him in awe.

"*Angeni-Cuauhtemoc--Angeni-Cuauhtemoc-*" they start chanting in unison, each reaching out to touch the red wool of his coat draped over his stout shoulders.

Adam later learns that the words mean a name. It is his new name translated as '*Angel of Fallen Eagle*'. This name destined to be definition of future consequence

Adam quickly becomes accustomed to these pleasant people. He learns that they call themselves Aconee, which means, as close as he can comprehend '*Born of Water*" or maybe the name means '*Water Frogs*'. They try to teach him the basic principles of their dialect: what it means to be hungry or thirsty, too hot or too cold. He learns the meaning of touch and laughter, the words for rain and for sun. Their word for love inclusive of everything applied with value and respect even to consumed plants and animals. He notes that they have no words to convey hate or prejudice, and that the concept of death is simply untranslatable. Something either is or is not. Particularly curious to Adam is the common way they greet each other. Each morning they say "*Shelecheyanu*," a sound incongruous to other speech congregations. And each night before returning to their tents, they say "*Shelecheyanu*."

As nearly as he can understand the word means blessing or an acknowledgement to a creator that bestows a meaning to all living things and things not living through acceptance of divine providence. It is difficult for Adam to appreciate fully the significance within context or its root of origin. Like so many other mysteries defining the unusualness of these people, the meaning of *Shelecheyanu* will remain the greatest obstacle for Adam Pixley when the time comes.

It is slow progress to pick-up their language in everyday communication, forcing him often to rely on signs and gestures to convey his desires. They, however, are far more astute, and a few even begin to speak English back to him, rather than merely parroting his own words. Once the curiosity gone, Adam becomes accepted as an honorary member of the tribe, allowed free access to come and go as he pleases. In time, he finds life here pleasant compared to being a scripted soldier of the Royal Army. Even though these Aconee Indians do not openly restrict his movements, Adam has little desire to explore too far from this simple domain. Eventually, he realizes the tribe inhabitants of an island surrounded by impassable barriers of dangerous marshland. Further, he feels here peace and sense of welcome never felt before, even by his own family.

One of the older men proves more clever for discerning sound of his voice than the rest and soon begins to actually speak back complete sentences. His name is Tahmoh, a meaning that he says is untranslatable. Tahmoh is descended from a linage of chieftains going back to the beginning. No one seems to know how long ago that is. Despite his titled position, Tahmoh revered no differently than anyone else in the tribe, except for his excellent skill as a hunter. For some inexplicable reason Adam does not particularly like the sound of the name Tahmoh. He calls the man Jack instead. Jack is the name of his older brother killed during one of England's military campaigns. The Indian happily accepts Jack as his new name, and calls Adam the English word 'Angel' in reciprocation.

The only surviving memory Adam has of his real brother is a crumpled letter written in a shaky hand on the eve of a decisive battle. As a boy, he read that letter often, memorizing every word, as one might a canto from a lost scroll. In one way it comforts him, in another terrifies his senses. Nevertheless, he reads it almost every night before retiring to bed.

"It's a bloody peaceful night…too bloody peaceful. Tonight I would give me rifle for some of mom's Sheppard Pie. I wishes that I could just walk away and say to the King: 'call me when the war be finished.' I think over the hill they must be thinking the same. The Sergeants on the line tell us this be the battle that will decide England's future. They said that before. There be a full moon in the night sky— a moon to kiss a lass, a moon watched by a young boy from under a tree…. and dream. The odor of cannon powder fills the air like an evil perfume. Me best friend was killed in today's skirmish. A musket ball passed into the soft of one of his eyes, and he fell beside me like slain Goliath. He says to me just last week that his wife bore him a new son. He says that at least his son won't have to fight once England wins the peace. Tonight he rests among England's fallen sons; his only son without knowledge, asleep in a cradle beneath the protection of this same wondrous moon I see far from British soil. Me thinks that maybe tomorrow I will join his brigade. I pray I die a hero as did he. I hope that me own brother uses a plow shear instead of a sword as the words of the Lord's book promises. I pray this be England's last war…"

This was not Great Britain's last war, nor would this present war be the last. Adam Pixley had chosen to follow in the steps of his brother, and all the sons and brothers before him. It is better than to starve to death. Adam's father witnessed the violent murder of his father by men wearing British uniforms during the Jacobite War. As with all conflicts, there were two sides, each believing their caused on the side of righteousness; but in the end, only starvation, pestilence, and death overshadows all. Adam's grandfather just a simple farmer trying to protect his crop fields from the torch. That is just the way of things then-- and so little has changed since. Today at least, those allowed privilege to serve in the British military walk with a full belly, even if they are treated second class. Adam hates this aristocratic measure of a man. The Irish made to feel inferior in the presence of lesser men-- having always to lower your head just because of birthright. Just because of the blood that courses through one's veins! It is for this reason, Adam Pixley feels less patriotic to the calling of the King's service.

Deep down Adam feels envious of Jack's simple Indian way of life. Here is a man who has never fought in any campaign of war, a man whose greatest ambition to hunt and to fish. Through simplicity of his nature, Jack sees the moon as a spirit to guide him, the earth as mother, and the sun as a father of life, inspiring meaning to all things in season. He is heir to the *water people* carried across the great river, born guiltless and free. Adam starts to think of this man as dear of a brother as ever he could have. But also thinks the other too pure, which provides opportunity for jealousy.

After awhile the two men begin to grow closer. Not the closeness of affection, but a bond based on mutual respect. Adam learns quickly the Indian ways, excited to learn all that he can. Jack proves the ideal mentor, willing to share all that he knows about hunting prey. Familiar with the ways of the swamp, Jack shows paths of safe passage through maze of deceptive bog pits just by smell. He claims monster-size Cat Fish weighing more than a man that lie on the swamp bottoms if one knows where to fish. He says that according to Aconee legend, the deeper marshlands inhabited by large prehistoric creatures with enormous razor-toothed jaws that can easily tear a man apart with one bite. Adam has read about Alligators and Crocodiles that live on the southern continent. It intrigues him that such creatures could be part of this wetland ecology as well. Jack speaks reverently of another creature, a creature, neither man, nor animal: a creature as much imaginary, as anything incarnate. To these Aconee he is a guardian spirit resurrected in times of special peril to protect and guide his chosen children. To those from outside, he is a dark emissary wielding a two-edged sword of death and life. To some salvation, others reserved to final judgment. Without doubt, this fabled creature responsible for saving Adam Pixley from certain death.

"Angel special frog," Jack says, referring to the morning one of the women found the man wearing a red coat laid at the edge of their village. "Angel fall from sun and not die –You Adam-- special frog!"

"What do you mean by frog?" Adam wants to know.

"All frogs children of Xeantee— all sing free his name," he replies sincerely.

"What is Xeantee?"

"Xeantee everywhere," he says spreading his arms apart, "all children of Xeantee— Xeantee Aconee *Shelecheyanu*!"

"So this…thing– this monster– he protects you?" Adam ventures.

"No monster—*Prince of Frogs*– all frogs sing Xeantee Aconee when he comes. His shadow great in the swamp– Jack knows– Angel has seen! He appears to all-- but only through soul of Aconee is he *Xeantee*."

Adam still does not fully understand, but declines pursuing the subject further. There would be time enough to ponder at least some part of this simple wisdom. One thing he cannot deny is that the being he saw a thing never seen before, even in imagination. No mortal arm raised his body from jaws of death, as though he were an infant. Nor the eyes that shined through a dark cowl those of some mindless animal.

Jack is right to believe the creature supernatural. Only Adam is unable to accept this so simply. Perhaps this perception based on measured experience, which could have made difference at the end. Except Adam's European mind trained to reject anything that cannot be touched or seen. Therefore, final judgment reserved because of an unwilling nature to believe simple testimony of something contrary to rationale.

Before long, Adam Pixley recognized as a full-fledged member of the Aconee tribe. He learns well the art of how to choose a straight shaft of wood to make an arrow, or strong dried bamboo for a spear. He learns how to attach a piece of slate-quartz shaped into a pointed tip, and how to hewn pieces of flint for a sharp blade. From tangles of thorn bushes, he learns to make snares. Wood that is more flexible produces a better Hunting Bow, and dried sinew of a deer the best for taunt string. The more effective weapon, at least to those with most skill, is a leather thong made into a sling. Only a few—Jack being perhaps the best—are able to deploy this weapon with the most deadly accuracy. Jack patiently teaches his friend the Indian way of hunting: how to move without making sound, and the difference between being upwind and downwind. Adam learns that it is not in the strength of the arm, but in the release, which most effectively downs a prey. In time, he can see just by hearing, and knows a presence by feeling. Jack, indeed, becomes the older brother he lost. The brother he never knew.

The men often hunt in bands, preferring to herd their quarry into a waiting ambush. The bigger Bucks prove the more difficult to kill. Strong and quick, with hides thick as tree bark and broad antlers capable of ripping open a man's flesh. The hunters approach these larger animals cautiously, with the goal of piercing them in the soft area just under the throat. Even then, the creature might rend one of the younger, less experienced braves, whose enthusiasm causes him to venture too near too soon. Thinking one of these large creatures to be dead during a hunt, Adam reaches out to touch the antlers. The animal bellows loudly, tries to rise, shakes its head ferociously, knocking the surprised hunter to the ground and inflicting a nasty wound across his arm.

"Angel fall when Buck rise from dead!" Jack laughs, helping the stricken man to his feet.

The cut turns infected and starts to pulse by next morning; therefore, he must endure several days of a foul smelling plaster composed of a mixture containing swamp herbs, black bog mud, and urine taken from the dead animal. Just the idea of this concoction makes Adam ill. Nevertheless, Jack's foul remedy proves effective. In future, he is careful never to make the same mistake.

Even smaller creatures such as raccoons, skunks, and possums might prove unpredictable and dangerous when cornered. Especially difficult are possums, whose nocturnal habits make it a night virtuoso, with eerily reflecting silver eyes in the light of a full moon. Particularly disturbing is the instinct to emit a foul odor while playing dead. By assuming a ghastly posture, eyes red and lifeless, tongue hanging out, it will just lie there when no other escape possible. However, if sufficiently prodded, this deceiver will leap to the offensive, gnashing with sharp piercing teeth and razor claws. The Aconee particularly enjoy possum stew, considering it a special delicacy. Therefore, every full moon the men organize a hunting party to peril the night in search of these rodent-like creatures, enough to feed a tribe of more than a hundred.

Another nocturnal creature favored by the Aconee is Raccoon. They are a quarrelsome species, bold scavengers that know how to slip into the tents through the cover of night and steal provisions without the knowledge of the sleeping inhabitants. They are prey most desirable during the winter months, when their coat grows thickest. The warm soft fur used by the women to fashion hats and gloves.

Fat Quail scurry about the island in abundance, as do squirrels and rabbits. The most difficult to hunt, and most wily of all the wildlife creatures that inhabit the area, a large North American bird called a Turkey. The ingenious markings of these creatures make them almost invisible. Having keen eyesight and elevated senses, they can hunker low to the ground with elongated neck extended horizontally and race swiftly through the underbrush. Hunted in the fall when they are fattest, the foliage providing the least amount of protection, this large unusual fowl provides occasion to a rare feast. Successful harvesting presents enormous challenge to even the most experienced hunter. Only those endowed with stealth and cunning able to bag even one of these magnificent birds. Rarely, one might get two after many days of stalking the underbrush. Jack is one such hunter inbred with intuition of instinct that defies the odds, sometimes bringing back three after a single day's forage.

During these many hunting excursions, Adam becomes increasingly aware of the geography. The tribe rests near center of an island, surrounded on all sides by dangerous swamp. Because of personal experience, he knows there is a passage to higher elevations, but remains ignorant of the way. Nor will Jack answer him when asked. For the first time, Adam begins to feel a prisoner to his surroundings, as one might feel the impediment of dwelling on an isolated pleasant island. Free to go where he pleases without supervision, free to participate or not in the tribal activities, he still feels trapped. Like the Aconee, he is limited to the boundaries of this appendage landmass. Thought of this restriction begins to torment him, mainly because of his memory of a greater world beyond. Often, he finds comfort in rubbing the foreign inscription stamped on the gold coin found in the beginning, glittering reminder of civilization beyond, which increasingly haunts his dreams. Not that there is really anything beyond for Adam Pixley, except a court martial and possible execution; nevertheless, his real world is that other material world glimmering in distant illusion of happiness not very happy then.

The rich diversity of wild game is not the only favorable attribute of this inland refuge. The black diluvium soil proves uncommonly fertile, producing enough fruits and vegetables in such quantities as to feed a tribe five times the present population. A variety of beans, squash the size of a man's arm, tall forest of corn, and swaying fields of yellow sunflowers networked together in such a way as to lend protection and support to each other. The corn stalks act as pillars for the twisting bean vines, while large squash with broad spreading leaves form a barrier to block encroachment of weeds. There are other varieties of vegetables as well, some altogether alien in appearance, such as a potato-like root bearing globes of yellow fruit growing wild on the ground requiring very little attendance; and another unnamed plant belonging to the beet family with leaves that resemble the webbed foot of a duck or goose.

A battalion of bright-faced sunflowers stand guardian over these natural food sources by attracting certain bugs and flying insects. They not only protect the vegetation by ample provision of supplement contained in the sour-sweet kernel of their yellow center; but also considered an edible nutritious snack by the agriculturist tending the fields.

A constant blight of crows proves particularly annoying, so Adam erects a stick-figure scarecrow, and drapes his British red jacket over the shoulders. This works even better than expected. Therefore, the red-jacketed effigy becomes a permanent member of the tribe from this point on, bearing an honorary name meaning *Chief Red Jacket*.

Cotton and tobacco, cultivated in a separate area from the food plants, represent the social life-blood of Aconee communal activity. The Aconee women, exceptionally skilled weavers, break open the boll, separate the fibers from the seeds, and make yarn using only their fingers. They then dye the strands different colors with wild berries, and produce most exquisite cotton garments embroidered with intricate designs rivaling any European design.

The men on occasions enjoy sitting around a campfire at night and share a pipe made of bone packed with dried tobacco. Here they brag the prowess of their past hunting victories or stories about exploits of their father's fathers going back generations. It is during these times that Adam hears many harrowing tales referring to the mythical existence of Xeantee. It becomes clear in his mind that Xeantee is not only a person; but also a spirit in time, referencing a place not completely associated in the physical world. At least not the world predicated on the prescribed actions of men conducted through daily course. In Adam Pixley's practical mind, Xeantee represents an existence bordering shadow and light, neither present, nor past, but a condition where some eternal battle rages continually between forces of light and darkness. The good spared through submission; the evil exiled in a place called *Valley of the Frog Prince*-- hunted by the arm of swift judgment.

"*Prince Xeantee—Prince of Frogs— Shelecheyanu*" Adam hears this over, and over again, as he struggles to fit the meaning within context of present reason.

These images enrich his curiosity, but also terrify his senses. Through course, Adam Pixley begins to comprehend choice of many possibilities...and more.

CHAPTER 8

Trial of Shadows

The one called *Angeni-Cuauhtemoc* particularly enjoys the communal activity of planting and harvesting. It is customary that only older folk, unmarried women, and some of adolescent age participate actively in agriculture. Since Adam a farmer at heart, the soil remains in his blood. In earth this rich he could have planted anything back home and it would have grown. It is here that Adam sees a shy young pretty woman named Mitexi. Jack introduces her to Adam as his younger biological sister sired by a different father.

"What does Mitexi mean?" Adam asks, entranced by her feminine charm.

"Mitexi means *Sacred Moon*." Jack says. "Since she likes you, my brother, Mitexi gives you permission to call her by your English translation."

In time, Adam and Mitexi become close, often laughing together, or just lying upon a hill watching the sky. Particularly funny to the young woman is Adam's sacrifice of his red coat suspended by skeleton of sticks to keep away harbinger crows. After this, she openly calls him '*Red Angel*' during community activities, but he still remains just '*Angel*' when he goes out hunting and fishing.

Sacred Moon is as soft and delicate as the promise of her name. Always she wears around her soft neck a turquoise-blue amulet carved with some kind of insect tied on a string of sinew. It sparkles when light hits it just right, with scorch marks, exhibiting evidence that the medallion exposed to extreme heat sometime in the past. Along the edges melted copper and brass, making it appear crude and worthless in Adam Pixley's cosmopolitan mind. However, he determines this not of Indian design, but provided no explanation of its origin. It will remain as enigmatic as the gold coin in his possession.

Mitexi protects her hands from damage by using rabbit skins to pull-up unwanted weeds, and keeps her head covered by a hat arrayed with Turkey feathers as protection from the sun. This makes her cunningly attractive to the imaginings of a young man. She is in Adam Pixley's mind a child and a woman. Her face and presence begins to creep into his dreams and fantasies.

After a time, Adam looks forward to going to the crop fields just to watch her, to see the movement of her slender body, as she bends over in attendance of her duties. She learns English quickly, and after only a few months speaks with surprising proficiency. Mitexi is neither the youngest, nor the prettiest of all the available Indian women. Except, she alone has the power to tug at Adam Pixley's soul, like passage of the moon disturbs ocean tides.

His desire begins to grow disproportionately, intoxicating, clouding his reason. Before long, Adam thinks about nothing else. Finally, he submits to his passions, convincing himself that the shadow of this rare reflection born from the heaven of a new world sufficient to make him forget his past, his traditions, his rage against authorities, and even the lust for things material.

"Jack since you are a blood relative of *Sacred Moon*, I wish to ask your permission to marry her according to Indian tradition."

"You are welcome my brother, for then we truly will be brothers. Mitexi has agreed already, willing to walk the *Trial of Shadows* in accordance to the way of *Shelecheyanu.*"

The Aconee Indians have a way of matrimonial consent that is different from other cultures, even other Indian cultures. If a man wishes to take a woman, and if she should accept his advances, then both are required to undergo a ritual of purification. They must walk together a spiritual corridor called the *Trial of Shadows*.

The couple bound together by a single cord and placed on opposite sides of a specially constructed tent. The *Trial of Shadows* prescribed passage through a realm the Aconee call '*Xeantee*' traveled only on the first night of a full moon. Adam thinks the tradition superstitious, but Mitexi insists that it is the only way of consummation.

"It is by passing along the *Trial of Shadows* that we must find each other. Have faith my husband. This is the way it has always been. In time you will understand."

As near as custom permits, Jack agrees to become his best man, appointed to stand guard outside the dwelling.

"Angel soon born again Aconee," he says with enthusiasm on the day of ritual.

"What does that mean?"

"It is said that our people once traveled across the great water, led to this place by a spirit holy. Here a new seed planted and made to grow, as meant in the beginning. Here Aconee born Xeantee. *Prince of Frogs* is everywhere, and even now prepares in river of his name."

"What river, Jack– I see only swamp," Adam insists.

"Angel see with mind, not with heart. River always near, like Xeantee always near– soon Angel know all that Aconee brother know. This is the way of *Shelecheyanu*."

Adam is not so certain. He has grown to respect these Indians and the way they live. Has even learned to embrace the simplicity of their existence and submit to their customs. *But can he really become one of them in spirit?*

In these people is the living legend of stories heard during his childhood about the noble magnificent tribes that inhabit the New World. He remembers his grandfather telling him the story about an Indian princess named Pocahontas, who traveled across the ocean to visit England nearly two centuries earlier. In young Adam's mind, it is a wonderful, yet impossible fairytale to live free in nature, free from authority and without restraint. Here he is in the midst of those people in the flesh. Here he prepares at the threshold of an important ritual, promising to make him a true member of this unusual and extraordinary society so longed for in youth.

The evening air crisp with a hint of fall and orb of a full moon hangs precisely over a uniquely prepared ceremonial lodge constructed of tree bark. Jack and two other young braves wearing black painted faces escort Adam to the edge of the swamp, instructing him on what is next. This structure is unlike other Aconee teepee dwellings. Those tents consist of an outer shell stitched together with layers of bear and deer hide, dried and stretched, and then sealed with tree sap. This one is made entirely of wood, shaped octagonal, and reinforced by a complex outer web of sticks fitted together in such manner as to form a tight-knit cage. Another oddity is that it has no opening, except for an expanded flange at the top belching steam like vent of an active volcano. The painted braves produce two makeshift ladders constructed of pine, positioning them against one side of the building. Next, they proceed to strip away the groom's clothing.

"What is this, Jack?" Adam protests.

"Angel begin purification with Sacred Moon. Soon you walk the *Trial of Shadows* together and know true meaning of Xeantee-- then Angel see-- born one soul with Aconee "

Without further ceremony, the two young men lift Adam by the arms, climb up the positioned ladders, and lower him bodily with ropes through the shaft opening. Adam squints, his eyes unaccustomed to the dim interior made even more obscure by an escaping vapor rising from a shallow basin containing fluid and herbs, surrounded by a ring of hot coals. The table is actually the flat surface of a smooth white rock engraved with pictograph symbols. A few shapes he can make out, but most obscure in reference. On one side of the basin is a black book, a leather satchel stamped with the Spanish Crest, along with tarnished brown sheet of a rolled parchment. Upon further examination, Adam realizes the book a Latin Bible. The scroll contains unusual scrip he thinks could be Jewish writing, a Semite text called Hebrew. This same lettering once he saw on the sign of a merchant shop in London.

An intoxicating balm pushes into his nostrils produced by the Sage herbs seeped in the basin. As his eyes adjust to the dim interior, Adam realizes he is not alone. On the opposite wall is Mitexi reclining on a couch covered by an animal skin blanket

"You are beautiful," he says to his bride to be and begins moving toward her.

"No!" She commands. "It is not allowed we touch until after we walk the *Trial of Shadows*. Adam must go to place prepared other side Rock of Foundation. There you must tie cord of life on right wrist. This begins our journey together."

Adam obeys. He finds another bed identical to the one his bride lays upon on the opposite side of the chamber. Just as she said, there is a cord made from animal gut, which these Indians use as rope. Tying the cord as instructed, he lies down and waits expectantly.

In the twilight of smoke, he imagines the embrace of Mitexi, anticipating the joy of their future joining. He imagines her naked in his arms, their bodies entwined together beneath shroud of animal skins. How soft her flesh would be, the honey sweetness of her sweat. He is thinking this and other things-- things that do not even make any sense. In fact, his mind has begun to hallucinate, wandering wispily between the lust of his desire and the elevation of his dreams. As he stares across the vaporous expanse, Adam can see the disembodied eyes of his Sacred Moon reflecting supernaturally in a void. Then by decree beyond his comprehension, the two translated to another place and time.

It is night. He and Mitexi side by side in a valley of crawling mist. They stand naked.

"How did we get here?" Adam demands confused.

"We have crossed the way not remembered." Her voice sounds clear as a mountain brook. "Together we walk the *Trial of Shadows*, as have all people walked before us. Adam now in Aconee heart– now sees with Aconee eyes! We stand together on the path of *Shelecheyanu*."

"We were in a tent. It seems only a short time ago…"

"*Shelecheyanu* is the beginning. *Shelecheyanu* is the end. Angeni-Cuauhtemoc and Mitexi are now one. This is all that we are-- all that we may know. Time is forever now."

This simple wisdom overwhelms his reason. Time and existence meaningless concepts– all that is past and future, only shadows. Only this moment are they joined in mortal presence as man and woman. Adam has never thought about it this way before. For him marriage and position defined by biology: a condition perceived in context of tradition to create family linage and bloodlines of nations. Here in this strange new world, it is something altogether different, altogether real, and altogether essential. He takes his place beside Sacred Moon to follow a prescribed trail of destiny set before them. He does this– not because of conviction– but because it is the only path presently most expedient.

Time has no dominion on the *Trial of Shadows*. It is as if they have always been here– will always belong here. A living fog slithers through a channel, as a great incandescent serpent showing the way not traversed. Adam feels himself energized in a way not felt before, a purpose of being unimaginable. His thoughts as air; his movement slow and labored revived from the shadows of fleeting dreams.

The mist parts suddenly, revealing the blackened skull of a garish new moon rising out of an eclipse of shadows.

Chorus of frogs begin to sing from within invisible crevices. Then a chimera figure appears in the way. A head forged of purest gold--with eyes as many burning suns--his countenance as the son of man seated upon a glorified throne in a realm without end!

Here stands the judgment Adam has always most feared: a seraph wielding a great burning trident, and with eyes changed to flame. Gripped suddenly by mortal impulse the man wishes to turn away from this bright apparition, yet unable to avert his gaze.

"*Xeantee Aconee Shelecheyanu!*" Mitexi cries, dropping to her knees and falling prostrate.

All is quiet. The slow pulse of a clockwork universe wanes in and out like a dying star in the center of constellations circling ever so slowly. With swift accuracy, the monarch presence plunges a fiery trident into invisible darkness, lifting a withering gold bullfrog into the heavens.

Again, choruses of frogs begin singing deliriously his name, a name spanning the beginning of creation and beyond. A name Adam knows, but cannot say. It is a name written in blood since fountains of the deep covered the world. The one called Angeni-Cuauhtemoc, *Fallen Angel*, raised inevitably into a matrix of quivering stars, and plunged into blackness of night without end!

Adam opens his eyes. He finds himself in the soft bosom of Sacred Moon, his new wife. It is now morning of another day and they are back in the familiar enclosure of their own Indian dwelling. The octagonal structure has vanished, along with the white rock in the center and the collection of several artifacts.

Adam wonders if all this only a dream, a grand hallucination through some concoction of Sage herbs released in the vapor of that air. Deep within Adam Pixley knows that he has witnessed a premonition of some event yet to come, a phenomenon of consequence at the end of mortal existence. Moreover, in spirit he understands with terrifying acuity the truest meaning of Xeantee!

When asked, Mitexi only replies, "We have passed together the *Trial of Shadows*. This is the Aconee way. Xeantee not the same for all, except now we are one, my husband: one plant, one hunt, and one to give life. We are now the meaning of *Shelecheyanu*. Beyond is the promise of Xeantee always. Trust only in this my husband."

No matter how much he urges, his beloved wife will answer nothing more.

"Why Angel asks what already he knows?" Jack says in response to an interrogation.

"But that's the point Jack— I don't know what really happened. It was night when we entered the ceremonial tent. We were on cots opposite each other. Then we were walking together in the dark heart of a frightening swamp. I'm sure I didn't sleep. I remember in terrible detail a giant presence with a pitchfork and frogs singing. None of it makes any sense."

Jack looks deeply into Adam's eyes, affectionately clasps his shoulder, and says solemnly, "Beware of dark Angel— his is the mind of world outside. It is not too late. Allow Aconee in your heart, my friend. Forget the confusion of past shadows and embrace the love through this passage with Sacred Moon. She is now Mitexi, wife to Angeni-Cuauhtemoc. I have gift for brother."

Jack retrieves from his pouch an alligator tooth with unfamiliar markings engraved on it. Something about the symbols makes Adam shiver with a sense of foreboding-- something that has not yet happened, but could happen still.

"This is the name *Angeni-Cuauhtemoc*– your name witnessed in heaven. Wear this always, and never remove from your heart. It will protect Angel from dark Angel that still walks *Trial of Shadows*."

Adam remains stunned by Jack's words of warning. Not that he understands, exactly– at least not with his mind. The words are as a dark prophetic vision. Nevertheless, this gift given freely by his Indian brother greatly pleases him. One symbol is the head of an eagle, the name given to him by this tribe upon arrival. Adam also recognizes another symbol. It is effigy of a scarecrow with a coat draped over stick shoulders. Between these two is a third symbol, reminiscent of a pyramid with a star at the peak.

Adam places the talisman reverently around his neck and thanks Jack. Yes, he still has a choice. Sacred Moon will be his guide through hours of confusion. This represents resurrected hope of a future destiny not written. Perhaps still a way of escape to Adam Pixley, a chance he may yet avoid his destiny. Moreover, the simple observation spoken by his Indian friend is undeniable. He does love his new wife more than life itself. Even more than the glitter of riches left behind. Jack is right about something else as well. They are truly brothers now, bound by nature of manhood, by tribal community, and by a mysticism that almost his mind grasps. Adam Pixley, the man who brought the red coat to keep away the crows, the man known as *Angel of Fallen Eagle* submits to earth of this unworldly position, taking his place among *Frogs of the River*, determined to banish all illusions past and future. For a while, he even forgets about the gold coin in his possession, considering it of little value compared to these newly discovered riches.

Their first year together Sacred Moon bares a son with intense light blue eyes and Viking red hair that stirs to the surface within Adam innate prejudice. But more than this, the child born with slightly hunched shoulders.

"This not the fault of Adam," consoles Mitexi. "This is a thing that happens sometimes-- not all things made straight in the beginning."

"The hair—where does his red hair come from," Adam interrogates, attempting to remain calm.

"There is another child of the village with the same mark of fire. It is nothing to make afraid. Our son will be called *Etu-Ninaha*, which means *'Fire of Sun'*. This is the gift of *Shelecheyanu*, my husband, our fruit of tomorrow."

Although his wife proclaims the child providence of *Shelecheyanu*, to Adam Pixley it is evidence of some forgotten sin made in the past. A randomness of forgotten ancestry settled along the Antrim coast, corrupting better blood even before Belfast a port city. During this time in history bans of notoriously savage men of Nordic descent would come ashore at night to raid villages, killing and raping. Some of those left alive bore children, allowing the ancestry of these violent marauders to mix into the Anglo-Irish bloodline.

Adam can see clearly the Indian features of his mother's lips and nose. The red of his hair and the Nordic blue of the eyes definitely not those of traditional native people. The only characteristic uniquely his own, maybe a mark of seriousness stamped on the infant's young brow that reminds Adam too much of his father. Therefore, he accepts the hump on the infant's back a sin of nature he must accept for the sake of mortal love.

In accordance to his paternal right, Adam also christens the child Jason, after the name of his father. It saddens Adam that Jason might never know his grandfather; or that his father will never know, he has a grandson. He wonders would his father even be glad to discover his grandchild half-Indian and humped-back. Although Europe less intolerant about such things than the American colonist; nevertheless, a deep-seated animosity exists that lingers just beneath the veneer of fascination, a prejudice of color and breeding—as everywhere, He knows from experience that blood and gentry everything in the end. Mostly, Adam knows in his heart that this offspring falls far short of many standards associated with human perfection.

Nevertheless, these prove the happiest days in the life of Adam Pixley. Days of solitude, of peace, and a sense of belonging, he will never know again. Sacred Moon teaches him daily the Aconee language, which he realizes to be a mixture of words and inflections familiar to him, not all originating from North American Indian dialect. Some words and pronunciations sound like those he has heard Norsemen sailors speak on the docks of London. She keeps referring to a book called *Espiritu Santo*, which he knows in English means *Holy Spirit*. She equates their present happiness as fulfilling proof of *Shelecheyanu* through the *Espiritu Santo*. For Adam the words *Espiritu Santo* remind him of someone from his forgotten past; someone who once shared with him many things before Adam marched off to war.

This name *Espiritu Santo* first spoken to him by a Portuguese cook named Miguel taken for a while prisoner in one of England's wars. It was young Adam's third month of inscription. He is for the first time away from his family and with few friends. Because of his Irish ancestry considered by some inferior, he chooses to keep mostly to himself. Adam never did make friends easily. The older man speaks some English, enough to get by, and suggests that he teach Adam how to play a game called *Draughts*. They play nearly every night after evening meal. Miguel has an annoying habit of drifting between English, Spanish, and his native Portuguese dialect as they play. Mostly the older man likes to drink ale and talk during the game. The last evening before Adam receives his first posting as a line duty soldier in Her Majesty's Royal Army their conversation turns religious. To Adam's surprise, this gruff, unkempt man believes in miracles and the existence of an eternal soul.

"I am named after a long lost ancestor that was a man of God. He devoted his life to the Spanish missionary sent to live among local Indians in the Americas. According to family history he perished in a shipwreck while returning to Europe." Miguel pauses here, takes a deep breath, and stares steadfast into the young soldier's eyes. "Men of God– those reborn through the '*Espiritu Santo*-- do not perish in time as do others. I have seen him more than once in my dreams, standing victorious among Angels. I have also seen you, my proud young friend, fallen from the heavens as a bright and burning star. Beware of the shadow grief– it is darkness to devour the soul. Your name Adam means first formed by the hand of God from clay of this world. Pray that you too do not fall soulless through temptation."

These are the last words spoken between them-- words altogether forgotten, until now. This represents the first testament of *Espiritu Santo* spoken to him long ago. When pressed how she knows these words, Sacred Moon only replies to him.

"It is not the way of the Aconee heart to question. The *Espiritu Santo* is the promise given to Xeantee Aconee in the beginning. It is to the Aconee people promise of resurrection fulfilled in *Shelecheyanu*, sign of peace to the Aconee soul. This, my husband, you must accept by faith only, and by nothing else can you know. There is an end to this way; but the way of Xeantee Aconee never ending."

Adam asks his wife no more questions on the subject after this, accepting there is more to the mystery than he can ever know by reason. He and Jason become as close as father and son can be. He teaches his son how to swim, how to fish; and when he becomes old enough, Adam teaches Jason how to stalk small and large game. Because his brother Jack had taught him well, Adam becomes a good teacher to his only son. Above all else, Adam continues to love the mother of his only child, as a man might cherish the image of an idol. This will prove to be the greater downfall of Adam Pixley.

In the one hundredth moon of his happiness, Mitexi falls ill with a fever. Men and women of the tribe congregate together in prayer, feed her medicines made of herbs, and chant incantations; but she only gets worse. Before succumbing, Sacred Moon calls Adam and their son to her side.

"You must be strong my husband and not forget! You are Adam, father to our son made perfect in the name of *Shelecheyanu*. Keep this meaning always so that your soul may not darken."

Mitexi gazes into bewildered eyes of the young boy. She then slips the turquoise blue amulet from around her neck and places it around the neck of her only child.

"You are Etu-Ninaha, son of Adam, my pure reflection. Keep this always near your heart. It is the way of *Shelecheyanu*."

With these words, Mitexi exhales one last time and is dead. The drums and the chanting stop and only silence remains.

Adam collapses inconsolable, altogether consumed by grief. Soon the grief changes to bitter anger. He weeps over Sacred Moon's lifeless body for two days, refusing to allow her proper burial. When time to surrender the body comes, Adam struggles defiantly, causing the talisman tied around his neck to rip away.

"Let me go Jack!"

"Sacred Moon gone, my brother," Jack consoles; "All water returns to water. It is the way of Aconee, the way of *Shelecheyanu*."

Jack picks up the alligator tooth and hands it back to his brother. Instead of placing it again around his neck, the distrait man flings the talisman into the fire.

"I want nothing more to do with your *Shelecheyanu*!" Adam curses and runs away.

With the aid of two younger braves, Jack takes up the body of their sister, Mitexi, and carries her to a special

place in the swamp. Adam follows from a distance, watches in agony as they lay the body of his mortal love on a bed of Water Lilies according to custom. Silently he sees her face sink slowly into the stygian deep. Wife of Adam Pixley–
reflected light of his beautiful Sacred Moon-- vanishes into swamp water forever lost!

CHAPTER 9

Sin of the Father

Isolating himself in his own tent, Adam continues to mourn for many days, refusing to eat or sleep. Jack takes young Etu-Ninaha and places the boy into the care of a childless couple, who accept him as their own. The orphan needs a father and mother, especially now that he has neither. Adam continues to change for the worse after the death of Sacred Moon. Every aspect of this idyllic environment reminds him of the paradise lost. Reminds Adam he is prisoner on this island surrounded by swamp. He altogether rejects his past happiness here-- rejects his son, Jason, as though the child somehow responsible. Most of all Adam Pixley rejects the peace he thought to find here. Jack tries often to reason with him, but on each occasion Adam just turns and walks away.

"Think about Etu-Ninaha, son of Adam," Jack pleas. "It is against nature to hate own flesh."

"He is your son, now– the son of an Indian!" Adam spits back without even looking at the boy. "Teach him the Indian way– the way of *Shelecheyanu*! Teach him about the monsters in your holy book, and about this prison of Xeantee!"

Adam becomes outcast to the people that once accepted him with open hearts. He eats alone, hunts alone, choosing to set his tent apart from the community. A year has passed since the death of Sacred Moon, and then something happens that inspires Adam Pixley with a bitter new objective.

While gathering potatoes from the garden, he sees something fall unnoticed out of a pouch Jack always wears on his side. Upon examination of the object, Adam recognizes it immediately as a musket ball. Not the kind used by the British or the Colonist in modern weaponry; rather it is much larger, very old, and irregularly round. Then Adam remembers that once while fishing for a monster catfish, Jack had squeezed a slither of metal-like material along the line of gut so that it would sink completely to the bottom. It did not occur to him at the time to question how he came in possession of this weight. He was too much in love with Mitexi to care about anything else then. Now he cares. Now it makes sense why Jack's stones always seem to travel further and more effective for the kill. Most on Adam's mind now is where Jack gets his unusual lead. He says nothing, determined to find out everything about the secret activities of this detached Indian.

It occurs to Adam that he actually knows little about Jack. In all these years never has he been inside the other man's tent. Jack lives alone; has always been alone. His dwelling positioned separate from the rest of the tribe. Adam never thought about why this is. Now he is inspired to discover the truth about this unusual fellow. Maybe there is another reason why Jack befriended him since the beginning. He secretly starts observing Jack's movements and routines closely. In time, he realizes that the Indian conducts many of his activities in accordance with different phases of the moon. During the new moon he can often be seen sitting beside a campfire outside his tent bobbing and praying in a strange language that is neither English, nor is it Aconee. Rather, it is a strange language never heard by Adam. Through the course of the lunar month, Jack goes hunting for different game, always successfully bringing back a kill. On the first day of the full moon, the Indian rises particularly early, adorns himself in animal skins, and disappears into the deeper swamp, not to return until late evening. Where did he go and for what reason?

One morning, after Jack has departed on one of his hunting trips, Adam decides to enter the other's tent for a further investigation.

The interior is unlike the dwellings Adam has visited. There are ample animal skins, even one reptilian hide twice the size of a man flayed beside the skull of a crocodile with an extended jaw of sharp studded teeth. The thing that attracts Adam's attention most is the table of a white rock. The same rock remembered inside the ceremonial lodge. Neatly arranged on the top is the Latin Bible, leather satchel bearing the Spanish insignia, and familiar parchment scroll with Jewish writing. Inside the leather satchel is another book bound in tanned Corsican leather and embossed on the face the word LIBERTAD, along with other words that read *Registro de la Nave*. Here is the Ship's Log belonging to a Spanish Captain– perhaps his vessel the same ship that transported the gold doubloon discovered that first night in the swamp interior. Where there is one, there must be others. After a thorough search of the dwelling, no more gold coins found. Now Adam knows without any doubt that these Indians not what they seem. This goes especially for Jack. Were it not for his consuming love for Sacred Moon, he would have suspected sooner. Adam feels the fool. He had so desperately wanted to believe in the dream of this noble native existence. Wanted to be part of that dream and live a life of leisure in the bosom of nature's bounty. Now he wants only to escape this island of purgatory!

Another month passes. Adam continues secretly to study the activities of Jack. As the first night of the full moon approaches, he devises a plan. First, he makes a bag from a batch of rabbit skins used by his Mitexi to protect the delicate femininity of her hands when doing manual chores. He rises particularly early and scouts out a position near Jack's teepee. His plan will not be easy. His mentor of many years possesses senses exceptionally keen, but Adam has learned much about the art of Indian stealth. Moreover, Jack will remain unsuspicious of this well thought-out plan.

The chill of fall is in the air again. The swamp has already begun to change in recent weeks, becoming more skeletal. Its true face of death unmasked. Adam chooses a dry socket beneath the decayed trunk of a fallen Cyprus tree and waits all night. Just before sunrise, he sees the familiar shape of a man moving silently from shadow to shadow. To anyone else the apparition would have appeared to be no more than a wisp of air disturbing the underbrush. Adam sees now through the eyes of an Indian; sees without really seeing; sees the detail of everything, not as the illusion they appear. As is his ritual, Jack first goes to the communal spring to fill his flask with fresh water. Adam takes this opportunity to slip into the Indian's tent and steal the Ship's Log, the Bible, and the parchment scroll. He knows Jack will not return here before evening. He then waits in the shadows for the unsuspecting man to begin his journey.

Jack pauses, sniffs the air, as animals do before making a move, and begins his trek through meandering twilight following trails he knows by heart. By mid-morning, they have penetrated more than a mile into the neither region, skirting along banks of quicksand fleshed with black water, through dark passages of vine-chocked alleys, and crossing over churning dangerous pools on the backs of protruding barks positioned precariously requiring precise export footing. To Adam's despair, they seem to be passing ever deeper into the swamp, ever farther from the promise of solid land.

Then Jack stops at the edge of a narrow mote where the water appears deeper and flows slowly. At first glance, there appears no way across except to swim. Moving carefully near the edge, Jack pauses beside a large Weeping Willow. Shimmying up the tree, he perches on an extended bough of an overhanging limb and walks across to an opposite bank by balancing with his arms. Once over this expanse, the Indian swings down on solid ground and continues his stride.

Adam attempts to follow these moves. He loses his balance and almost falls into the swill of slow churning sludge. However, partly due to the tallness of his stature manages to recover and swing the remaining distance to safety on the other side. Here the earth feels more solid, drier like the earth he has forgotten. Quickly picking-up Jack's trail again, he discovers the path has changed rockier, the foliage a little less green. Even the trees are different, taller, straighter, and in greater variety. Soon Adam detects the audible sound of river rapids, a familiar dry wind blowing from the West. The path opens unexpectedly into the bottom of a narrow ravine with trickling streams of several small waterfalls cascading softly along a canyon wall on the opposite side of a river cutting through a steep canyon. It is far below the waterline, meaning that in spring the river three times larger than it is now.

Adam quickly hides behind a white boulder etched with strange symbols near the water's edge. Jack stands beside one of the larger rocks about a hundred yards downstream with his hands raised toward the sky, once again chanting in that same unknown language Adam does not understand. The Indian must have sensed something, because he spins suddenly around and stares intently in Adam's direction. Satisfied that nothing is there, he searches along the riverbank, until finding a series of crossing stones fleshed even with the flow. Once across, he vanishes behind the curtain of a waterfall cascading down the rock face on that side of the river. Several minutes later Jack emerges holding something in his hand. From a distance, it resembles a silver dagger, but Adam cannot be certain. Carefully wrapping the object in a leather napkin, the intrepid Indian retraces his path back across the river. Once again he pauses, meticulously surveys the area, scrutinizing with his senses what eyes do not see. Then soundlessly disappears into the surrounding foliage.

Adam does not move, but remains crouched in the shadow of his hiding place. He knows Jack to be wily and patient–knows that he can sense a prey as well as any animal. Adam had been careful to remain always downwind, careful to remain invisible at all times just as his friend had taught him. Finally he is convinced the Indian gone. He steps cautiously along the riverbank, finds the path of stepping-stones, and crosses to the other side.

The bright narrow passage, camouflaged behind the waterfall, barricaded by carefully placed rocks to keep out larger animals. Never would Adam have found it had he not seen Jack enter here. Removing the barrier, he squeezes through a narrow corridor to discover behind the cascade of water entrance to a shimmering crystal cave. The brightness within emanates from a translucent quartz window above, sunlight sparkling along the sheer cavern walls laced with streaks of mica, and sweeping through a glittering stream of golden coins.

This like no place Adam has ever seen. Now he knows why Jack makes clandestine excursions to this secret domain. This is no ordinary cave; rather a preserved treasure house enshrining cache of worldly desire to ensnare this embittered man of perdition. Here sparkles the frustration in his being, the true promise of his deserved birthright on earth.

The gold doubloons, bursting from bags of rotting canvass and strewn on the cavern floor, fills the emptiness of his soul as nothing he might have imagined. Gold plentiful as stars in heaven here for the taking-- now all belonging to Adam Pixley!

No more will he bow to authority. Never again to be treated without respect in the world. He is now his own king on earth, a man of means to receive a mantle of adornment. Dropping to his knees, Adam Pixley runs his fingers through the cascade of minted gold coins stamped with a Spanish inscription, only vaguely aware of the human skull and bones entwined in the rags of a tattered robe.

Were it not for his delirium, Adam may have realized that he is in the hallowed tomb of a saint from another era. It never occurs to him to question the significance of this corpse or the meaning of the gold. Then his hand finds something else buried under the mound.

Except for a little surface rust, the ornate pistol appears still serviceable. Adam is familiar with this type of flintlock from the early days of his military training. Similar to the function of modern firearms, except lacking a few refinements in ballistic design for quicker load and better accuracy, the weapon as potentially deadly as the day fashioned. Detaching a rod running along the barrel, he rams in the shot that dropped out of Jack's pouch weeks earlier. Adam is little surprised that it is precisely the right gage. Engraved on the handle are the initials JB, which Adam presumes is the name of the previous owner. Although the hammer a little stiff, it quickly loosens up after only a few cocks. Finding a pouch of dry black gunpowder near the skeletal remains, he primes the flash pan and steps outside to test this surviving antique from another history.

"Angel go back with Aconee brother!" Speaks Jack without ceremony.

He is standing near the water's edge, holding what appears to be the silver dagger clutched in one hand. In the other, he holds his prepared sling. The Indian had not left after all. Adam should have known Jack more cunning than the average person, endowed with the keen instincts of an animal. This moment he appears in Adam's mind somehow different. He is not the same Jack known these many years. Not the man he has laughed and joked with since those early days living on this swamp island. In the presence of this moment, Adam sees him as he truly is for the first time. The broad and powerful shoulders draped with animal skins, the purity of his eyes glittering in the morning light. He is the one all along! His is the mighty arm that lifted Adam Pixley from certain death of a bog pit. He is the one that carried him delirious to the village so that Adam might recover in time. His name is Tahmoh, a Prince of Xeantee, heir to a throne not of this dominion.

"No– there is no going back! This is the promise of my world. There is enough here for both of us. Think how much better you can live. No more cold, or fever, or fear of Xeantee."

"Children of Xeantee have no need for bright metal," he says shaking his head sadly. "Angeni-Cuauhtemoc fall from high. He share Aconee heart– see through Aconee eyes– make Aconee son with sister Mitexi—"

"I have no son!" Adam screams enraged. "I'm not going with you, Tahmoh! There is nothing left for me here– nothing except death and the reminder of death! I want no part of your *Shelecheyanu*! My promise is here and now!"

"It not too late for Angeni-Cuauhtemoc," pleads the Indian.

"Yes, Tahmoh, it is too late for everything!"

What Jack may have intended to do next, Adam cannot be certain. It seems in the moment that he raises his sling, as often was his habit when ready for a kill. Without hesitation, Adam takes aim with the flintlock pistol and squeezes the trigger.

It functions all too well. The sound of the shot ricochets through the stretch of canyon and fades into the distance. Tahmoh just stands there frozen in time, his arms hanging limply at his side. The silver dagger falls from one hand, as does the loaded sling from the other. He looks dazedly up into the blue morning sky, drops to his knees, and keels slowly backward.

The shot has passed cleanly into his right eye socket, killing the man instantly. Adam convinces himself that he did what he had to. It was, after all, him or the Indian. The terrible wound, painful to look at, convinces Adam Pixley that all things finish in the grave. Jack had been the brother he never knew, and a friend he will never again have.

Without further thought of the deed, he strips away the Indian's clothing. These will make strong leather bags for his gold. He next digs the single shot out of the dead man's brain. Without remorse, Adam lifts the naked body on his shoulders, carries it to the river's edge, and drops the one named Tahmoh into the shadows of the deep until judgment day. Only now does Adam realize that what he thought a dagger is actually a pewter cross. Although of little value, he decides to keep the relic, adding the souvenir to the other stolen artifacts.

Evening has already begun to descend, announced by the auspicious call of a black crow taking position in a nearby tree. Igniting a fire inside the crystal cave, Adam huddles near the cold warmth of his gold. The human remains make no difference to him, for he is now as dead inside as these dry bones. Against the opposite wall, crouches flickering shadow of a dark presence grotesquely bowed beneath folded hump of Seraph wings. The spirit of fallen angel earthbound, as assuredly, the '*Espíritu Santo*' flees from his presence forever.

The next morning Adam Pixley prepares four sacks made from the Indian skins, but is able to carry only one. The single coin he had found first in the swamp inadvertently slips from his pocket and lodges into the crevice of a rock where it will remain hidden and unnoticed long after Adam Pixley is gone. Nor will he find it later upon returning for the balance of his treasure. Here it will wait through nearly two centuries, until resurrected by the curiosity of another generation.

Marking the place well, he reloads his Spanish pistol with the bloodied ball, slips the pewter cross into his belt, and sets off with expectation of the future that awaits him. To his satisfaction, he comes across a peaceful settlement after only a day's journey. They immediately take him in, feed him, and convey news that the war with England ended since many years, leaving the new America alone to make its own destiny. Now that the Colonial War over and withdrawal of Great Britain's army, he finds himself a man without a history.

Adam Pixley gains reputation as an eccentric frontiersman, appearing out of nowhere rich with a bag of minted gold coins bearing insignia of the Spanish Crest. Because of his great wealth, Adam Pixley becomes the most powerful man in the community, even the entire district as far as the Charleston coast. There is nothing his money unable to buy. He makes a legal homestead and lays claim to all land from the Piedmont hills to edge of the wetlands, including the secret cave containing the rest of his gold.

Upon the cliff above the Quartz rock, he builds a mansion with a grand balcony that overlooks the river so he can keep a watchful eye below. Adam christens the swamp basin Liberty, translated after the name of the ship listed in the maritime Captain's logs. Because of this, Adam Pixley hailed a patriot, many believing the coinage in honorable dedication to the famous Bell of Independence proudly displayed in Pennsylvania. By some reports, Adam Pixley immediately hires mercenaries, some renegade Cherokees from the north, to serve as his personal army. He soon gains the reputation of being ruthless in business; and anything his money unable to buy, acquired by force. Still there is one thing he wants more than all other things of this world. He wishes to erase his past and repossess the grave of his innocence.

By his own reason, Adam convinced that where there is no past; then there can be no sin. He gathers from his army a band of forty men, most of the less savory type, some local half-breeds, and a few young Cherokee braves. These he leads personally to the edge of the swamp near the secret cave beside a river later named Aconee. From memory, Adam Pixley draws them a map directing his army precisely through a dangerous maze of marshland to the inhabited dry Liberty Island.

"Especially the children," Adam emphasizes, his eyes squinting evilly. "Every man, woman, and child– but especially I want the scalps of all the children below the age of fifteen years!"

Pixley arms each man, giving a gold coin with the promise of another for every scalp brought back. He waits alone at the edge of a slick rock skull later named Devils Fall and watches the sun climb across the sky. All afternoon shots ring out amid muffled sounds of screaming almost he can hear.

In his heart, he dares the Prince of Xeantee to come. What good might his trident be against guns and blood lust? All but eight of the forty return. The Cherokee are the last to come back. Many bring him pelts of raw bleeding scalps. One among them is a bright Viking red. Adam Pixley now content that his past sins truly dead.

He will place the scalp tied to a white river rock, along with the Latin Bible and cryptic scroll, sealing them inside a coffin in the cellar of his newly constructed mansion. He later adds the embossed leather satchel containing the Captain's Log without reading it once. He thinks that by preserving these he will somehow find forgiveness, hopes they will keep away the demons of his nightmares. When the demons come anyway, he pays an Indian whore to come and keep him company. In the course of time, the demons win.

For many years, those who came back alive from the massacre will tell tales of a creature half man and half frog that swoops out of nowhere, taking the lost eight one by one. They agree that the Aconee Indians never put up a fight, many shot in the back as they ran– all thrown into the mass grave of a bog pit. Those foolish enough to surrender executed on the spot in accordance with Mr. Pixley's orders.

The genocide of the Aconee tribe remains to this day clouded as a shadowy event unproven by history. Some of the young Cherokee braves secretly spare several women to take as wives, and even their children. This impropriety they will keep from the knowledge of Adam Pixley. Today all that is known about the legend of Xeantee are bedtime stories told by mothers to their children about a mythical tribe of Indians known as Aconee passed down from generation to generation.

Each mercenary receives his remaining wages, sworn to an oath of secrecy, and summarily sent away. The land records show that Adam Pixley purchased at a fair market price all the surrounding land from the upper piedmont to the Aconee River, and from the Aconee River, to the inaccessible graveyard land of the swamp peninsula. The house he built overlooks the river valley to the east perched darkly on a high ridge opposite the hump of Hog Back Mountain. Rumor is that any given night he can be seen standing like a dark angel on the precipice of his balcony surveying the swamp terrain nestled between the Aconee River and the Piedmont Plateau. They say he always has a bottle of spirits in his hand, drinks until nearly passing out. Only then do his servants appear to help him to bed. In time, he adds slave quarters and homes for his bodyguards. It is no secret he has a special interest for Indian women, and that he has sired many half-breed children.

Adam Pixley will eventually marry to a good protestant woman and produce proper heirs to his name. In generations to come a town and county spring up to the memory of this respected citizen. The rest of the gold he hides safely in a vault of his own making.

In course of time, a wooden bridge constructed, connecting the island peninsula to the mainland. Later that bridge replaced by a land access made with tons of bedrock transported from elsewhere in wagons. Pixley's heirs will erect rival plantations and live sumptuously, until days of America's Civil War marks an end to slavery. During the revival age of modern industry, Liberty Peninsula inaugurated home to one of the south's first cotton mills, creating jobs for those dispossessed after the reunification of North and South.

Adam Pixley grows old and pale with deep wrinkles caused by years of bitterness. The scar slashed across his left temple turns hideously black, resembling something wicked; and common report is that something evil reflected in his red demonic eyes. A creature angry, glaring out between folds of sagging wrinkles, with the breath of old graves. This Angel indeed fallen, now to inherit the earth. His truer nature revealed.

There would be many legends about Pixley's gold and from where he might have come. Only Adam Pixley knows the whole truth. Only he will know meaning of the silver-plated dagger resembling a cross and the origin of his antique pirate pistol. Only he knows the softness of Sacred Moon, the true nature of his Indian brother, and erased memory of his Indian son named Etu-Ninaha murdered in innocence. Within the crypt of his heart echoes continually, screams of those slaughtered dead. From sunset, until rising of the morning star, Adam Pixley waits for the harbinger of his fear to appear. He is *Angeni-Cuauhtemoc*, Fallen Angel, curse of the earth; a name cast out of heaven and condemned eternally to walk alone the *Trial of Shadows* until judgment day of *Xeantee Aconee*.

According to the official documents, Adam Pixley waited through many long years, and glad when the waiting finally ended. He is the first white man buried on the Liberty Peninsula in an embellished mausoleum erected below the fortress of his grand plantation estate. In later years, this tomb also marks the beginning of the old cemetery. It is not a place for children; nor is it for the faint of heart. A gravesite cautiously avoided; a building of architectural design void of the presence of what the Aconee Indians call *Shelecheyanu*. Chiseled into the black stone that enshrines Liberty's founding father are these words of forfeited promise: **"UNTIL THE KING SHALL COME.**

BOOK THREE

Until the King Shall Come

CHAPTER 10

Nela

Nela Smith lies troubled in her bed, her rest disturbed by specter of an unpleasant dream. Moist blanket of humidity in early October means approach of a storm brewing somewhere in the Atlantic. To most, this change would have been indiscernible, except Nela acutely aware of every detail, inspired through ever escalating meaning new and old in the south she knows. She feels suddenly worn, feels apprehensively the minutes and the hours composing fragile string of her existence. She feels for the first time what it really means to be born of gentry within historical context of a proper family; now the last of her kind. Finally surrendering to the knowledge that further sleep impossible, Nela rises out of her bed, gets dressed, and does what often she did when confronted by unrest.

The 1948 motor car starts without hesitation and *"hums like a sewing machine"*, as the Good Doctor would say. Nela pulls into the lane and begins confidently navigating along the empty roads from the Liberty Peninsula to Hogback Mountain. These are her finest moments; moments, the moments of noticeable importance.

Nela might have traveled to the Pixley side, but more prefers the mountains. Even with the windows rolled up, a pungent odor permeates the air, reminding Nela that fall has arrived and soon nearly all the trees will fade into rich color. When the color gone, then the Liberty swamp will have a face truer to its nature, a nature closer to her own nature, having witnessed this change, year after year, for as long as remembered. This is also part of her legacy, truest bearing of what it means to be heir to this region.

Nela has always been a proper child, first daughter to a family of wealth and means, whose lineage goes back almost two centuries. Nela never knew what it is like not to have plenty. She is, after all, last descendant of the founding father that purchased and settled this land from the Piedmont hills, through several miles of swamp basin, and to the foothills of Hog Back Mountain. Here the two elevations almost meet, creating a narrow channel that will be the site of the future Aconee Dam project.

The Pixley Estate was the first built and the only one still standing. It has survived the ravages of America's Civil War, as well as the economic recession on the heels of world depression. Through it all, the Pixley family manages to hang on by playing both sides. Even when the northern alliance burned other cotton plantations to the ground, the elegant grandeur of the Pixley home continues to prosper through greed of private interest and deals of secret negotiations. Some say all this made possible by a legendary chest of Spanish gold coins. Others, that the Pixleys are just good in business dealings, knowing the difference between concession and survival.

Nela's great grandfather responsible for establishing the First Liberty Cotton Mill on the peninsula. This is a remarkable accomplishment; one that inaugurates beginning of an industrial revolution reviving economic potential to a trodden south restored. She remembers little about the old man, except the way he smelled. To this day, it remains in her mind odor reminiscent of something ancient and moldy, something that should have been disposed of long ago in the past. Just memory of that smell continues to contaminate her senses to the soul.

As young children, Nela and her older twin brother Nathaniel, born only minutes apart, tutored by the best private instructors money can buy, both well versed in the ways of refined etiquette and modern science. Because nearly all their clothes imported from the big cities of the world, they prosper in the knowledge that they are born better than everyone else, sprouting from the rich soil of the *Old South* as firstlings of a preferred crop.

Nathaniel has a particularly inquisitive nature and smart as a whip. Perhaps too smart, making him the more sensitive of the two. Maybe, also, because he was a boy and named after their father's only brother that Nathaniel felt always greater responsible for preserving the family name. This uncle, a relative they never knew, perished in the trenches of World War I without an heir. Like his name, the weight of future generations falls on Nathaniel's shoulders. Of course there was always Nela, but for some reason she did not count the same.

She and Nathaniel enroll at the same time into a prestigious English university abroad in London. How invigorating to get away from the boredom of wealth and family responsibility. Women in Europe had opportunity to be anything, so long as they were smart enough. And Nela has always been very smart!

Having access to libraries containing volumes of worldly knowledge, Nela finds herself irresistibly drawn into light of that knowledge. Although encouraged to major in the humanities, she secretly studies history of war tactics and important role of economic resources to maintain and control local populations. These early years abroad, the only time in Nela's life feels truly empowered to choose her own destiny. Feels she counts more than just a daughter born into wealth.

It is here that Nela also discovers the true meaning of fashion within the social context of a world larger than ever dreamed. She begins reading the Greek Classics, which inspires her imagination with images of those marvelous Gods of antiquity overshadowing the virginity of mortal women with their passion. Secretly she wishes that such an anthropomorphic being might descend from Olympus to consume her body and soul by his immortal presence.

Liberty Epic of Shadows

Once, Nela thinks this almost possible during summer-break at the Carolina family mansion.

It is a hot August afternoon when a black hireling catches her adolescent attention as he tends the gardens. His flesh dark exotic wood; his eyes deep wells set within hollows of a strong sculpted brow. The young woman enjoys nothing better than to watch him work, while pretending to read. Occasionally she glances up from her book and makes immature attempts to engage the man in idol conversation. Although he pretends to ignore her advances, she knows instinctively his interest more than casual. However, her father put a stop to that. Even though it not the man's fault, Nela feels betrayed in her imagination, never forgiving him for leaving without even saying goodbye. Many years later, this woman of worldly frustration would find fulfillment to her unwholesome fantasy in the presence of another mythical chimera made of light and shadow. Only by then her dreams less pure, consumed by lust of a dazzling creature with fangs full of bittersweet poison mixed in mortar of deception.

After graduation, Nela and her brother return to the plantation style home of their youth. Nathaniel just turned twenty-one when the Second World War begins. In beginning, he objects, sharing the beliefs of so many others at the time. Even her parents proclaim that Europe should fend for its own. Because her father dying of cancer he wishes to protect his only son from potential harm. This has always been the Pixley way. For three years, her brother watches from a distance as many sons of the cotton mill hands march bravely off to conflict on distant shores. Even months after the death of his father, he often sits up at night listening to the radio news broadcast of the war to end all wars. Then the Japanese bomb Pearl Harbor in the Pacific. This is more than Nathaniel can bear.

"Please say you will not go--" mother pleas. "We are the ones that give them life and purpose. No matter which side wins this war, we will still be here. Now you are the only one left. Think of how important that is!"

"I prefer to die in honor, than to know so many others died to the end of my dishonor. It is everyone's patriotic duty to lay down their life for a greater cause!" He then looks into the eyes of his sister in such a way as to say, *'even you could do something more than to serve the dilettante ends of this worldly estate'*.

"Then you will die like your uncle!" Mother prophesies.

Nela's brother enlists into the Marine Corps very next day and within a month ships off to Paris Island for boot camp training. She remembers how her mother broke down into hysteria six weeks later when her only son receives orders sending him to Guadalcanal and later Iwo Jima. Nela's mother cries inconsolably the morning he leaves; and continued to cry for all the months he is gone. After the body shipped home, she stops crying and never cries again. Nela also refuses to cry, not even the day her brother's body laid to rest in the new V. A. Cemetery in Pixley nearly the newly built V. A. Hospital.

In the fall of that same year, Nela's mother commits suicide, leaving her all alone. Only she remains to carry on the Pixley bloodline. As is usually the case of people with means, her parents had taken care of all the legal arrangements to ensure that the surviving heiress would never need to work a day in life. Nela acquires control to all shares of business related investments. Nela Pixley, less than 30 years old, now owns things she did not even know about. She hires a personal lawyer from the Tootersville directory named Hannibal Smith. He is a smart young man with an ambitious nature she can appreciate. *Hannibal would have made a fine Pixley!* During an arranged meeting in her lawyer's office, Nela meets his older brother Bill, introduced as a doctor of medicine.

Bill Smith is a humble man, tall and dignified, but with a slight hunch in his back compensated for by a solidly built stature dwarfing most men. He has wintry blue eyes, hair flaxen like August hay rolled in the sun, parted in the middle by a shock of auburn red that runs Mohawk fashion through middle of his head. Yet, these few imperfections seem somehow to make the older Smith brother more interesting in the younger woman's eyes. Nela instantly reminded of a character named Smiling Jack in an adventure novel series read often as a child, while curled beneath the warm covers of her bed before drifting into dream. Bill Smith is almost every bit this Captain of the Skies imagined through many extraordinary exploits of adventure.

"You are the loveliest lady I have ever had the pleasure to meet," he says, peering deeply into her face. "My name is William. May a gentleman be so bold as to ask a handsome lady out on a date?"

Intrigued by the confident twinkle in his eyes, the almost mischievous way his full upper lip spirals up ever so slightly when he smiles, William Smith begins to swirl deeply into her imagination. Nela did not believe in love at first sight. The truth being, she has never really been in love. Therefore, she accepts invitation from this dashing Smiling Jack of her innocence that will change course of Nela Pixley's life.

William is nothing like her father, which makes him all the more attractive. The two brothers bear little family resemblance, even their hair color different. However, the most striking contradiction is their way of seeing the world. William wants to make the world a better place. Hannibal a man, whose only interest is his own interest. Nela will trust Hannibal with her money, only because she knows he has no heart.

Nela is certain that Nathaniel would have approved immediately-- would have liked William as much as she-- not because he is the same, but because he is not the same. A man made from a different mold, a man born with a nature inspired by values more humanitarian. Taught kindness and gentleness qualities of weakness, Nela has learned to embrace the doctrine of *Social Darwinism*. Yet, her heart now confronted by a man committed to a code of compassion, believing in the dignity and equality of every human being. This is something new to her way of reason, something with greater substance than found in the ledger sheets of an accountant. His only true failing is that William Smith falls just a little short, when compared to her imagined gods of antiquity.

Nevertheless, flesh and blood proves stronger in the end. Three months later, they decide on a simple wedding in a Baptist Church located on the outskirts of Tootersville, the small town where he and Hannibal grew up. Bill never was one for large social gatherings. The night before their final vows, they take a stroll along avenues of his childhood memories.

"My great grandfather had a good-paying office job with the railroad," he says as they walk together affectionately holding hands. "He took Hannibal and me in after the sudden death of both our parents because of an automobile accident on Hogback Mountain. He was always a quiet man, rarely commenting on anything happening in the world, not even politics of religion. Yet, the one thing he valued most was education. He always said that an educated person obtains power of choice: to make the earth a place better or a place worse. For this reason, my brother and I both went to college in Atlanta. I will always respect my grandfather for that."

"And so you should;" Nela remarks. "It is men of noble character, who make the rules for a better society. I think this the reason I have fallen in love with you. Your heart, William Smith, is made of better stuff than that of most men. Through you I am also made better."

"This belonged to my mother." William says reaching into his pants pocket and retrieving something glittering greenish-blue tied to a crude string. "I remember as a young child her saying that it is something very special to our family heritage, only I was not old enough at the time to understand. I want you to have it, Nela, as token commitment of my love for you."

Taking the object in her hand, Nela realizes it to be a piece of jewelry. Nothing particularly special, except for the present meaning conveyed. With this perception, she will wear it for a time, believing it valuable for the simple reason it is a gift from her husband.

William pulls the woman he loves near and kisses her in pale light of a third crescent moon. As their lips touch, Nela feels a jolt race through her body never felt before.

William Smith wants no part of the Pixley Estate, declaring they should buy their own place and start a new life together. During the first several months, these newlyweds reside in the Atlanta suburbs near the hospital of her husband's employment. However, William expresses dissatisfaction at being one of many doctors in a big city, when greater need for a physician exists in poor rural areas closer to Nela's roots.

It is a real-estate client of Hannibal, who finds the couple a perfect place on the southern tip of the Liberty Peninsula, located at the edge of the swamp. The small mansion built near the ruins of a once elegant plantation burned to the ground during the Civil War of the 1860s. In the back rests a shallow pond surrounded by a perimeter of natural stones and inhabited with many tadpoles. A place William finds immediately peaceful. There are several fruit trees bearing apples and persimmons, which is also home to many Wasp.

William loves the place immediately. Nela less so, but remains content to accept this humble dwelling as her future home with insistence that certain amenities added once they move in. By end of the tour, decision affirmed that this to be the first real home of the Smith family.

Immediate task is to sort out the affairs of her heirloom estate. Little known about the family genealogy before Adam Pixley homesteaded this region nearly 200 years earlier. Rumor has it that he was a shrewd businessman, a man of wealth and European taste originally from somewhere across the seas, responsible for bringing civilized prosperity to the region. Legend persist that Adam Pixley once an Indian fighter, who just one day drifted into a local trading post one day carrying buckskins bulging with minted Spanish gold coins.

In the main entrance of the Pixley home hangs a life-size portrait of a man dressed in eighteenth century hunting attire with Irish blond hair, cold steely eyes, and a scar slashed across his left brow. He holds in one hand a leather satchel and a musket pistol in the other hand.

For some inexplicable reason this effigy always sends a chill along Nela's spine, a sense of dread that permeates into her bones each time she passed the looming presence, as though those eyes follow her every move. And even after all these years, she still feels uneasy.

Nela has decided to donate some of the furniture--including that dreadful portrait-- to the state museum in Charleston. By the end of the second week, Nela has sorted through everything on the main floors of the estate. Now it is time to penetrate into past of the unknown.

Growing up, Nela and her brother forbidden entrance to the basement, the haunted darkness barricaded by a securely locked door. Following her mother's suicide there, it becomes a place of particular dread. A lair she never cares to venture into, remaining off-limits in her imagination. Even after removal of the door, and the passage covered by a black curtain, Nela avoids impulse to go down there. This day she has determined within herself to descend into this dark heart of the Pixley Estate and unleash the many demons that have plagued her mind always.

Without even a curtain now, the passage reeks of death, like pungent odor of a centuries-old crypt, stagnant and foreboding. For reasons just as clandestine, electrical lighting never installed here. Discovering a lantern hanging from a rusted hook attached on the doorpost just inside the entrance, Nela lights the wick and apprehensively descends the creaking wooden stairs not knowing what she might find.

Hidden here a family history kept from the knowledge of this only surviving heir. The chamber is smaller than expected, cluttered with old furnishings, family portraits, and art collectables covered with sheets of cotton yarn, all bound in strings of cobwebs. Many worldly artifacts gathered through generations of Pixleys spanning centuries resurrect from the shadows. In one corner, her brother's Sherlock Holms book collection, along with boxes of clothes, a hunting rifle, and stacks of medical journals that continue even now to come in the mail.

The remains of every Pixley that has ever lived gathered in this musky keep, a macabre catacomb enshrining the ancient dead. Large-game hunting guns and ivory horns taken from dead elephants carved with intricate designs. Strands of fine silk material hang along the walls; spindles of machined cotton threads gathered in bins of exotic dress patterns with printed labels written in French, Italian, and even some in Russian. There are several pieces of furniture finished in rich black lacquer, consisting of a small chest overflowing with costume jewelry, an empty wardrobe, a midsized dresser drawer, and two end tables with mother of pearl inlays etched into the wood depicting exquisite oriental designs.

Nela finds an open safe behind a grand French provincial buffet dating back to the Civil War days. It is empty, except for a few rat droppings. Concealed behind the dresser drawer is another locked door. At first, Nela thinks of trying to break open the barrier with a hammer and chisel found in the storage pantry. Then she remembers two unusual skeleton keys that always hung in a wardrobe armoire in the room where her grandfather died. It is the same room once occupied by her great ancestor, Adam Pixley, the only room with an overhanging balcony.

Nela climbs back to the top floor. It feels strange to enter this room. She feels his presence; sees vividly image of her grandfather covered under a white sheet bedridden in the end, the sound of his breathing as a disembodied spirit that haunts the place still. This his final resting place for scores of months after the tragic accident of his wife.

According to the official report, she ventured too near the edge and fell down. Her body found next morning with neck broken at bottom of the southern ravine by an angler casting along the overflowing banks of the Aconee River. Nela was too young to remember much about her grandmother, except for the smell of her hair, like fresh lavender, and the unhappy sound of her crying in the night. So many things Nela does not know.

She must pry open the armoire, but the keys still there, right where she remembers. One of the two keys turns the lock making a resounding click. The solid oak door proves more difficult to open than expected, but finally gives way to the full pressure of Nela's body, swinging unexpectedly inward. An oppressive odor invades her nostrils with stale trapped air rushing out. Covering her mouth and nose using the hem of her dress, she cautiously enters. It did not smell like anything dead, exactly-- nor is it of the living. The flood of lantern light exposes corpses of many more ghosts trapped inside.

Arranged artifacts and forgotten oblations leap from the shadows of this unholy shrine sealed against time. In one corner stands a weathered British red coat, like the kind worn by the King's soldiers during the Revolutionary War.

The skeleton of several dry brittle sticks provide a body entangled in the moth-eaten sleeves. The room, no larger than a small windowless study, void of ventilation, constructed more as vault of a burial chamber designed to inter things long dead.

Dominating one wall leans a life-size portrait of Adam Pixley painted during his later years. It is not like the one that hangs upstairs, capturing him as a handsome pioneer first settling this land. In this portrait hunches a man with bowed shoulders, his hands grasping wretchedly an English briar walking stick. He looks altogether wicked, made even more evil by a black scar slashed above the left temple of a blood-red eye, seeming to watch Nela's every move like the soulless glare of a wild animal studying prey.

She wonders if the artist had captured the true countenance of this distant relative, or the visage of some other demon that still harbors within. Below the portrait are two trunks positioned side by side, both very old. The first opens easily with only a brass ornate hasp embedded into the polished wood; the second resembles more a weathered pirate's chest, secured by a blackened padlock.

Contents of the first trunk mostly consist of clothing worn by early frontiersmen: a buckskin jacket, pair of moccasin boots, and a dried dark-brown leather satchel embossed with a Spanish Crest. This is the same satchel and the same clothes worn by the younger Adam Pixley in the upstairs portrait. Here, also, the famous flintlock pistol engraved with an elegant design and the initials *J B* carved into the handle. Inside the satchel are thirty pieces of minted Spanish gold doubloons.

Just the sight of the shiny coins makes her heart skip with excitement, Nela's senses stimulated in a way not experienced before. Her inherited estate is worth a hundred— maybe even a thousand times more than these few golden coins sought by pirates and gold hunters of the world since age of the Conquistadors. Yet, there is something about seeing– yes, even the tangible sensation of touching these magnificent coins quickens her senses, awakens desire inside Nela unknown until now.

Closely examining one of the coins, she feels aroused by more than just the shiny element in her trembling hand. Stamped on one side of this perfectly preserved currency is a lion representing the once grand Spanish Empire with the inscription "HISPANIARUM REX," meaning Kings of Spain. The word "MREXTOO," or gold coin, written along the circumference. For the first time in her life, Nela's European Latin study truly pays off!

"Gold coin belonging to the King of Spain," she proudly repeats aloud.

On one side, the unrecognizable face of a monarch along with the Roman numeral date of 1640. On the opposite side are symbols she thinks pertains to valued weight.

Nela feels truly rich as never she has felt before; feels as only a Pixley might feel, running her fingers through the remaining pieces of gold doubloons. These she will put into a safe place and keep their existence secret until the day she dies. Nela is-- after all-- born a Pixley, and rightful heir apparent!

The only remaining inventory in the trunk are a few disintegrating articles of female attire *"no proper lady"* from any century would ever dream of wearing on her own.

Nela quickly surmises that the second key belongs to the padlock securing the pirate's chest. The lid creaks open with only a little effort, its many specters unleashed.

Nela shudders with apprehension as she bravely sorts through the contents of this second coffin. Here the enigma of a story speaking the true confessions of notorious events no Pixley heir should know. The first to catch her eye is a handwritten diary recorded by her great ancestor. This she will read in more detail later and will never tell anyone the truth of what she reads. There is a

Latin Bible with a piece of paper tucked between the pages, and the words '*Espiritu Santo*' written by the same hand that wrote the diary. Beneath it is a more durable parchment scroll printed with strange lettering, which William will later confirm as Semitic writing. At bottom of this trunk rests a richly leather-bound volume embossed with lettering that Nela translates in English to mean *Ship Log of the Libertad*.

"This is very old Spanish, and some of the words Castilian," Nela proclaims in excitement, again referencing her European education.

She quickly skims through the many entries, deciding that although the language similar to the dialects exposed to during university academics, many words unrecognizable within context. This, too, she thinks to reserve reading for a later date. But never will. She is about to close the lid when something wadded and tucked into a corner flames to attention. Upon first glance, she thinks it to be ball of frayed red yarn tiered around a white stone etched with symbols that appear drawn by a post-grade schoolchild.

"What in the Lord!" Nela breathes involuntarily, raising it into the light.

The dried human scalp grown with a long streak of bright Viking-red hair represents something ghastly in meaning. How did Adam Pixley come in possession of such a macabre souvenir? What significance did it have; and why had he kept it?

Involuntarily Nela voices another question in her mind just as disturbing: "Is she the first Pixley to open this trunk of dark secrets hidden here for nearly two centuries?"

Later the same day, Nela sends message to her new husband, informing him that she has found a trove of family heirlooms she thinks he can help decipher. She is careful to leave out the part about the gold coins and the diary. These she will keep always secret to herself-- as any Pixley would!

"I have a patient, whose son a junior archeologist working for department of criminal forensics in Atlanta." William volunteers after inspecting the remaining contents. "I think we should get him over here."

Nela cannot agree more. Several days later, a young man named Jeremiah Wake meets them at the estate dressed in clothing unaccommodating to the hot humid July weather. He looks barely old enough to be out of high school and has a slight stammer in the beginning. The stammer quickly dissipates, as he begins carefully cataloging the contents of the trunk by numbering each artifact, taking numerous photos, making extensive notes scribbled into a spiral notepad.

"What do you think it all means?" Nela inquires after the inventory complete.

"I-I can't be s-sure, but I think w-we are looking at more than one history here." Jeremiah Wake begins, clearing his throat, his Adam's apple racing up and down along an elongated scrawny neck. "The ships log and Bible are def-definitely from early to the middle 1600s. The scroll comes from a period much earlier th-than that. You are right Doctor Smith, t-the writing is Semitic. To be precise, it is the ancient *Paleo-Hebrew* alphabet, a reference taken f-from the Book of Isaiah prophesying the coming of Emmanuel, the Messiah -Be-Ben Joseph. The scalp is more in line with age of your founding fa-father ancestor, Adam Pixley; and ju-judging by the incision marks, removed by a Ch-Cherokee Indian. As for the wh-white rock, it is indigenous to many such rocks f-found in the local area with a unique script of Indian symbols, very different from othe-other native tribes. My fa-father was the boss Foreman during excavation for the se-second Liberty Cotton Mill. He claims they dis-discovered ma-mass graves with skeletal remains, many bearing ballistic wounds in the ba-back of their skulls. Only there is no historical record of su-such a massacre ever taking place here. The mill people ordered a co-cover-up of this discovery so not to delay the project. The excavators al-also found a large white rock engraved with pic-pictograph symbols. Sym-Symbols that are very similar to the ones found on this s-smaller rock. Da-Daddy ordered his crew to roll it to the top of an uncultivated hill wh-where it remains lost to this day. I tr-tried to find that rock as a boy during the years we lived in these parts. I f-found a lot of other interesting pieces of the pu-puzzle, but never that rock."

"Can you tell us what the Indian symbols mean?" William wants to know.

"No- Not precisely," Wake replies professionally. "I am mi-missing some important cipher keys, b-but basically the symbols on this rock literally translate *'Last Days of Fallen Eagle"*.

"That is a most strange meaning," Nela says partly to herself, fondling the ornament attached to a leathern cord tied around her neck.

"H-Have you recently traveled to Egypt?" Wake enquires, glancing at the stone engraving.

"Heavens no-- this is a gift from my William on the night before getting married."

She says this, sounding almost apologetic. Wake decides the pendant a rather interesting imitation, but a fake all the same. From his perspective, it appears as though the blue-green paint has begun to chip and fade, the common metal used to make the frame scored and tarnished. He cannot help but wonder why a woman of her wealth and reputation would wish to wear publicly a damaged piece of costume jewelry available in any gift store.

The couple thanks Wake and gives him the trunk with its contents for eventual donation to the Atlanta Museum of Archeology after his investigation concluded. The Pixley Town Committee later vote to buy the famous landmark estate at a fair market price and turn the home of the first founding father into a historic monument. They even take nearly all of the furniture, making it that much easier for Nela and William Smith to start their couple life fresh in the newly renovated Liberty home.

The years pass peacefully. William devotes his life to provide medicine to the poor living in, or near the mill village community. His clientele barely make enough to feed their families after drinking away their meager wages to salve sickness of depression at a local bar owned by a despicable gentleman named Homer. If not for Nela's money, William Smith would have been poorest of the lot.

The qualities Nela loves most about her husband are also things she finds most difficult to respect. Alien to her way of instruction is Bill's sense of social justice to believe all men equal, his attitude of reverence, even for those most poor. Nela's truer nature rises to the surface during a difference of opinion in the early months of their matrimonial union having to do with the cost of building a garage for their new motor car, which he considers wasteful extravagance. Bill learns to avoid conversations about money after this.

Her husband has little interest in domestic arrangement, allowing his wife full reign to remodel their home into her vision of Camelot. He only nods approvingly to her choice of decorations and the colors for each room. Nela decides on the landscape of the lawn. She is free to choose where to place the gardens, which trees to keep, and which to cut down. Only the barrier of the rock pond off limits with insistence it remain as is.

Twice during the renovations, she sees a large Negro man in dirty clothes standing at the edge of her cultivated property. The second time their eyes meet. The man quickly turns away and lumbers back into the swamp. Sometimes in the night she can hear someone singing, a woeful baritone voice, songs remembered as a child sang by black servants that tended her father's fields. He is down there*! Somewhere near that nasty old black man is encroaching on her property!*

"Okay, Nela, I will go down and find out who this man is and why he is here." William promises, slipping a revolver into his pants pocket.

"You will be careful?"

"It is probably just a vagrant. If he meant us any harm, I am sure he would have tried something by now. This is just a precaution. To be poor does not automatically make someone a dangerous criminal."

Nela cannot help but respect the humble bravery of this man. Even if she were not married to him, this moment William Smith shines noble in her mind. He walks alone down into the darkness of the Liberty swamp to confront a Nubian giant capable of anything. Upon his later return, William says the man's name is Abraham, and that the shanty in the swamp where he now lives has been the home of his family since the days of the Civil War. He left as a young man to discover the world, only to come back here. By then the home of his youth abandoned, his family gone.

"He now lives there alone, no electricity, no plumbing, and with only an outhouse. But he seems like a happy and peaceful fellow, so I have decided to let him stay. Don't worry, Nela, Abraham is a good man. And there are so few good people in this world."

Abraham– there is something familiar about the name– something about the man that causes Nela to remember someone else in the past, when she was just a girl. What difference should that make now? Her husband has chosen to allow this encroacher to remain. Because Bill's demands so few, Nela reluctantly accepts the presence of this stranger from the past to infringe upon her cultivated estate.

There are times she becomes jealous that William shares an affinity with this gruff looking Negro, a connection completely lacking in their communication as man and wife. He is this way with most everyone encountered: poor land-squatters, Indians, and Gypsies-- all considered equal in his eyes. Each time it happens, Nela feels rejected, a feeling familiar and without reason. Always there lingers that feeling, a feeling lacking substance, reminder of something that happened long ago, as though from another lifetime. Therefore, Abraham stays-on, like a familiar shadow in her mind; and will continue to remain even after William Smith departed.

In the eighth year of their marriage, Nela and Bill resign themselves to the fact that they will remain childless. She sees in his eyes the profound disappointment. Not contempt exactly, but a look that makes Nela feel insignificant. She is not accustomed to feel this way, and to feel it now makes Nela angry. Nevertheless, they love each other. What disappointment can be stronger, than their matrimonial bond of love? What greater meaning of happiness can there be in life... except maybe Nela's money? Perhaps, had she done things differently, things would have turned out different. Admission of guilt not the Pixley way; and this the way it has always been.

Arriving back home, Nela parks her car in the motor garage, the last addition to their home before William's death. It will be morning soon, and she desperately wants to fall asleep again. She has many things to consider in days to come. Once it was so peaceful here. Once she believed this world made of better things. That was a long time ago, so many things different now. Change stands at the door and soon enough all will know the truth!

Unable to go back to sleep, Nela abandons all further attempts. She is out of elixir. This is good reason to make a surprised visit to Homer's in Liberty Town. She steps carefully toward the Widow Pond behind her house. Here is the place where William died; the place she most finds solitude. Nela is long pass the fear of ghost and hobgoblins. She knows only too well the monsters that dwell deep in the Liberty Peninsula-- and those monsters know her-- time being the greatest harbinger of all!

She sits by the water's edge and peers into the black mirror. It is Nela as she truly is. Just a shadow darkly reflected before light of encroaching morning.

CHAPTER 11

Prophecy of Xeantee

Only Homer's *Bar and Liquor Store* continues to survive year after year without change. Maybe because gossip and a few drinks are all that folks in the little ghost of a town have to keep them going. Maybe it prevents them from becoming altogether bored. Becoming like the damp cellars and musty odors in the cramp mill village houses built before anyone can remember. Anyone–that is–except maybe Homer. These are the whitewash of appearance. A graveyard of weathered bones, apparently peaceful, apparently tended by stewards devoted to the simple life and filled with glad tidings. However, deep down all know the truth. It is the redbrick cotton mill, which breathes life into Liberty.

The town of Liberty itself is little more than a collection of old buildings, better condemned along with the dream of becoming a big city before the Great Depression. Storefronts boarded up every few years, inviting someone new: someone brave and foolish to pry them open, sweep away the dust, and try where so many others have failed before them. Few of these pioneers last longer than a season. Usually in less time than this, the premises vacated, the old familiar 'For Lease' sign hanging despairingly in the window.

Most all the property owners live in neighboring Pixley, nestled on the opposite side of a humped hill appropriately named Hog Back Mountain because of its protruding shape. These absent landlords have not so much as visited their estates in more than two generations. And except for the occasional inspection by Pixley's Indian Sheriff– for whom

Homer always pours for free– one might think them as dead as the town.

The present town of Liberty rests on a narrow swamp island shaped like a crooked appendage extending into bosom of a swamp valley. Miles of marshland surround the island on all sides, except northwest. Here is a natural mote breached by a narrow man-made land bridge connecting it to the rest of the world providing only one way in and one way out. Since then the island called Liberty Peninsula. At widest point, the Liberty Peninsula measures less than two miles wide and extends just under four miles to the southeastern tip. Geographically, this anomalous landmass rests dead center of a valley between foothills of two separate mountain chains tapering into the thick piedmont marshlands that meander to the coast. A single access road named Paul Revere Avenue travels clockwise around the perimeter, loops over on the north end of Main Street like an inverted figure eight, and then intersects again on the south end of Main Street now running counterclockwise. There is only one lane, distressingly narrow for modern automobiles, with deep potholes and sticky tar pools during the hot summer months. On occasion teenagers drive their proud hot-rods across Hog Back Mountain at night, down to the access road, and along the circle to find a secret place to neck. That stopped after Whitey Miller beat a boy to a pulp that he caught parked on the roadside near his house.

Because Liberty's Main Street slices diagonally across the middle of the peninsula, it often creates some confusion for none residents. On one side of town, the street named East Main and Paul Revere, and West Main and Paul Revere on the other side. This has happened more than once with a visitor that just happens to be passing through. Homer joked for weeks about the man from Atlanta unable to find his way around. Like every town, Liberty has its old and has its new. The original mill went bankrupt during the Depression. Then good times return; a more modern and bigger mill built. A crumbling smoke stack and a few exposed cotton gins rusted beyond recognition far to the southeast are all that remain of the original structure. A rumor persist that a headless demon haunts the chimney. In the end the only demon residing there is the town drunk, who crawls each night into the blacken interior until stung awake by soberness.

The new mill founded on the northwest side, physically removed as far as possible from the old, represents a wonder of modern technology. It stands three stories tall with two crimson-lipped chimneys rising more than seventy-five feet above the tallest trees, belching a body of black smoke night and day, like a taskmaster shadow looming over the peninsula. Nearly everyone works a shift in the mill. Everyone except Homer, old widows, some wives, and youngsters not yet old enough since creation of laws prohibiting child labor. Of course, there are also the occasional shop owners. These never seem to last long enough to be counted. There are others existing in the shadows uncensored, to whom the sharp piercing whistle marking a change in shift represents intrusion into the tranquility of the surrounding swamp. To these the mill and Liberty represents something altogether different.

Once upon a time, the entire Liberty peninsula sprouted with fabulous cotton plantations creating a dynasty of wealth. According to southern legend, these viceroys of the period ruled the land with an unbridled iron fist, and guarded their women with equal diligence. Black slaves were often beaten, traded, or even executed for just looking at a white woman in such a way as their owners might interpret usurping. In those days, justice resided in the hand of one holding the larger whip. Provided his color right and he had enough money. Little would change even after a hundred years. Even long after the pride of these cruel barons withered as cottonseed scattered in the wind.

These former slave generations lived in small paint-less shanties at the swamp's edge. Through these fringe populations survive tales of the monster remembered. The more popular theory is that the stories inventions by the plantation owners themselves in order to breed fear, thereby reducing runaways. If this was the ploy, it works all too well, and continues to work long after that generation lost in the chorus of time. Now only one of these shanties remains. This homestead never included in Liberty's property menu; nor is its present inhabitant numbered with the rest of the town folks. Except for the knowledge that the rotting timbers refuse to collapse, it remains lost behind a barrier of creeping cattails that grow thicker with each year.

The host plantation farther to the south fared less well. Only a crumbling foundation remains, a few charred ribs, parts of broken columns, and smashed edifice halves of what may have been pieces of a large oval balcony. The ghost of a garden appears nearly invisible beneath clumps of Milk Weed and creeping vines of Poison Ivy. A stagnant black pool opens menacingly in what was probably the center of the garden. Perhaps it once mirrored clearly the sparkling dignity of bygone days in the old south, but now altogether without reflection, a tomb of many unfortunate creatures that drown mysteriously in the shallow waters.

Adjacent to these ruins is a neatly trimmed hedge. On the other side of this hedge, the gleaming elegant white house belonging to the widow of the good late Doctor Smith. It is worth mentioning that the Smith estate is architecture without equal, elegantly constructed, and regal beyond comparison to the cheaply built mill village houses characteristic of Liberty. The well-groomed front lawn would have served wonderfully as a football field– had there been enough idle kids in town to make a team. The sound of a lawnmower echoes every Saturday morning from the Smith estate, except on rainy days, the wonderful lawn remaining thick and green for most of the year. There grows a Pear tree and an Apple tree on either side of the grand front porch. For some unexplained reason neither tree ever bore fruit. Just as well, too, since the widow would not have liked the idea of a boy climbing her trees, or the litter of fallen fruit. However, she did have an annoying problem with insects on the large stone back patio, and remains forever at war with the encroachers. Few people have ever actually been inside. Rumors are that many of the furnishings expensive antiques imported from France and England costing more than a mill worker makes his whole life. A handsome motorcar garage, unconnected and added later, houses a tan 1948 Buick Sedan maintained in mint condition. The widow rarely goes anywhere in the day since the death of her husband. When she does, people take notice; and it is never long before the news reaches Homer.

The Liberty peninsula has yet another kind of history: a history that no one wishes to remember. Legend persists that the original inhabitants of the land track were a small tribe of Indians called Aconee. They were a friendly people in the beginning, welcoming the first white man with open arms and gifts of thanksgiving. Nevertheless, they were Indians just the same. It is to the thanks of the early pioneer named Adam Pixley, who with a band of patriots put a stop to an Indian uprising. Because of so few documented accounts, only a few rumored stories survive. By some, Pixley is an American hero after the order of Daniel Boone. By others, he is the worst kind of monster. According to at least one historical record, an Indian shaman left a curse to avenge treachery dealt to his people. However, in time this, too, lost and forgotten, until many generations later the excavation of something unusual from beneath several layers of bog.

While digging the foundation for what will become the New Liberty Mill, the workers unearth a large smooth white rock with a shallow depression on one side. Engraved on the face are several strange symbols of Indian writing.

Realizing the find to be significant, but not knowing what else to do, the supervisor in charge orders the rock rolled to the top of a nearby hill. In later years, that hill marks the outer boundary of Liberty's cemetery. The unusual find once again lost among the silent memories of the dead. Until one unseasonable hot spring day, someone arrives in town to resurrect the memory and the meaning of the white Indian rock rediscovered thanks to a late-night radiobroadcast announcing testimony of a young girl once local to the region.

Jeremiah Wake, a Professor of Anthropology at the University of Georgia, whose main interest ancient cultures and their languages, arrives excitedly and unannounced into town. No one has ever seen a professor before and unanimously decide that the surest courtesy is to shun him completely. Wake wastes no time. He rents a small, but clean room above *Mabel's Garage,* and spends the next few days in the cemetery unraveling the greatest mystery of his career.

Homer lazes in his bar as usual. Things are always quiet during the day. Oh- he had his occasional customer- but not like at night. He knows all about Jeremiah Wake even though he has yet to lay eyes on him. He is therefore only a little surprised when the tall lean man with clear auburn eyes steps into his bar, an unlighted briar pipe pried between thin lips.

"What's your pleasure, Mr. Wake?" Homer demands triumphantly, as always he did.

"I am told... you are the nearest thing to an official that there is in Liberty?" Wake enquires awkwardly, removing the pipe from his mouth.

Homer only grunts, as he sets up a glass.

"No, thanks, I don't drink," Wake declines, and then clears his throat. "Are you familiar with the Indian Rock in the cemetery?"

Homer has heard about it, not more than that.

"My father was the Foreman, who ordered the rock moved up there." Wake continues clearing his throat. "They found some other things, too: broken pottery, Indian jewelry, and jumbles of human bones indicating a massacre. The mill people gave orders to throw everything in the swamp. Father told my mother and me the story many years later. He claims to have found more than a hundred skulls with bullet holes scattered about, the skeletal remains buried in mass graves... and the children– so many children! It was more genocide, than a war!

It always puzzled my father how anyone could murder innocents that way. He kept the souvenir of a petrified charred alligator tooth engraved with Indian symbols unearthed from a heap of decayed rubble. Judging by the shape and a hole drilled through it, I think this to be a talisman worn by a Shaman chieftain. It remains an heirloom placed on the mantle of our family home for as long as I can remember. I visited this area for a second time several years back after retiring from the Atlanta Criminal Archeology Lab. During this excursion, I found skeletal remains in a shallow grave near the dry riverbed that I think dates back to approximately the era when the pictograph history begins. I was the intact skull of a young male with teeth and bone structure characteristics of an Eastern European during the Habsburgs Monarchy."

Wake hesitates awkwardly at this point upon realizing the gnarly arrangement of this bartender's few remaining front teeth, and even these yellowed and dark. A failed attempt at politeness, he continues.

"In the dry river bed itself, I later discovered the remains of two other men dating back to the same period. These unfortunate fellows seem to have drowned together in a deadly embrace, both wedged together in a dry sinkhole, no doubt submerged when once the river flowed unimpeded. For some odd reason, one of those skulls went missing from the forensics lab about a year ago."

Homer only grunts as he searches under the bar for something he thinks more important, reminding Wake of an unkempt pig searching for truffles, which he once saw on the cover of a National Geographic Magazine.

"My father was quite the artist and made drawings of some of those symbols. He always wanted to know what they meant. I suppose this the main reason I chose the path of my education. You might even say his desire to know branded me with a destiny. Even though he is gone now, I think he will rest better. Now that I have had a chance to study them in more detail, I'm beginning to understand some things about this lost culture and their spiritual beliefs."

Wake produces a piece of paper from a notebook filled with papers and some photographs of the white rock in the cemetery. His hand trembles slightly as he hands the paper into those of the gruff bartender.

"This is a copy of some of the translation. I think it only right that the folks in Liberty Town should know about this first. After all, it is part of your own local history."

Homer takes the paper as though handling a snake, careful not to hold it too much near. Despite his several failings, Homer reads well. For some unexplainable reason what he reads bothers him, turning in his gut like a feeling he has known and feared all along. As he continues to read, the fingers on his hands begin to contract, his mouth dryer than his driest (howbeit a little watered-down) whiskey.

His star wondrous appears in heaven bright
Shadows awake from ancient sleep
Prince Aconee borne upon wings of night
Frogs congregate children at his feet
Peace made in Valley Xeantee

Face in a canyon grins sepulcher white
Place Fallen Eagle makes his nest

And walks still an Indian spirit blind of sight
His soul stripped naked without rest
Bones forgotten in Valley Xeantee

Blood weeping at first morning light
Recalling sin of the father's shame
Summer flies consume his flesh into twilight
The beaver proclaims treachery of his name
Violence remembered in Valley Xeantee

Xeantee Aconee where fountains meet
Frogs singing his chorus tonight
Souls rise from graves buried deep
Legions resurrected into hoary flight
Days restored in Valley Xeantee

At the bottom of the page, it reads Translated by J. Wake. Homer turns altogether pale, as he lowers the paper to the bar. He did not understand it really– that is-- not with his mind. Nonetheless, he feels the meaning as acutely as he can feel the gnawing of his ulcers. Homer is too proud to admit that he does not comprehend something right in his own backyard. He says what he does to all his customers sooner or later. Homer tells a lie.

"My daddy showed me that old Indian rock before I was knee high to a grasshopper," he affirms with unmistakable authority. "His great great-great grand daddy was one of them that helped clear out them savages. –Don't make no doubt about it-- they was savages! Look around you today and tell me which is better."

Wake raises dolefully his eyebrows, attempts a smile, fondling the polished neck of his briar pipe.

"Of course there is more. I haven't finished deciphering it all. Something about an Aconee warrior incarnated somehow into a creature half frog and half man, who is both a judge and a deliverer. Written there is what anthropology calls the keystone to the legend. There might be more pieces to the puzzle somewhere, if only one knew where to look. Have you ever seen any other rocks or trees with these kinds of symbols on them?"

He presents Homer with the pictures he has taken, as well as notes on other pieces of deciphered text. Homer only wags his head and yawns like a hippopotamus.

"It's a prophecy of some kind, maybe even a curse!" Wake urges desperately. "It's very unusual, and many scores of years old. If you like, I can send you the rest when I'm finished."

"You don't say?" Homer grunts again.

Whatever impression Wake hoped to make remains wasted on this rude bartender. All the same, he has fulfilled his purpose as an anthropologist by restoring life to a culture forgotten, as well as keeping a promise made to his deceased father. What Liberty did with her discovered truth is none of his concern. The afternoon train from Pixley to Atlanta leaves in two hours. It is Wake's intention to be on it.

"I trust you will see to it that everyone has an opportunity to read this? Maybe someone can provide more information. I can be contacted at this address."

He presents Homer a faculty business card with his name printed on it, and begins drifting nervously toward the door. Upon reaching the opening, he returns the bitten stem of the briar to his mouth, and quickly exits. Homer just shakes his head dumbly.

"There has got to be something wrong with a man who doesn't drink," he is thinking to himself.

Homer will continue to think about it all that day, until the paychecks started coming in. Whitey Miller passes Wake outside as he is leaving. Whitey has just finished working a double shift, and is dog-tired-- but never is he too tired to spend a few hours in Homer's bar.

"I swear if that fellow don't look like a new-born turkey!" He remarks sourly.

Automatically Homer pours Whitey a dose of his usual poison.

"He claims this here what's written on the Indian Rock up in the cemetery," Homer says pushing the paper toward Whitey.

Whitey leaps back and hisses.

"Badger, you know I don't read! Besides, why should I give a damn about what was writ by some `Injun' before ever I was born?"

Homer takes a deep breath. Sometimes old Whitey made good sense. He locates a nearly empty Gin bottle under the bar. Taking the last swig, he rolls the paper into a scroll, pushes it in along with the business card, and seals it forever with a cork. In his own way, Homer likes to keep things organized.

"It'll be safe there," he says, returning the container to its original place.

In time, Homer forgets about the paper. He forgets about Wake and the Indian Rock. Nor will he remember later when strange and unusual things begin happening in Liberty-- things that no one able to explain. Like when James Anderson, whose farm rests nearest the eastern tip of the peninsula, sends a third message from Mabel's telegraph service to Pixley's Sheriff's office one morning complaining that his lower pasture has flooded again during the night drowning two calves. Later the same day the mill lays-off twelve men without any reason. This only the beginning signs of worse things to come.

CHAPTER 12

Davy's First Job

That year the Shriners finish construction of a new wing added to the old V.A. Hospital in Pixley. Chevrolet markets a 1962 sedan that promises one day to become a classic, streamlined and chromed to the kind of excess that sparkles in the young mind. Rumors of another escalating war drift across the sea from the Far East, another war that guarantees the end of tyranny and evil.

This same year a Jew and his son move to Liberty and open a watch repair business. The first thing the time fixer does is to letter a fresh new sign that reads *Weis T Baily & Son*, which he displays with spotlights every night. Why he did this is a mystery to all. Homer suggests that maybe this how they do things in a big city.

"Damn Foreigners!" Homer often swears. "Someday they're going to take over everything;" adding with a wink, "just like we did to the Indians!"

Local residents at first resist the idea of Jews– especially big city Jews from the north-- invading their community. There are those who would have cast them out had Pixley's Sheriff not been a half-breed, therefore encouraging tolerance for differences. However, in time even these white-robed vigilantes forget their vows, as one by one Liberty's clocks stop, and *Weis T Baily & Son* makes them live again. By renewing a worn spring, or making a minor adjustment, the watch smith quickly restores the oracle of time to their lives. They often even marvel at his skill to perform miracles before their very eyes, and in time altogether ignore the fact that he is a Northerner Jew.

Lucy Tracy rushes nervously about the kitchen preparing the last remaining details of a picture perfect breakfast arrangement from an open Sears's catalogue on the rough butcher-block counter. The only detail that really matches the picture is a green checker tablecloth recently ordered for $9.95, plus tax and rail shipping to Mabel's, including a matching green curtain. Of course, Lucy could have made it cheaper, provided she could find the material. But there is just something special about store-bought! These new colors contrast poorly with the faded yellow pastel walls and the dull cracked plaster ceiling blighted by a rat hole stuffed with tin foil. The morning sun streams through the open glass window embellishing the rich new pattern with a luster that brings Lucy near to tears with pride—oh how Homer was going to like it! He liked most anything new; the newer, the better he likes it. Glancing up at the clock, Lucy nearly upsets one of the chairs as she races from the kitchen, through the den decorated with old furniture inherited from her parents, pausing at the entrance of a closed door. To most everyone in town she goes by the name of Lucile, including Davy, her sister's only surviving son. Just Homer and few paying clients call her by the preferred name of Lucy. A name that makes her feel still young, still attractive in the eyes of a man to desire more than just the attention of a wife and mother.

"David, are you awake?" She inquires harshly.

"I was just getting out of bed..." an inhuman mumble crackles from inside.

"Well, you best hurry. Nela Smith called nearly an hour ago, and she's expecting you early."

A sudden hurried bumbling on the other side of the door.

"She– She wasn't mad... was she?"

"She said to tell you that only the early bird catches the worm." Lucile's voice trails, as she clicks her way back toward the kitchen.

Davy can tell by the sound of her walk that Lucile is happy. He knows from experience that this can only mean that old Homer will soon arrive. She is a good woman, as good and self-sacrificing as a person can be. She works six days a week mending clothes. Rarely might she receive a special order for a new dress because someone is getting married. As a rule, Lucile is the only woman in town who wears new clothes. She goes to church every single Sunday and sings in the choir; her only mortal vice being that she loves old Homer, tender at Homer's Bar and Liquor Store. You might say he is her thorn in the flesh. That piece of earthiness that anchors Lucile, and prevents her from flying off in the rapture. She is after all past forty, past the prime for marrying, a solitary soul that has devoted her life to abstinence since the cruel death of her first true love. Her only living legacy is Davy and the only joy she truly admit to. Lucile has taken upon herself to raise him alone and as though he her own after the younger sister perished in a fire. This is as much as she will tell Davy, making him promise never to say anything more to another soul.

"It must always remain our secret," she reminds Davy often. "Some people have nothing better to do than gossip, and say hurtful things. What business is it of others? Your mother would have wanted it this way."

Davy knows little about his real mother, except her name Lori, who Lucile reports as a living angel, further supported by a few faded pictures of an attractive smiling young girl kept in the family album. He prefers not to think too much, as he considers Lucile the best mother he could have. Nevertheless, he often thinks about an enigmatic father no one seems to know anything about.

Lucy still retains a glimmer of youth and vitality, and has determined in herself to snare Homer with her remaining charm. Homer is smart and slippery as an eel, but too easily given to natural appetite. It looks that given enough time; Lucy Tracy might have her way.

Homer is sitting in one of three Black Walnut wooden chairs sipping a cup of fresh coffee consciously admiring the new arrangement by the time Davy gets dressed. There had been four chairs, but the fourth cracked under Homer's weight last time he was over because she claims he leaned back too far; and even though Lucile considers the chairs precious heirlooms once belonging to her parents, she shrugs-off the unfortunate incident as the calculated price of his corpulent presence.

Homer's twinkling brown eyes, impish and alert, look up as Davy enters. By gosh here was a boy with expectation-- a boy heading into his prime— a boy not so much unlike himself once upon a day!

"Son, you sure are getting big," he says admiringly.

"Takes after his grandfather Tracy," Lucile interjects; "he was tall just like that– and Lord the way that boy does eat! I swear, Homer, I'm going to need to get me a job in that sweaty old cotton mill just to keep him in feed."

"You wouldn't want to do that, Lucy." Homer replies protectively. "A pretty woman like you wouldn't last long in that hell-hole."

Lucy blushes sweetly. She likes it when Homer calls her pretty, likes his words as honey on her lips. Without saying a word, Davy sits down and begins shoveling grits and eggs into his mouth from a plate that Lucile has judiciously placed before him.

"I had that dream again." He says to her between a mouth full of scrambled eggs and annoying slurps of coffee.

Lucile only squints in agony.

"What dream is that?" Homer wants to know.

"It's not all clear," Davy begins after swallowing the last mouthful. "I'm in some kind of bed, except it's more like being inside a cage with fire and smoke all around. Then the bed starts burning, too. I feel the flames like hot tongues licking all around me, but for some reason I'm helpless to do anything about it. Then I feel my face melting like a candle, the hot wax of my flesh sizzling and flowing. I scream and scream, and then I awake."

"That's a dream sure enough!" Homer agrees.

"I'm sure," Lucile cuts in tersely, "that's because of all those monster movies you watch on television each Friday night."

"It seems so real– not anything at all like a movie! Sometimes I wish I could stay in the dream long enough just to see how it might end."

"I'm certain Nela Smith wouldn't mind waiting for you to finish your dream–"

"Mrs. Smith!" Davy exclaims jumping up, and then winks across at the pandering figure seated opposite him. "I'll be seeing you Homer. A few more months and I'll be eighteen, and you can serve me legal!"

"You better not!" Lucy threatens both of them. "I want at least one Tracy in this family to amount to something!"

The back screened back door snaps shut; and Davy is gone. Homer looks across at Lucy and winks mischievously, as always he does when they are alone. This is his way. The way Lucy likes to feel in the glint of his eyes, making her feel desire, as never she has felt for a man before.

Nela Smith stands watering her flowers when Davy arrives. She looks like a flower herself. A budding head covered by a wide brimmed yellow hat, wrapped around with a green polka-dot scarf as new as the day bought. She wears a peach colored housecoat gathered at the sleeves. Her soft white hands concealed inside pink gloves. The figure of her body twists slightly in a green shadow, giving the appearance of suddenly sprouting out of the soil. Like her many flowers, Nela Smith blossoms as a southern Magnolia rarely beautiful.

"Good morning, Mrs. Smith. I'm real sorry that I'm late."

Nela, deaf in one ear, the other slightly hard of hearing, often dwells in the rich silence of her own thoughts. Therefore it little surprises Davy that she completely ignores his presence, continuing to water and pluck out unwanted weeds stolen among her chosen favorites since the last time she performed this morning ritual.

"Mrs. Smith," He shouts again, "I said I'm real sorry–"

"Oh, it's you!" She exclaims understandably surprised.

"I guess I over slept. I came straight over as soon as Lucile told me you called."

Her face changes vacant, as if suddenly, just now the motion of time invented for her. Nela must be well past fifty, considering that she and her late husband, the honorable Doctor William Smith, were married nearly two decades before he died accidentally. That was about the same time Davy born, which to him is a lifetime. Yet, Nela Smith remains blessed with an ageless vitality. Not only did she seem younger than her years, Nela somehow commands presence of beauty that continues to renew itself, refusing to submit to nature's irresistible command. The strong fiber of her being as the ebon polished brilliance of her life, the exquisite fusion of all that is painful and all that is exhilarating, composed of rich moments that inspire more than the dormant clay in Nela's garden.

"My– how time just winks past us!" Then adds sweetly, "How about a glass of lemonade, and then I have a special errand for you to do for me today."

"Thank you, Mrs. Smith. Maybe after–"

"Nonsense–" she snaps leading him to the back patio where two elegant glasses are already prepared on a silver tray. "I made a fresh batch just this morning. As the Good Doctor always said, `Health is wealth; drink insurance'."

This prescription by the late doctor did not make Davy feel any more at ease. After all, if a physician unable even to save himself, how can his remedies be good for anyone else? No sooner do they sit than a cloud of angry Yellow Jackets begin swarming around them.

"Oh, dear –dear–," Nela cries frantically waving her hands. "I burned their nest early this morning. I thought they would be gone by now. Come along, Davy, we must sit in the parlor. Besides, it is much cooler in there."

Raising the serving tray precisely, she glides into the house. Davy follows quickly, fledging the air with his arms. The angry horde seems altogether uninterested in Nela, choosing instead to blame this new arrival for their untimely eviction.

The parlor is the largest room of the Smith home, located nearly center of this grand architecture resembling a miniaturized amphitheatre. The high concave ceiling painted brilliantly white has begun to exhibit some signs of age with rather noticeable cracks. Only Nela seems not to notice, or else refuses to acknowledge that her Camelot not meant to last.

Ornately carved baseboards and intersecting lattices surround plate of a large bay window. Diamonds of a glass chandelier with pink bugle bulbs hangs respectfully in the middle of this room above a nineteenth century divan and two Napoleonic chairs comfortably arranged around a polished oval pecan tea table. This altogether creates an enchanted setting, resurrecting an era of splendid plantations and worldly richness.

One entire wall devoted to a mural depicting life size pink Flamingos floating timelessly above a shallow pond; others already landed, standing upright and stoic on stilted legs cut off below the knees by the still water. Overhead, perched discreetly on a green bough, watch two hooded Blue Jays in frozen curiosity. An intricately designed circular rug, the same pastel hue as the pool, splashes over the floor with white floating lilies arranged in a natural pattern, as feeble attempt to subdue the polished grain of a light oak hardwood floor underneath. The unused fireplace swept clean and made with stones of imported granite dominates wall opposite the mural. Hanging above the mantle and haunting this elegant chamber is a larger-than-life painting of the deceased Doctor.

Nela seats herself briskly on the divan and motions for Davy to sit beside her. She is every stitch part of the fabric in this room. It is as if the parlor preserved tapestry of a bygone era, Nela Smith trapped in the weaver's pattern forever ageless, forever young.

Nela looks unblinking into Davy's eyes. They are beautiful eyes, eyes that make her remember days long gone. She raises the glass gracefully to her lips; her own eyes clear and deceptive, as swift river currents tugging at his inexperienced soul.

"You are a very nice boy," she says, lowering the glass.

"Thank you... Mrs. Smith." He blushes.

"Please, you must call me Nela. You are practically a man now, and a woman likes hearing her name spoken by a man sometimes."

"Yes Mam, Mrs. – I mean, Nela."

It also makes Davy feel good to call her this.

"Lucile has done a fine job raising you Davy. I am sure you think of her in a very special way– mother and son– so wholesome a relationship! She has such a good Christian soul, that woman, so good that it makes your heart just ache."

"Yes... Nela, Lucile is the best mother in the whole world!"

True to his promise, Davy has never told anyone about Lori being his real mother. Lucile right, it is better this way. Those few who did know kept the secret darkly to themselves. Yet, always it is the forgotten memory of Davy's absent father that haunts him most, covered in a shroud of complete obscurity, without even a photograph to remember. Not even the location of a grave known with any certainty, since his family in another county. Final instructions were that his remains be buried there. Once when drunk, Uncle Frank said he had pictures of him that he would try to dig up.

"By God, they are around here somewhere— but lost in some hell-hole corner like everything else since getting married!"

Then Aunt Lucile spoke something harsh to him beyond Davy's hearing. Later Uncle Frank denies ever saying any such thing.

"Oh yes, mothers and sons– just a perfect… perfect relationship!" Nela repeats. "I always wished to have a son of my own, but it just was not in the Lord's plan for the Doctor and me."

Davy wants to say he is sorry, only he lacks the proper words, or any word at all that may have given Nela comfort. Sensing his helplessness, she only smiles, her eyes glassy. Then tenderly reaches over and squeezes his arm, as if to say that all just a dream from long ago, a dream that no longer matters.

"Tell me, Davy, what does a young man like you do when he is not doing yard work for an old lady?" She enquires, rubbing her finger around the rim of her glass.

It begins to hum magically. At first low, almost not even a sound, ascending higher and higher, rising into crescendo, altogether filling this specially constructed chamber. Davy truly amazed by this unexpected trick, opens his mouth in awe.

"How do you do that, Mrs. Smith?"

"This is how you can tell true crystal, Davy." She replies quietly. "Something true always sings a special tune. It is what separates the voices of angels from groaning in the earth."

Nela's voice begins to melt into the ringing echelon.

"It's very beautiful…Nela."

"Davy, do you have a sweetheart in school?"

Looking into his soul with sorcerer's eyes, Nela's voice harmonizes with the celestial melody. The sound of her words change to a chant in young Davy's mind, as she continues to run her finger around lip of the glass. It seems in this solitary moment that only he and Nela exist in a universe of her own conjuring.

"No, Mrs. -- N– Nela– but I am thinking about getting a job at the mill soon. I graduate High School in a few weeks. I heard rumor in Homer's that they plan to be hiring about then."

Immediately the ringing stops. Nela places her glass back on the silver tray, her expression suddenly tense, suddenly old.

"Then... I suppose you'll no longer be coming here on Saturday?"

Because of some reflex, Nela has retreated into a secret place; the corners of her mouth begin to twitch. This is another side of Nela Davy has never seen.

"No, Mrs. – I mean yes, Nela. I promise to keep coming at least until the end of summer..."

Nela Smith had a way of making people feel obligated, even guilty. For the last three seasons, Davy has been coming every weekend to mow her lawn, trim the hedges, and any other odd job around the house she needs done. He originally asked for five dollars. Lucile said that he should not request more than four. In the end, the good Doctor's widow determines two dollars and seventy-five cents more than adequate. Nela takes traditional pride in the outward appearance of things. She especially loves neatness and orderly fashion. However, this is not the only reason Nela keeps Davy coming back week after week, season after season. Rather, it is something more needful than her garden estate; something altogether not wholesome, and selfish, that can never be more than a dream. Often Davy finds himself wishing to be free from Nela's ever-watchful eyes.

"I am so very glad;" the tone in her voice pitiful. "A poor lonely widow in her years has so little to count on. It's good to know that at least some things need not change all at once!"

Nela rolls her eyes around, the sudden enormity of the room reflected in the dull blue of her eyes. She seems as a child abandoned in a grand scheme imagined by a grown-up world-- a world not her own. No, Nela has never really been part of Liberty's world. Then her gaze meets the painted visage of the doctor, and calm returns to the older woman's face. Here is the source of her strength, the moral rudder that saves her continually from dashing upon the shoals of reality.

"But God gives us comfort," she sighs, a smile pursing the lines on her thin lips. "In the hour of our need, he is always there."

"Yes, Mrs. Smith, I thank God every day that I'm alive!" Davy proclaims sincerely.

"And so you should! A young strong handsome man like you with all of life still ahead-- the Good Doctor was once almost just like you! You do know Davy that he chose to devote his life to helping others. Most people never paid him-- at least not with money. It is such a wonderful thing to be a Doctor, Davy, all the time helping others. If it were not for him, maybe you, and a lot of others, might not even be here. There were so many. But you were always very special to him. Do not ever forget that Davy. I will always remember his words to me concerning you: `Nela,' he said, `*I'm going to see to it that boy has a chance in this world! Maybe one day he will choose to be a doctor, too. The world can always use another doctor.*' It was not long after that William had his accident. But I know he meant every word spoken."

Nela often tells him this story, as though she is afraid that he might one day forget it. Davy never certain if what she said true. Just the same, it makes him feel good and somehow special. Even though he knows little about this respected figure, the proclamation validates Davy, elevating him above everyone else in the small cotton mill town of Liberty.

Because Nela did not share the weakness of gossip, as did most in the mill community, her words carry greater weight. Maybe it is her better education, or the fact that she is more worldly, Nela presents herself with undeniable presence. Nor has she always lived in Liberty. Nela knows many things that she keeps hidden within, wonderful and sad things. She knows things that can save, as well as things that can destroy. All this knowledge she will take with her to the grave. It is doubtful that anyone in Liberty would have listened anyway. If ever Nela lied, she did it always for a greater good. This is both penitence and curse of Nela Smith.

"Well, enough of this!" She announces at last. "Would you mind being a dear, and running that special errand for me before cutting the grass?"

Davy reluctantly nods his head. What else can he do? It would not have changed Nela's mind even if he should refuse. In retrospect, there will be few things left in the world certain after the passing of Nela.

"Bless you, Davy!" She exclaims sweetly and produces a gilded pocket watch from her blouse.

From his angle, Davy can see clearly that Nela is still a woman in the vital sense.

"This belonged to William. I wish to have it properly examined after so many years. Now that we have a time fixer right here in town, it is high time I have it done. Here is five dollars. If it should come to more than this, ask Mr. Baily if he will give credit for one week. Just until William's pension arrives in the mail. Jews are hard money people– not at all like Christian folks! So be sure to tell him it is for the good Doctor's wife. Maybe then he will be more gracious."

Of course, Nela does not need her late husband's pension. Maybe pretending that she did makes her feel more like ordinary people. Deep down, Nela always did want to be considered the same as everyone else.

"I'll tell him what you said... Mrs. Smith," he promises, taking the money and glittering medallion.

It is without question, the finest watch Davy has ever seen. A ring of tiny jewels circle a golden sundial face with red enamel of a painted cross on the back and etched between two silver embossed serpents entwined together. He dares not ask if it is expensive. It is important, and this is all that really matters. His hand trembles as he touches it. Nela also is trembling.

"You will take care not to lose it?" She says, searching his young beautiful face.

"Yes, Mrs. Smith, I promise."

"Nela, Davy, call me Nela."

"I promise, Nela, I promise."

CHAPTER 13

The Story of Weistmeister

Weis T. Baily and Son is the only shop in town that posted real business hours, and the only one that closes early on Saturday. In the beginning, Baily did not open at all, but soon discovers that most people paid cash only on that day. Always Homer has first pickings. The more prudent wives stay awake on Friday night and empty the little remaining change in their husband's pockets while he slumbers in oblivion. This had to be stretched far to support a household. Baily soon accepts that he must compromise some part of his Sabbath in order to survive. Shortly after arriving with his son, he begins posting new hours, opening every Saturday from eight o'clock, until twelve noon. Even then, people were not completely satisfied, but in time got use to it as they did most everything else.

A bell jingles above the door as Davy enters Baily's shop. It is dark within and takes some time for his eyes to adjust after being in the bright sunlight. The clamor of ticking, grinding, clatter of gears and springs-- so many ticks and tocks fill the little shop made by so many clocks. All time in the universe compressed into this seemingly insignificant chamber surrounded in an insignificant town on an insignificant world circling a star clustered in an insignificant galaxy. Guardian shadows positioned everywhere, standing or crouching, some gigantic, others dwarfed. One particular shadow rises cabalistic above them all bobbing back and forth.

Slowly objects and shapes fade into vision. Old world Cuckoo clocks, richly painted Russian clocks, clocks with faces of men, others altogether faceless and unrecognizable.

It seems impossible in Davy's mind that all these clocks might be gathered into this one place.

Mr. Baily appears, dissolving out of shadow wrapped in a shawl and wearing round head covering. He remains religiously bent over a table supporting eight burning candles set upon a bronze menorah positioned above pages of a large open black book. He seems oblivious to Davy's presence, continuing to bob slowly back and forth

Approaching cautiously, Davy is about to say something when a grandfather clock standing monarch and ancient in an obscure corner suddenly rumbles to life. The hollow baritone chime seems to strike uncertainty into the very core of the world. Battalions of feathered birds leap out of concealment and begin screaming incoherently. This triggers a bedlam of chimes and squawks in all directions. Some of the mechanisms surely possess a tune– but that melody lost in confusion, becoming din of droning torment. Just as quickly, the wailing ceases. Only the final chime of the deep reverberating grandfather clock lasts into silence.

The end is not yet. For on a counter, alone and separate, rests a clock fashioned after the design of a royal palace. Exactly thirty seconds slower than all the other clocks, it begins an automated scenario. A drawbridge unfolds lowering mechanically down. A door opens, releasing an elegant ballerina wearing silver-laced shoes, which begins twirling with elegant slender arms held high over a face of empty countenance.

Appearing from another door and moving into position on a balcony overlooking the courtyard, stands a distinguished soldier dressed in German uniform. His expression sad, a melancholy born of the worse kind of rejection, he stoically watches her dance. The ballerina moves round and round in homage to another imagination, unaware of the pain she causes. Through intricacy of design determined from beginning and long ago, the ill-fated lovers retreat back into the castle to remain hour by hour forever separated.

"You like my clocks— yes?" A voice says once the drawbridge rises back into position.

Davy turns to see Baily now looming over him. He is a large man, larger than he had thought. His presence almost threatening, he looks exactly the way Davy expects a Jew should up close. His brow, cracked and wrinkled, creates a grim countenance. He has a thick black beard that completely smothers his mouth and chin. His cheeks hollow, horribly scarred with pockmarks. Deep lines furrow from the corners of his eyes; his lips drawn and puckered. Stitch scars tear unevenly across the breath of Baily's nose, altogether dominating his features, and would have been monstrous did he not wear thick wire-framed glasses. This compensates his features by magnifying his dark eyes proportionately. Davy has heard many tales about Jews, mostly bad, and mostly from Homer. Baily matches every description with unfailing accuracy.

"Did– Did you make all..." he stammers, sweeping his arms around the room.

"Heavens no– most are older than even I am! Some are masterpieces of tradition in honor of Counts and Countess'. Some for kings, some for presidents, and some for dictators– all works of art-- each created out of a soul! There are as many clocks as there are people in this world. How many you cannot imagine! And when there is no longer anyone left to wind them up, then they sleep, and wait, and perhaps never again awaken."

Baily's accent sounds strange, the tone soft and compelling. Davy finds himself listening to him as he may have listened to Homer– and Homer knows more than anyone Davy ever met!

"My Uncle Frank has a grandfather clock!" He says importantly.

"Grandfather clocks make good companions."

He smiles, stepping into the dark corner that partially camouflages the snoring giant that instigated the recent commotion.

"But not all clocks are happy," he continues. "No, some are witnesses to very sad happenings."

Stepping back into the light, he approaches the castle clock on the counter. Taking a deep breath, Baily delicately runs his slender fingers along the contour of the castle roof.

"Such is this creation."

He pauses, removes his spectacles, and begins wiping them briskly. Davy is uncertain if the tears real, or if his large globular eyes just tired from staring all day into a magnifying glass.

"What happened?"

"It was fashioned for a nobleman, a flying ace in the German Air Force during World War I. He caused many young men to die, to crash to their death! He was merciless in the sky against Germany's enemies. The British had a name for this fearless aviator. They called him The Red Baron. There is yet another side to this Baron of the skies; a side not found in any war record. You see, the Baron was a man of culture, a man with refined taste. He loved the upper seats in concert halls, worshiped masters of musical genius, his greatest love being the ballet. And it is this worship that would finally destroy him."

Baily pauses here, looks reflectively around his shop at his many clocks as though he hears something, something familiar, and not heard for a long time. Then he shrugs his shoulders and sighs. Whatever it might have been is gone now. His ghosts have a way of coming and going that way.

"The Baron first saw her while on leave in Berlin. She was the star dancer in Tchaikovsky's Swan Lake, pure as the music, delicately radiant as a snowflake of reflected light sifting through shadows of his war-weary heart. At long last, he had found the thing that always eluded his imagination. Through vision of this dancing ballerina glimpsed vision of salvation capable of cleansing his soul!

Germany's royal Ace of the skies determines in his heart that he must have her; and that nothing must stand in the way. Making all the necessary arrangements, the Baron spares no expense, sending the ballerina flowers and inviting her on exquisite dates.

Of course, this young lady is flattered for someone of his reputation- someone with noble blood to be interested in her! The weeks that follow are special to the Baron. He dreams as never he dreamed before. In his dream, he is no longer a soldier bound by duty. No longer do the skies interest him. As for the ballerina, she accepts his wine and his gifts, even accepts his family ring. After all, her country was at war, times very difficult; she therefore blameless for the dream she could not be. The Baron had even gone so far as to commission a *Time Smith* to build this clock after a design conceived in his own heart. –Ah, it could have been such a wonderful love story!"

Baily pauses, looks up, his cheeks moist, his voice trembling. It is as though his eyes see these events happening again in the present.

"She left him, vanished one night as all illusions do. He traces her steps to the door of a certain jeweler who had purchased the ring with the Baron's insignia from a lovely woman accompanied by a handsome young consort.

'He was a musician, I believe, Herr Rittmeister," says the jeweler. "From what I could gather they were engaged to be married, and wanted the money to honeymoon. Of course I will not hesitate to sell it back at no profit, now that I know it belongs to you, Germany's greatest hero.'

The Baron says nothing, buys back his ring, and returns to his Flying Circus squadron. The next morning his red plane lifts into the clouds never again to return. Some say his plane shot down and that he perished in the ashes. –But I know it is a broken heart killed the Red Baron. Only this clock remains. Now the tragic performance finished. The ballerina shriveled old and died long ago; her love of another a cold inscription on a tombstone in a small German cemetery. As for the great Red Baron, his legend remains written in the skies to this day. Yet, still she dances immortal in his heart, dancing on and on, heartless to the suffering she causes...”

“Were you the clock maker?” Davy enquires with wide-eyed amazement.

“No,” Baily replies solemnly. “It was not me.”

He turns the clock over. On the bottom is a bronze plate with the word *Weistmeister* stamped on it. Davy wonders if this is a place, or someone’s name. Baily does not say. He places the clock back in its original position, examining that nothing has been disturbed. No matter who made it, the clock belongs here. Belonging always among this collection of amorphous reality, timeless, a solemn keeper made to keep time forever.

“So, what other curiosity brings you today into my shop?” Baily’s eyes suddenly brighten, becoming almost hypnotic.

Davy has completely forgotten the reason he came here and begins fumbling in his pocket like a little boy in search of lost treasures.

“Mrs. Smith asked me to bring this by for you to look at,” he says, producing the late doctor’s watch at last.

“Hum,” sighs the older man, holding it up toward a small lamp affixed to his workbench; “and just what seems to be the trouble?”

Davy shrugs his shoulders. Until just now, he has never considered the meaning of time.

“Then I’ll just have to see for myself,” Baily continues slyly.

He then takes a small tool resembling a long thin screwdriver, and with a quick professional twist, pops open the back plate to expose the hidden reality inside the watch.

Lowering a monocle attached to his eyeglasses over his right eye, he begins to hum and grunt, whispering words altogether unintelligible and foreign. Then he breaks into a singing chant. Balancing precariously on the edge of his stool, Baily begins prodding and twisting with different instruments, like a surgeon performing some critical operation. Davy watches silently amazwed, as though witnessing a miracle without even knowing it. He momentarily turns away and notices a boy watching him from an open door at the rear of the shop. Judging by his size, he is about Davy's age, maybe older by a year, with black curly hair, the beginning wisp of a mustache, and eyes, small and dark, like those of an animal. Realizing Davy sees him, he darts back, quickly closing the door.

"There! The good doctor's watch is almost as good as new!" Baily announces triumphantly. "Just a speck of rust gathered on the pendulum plate– so much trouble caused by small things!"

He snaps the back into position, sets the time, and begins winding the stem. His right eyebrow raises wily, reminding Davy of a Fox that stole often Uncle Franks chickens, until one day his uncle made his wife a fur hat from the animal's hide.

"How much did Mrs. Smith think it would cost?" He asks shrewdly, peering hypnotically through the thick lens of his glasses.

"Five dollars…"

"I think five dollars will be enough. Tell Mrs. Smith to bring it back by sometime for a proper cleaning."

The five-dollar bill disappears, as if by magic, and in the boy's palm is the glittering timepiece ticking gaily away. Even more sprightly, Baily ushers him to the front door, saying it is already past noon and past closing time.

No one else walks the sidewalks. Perhaps this is because there are no other open businesses, except for Homer's at the end of town; and it is still too early for his kind of customers. Nevertheless, Liberty is a town– at least on the map– and that sometimes promises enough to attract the bored and the curious like moths into a dim light.

Beside the watch repair shop, stands an identical building with an identical entrance and a sign above the door that reads *Shaves 5 cents - Haircut 20 cents*. The windows are mostly all broken and boarded up, the battered front door chained with a heavy padlock. Through one of the surviving cracked panes, Davy can make out several mortified shadows standing or propped against the wall and covered by sheets. Odd pieces of broken glass litter the floor, and the decapitated head of a broom lies nearest the door completely mummified in dust.

"You see ghost in there, boy?"

Davy leaps against the wall startled by a large shadow that rises behind him changing the glass opaque.

"Maybe you seen something that old Abraham seen all the days of his life."

Abraham is the big black man that lives in the swamp. Not too deep, but further than anyone else dared. There really is not that much known about the old Negro, except that he plays a harmonica, a mournful sound that sometimes travels along Main Street, rising at night on the swamp mist. There are rumors that Abraham once was a blacksmith before the invention of the automobile. There are also other rumors-- rumors to make people afraid, causing them to worry. If these rumors true, then Abraham is possibly older than the first laid foundation of Liberty Town– *and perhaps much older than this!*

Yet, he appears harmless enough, coming into town only occasionally to trade fresh frogs for provisions, or to sell frog legs at a fair price of three cents each. Since few brave enough to venture into the swamp at night, and since Abraham always seems to have plenty, he never has any problem striking a bargain. Because frog legs are a popular item on almost everyone's diet.

"I- I don't see anything–" Davy manages, frightened by what this Nubian giant might do next.

Abraham only smiles, his teeth the same yellow hue as his eyes.

"Then you ain't looking right. Now old Abraham, he sees things. Like he sees a white boy who has got something shiny bright in his hand. And just what might that be?"

Remembering his promise to Nela, Davy quickly pockets the watch.

"No, Abraham, it's not mine!"

"So it ain't." Abraham says pleasantly. "Little there be that a man can call his own in this old world." He chuckles loudly. "Ask a man, and he'll say he be master of the dog. When the dog gets hungry, the man feeds him. When the dog gets cold, the man makes him a house. But if the man gets hungry and cold, he will kill that dog for meat and a coat. It's the stomach that be master of us all! And Lord what a master it be!"

Abraham pats a withering sack hanging from his side.

"Why don't you let old Abraham just look at it," he says, a pandering grin spreading across his mahogany face, the dull brown iris of his eyes suddenly clear and alluring.

"You got to promise to give it right back."

"Of course... of course..." he says in a tone soft like the passage of a mountain stream, reaches out, and gently takes Davy's hand.

Davy is amazed that the brown, pitted stone of the old man's flesh as warm and soft as is his own. For some reason that he cannot explain, he always thought that the touch of black skin would be different somehow. Aunt Lucile– who swears that she did not have a prejudice bone in her body– maintains that there is a spark of good in most all of God's creatures. Nevertheless, one must to be careful when it came to Negros. It seems that spark did not necessarily apply to all in Liberty, as always there is at least one exception even to rules of the divine.

"Mighty fine time piece," Abraham says, cupping the gold watch in his two hands, as though he fears it might try to escape. "I did know a man once who had a time piece like this. He was a good man… a man who died mighty mysterious. Look how it ticks along just the same, as if he was still alive and breathing. It will keep like that even after the old widow lady done past on too. Had me a watch once, but I give it to a mean old Boss Man so as I could ride in the pig car on his train. Just so I could come back here and live poor. Lord the things a man does without thinking!"

He smiles, shakes his head. The memories he might remember, and the many tales he could tell. But who would listen?

"As the good book say, everything has got to happen for a reason. I bet you know just what I'm talking about-- don't you white boy?"

Davy nods, even though he really does not know at this time why.

"Sure you do. Maybe you don't know it in your head just yet cause nobody told you. You know deep inside that you ain't alone. The man who owned this watch knowed it, too– and what he knowed I know."

He then gently places the watch back into Davy's trembling hand.

Suddenly a figure charges around the corner, brushing Davy aside. It is the boy in the doorway at the rear of Baily's shop. His stature short and stocky, he approaches only chest high to the black man's enormous presence. Yet, his momentum strikes as the charge of a locomotive. He fiercely grabs Abraham around the waist tackling him to the ground. He must have hit him once or twice as well– from Davy's angle of vision it is difficult to tell– only that Abraham begins crying out repeatedly.

"Oh Lord –Oh Lord!"

"What do you mean coming around here bothering our customers?" He swears, hovering menacingly over his shaken victim.

Abraham is past words. During the encounter, the frog sack has come undone. Blood and slime spills over the sidewalk, as well as several frog bodies, most dead, some only wounded.

"I weren't bothering nobody." Abraham sniffles, looking down at the massacred brood.

"Well you see that you don't around here. You come within ten yards of this store, and I'll personally kick your dark hide every foot of the way back into the swamp! —And you'll wish you never laid eyes on Bubba Baily!"

This Bubba was tough. How tough, Davy did not particularly care to find out, not just now. Abraham also decides Bubba is tough. He kneels down and silently begins gathering the slaughter back into his sack. When he has collected every single frog, he throws the sack over his back and steps quickly to the opposite corner.

"You don't forget what I say, white boy!" He shouts back over his shoulder.

Bubba makes a threatening jester, and the old man shuffles hastily away in the direction of the swamp. Davy is glad to see him go. Glad because what Old Abraham said makes no sense at all.

"Thanks," he says, trying to sound tough.

"All that garbage about the Red Baron doesn't mean anything!" Bubba sneers. "That clock came from an old dead widow's attic on East 30th Street. She wasn't even German. I'll be seeing you around."

Without saying another word, he vanishes through a side door into his father's shop. It will be a while before Davy sees Bubba Baily again. He can still feel him watching even though the shade pulled down, deciding even then that he likes him. Maybe it is because Bubba born a Jew in a grand city to the north far away from

Liberty that makes Davy enviously curious to know more about him.

"Five dollars," Nela hisses when he returns. "See, Davy, I told you about Jews! They will rob a poor widow blind, if one not careful! Imagine him charging me five dollars for that!"

Nela Smith then drops the watch back into her jewelry box, immediately forgetting all about it.

CHAPTER 14

Candy Morgan

Candy Morgan is the typical nice girl. Always clean and neat, attends church every Sunday, and even sings in the choir. She always receives good grades, never absent from school–except with good reason–never swears in public. And never would have gotten caught smoking in the bathroom had it not been for the untimely attack of diarrhea that sent Mrs. Hall, the third period Home Economics teacher, rushing unannounced into the girl's student toilet. Even then, Candy manages somehow to remain un-tarnished by repenting of her wrongful deed and submitting herself to martyrdom. Confessing her sin before the Lord's mercy seat, she readily submits to the punishment of their sinless hearts. Thereby, Candy receives no punishment at all; her pious image perfected in the eyes of persecution. Maybe because Candy is the Preacher's daughter that they are afraid to punish her like other children. I guess deep down they decide that she just must be better.

Most agree that Candy is pretty, but none can imply that she has even one ugly bone in her body. Her hair dyed peroxide blond, sealed with enough sprays so that not one filament ever falls out of place, even when the wind blows. Because she has bad acne, Candy wears a lot of cheap make-up. Her eyes are an Irish green color, but too small, adding a general fleshiness to her face. Yet, all of these seeming imperfections blend somehow, creating a voluptuous illusion, making Candy Morgan sensuous and desirable, exceeding other girls her age.

Davy has known Candy since the fifth grade when Preacher Morgan initially took up residence at Liberty's First Baptist Church. Then she went by Candice, but changed it when she got older to Candy, because she says the other sounds too much like a preacher's daughter.

"Boys just naturally expect the daughter of a preacher to be different," she later confides. "I like the same things any girl likes– maybe better– because I've spent my whole life denying that that's what I want!"

No one will ever know what Candy really wanted. It is doubtful that she truly knew herself then. She should have stayed in Liberty, gotten married, and had a baby like any other girl. Except Candy was never like any other girl. Always there remains something guilty inside her, something tormenting, refusing to allow her peace-- something that happened long ago in the past. Maybe it is because her father had not always been a preacher, or because her half-Indian mother ran off with another man before Candy turned six. Maybe it is because her father too stern in the beginning. Maybe because he beats his only child cruelly one night when she would not sleep and kept drying for a mother that would never come back for her. When Preacher Morgan could blame no one else, he runs away with the daughter that reminds him continuously of her, and tries to forget. They travel west; sleep in dark valleys beneath enigmatic stars. She remembers vast prairies polluted with restless oil drilling equipment. Candy has seen dams that squash the imagination, dignified mountains so high that nothing grows on the bald peaks, frighteningly desolate in her young eyes, as though visions of a journey too near the end of this world. She has witnessed other things as well, things she cannot tell– will never tell anyone! Perhaps because Candy becomes every day more like a yellowed photograph of her estranged mother that the Preacher begins to fear most for her soul.

"You are too much like your mother, Candice!" He condemns often each time she does something he thinks disapproving. "I prayed that God would spare you for my sake, but as the scripture says, `you will know them by their fruits!' –Repent child! -Repent before it is too late– before you become every bit like her!"

Reference to the indisputable scripture often plunges Candy into sometime violent, inconsolable passions. Many times she might have killed herself, except considers this to be the one un-pardonable sin. Candy grows to hate the woman who brought her into this world, only to abandon her. She hates herself more, because Candy knows that she must be just like her, wicked and undeserving. As every day, something unclean and burning grows stronger inside-- something that hates the preacher even more! Candy Morgan also has another kind of reputation among the boys at Pixley High. Only those that really did, know for certain; and those who did not, only dream, or wish it. Davy will later doubt that all the stories about Candy true. At least he will always hope that most these rumors based on lustful fantasy.

It is Wednesday of the last week before summer break, Candy sitting beside another, not so pretty girl named Beth Ann, on the bus that takes Liberty's children every day to and from school. Beth Ann is a freshman, her teeth slightly bucked, her skin greasy looking, and jet-black hair that falls limply over her shoulders like a dirty rag. Beth Ann exists as a dull painting compared to Candy Morgan. She always seems to be wearing the same red plaid dress, her ostrich neck flowering from the stem of a long shapeless body. She never wears socks, her ankles always a red mud color, the hem of the dresses never finished. The same uninteresting scuffed black shoes, the same featureless face stamped without emotion, except the time Candy got caught smoking. Even then, her countenance little changed; except for the glimmer of a grin on her thin expressionless lips.

Candy is every bit alive in contrast. Her face radiates charm, flashing with excitement, a smile intoxicating, or else her lips seductively sulky and silently arousing, but mostly invites curiosity. Her eyes always moving, always they search for something that can never truly exist, but promises possibility that it might exist. Today Candy is wearing a white see-through blouse, a short blue skirt ahead of the fashion– and where Davy is sitting, he can see without any imagination that Candy is not wearing panties! Then, unexpectedly, she looks straight at him, spreads her legs apart on purpose, and smiles deliciously. Davy flushes with embarrassment, but unable to take his eyes off her. The bus comes to a full stop; the door opens. Candy gathers her books, whispers good-bye to Beth Ann, and steps down the aisle. She continues to smile at Davy, her eyes like those of an experienced hunter stalking a rodent.

"Hi, Candy," he manages shyly as she passes.

Candy turns around, looks at Beth Ann, and starts giggling. Again, she faces Davy.

"Hello Davy," she says in her thick `nice girl' voice. "It sure is hot out. These books make my arms feel like they're going to fall off!"

"C- Can I help you carry them?" He volunteers, his tone sounding more a plea, than offer of a kind act. Candy knows already what this means.

"But then you would have to walk all the way home from the church." She knows he will not mind. "They are awful heavy though..."

Candy smiles so sweetly that had she provoked the rage of the Minotaur he would have spared her just because of her pouting lips. Davy scoops her books in his arms, follows Candy's slithering movements. Moments later, both stand alone in the sun, the bus vanishing in a mirage of dust.

They walk several yards down the road without saying a word to one another. Just beside is the cemetery, an observation that Davy particularly chooses to ignore.

"Here," she says, taking a well-traveled path leading between columns of white gravestones.

"You mean we got to walk through the graveyard?" Davy gasps.

"Of course, silly-- you're not afraid, are you Davy?"

Candy actually seems to be challenging him. He is afraid. Not that he knows why, only that he feels weak in his stomach, his feet cold.

"Well are you, Davy?"

Sweat runs down and along Candy's bare legs as something sweet and inviting. Something he wants more than all else. He does not know what exactly, because he has never wanted a woman before. He remembers fantasies of flying, imagined pleasures while reading the adventures of Super Girl and Wonder Woman. This is a different kind of feeling, somehow more real, more dangerous. Davy becomes instantly brave, feels as he has never felt before.

"I ain't afraid of anything!" He proclaims taking a position behind her. "It just seems somehow not respectful walking on people's graves. If I died I wouldn't want people walking on top of me!"

Candy only smiles back at him, as if to say, but of course, they will; only you will not care then. Perhaps Candy actually looks forward to the day when she will feel nothing ever again.

"Really there's nothing here to bother us, Davy," Candy sooths, dropping back beside him as they stroll among the headstones. "The truly dead don't come back. Father says that one day there is going to be a resurrection and judgment." Then quickly adds,"–but I don't think we need to worry about that today!"

Davy is not altogether convinced. He has begun to question within himself the sanctity of their purpose. Candy senses this, and teasingly begins to change the subject.

"Do you have dreams, Davy, I mean special dreams?"

Davy is not sure what she means by special. Everyone has dreams– often he has the same terrible dream when he feels trapped, helpless in a burning room. However, he cannot talk about it-- not now-- not even later with Candy.

"I dream a lot, Davy– beautiful, romantic dreams– dreams that wake me up hot at night! Like last night, I dreamed that I met a frog wearing boots– silly looking thing! I laughed until I cried. Then I kissed him because that's what a beautiful princess does in a story I read as a little girl. Do you want to know what happened next, Davy? He changed to a handsome Prince just as I knew he would!"

Candy pauses as if she has chosen to delete some portion of the experience. She turns and begins skipping toward a grove of very large, very old trees. It is all that Davy can do to keep up without dropping his load. Once beneath the shade of the trees, Candy slows her pace. Davy is breathing hard by the time he catches up with her. She seems pleased, almost as though Candy enjoying his difficulty.

"It's hard carrying all these books..." He manages between breaths.

Candy giggles, and cries out something nonsensical.

"The beautiful damsel walks forever in shadows; her brave prince a fallen shadow behind!"

It is not so much what she says, rather, how she says it. Almost as if she is teasing him, wanting Davy to do something that he might later regret.

"There is a castle here, Davy, and who knows there might even be a dragon inside! You're not afraid of dragons, too, are you Davy?"

"That's crazy talk, Candy!" He replies at last.

"Is it? Look over there Davy!" She says, pointing.

The mausoleum wedges tightly between two black oak trees, constructed entirely of marble, pale, dripping with dark stains. The vault itself is square, surrounded by ruins of what had once been a porch supported by two fallen classical pillars. Like the grandeur of history it mimics, this architecture evidence of gradual ruination. The earth underneath has given way on one side, causing the remaining structure to tilt at an unsettling angle, fractured with cancerous cracks throughout. Chiseled on the front in large blackened letters are the words **"UNTIL THE KING SHALL COME."** This tomb housed the remains of Liberty's first founding family. Once upon a time, there had been an elegant white cotton plantation nearby, tended gardens, and fields of new cotton snowed upon the horizon dotted with black slave hands. Now it serves only as a marker to designate the end of the old Liberty cemetery. From this point battalions of white crosses stand at attention, paying dedicated homage to its decaying presence. How old this crypt, few know for certain, only that it marks the beginning of a necropolis that on occasion still receives the remains of Liberty's finest.

The Veterans Administration purchased rights to the adjacent grounds to inter fallen soldiers after the First World War. It is amazing how quickly the graves appeared, during and after the wars that follow, covering hills and filling in shallow valleys. Before long, it is as a white river of crosses flowing through the center of the peninsula, tireless sentries guarding the little town on both sides. Before the end of the Second World War another Veteran's Cemetery inaugurated on the Pixley side nearer the new V. A. Hospital, considered more fitting to receive future sacrifices. There is a much smaller portion of the grounds allotted to Liberty's Baptist Church, for disposition as the time arises, to receive one of Liberty's poorer citizens. However Liberty lacks an undertaker; therefore, a dispatch from Pixley must come on occasion, something like a doctor making a house call.

The older cemetery remains somehow sacred and intentionally undisturbed like an untended sore darkened with overgrowth surrounded by hordes of white corpuscles. Rarely anyone ever comes here now. Why should anyone bother? Perhaps this based more on fear, than act of respect. This unkempt hill surrounding Pixley's tomb littered with tilting headstones, some raised surreptitiously, others fallen, many erased and forever nameless. Thorny weeds sprout out of sunken cavities, as webby fingers of red and green fungus creep out of the ground along the blackened markers making them appear altogether evil.

"Let's stop here and rest!" Candy decides.

She then runs playfully ahead and curls into a jade shadow at base of a large white rock. Davy drops beside her, lightened of his burden at last. It is all becoming so wondrously clear– her hands, her feet-- Candy's neck– everything about this girl becoming a woman perfect as ever he could have imagined. It seems to him an enchanted region within her eyes suddenly opens, drawing his soul into their depths. He instantly desires to touch Candy Morgan, the daughter of a preacher, and be absorbed completely into mystery of this new sensation.

"This is my most favorite place in the whole world!" She exclaims turning over on her back. "Davy, do you like it here, too?"

"No– yes– I don't know... I guess that it gives me the creeps a little. But I don't mind so much because you're here with me."

Instinctively, he reaches out to touch her. Candy pulls away. Death everywhere around, but Candy is alive. Candy is now.

"Do you know where we are?" She inquires softly.

"Of course I know."

"Do you really?"

Davy looks around, feeling helpless, bewildered in this girl's presence. It is not what she says so much, but how Candy says it, making everything a proclamation of revelation providing purpose to his young flesh.

"This rock is since the beginning. Davy can't you see?"

Davy sits up and examines the white boulder. It comes up to his waist, smooth, flat on one side, and with a shallow depression creating a natural basin. At first, he sees nothing particularly special. Then symbol of the sun appears, and a structure of some kind. Above this a few triangles, or maybe Indian tents, mixed with herding animals. Just above the flow of Candy's auburn hair is the shadow of what appears to be a larger than life creature holding a pitchfork, partially obscured in a smug of dead moss.

"The Indian Rock–" Davy exclaims with boyish excitement.

He has heard tales of it only. Uncle Frank promised often to take his only nephew to see this legend, but never got around to it. Homer claims the Indians that use to live here were a bad lot, the rock cursed. He says that even if a person knew where to find it on a particular day that it is liable not be there the next. Then again, Homer has a way of exaggerating most everything. This ancient enigma requires little exaggeration to sustain its air of mystery. It is bone-white and must weigh close to half a ton. According to Uncle Frank originates from beyond the lower Aconee riverbed miles away. There is no one presently living in Liberty, who can say with any authority that these are indeed Indian symbols. However, if Indians did not make them, then who did?

"No, you're wrong " Candy corrects softly. "This is footstool to the throne of the Frog Prince."

"That's silly!" Davy scoffs. "I've heard about this rock ever since I was in diapers. My Uncle Frank says that Indian magic brought it up here clear from the old riverbed. –But Uncle Frank thinks everything is magic. Homer says it's just a rock rolled up here by construction men during excavation of the new mill. Homer should know. He's been here ever since the beginning."

"Did you ever see it before just now– before today?"

"No," Davy admits. "But–"

"Then you don't really know? I can prove what I am saying is true."

Candy sits up, wipes away the moss with stands of her lovely curls and begins tracing the symbols with a delicate finger.

"Look closer Davey. Can you not see the Frog Prince on his throne? Look closely at his footrest. See the raised platform at his feet. Do you not see how familiar it is? Here is the Lady knelling by his side. Not even a shred of doubt in my mind. This is that rock! If really you wish to see, I'm sure you will agree, Dave Tracey."

Davy gets on his knees to examine better the crude engravings. Candy is right! It is a frog seated upon a royal throne and holding trident scepter. She is also right about there being a woman with shadow of long flowing hair kneeling beside him in supplication. This very rock most definitely is his footstool.

"That still doesn't prove it wasn't Indians who made it all up." Davy insists.

Candy remains quiet for what seems a long time, her beauty increasing in mystery. Then Candy's eyes change suddenly sad.

"You don't believe, Davy?"

"Believe what?"

"In miracles– I see in your eyes that you don't. Poor Davy... you don't have any faith."

"So what if I don't?" Davy demands crossly.

"Then I guess you don't. But, Davy, if you have no faith– even a small little bit– then how can you ever believe that a hero can save you?"

"You mean like Jesus Christ?"

Really, he is thinking about Bubba Baily.

"He is the strength in my weakness!" Candy laments touching her forehead with both palms. "He is coming back. Someday he is coming back."

At this moment Candy is so much like a preacher's daughter that Davy's desire withers. Perhaps he has mistaken her intention after all. Perhaps none of the things he has heard about Candy true. Then he realizes how alone they are, how far removed from the eyes and ears of any other living soul.

"Look around you Candy!" He says, fighting a battle within himself. "No one ever comes back!"

"Don't they Davy?" Candy replies with practiced sweetness.

Davy looks around uncomfortably. At least he hopes that the dead do not come back. Just above a whisper, he asks the question most on his mind. A question this Preacher's daughter might know.

"Did you ever see a real miracle?"

Candy crosses her arms, looks divinely up at the sky, and shouts at the top of her voice something only a Preacher's daughter would say.

"I've seen more miracles than could fill chalice of this world!"

"Candy, you shouldn't scream like that. What if... what if someone hears you?"

"You sound just like my father when you say that. I will tell you a secret. He was not always a preacher. Sometimes men do whatever is convenient at the time. —But you got to swear never to tell that to anybody else!"

Davy swears. Really, he has no idea what Candy is talking about, but he swears all the same. To him a preacher is a preacher. What difference does it matter if that preacher did not believe in his own preaching.

"So who do you think that woman is?" Davy enquires, turning his attention back to the rock symbols.

Candy takes a deep breath, her gaze transfixed toward heaven, reminding Davy of Joan of Arc from illustration in a book he once read.

"She is the Holy Spirit of God sent to guide the Frog Prince in his way. See how meekly she knells beside him. Yet, she is his strength. It is so clear to me. He is the arm of judgment; she the heart of mercy."

"So why is he a frog?"

Candy smiles benevolently and sadly shakes her head.

"And does a frog as prince seem so foolish a thing to you?"

The way she asks the question makes Davy feel particularly self-conscious.

"Well, I mean why not something big, like a mountain lion or a bear? At least a bear looks more regal."

"Maybe it is because a bear too strong. What need do the strong have in strength? After all, Jesus was born the son of a humble carpenter. His apostles for the most part simple fishermen. That's why, Davy, faith is so important a thing to have. Without faith our soul cannot be saved."

Davy only shrugs his shoulders trying to seem indifferent to this legend of an Indian savior. Deep down he believes Candy might be right. He has such little faith, and what little he did have already pledged to the time fixer's son from a great far away city called New York.

"What if you are wrong, Candy, and there is no soul? What then? Maybe we all just die, buried, and remain in the earth. I see only graves."

"You see through the sight of this world, Davy. There is more to light in shadow than perceived by the eyes."

Her countenance changes to sadness. A change so imperceptible, it frightens young Davy; makes him think that maybe Candy too perfect in this world.

"My mother used to tell me stories at night. That was before she went away, before father learned to hate—and to drink, and hate even more! That was before he became a Preacher. She is part Indian on her mother's side, beautiful like a princess. She would tell me wonderful and tragic tales, tales told by her mother, and her mother before her.

Stories about children of the water, called Aconee that wander restless and find no peace. One of my forgotten ancestors was member of that lost tribe. He survived something terrible...something few know anything about. My mother says his name is an old Indian word meaning *One Born from the Sun.* I am not altogether sure what this means, except this boy not like other Indian children. It is not just his name, but also something different in the way he looked. He and his mother spared death because of desire of a young Cherokee warrior. They say Cherokees are a bad lot-- but not all! This one raised the child as his own, keeping the truth always hidden. This is what it means to truly love, Davy, to protect the ones you care about."

"So what does this have to do with faith?"

"In these stories my mother recited songs from long ago, singing lullabies about the secret kingdom of Xeantee Aconee, a place inhabited by the spirit of something she calls "*Shelecheyanu.*" In *Shelecheyanu,* there is only peace-- no death, no sorrow-- no waning of twilight. In *Shelecheyanu* all reborn perfect to sing his name forever. These stories helped me sleep at night-- the best memories I ever had! I remember her tears; the sound of her voice like a singing brook. Then she left and I never slept the same, until my pain changed to faith. Now I believe all will sing *Shelecheyanu* one day in the presence of Xeantee Aconee!"

"So you think this *Shelecheyanu* means heaven, and that this Xeantee Aconee a person somewhere in heaven?"

"*Shelecheyanu* is not just a place, Davy Tracy-- and Xeantee Aconee more than just a person!" Candy promises looking steadfast into his eyes. "There are times I can feel him near, as though his presence just beyond the fringe of my heart. I know my mother is there even now calling my soul to peace. I hate her sometimes because she went away and didn't take me with her. But did you know even hate has an end? Davy, this rock is the key, a testament to what happened here in the past."

Davy has never heard this version before. He honestly did not know much about Indian, at least not unless seen on Saturday morning television. Indians were just Indians in his mind. Then there is Homer's version.

"Murdering savages that massacred General Custard and his men at the Little Big Horn-- ain't no Indian in the world that don't owe something to the white man!"

He has heard Homer say this often in any conversation referring to Indians. Naturally, old Homer did not say this when Pixley's Indian sheriff visiting town. Still, it makes him wonder if maybe Candy is right, and if just maybe she is right about him having a soul. This singular thought causes him to reflect uneasily, as he considers the surrounding necropolis marking the bones of those, who once were, and are no more.

"Even now the Children of Xeantee sing!" Candy blurts loudly. "I know all these stories to be true, Davy. Just as I know that all will sing his name one day. If only one might believe!"

Of course, Davy again has no idea what Candy really saying. She is after all, a preacher's daughter. This singular fact alone makes everything she says seem somehow mysterious, somehow elevated above the knowledge of mortal understanding.

"So is that all?"

"No, not all; but you wouldn't want to hear more– at least not now. But this is the most important part."

Again, Candy is right. He did not want to hear any more about the testaments of legend or the actions of the sons of men centuries dead. Now it is his turn. This is his hour to live and to burn! Something electric is in the air, something of great power consuming both their flesh as stubble. Yes, this is their time! His bowels suddenly on fire; the burning lust he has heard Aunt Lucile speak of so often. In this moment, only Candy matters!

"Candy, I really think you're pretty," he says, and presses forward to kiss her.

Candy rolls naturally over on her back and pulls up her skirt. Again, she says nothing. Candy knows the moment for words passed. Davy awkwardly ascends over her, telling himself repeatedly that he is a man at last. Instantly the light vanishes from Candy's eyes, becoming dark abysses. He tries passionately to kiss her. She refuses to let him, as though to do so too personal, too near to being real. She then begins to groan and push him away. However, before he can retreat, she grabs him tightly and wraps her legs around his waist. Then she does something he will never quite understand. She begins sobbing like a little girl, whispering in his ear:

"Never again— daddy– I promise never – never again!"

The sun peeks curiously through upper branches, splashing light over Candy's naked shoulder. The headstones stare silently away, the distant steeple righteous and blind. Candy and Davy lay motionless beside white hump of the Indian Rock half awake, half in dream, half-alive, and half-dead. They are free, at least in the fleeting present. No longer do they feel alone: no more pain, or fear, or guilt—nor feel pain of emptiness that sifts the measure of their lives– the lives of all who live too long in Liberty. At least Candy believes their sin covered in the shadow of an ancient legend.

"I love you, Candy," Davy breaths at last.

Candy immediately pushes him away and begins buttoning the front of her blouse.

"Did you hear what I said, Candy? I love you!"

"I best be getting home," she replies coldly. "Father will start worrying if I come home too late."

She navigates a course directly in line with the church steeple. Davy quickly scrambles up the books and runs behind her. They break out of the grove and into the late afternoon sun on the other side of the cemetery hill, the white edifice of the church within a few stone throws.

"Candy, I love you," again he insists.

"Boys are really funny sometimes," she shouts, looking up into the sky, as though preparing to spread her wings in a vision of smoke. "Have you ever thought that maybe some princes are better to remain frogs? You ought to let yourself dream, Davy. Without dreams life becomes too much serious with nothing to look forward to."

By now, they are now in front of the double dove wing doors of Liberty Church. Davy is more perplexed than ever. What is Candy really trying to say? It is doubtful it would have made any difference even if he had understood.

The church doors fly suddenly open, and out steps the tall, thinly dark figure of Preacher Morgan. Today he is not wearing his Sunday morning pleasantry. He holds in one hand the hook of a bloodied garden spade, the other hand clutching the mouth of a squirming burlap bag.

"Where in blazes have you been, Candice?"

He almost begins to swear upon seeing the boy with his daughter, but thinks better of it. The Preacher's thin lips begin twitching nervously, his countenance less forgiving.

"Davy and me stopped in the cemetery to do homework together," Candy lies, her voice honey sweet and convincing as always.

Preacher Morgan looks doubtfully at Davy. He then decides it better not to pursue the issue further. Besides, this day he has other problems.

"Look at them!" He exclaims, and opens the bag. "They're everywhere inside the house of the Lord!"

Frogs– frogs of all kinds and shapes, green frogs, brown frogs, large and small, all covered in black swap mud. Where did they come from; and how had they gotten inside the church?

"I think it's the work of a devil," accuses the Preacher, casting a suspicious eye at Davy.

Davy begins shaking his head guiltily, looks at Candy, who appears an angel without spot or blemish. It is past five o'clock by the time he finishes to help the preacher gather them all. Preacher Morgan decides that he will take the whole lot to Pixley next morning and sell them to those hungry.

"The blessings from the Lord are strange indeed!" He piously adds.

Davy says goodbye to Candy. She only looks pityingly at him, her eyes distant, without emotion. This is what hurt the most. Candy Morgan never felt anything.

"Frogs are such sad creatures," Candy sighs aloud to no one.

She turns and follows her father waiting impatiently from within.

The next Sunday Lucile swore that she heard frogs during the choir service. It is not long after this other folks hear them, too. As for Candy, she would find her true prince someday.

CHAPTER 15

The Anderson Boy off to Vietnam

Davy never stops thinking about Candy. She comes often in his dreams, sometimes as a saving matron, sometimes as a tormenting temptress. When she is not in his dreams, she becomes the vision of what he hopes the future might bring. He has not seen her since school let out for summer break. Oh he observes her singing in the church choir on Sunday mornings; however this not the same as to really see her. He tries to talk to Candy a few times, but prevented by the ever-vigilant preacher determined not to make the same oversight twice. Once Davy makes a visit during the week and feared the preacher capable of committing a mortal sin.

"I think in future, young man, you should find your way to church only on Sunday morning," he warns, his eyes blazing with damnation, "and knell at the judgment seat of Almighty God to pray forgiveness!"

Candy only smiles meekly in the background, pious to the end, and as unemotional as a seraphim painted on the church stained glass windows. Davy continues to visit Nela Smith every Saturday. His job at the mill fails to come through– at least not yet. The Worse is talk of another lay-off that no one– not even Homer expected.

One Saturday morning he is trimming the front hedges that line the walkway leading from the plantation style white front porch– Nela likes to keep up good appearances— when up walks Homer. He has that fresh alligator look, which means this the morning he is washed and shaved, and that Lucy has recently done his laundry.

"Morning" he shouts robustly.

"Morning, Homer, Lucile sent you after me?"

"Naw, boy, I just come by to tell you that there is going to be a shindig tonight down at old man Anderson's place. His eldest got orders to go to Vietnam. He leaves Monday morning on the first bus out of Pixley so they decided to throw him a party. Everybody in Liberty has been invited."

"Everybody" Davy chokes with excitement.

Surely, the Preacher and his daughter will attend such a patriotic occasion as this!

"Well if it is not Liberty's devil himself!" Nela exclaims, gliding gracefully from the west corner of the house.

"In person Missy," Homer retorts with a polite nod.

"I haven't seen you since William..."

"It surely has been a long time... Mrs. Smith. Your husband was a mighty fine fellow."

Homer shoots a quick wily look in Davy's direction, grunts something about her still being as pretty as a magnolia.

"A magnolia unfortunately left too long out of water," Nela half laughs. "But you can call me Nela. A woman likes to hear her name spoken by a man. So what brings you around here, Homer?"

"I come to tell Dave here that there's going to be a dance party tonight. I guess you're invited, too; if you want to come."

Nela reflects for a moment. A vagueness of beauty flashes over her like a spark from the distant past. Her countenance suddenly years younger, her eyes vital and alive.

"I think not this time." She replies softly. "Maybe, Homer, you would join me for a glass of fresh lemonade. I know you're more use to drinks a might stronger, but it still goes a long way to kill thirst."

No further coaxing is necessary. Nela slips gracefully into the house Homer boyishly in tow. She did not even think to invite Davy along. Just as well since he is now too excited to think about anything else except tonight's dance. Candy will most certainly be there! She just has to be there! Liberty lacks reputation for social events. This in fact is only the third party occasion that Davy can remember. The first had been a Christmas party five years ago sponsored by the mill. Next day everyone forced to work overtime shifts straight through to New Years. Last summer Homer gave himself a birthday party and charged twice as much for drinks. This promises to be different. There will be real dancing. Mr. Anderson, maybe the richest farmer living in Liberty, has a reputation for being generous. More importantly, Candy Morgan will certainly be there!

It is past three in the afternoon by the time Davy finishes the last of his chores. Nela answers the door looking a bit tired, as though roused from a nap. When asked about Homer, she replies that he left hours ago by way at the back. She passes Davy a five-dollar bill and promptly shuts the door.

Davy spends the rest of the afternoon trying to decide what he should wear. How he should comb his hair and there still remains that unsightly cowlick that no amount of Vaseline able to tame.

"Damn if you don't look slicker than a pair of new shoes," Homer says when he arrives at seven to pick up Lucy.

Shoes– Davy knew something forgotten!

"Well, come along, Davy," Lucile commands, throwing the final touch of a white cotton shawl over her bare shoulders.

Lucile is rather attractive when all made up. Tonight she has taken special care. Has chosen a pink dress that she knows is Homer's favorite. Even though she knows that hungry mosquitoes will attack her exposed arms and back mercilessly, willingly makes the sacrifice. There are moments when a girl has no choice but to suffer. Especially now, because she feels something suspicious going on. Homer promised to drop by that afternoon before going to his bar, only he never showed up. If nothing else, Homer is predictable-- too predictable.

"You go on without me," Davy says nervously. "There's something I need to do."

Lucile shrugs her shoulders and says something to Homer as they walk out the door about never seeing him like this before. Davy runs to his room closet and takes out the shoeshine box. As he brushes the black across his shoes, some manages to jump on his white socks. He would have changed socks, except does not have another clean pair. He decides to turn them inside out. This helps some. However, during the process he discovers to his horror that a spot of black has somehow leaped on his shirtsleeve, and so on. At half past eight, Davy arrives, shirtsleeves rolled up, a double cuff in his blue jeans, and his straw blond head crowned with stubborn cowlicks.

People have already begun dancing. Davy spends the first half hour trying to find Candy. He did find the accusing eye of Preacher Morgan; only dares not ask him where his daughter might be. Davy helps himself to several cobs of corn and a glass of cold apple cider, the first fruit offerings from Anderson's very own orchard. Finding an inconspicuous corner, he positions himself determined not to move. It is just a matter of time before Candy passes by him. Most everyone else does.

Among them is Anderson's oldest son Raymond, the one shipping to Nam, with his blonde girlfriend from the other side of Hogback Mountain. Raymond has the build of a football player with enviable shoulders and handsome bones imparting a countenance of Herculean stature. There is certainty in his every move, a confidence born, not made, the very stuff of heroes. Here is the true apple in his father's eye. Every now and then, the old man's proud face appears out of the crowd– sometimes tearful, sad and far away. Sometimes he just winks or slaps his son on the back without saying anything. At other times, he can be seen turning quickly away glassy eyed and then shout loud excuses to someone at the other end of the barn. This turns out to be the liveliest event to take place in Liberty since its founding. Prudently, some of the less favorable elements warned to stay away. These choose to travel to Pixley for the evening where they might drink and curse as they please.

Anderson is a stoutly religious man, who thoroughly believes in the disciplines of the Bible and devotion to his land. He takes special pride in his prime breeding stock, and altogether lacks tolerance for backbiters. Siring three of the biggest, strongest boys in the county, his continued peace and security ensured. It also might be interesting to mention that these are also the only boys living on the Liberty Peninsula, who usually socialize and work elsewhere. Each owns a late model pickup and all have girlfriends from neighboring counties. The younger twins, Arnold and Oscar, share little interest in farming, conniving early in life to invest their future inheritance in a Farm Equipment and Feed business located in downtown Pixley. The only portion of Liberty that interests either of them, besides the comfortable rent-free dwelling of their father's farm, is the narrow land bridge that offers easy access of escape.

Raymond, on the other hand, is different. He loves the smell of earth, the miracle of birth, and wonder of watching his father's fields grow harvest rich. Only Raymond Anderson is the true heir apparent to continue his father's dynasty. However, Raymond dislikes mill people. He dislikes them with a passion born of violence. Mostly this is because Whitey Miller caught him one night necking on a portion of his property and nearly beat the daylights out of him. A beating he will never forget or forgive.

As for Mr. Anderson, he shares a certain sentimental attachment to his less fortunate neighbors, which is the main reason he has decided to share a portion of this patriotic moment with them. He has witnessed the little community sprout into existence, like untimely fruit on a vine, only to wither and remain stunted for lack of nourishment. Because of this, Anderson feels a husbandly connection to his underprivileged fellow citizens. He even remembers Homer when Homer was just a boy, but has never once stepped a foot in his bar– or for that matter-- rarely any business in Liberty. Except the time he hauls a Seth Thomas clock to *Baily and Son* for proper adjustment. But this might happen only once in a century.

There have been many offers to buy his land through the years. The first came from those rich *Mill* people, and then lately from that squirrelly fellow from an upstate real estate company, whose presence on his property he did not at all care for. Anderson loves his land with greatest passion, wishing now only to receive burial in the bountiful soil that has been the burden of his lifetime of toil. He reminisces himself as king Nebuchadnezzar, beholding his kingdom of spreading orchards and harvest rich fields with certain haughtiness. Such a tree of stoicism cannot possible stand forever, even though he is the best seed ever to take root on the Liberty peninsula.

It is nearly half past nine and still no sign of Candy. Beth Ann wanders clumsily by and makes a shy attempt to stir up conversation. Impolitely, Davy tells her to go away, feeling particularly self-conscious by her clinging presence.

"You wouldn't talk that way to Candy!" Beth Ann taunts. "But I know where she's at and I know who she's with!"

"Where," Davy demands.

"Find out for yourself, Dave Tracy!"

She then turns without so much as a ripple in her faded blue dress and vanishes into the motion of the crowd. Davy jumps up and runs after her. After several minutes of sorting through the activity, he sees her cowered beside a dark brutish man Davy recognizes immediately as being Mr. Macky, Beth Ann's father. Macky is Second Foreman down at the mill. Whispers behind his back are that he is overbearing and a `brown-nose'. Chances are that when a man fired or suspended, Macky stands somewhere behind it. He has become something like the mill's junkyard dog, thrown scraps of appreciation from time to time, while gaining a reputation of distrust and hatred from his fellow laborers. For this reason, Macky makes a point never to show his face in Homer's during regular hours, considering it safer to pour his drinks alone. His guilt of being a mill informant sometimes more than even he can bear, always isolated, and never confided in. He therefore takes out his frustrations on his wife and only daughter with a fury of verbal abuse heard a block away. However, Beth Ann loves her father. She has the habit of changing into a wilted weed when he is near, seeking the coldness of his shadow when hurt or afraid.

Davy is still trying to get her attention when Homer comes up beside him. He is wheezing painfully, his pale puffy skin slick as bee's wax.

"Boy am I glad to find you, Dave. That woman's got more energy than them turbines down at the cotton mill!"

Homer is referring to Lucile still fresh and dainty in her summer dress. Lucile has been saving herself for just such an occasion. Now that it is here, she is determined to dance away every minute of it. On rare occasion, she and Homer gossiped to have traveled up to Pixley from time to time in her car. Homer never learned to drive, and has never owned a car, so always she drove and paid the gas. However, the kind of places he knows all fall short on dancing. Even then, it is unlikely that Homer would have allowed himself to be 'bamboozled' into actually doing it in front of those he shares a bottle of respect. Tonight he has no excuse; and given the state of his health, Homer will surely perish before Lucile has had enough.

"Why don't you take over for me," Homer coerces; then winks slyly. "She can't take us both on!"

Lucile remains her distance, like an accused awaiting justice or mercy, whatever the verdict. How can Davy possibly condemn the only mother he knows?

"It makes me happy to be dancing with the most handsome man in the whole place." Lucile says as they engage to the tune of a hillbilly tune, then whispering in his ear, "Lori would have been so proud!"

Davy wants to believe her, but finds it difficult with all three of the Anderson boys under the same roof. Nevertheless, it pleases him that she said it. Maybe Candy absent, but at least he has inspired the compliment of one woman, even if that woman is his Aunt. Davy allows Lucile to lead. She is after all the one to teach him how to step. She does it so gracefully that no one else notices.

Then someone removes the record in mid-song and replaces it with a new Elvis hit. Lucile freezes, mumbles something about "*that horrible music*", and abandons Davy to find another partner. Davy sees and corners Beth Ann. Shyly Beth Ann accepts his invitation to dance. Her skin appears a little too mousy on the dimly lit dance floor. Her imitation of the American Band Stand Hour Twist so spasmodic, that it lacks any kind of rhythm. Davy's movements little better, as he tries to coordinate his left and right feet to match the discordant beat.

He is so intent trying to pump Beth Ann for information that he accidentally bumps Raymond Anderson's pretty girl friend, nearly causing her to fall.

"Look what you done you clumsy mill trash!"

Raymond is drunk and not at all in a good humor.

"I'm real sorry," Davy apologizes, turning quickly to the young woman.

"It's okay, Raymond–" she says hastily.

"No, it ain't! I'm about to go fight for this mill hick. He ought at least to have more respect–"

"Raymond—" breaks in the stern voice of Mr. Anderson; "that's just about enough, Raymond. These people are our guest. Now I want you to apologize for what you said."

There is a tense moment when it appears that Raymond might challenge even his father. Then his eyes catch sight of a familiar leather strap hung on one of the barn post. His lower lip sticks-out boyishly and begins to quiver slightly, as he remembers lashes from his childhood. Hanging his head, he mumbles what amounts to an apology. Mr. Anderson is about to say something else, when Oscar bursts into the barn, followed by a beautiful raven-haired girl sprinkled with straws of hay.

"Pa, something's going on down in the lower pasture!" Oscar puffs, trying to catch his breath. "Sounded like something big falling into a lake!"

"A lake–what the devil are you talking about boy? There ain't no lake around here!"

Anderson is a logical man, made that way by the elements through long years of hardship, nature being both his ally and his foe. He also knows that young Oscar (although a bit fanciful when it came to his girls and the hay house at the edge of Anderson's bull pasture) is not given to fanciful imagining. Nevertheless, what he describes impossible. There has not been a good rain in more than a month; and even at its wettest, the swamp border never reaches more than a few inches into the lower pasture.

"It sounds like an awful lot of water down there," affirms Oscar, his dark round-eyed girlfriend beside him wagging her head in agreement.

Without saying another word, Anderson marches out into the yard and swings up into the worn seat of a sun bleached John Deere tractor. As he starts the motor and switches on the light, a short stocky boy with dark hair and eyes appears near the corner of the hay house. With him is Candy! No sooner did the lights catch him, he is gone.

"Where have you been Candice?" Demands Preacher Morgan, as Candy steps forward, "and who was that boy?"

Candy chirps something about him just being a friend from school. Without further ceremony, Morgan grabs his daughter by the arm and roughly escorts her away. Davy is also stupefied– surprised to see Candy with someone else– but mostly, because he thinks to recognize the boy with her. He immediately decides that he must be mistaken. What would Bubba Baily be doing here? –And why was Candy with him?

As the tractor noses slowly forward nearly everyone, including the women and children, follow. The two large lights mounted on the front slice into the obscure realm of darkness with modern precision of a surgeon's scalpel, dissecting neat rolls of hunkered apple trees, easily shredding malignant shadows that ordinarily would have haunted the imagination for a lifetime. It is as if this solitary mechanism has freed an entire town from a dark age of fear and superstition. No one would have dared to descend this near the swamp alone at night. There is something about the lights and the noise, and being together as a mob that makes them uncommonly brave.

There are a few, however, who wish to go no further, except that a heavy darkness has closed the way behind them even more complete than before. The exodus has begun; and Old Man Anderson, their mighty Moses, determined not to turn back. The tractor stops suddenly, the engine shivering to silence. The sound of the motor now replaced by a drone of frogs never heard here before.

"Damn, if it ain't all swamp now!" Homer exclaims.

A few feet distant, a string of rusted barbwire fence marks the beginning of the pasture. Particularly frightening is the bottom strand lies submerged in several inches of dark water. Less than a dozen yards away is the body of Anderson's prize bull slumped dead under a sycamore tree. The beast apparently drowned after losing its footing amid the crawling roots. This is the sound Oscar heard, the sound of this tremendous animal drowning in less than a foot of water. Then former fears come rushing back, reminding everyone that night supreme in the end. All Anderson can do is bow his head and embrace his three sons.

The next afternoon Pixley's sheriff drops by to see the mystery first hand. He says something about there being an Indian legend that speaks about things like this. That it means something, something his mother told him, only he no longer remembers what. Anderson is in no mood for legends. His prize winning bull dead, his pasture turned to swamp. He is determined to know why.

"You are pretty near the swamp and considering the elevation–"

"I was here before this town was here!" Anderson scoffs. "I never saw it flood like this even after heavy rain. Something is going on Sheriff. I don't know any way to explain it, but it ain't at all natural!"

Sheriff Taylors promises to look into it. He also tells Anderson that he is not the only farmer around complaining. He reports there are others living below the ridge on the other side with similar accounts.

"A mighty fine bull," he comments before leaving. "It's a shame to go to waste like that. I hear your boy left this morning?"

Anderson nods his head abjectly and exhales deeply.

"I'll be praying he comes back safe," he says. "I guess you know I was in Normandy during the big one. Seems there's just no end to war and violence. They keep saying that one day we'll going to fight the last one. But I just don't see how that can ever be."

That same afternoon Liberty Mill issues a lay-off to twelve good men without reason. This marks only beginning of things yet to come.

CHAPTER 16

The Master of Margrette

It is little surprise to everyone when the news arrives that Uncle Frank lays sick and perhaps near death. He is overweight, drinks too much beer, smokes like an incinerator, and eats always too much of the wrong things. He is forever in heated dispute with his neighbors. Accused of poisoning pets, stripping fruit from their trees, and the often pillage of their gardens. He is especially disagreeable down at the County Office where he works. Nevertheless, Frank is the only one for miles around who can handle a Caterpillar, which makes him something of a tolerated fixture.

When he is not excavating holes to bury garbage, then he is pushing over trees or scraping away boulders so that the chain-gang crews can lay down new asphalt. What Uncle Frank lacks socially, he doubly lacks in personal hygiene. So much so, that there are days when even his wife, formerly Louise Eleanor, cannot tolerate the smell. On these days, Frank arrives home soggy with sweat, covered with black diesel soot, and sloshing with a barrel of beer in his gut. However, Uncle Frank does have one saving attribute. He enjoys playing practical jokes, and takes special pleasure teasing his only nephew.

Now is no time for jokes. Frank feels terrible, feels like his ten-ton tractor has backed over his chest, leaving him heaving and invalid. The county doctor predicts it might be a heart attack and wants Frank to go to the hospital for test. In his most unsociable posture, Frank refuses, saying that if he died, he will do it in his own home and not under the knife of some quack.

It is late Thursday evening by the time Lucile and Davy arrive. They would have come in the morning, except that Lucile just had to see Homer one more time before leaving. She waited until past eight o'clock. Homer came and was gone before nine. Always it is the same. Yet Lucile never seems to mind so long as Homer brings her a little something special from his bar.

"Howdy little sister," Uncle Frank bellows weakly as they come in, "and how about the little Toad Face! How you been boy?"

Davy only shrugs his shoulders and grimaces. He is not so little anymore, but no one seems really to notice that he has already excelled Frank in height. Uncle Frank has nicknamed him Toad Face ever since he was ten years old and got a case of warts on his hand.

"'Cause you have been handling them toads," Uncle Frank warns after Lucile informs him that Davy is always catching frogs in the back yard and bringing them inside the house. "Probably one of them peed on you. Those warts are just the beginning. I suspect that before the year is over you'll turn completely. Why I knew a boy once just about your age that used to catch frogs and put them in his bed. Now he's the biggest old Bullfrog in the swamp!"

Davy never caught any more frogs after that. To his relief the warts disappear in time, but the nickname remained. Uncle Frank stopped for a while, but then starts back when Davy enters puberty and develops a case of acme.

"Frank... lord if you don't look pale as a ghost!"

Lucile never was one for bedside etiquette.

"Doc thinks maybe it's my ticker."

"That's pure nonsense. You got a heart like a bull. I told you before it's the way you eat. All those biscuits and potatoes, and wolfing everything down without chewing proper. It's little wonder you haven't had problems before now."

"Lucy, you ought not to talk to Frank that way," interjects a timid voice in a chair across from Uncle Frank.

Louise is Frank's second wife. His first wife perished of an unknown blood disorder, and buried on a clay hill in Frank's back yard. Less than a week later, he sees Louise walking home with a bag of groceries in her arms. Frank gruffly offers her a lift on his tractor. The girl's parents are so delighted that they invited Frank to stay for supper, and somehow he gets engaged even before shoveling the last bite into his ripe cheeks. Louise is not very pretty. With shoulders permanently slumped over from a lifetime of abuse and humiliation. She has dirty-blond hair, tired gray eyes, and drained complexion. Louise trembles slightly as she looks over at Frank for support, then down at the dried gnarled talons of her hands, the tone in her voice more a plea than statement.

"You just shut your mouth, woman!" Uncle Frank snaps at her. "Lucy come clear from Liberty to see me. And I put a lot more stock in her than I do that quack doctor."

"Thank you, Frank," Lucile says with smug confidence.

She then glares across the room at Louise recoiled into her shell altogether paralyzed. Lucile never much liked Louise, and takes particular pleasure now to watch her miserably deposed.

"Now Davy you go in the kitchen and put some water on to boil." Lucile commands and produces a jar containing dried herbs and a pint bottle of T.W. Samuel's whiskey from her black Mary Poppin's purse. "This will fix you right up, Frank."

"I'm sure willing to try, Lucy. –By God I'm willing!"

Uncle Frank grunts, licking his lips and hungrily eyeing the bottle of whiskey.

An hour later Uncle Frank's cure remains uncertain, but he surely is no longer in pain. He starts laughing– mostly at his own jokes– and even jumps up and starts dancing to an old tune by Hank Williams playing on the radio. Louise tries to prevent him from rising, but it is like trying to wrestle a bull. Lucy takes more than a swig or two of her own, and almost immediately begins lamenting over her love for Homer to whom they both owe this recipe of medicine.

"To Brother Homer," Frank acknowledges respectfully, and downs last of the bottle.

Davy falls asleep across the ragged arms of a Victorian style love seat salvaged from a garbage heap that once harbored a nest of field mice. Just as Uncle Frank predicted on their wedding day, the mice all die off in time. The love seat, worth something once, continues to serve a purpose long after the matrimonial union of Frank and Louise a distant memory.

"You know, Lucy, Davy's almost grown now," Frank begins somberly. "He ought to know who his father is."

"You better just hush, Frank!" Lucile threatens. "He don't need to know nothing about that snake. If I was born a man, that monster wouldn't be alive today. As far as I'm concerned, he died with Lori– do you hear, Frank? Davy is better off knowing nothing about him!"

Frank only hangs his head, nodding shamefully. There is little more he can say, and knows it, as does Lucile. Nevertheless, deep down it just feels wrong to him not to say something. The boy has a right to know-- at least given name of his patronage.

Next morning Frank awakens with the stab of sunlight in his eyes. His tongue and mouth raw dried jerky. The hammering inside his head as he imagines inside the diesel engine of his Caterpillar. During the night, Frank experienced an unrelenting attack of diarrhea and failed to make it to the toilet in time. This morning the pain in his chest altogether gone and he begins to feel like his old self again. A cold shower, another swig of Lucile's tonic from a second bottle in her purse, and Frank begins to feel as right as rain. After Louise quietly prepares some eggs and sausage, Uncle Frank recovers completely, back to his usual obnoxious self.

"What did I tell you, Frank?" Lucile comments, assuming her most saintly posture, "Doctors are good for delivering babies, but its old fashion remedies when it comes to taking proper care of the body. Just the same, I'm leaving Davy here for a spell to help you out. Be sure to get him back by Saturday."

Lucile gone more than an hour by the time Davy rises out of bed. He is not pleased being abandoned this way without even asking his consent. Not that it would have made any difference, since Lucile has an insistent personality once she makes up her mind. Still, it would have made Davy feel more grown up; more that his opinions count. Nevertheless, he likes Uncle Frank almost as much as he likes Homer. Unwillingly, Davy decides Lucile is right and that he should do whatever he can to help his Uncle in this time of need.

"Come on Swamp Toad, what do you say you and me take a tractor ride," Uncle Frank says after Davy finishes consuming the last of the eggs and sausage.

He knows there is nothing the boy would like better. They are already outside and preparing to leave when Louise shouts at him from the door.

"You sure you ought to Frank?" She worries.

"Don't fret about me, woman," he shouts back crossly. "For now on its fresh air and good whiskey for me-- and if you don't like it, go back and live with your mama and papa!"

Louise shrinks back and vanishes inside the house. Davy can hear the sound of her crying, but Uncle Frank insists it is only the chickens brawling inside the barn. The county yellow bulldozer waits with demonic patience beneath the shade of an overhanging tree limb. The large front plate used to clear anything in its path, juts out into the sunlight as a bloodied weapon covered with the red dye of local mud. Often Louise curses the nature of this pestilent earth. Even after several washings, still the tint clings to everything her husband touches, or touches him.

A network of chrome hydraulic cylinders, like main arteries sweating with oil, extends from the machine body to the front blade. Although the appearance unsettlingly primitive, this contrivance of pumps and pressure hoses represents Uncle Franks only true affection in life.

With twinkling eyes, he shifts his clumsy weight up into the dozing caterpillar, melting naturally into the seat. Davy manages to find a comfortable spot on the solid steel plates covering the batteries. Black smoke coughs out of two long tubes rising above the driver's cage, followed by a roar like a crazed bull elephant. Even the big China Berry tree shakes and sways as the mammoth rolls past it, showering them in a rain of shriveled hard pellets.

With Frank's gentle touch, the machine noses into a well-defined path, the enormous tractor treads chewing into rubble any brittle appendage snared in its powerful teeth. Here more than fifty acres of farmland, including a barn and an apple orchard, all belong to Davy's uncle. However, Frank is no farmer. Wild grass, shrubs, and tall weeds chock the fallow fields. The orchard grotesque and barren, the barn falling apart, inhabited by rats and a few savage chickens-- all adding-up to signs of neglect.

Davy knows from experience that conversation all but impossible above the hydraulic howling. Today promises to be hot, but nothing compared to the simmering blast exhaled by the huge diesel motor. For some reason known only to Frank, he christened the rattling monstrosity with the name 'Margrette', a name that makes Louise cringe every time he speaks it. He always refers to this growling machine as "her" and at times even whispers tenderly, as one might to a beloved. Louise calls it quite something else, often complaining jealously, as though it truly is a living breathing rival. Regardless the name of this marvel of modern excavation, there is a great deal to respect. For Margrette could idle all day in the hottest climate without overheating, and grind through snow and mud without even a whimper of hesitation. As a beast of burden, there can be no equal. She effortlessly pushes over the greatest of trees, and scoops away mountains with powerful jaws. However, despite the Caterpillar's apparent invincibility, Liberty's swamp remains strictly off limit.

"There are holes down there deep enough to swallow houses," Frank once admitted. "If Margrette was to ever get stuck down there she'd be lost for sure. 'Cause there ain't anything in the whole county big enough or strong enough to pull her free".

Frank often repeats this indisputable fact with certain pride. Because it is true, no one can even imagine such a scenario. The Pixley Community Council approved purchase of the machine from a neighboring county fifteen years earlier in order to create (or so the rumor goes) a golf course for the presiding Mayor and the Pixley City Council Members. They hire Frank to maintain and operate the machine based on his military tank record. Frank lacked tact even then. He accepts the job under the written condition that he has sole responsibility for the machine, and that the county can never fire him. They wanted that golf course. In effect, they give Frank the Caterpillar for as long as he should live, a condition less than satisfactory to following administrations. If military taught Uncle Frank nothing else, he learned always to get things in writing.

Soon the council realize their hands tied and with few legal options. Oh, they tried. Like the time a new County Works inspector assigned to check Frank at his job. Every time he caught the inspector spying on him, the machine would develop some hydraulics problem or another, and be out of commission for two or three days while Frank continues to draw County pay as stipulated in his original contract. After firing of the inspector, Frank returns to his normal performance of duty– a well-learned lesson taught. County officials from that day forward exercise more diligence to ban any kind of Union from the region, determined never again held legal hostage.

A wave of instant relief as the tractor crawls into the shadow of an adjoining forest. With burning element of direct sun eliminated the raging noon furnace now more endurable. Uncle Frank manipulates the controls with automatic sureness, as though he is an automated extension of the machine. The great scoop on the front rises and falls, feeling the terrain as it goes.

Davy loves these moments. Ever since he was a little boy, always a ride on his Uncle's tractor promised exciting adventure. The first time on this terrible machine, Davy hung around this strong man's slippery neck, crying the whole time. Once the trip finished and the terrible rumbling screams silenced, the boy's apprehension changed to laughter. Never again did he fear the growling monster made tame by strong presence of his Uncle Frank.

They navigate for nearly an hour between sentries of southern pines, avoiding companies of oak and ash groves, and crunching over fallen logs. Pushing through a ditch, and smashing a briar patch house belonging to family of rabbits, the Caterpillar comes to a stop, coughing to silence.

The machine rests ominously at the edge of a red clay ravine washed slick by flooding during heavy rains. This is the clef between two ridges: Hog Back Mountain and the Piedmont Plateau, known to local inhabitants as Devils Canyon. Further southeast down in the valley lays the cut-off appendage of Liberty Peninsula surrounded by congested swampland.

"Listen... just listen real quiet," Uncle Frank says after a few minutes.

Davy stands up and cocks his head, unable to hear anything at all, except a ringing hiss that always accompanies the end of a long ride. It is a wonder that

Frank can hear at all. He claims to know a way to close his mind to noise. A gift he picked up during the artillery shelling before the Armistice that created the 38th parallel. Davy listens, and then hears other sounds rising up out of the hole. A familiar rumbling squeal made by-- not just one-- but many vehicles of heavy machines.

"Is that an echo?" Davy wants to know.

"Nope– I'd say seven, maybe even eight Cats just like this one. By the sound of it, I'd say they are real busy."

Davy surveys the enclave from its narrowest path to where it spreads out tapering into a shallow valley. It must be in excess of a hundred feet at the deepest juncture, and at least four times as wide. From this point, the two ridges jut southward, bow-out in relation to each other, and then begin narrowing again traveling due east. It is in this direction that the excavation taking place.

"Uncle Frank I don't see anything. But I hear them!"

"Course not Toad Face!" Frank remarks and spits a wad of black saliva into the hole. "I figure them to be pretty near five miles away. Down in that direction."

He points to a position where the two ridges appear almost to join. His eyes squint and deep wrinkles on his leathery forehead appear more pronounced, as he thoughtfully considers greater bearing of deeper meaning.

"What I can't figure is why they'd be working in the old river valley down near the delta mouth. It doesn't make any sense. There be something else that don't make sense. Jim Pigeon, a friend of mine down at the county office, said that just in the last two years somebody living in Liberty has bought up all of the useless high country along the northern ridge of the Piedmont Plateau. He won't say who, only that he's got good connections. Mark my word, boy, there be something fishy going on here. And it got nothing to do with catching them old river bass!"

Davy shakes his head in agreement. He knows better than to disagree. Not that Uncle Frank violent, but he is sometimes unpredictable. Like the time he swiped Davy upside the head just because he accidentally knocks over his uncle's beer while playing. There remained a knot behind his ear for over a week, the memory of that moment still sensitive.

"Uncle Frank, why is it called the old river valley?"

"'Cause that's where the Aconee River used to run deep. That was all before the Hydro Electric people come in and began rerouting the flow to the water reservoir on the Pixley side. It was once the damned best fishing hole in the county hopping with Brim and Crappy twice the size of a man's hand, and Big Mouth River Bass able to snatch a fishing pole out of your hand if you aren't paying proper attention. Me, and old Homer used to go down there every Sunday. Now there's nothing left except a dry bed full of them white rocks."

"You knew Homer even back then?" Davy blurts in surprise.

"He was older than me by a few years, but he took me under his wing and showed me things that I never knew. Once, he showed me a cave made of rock crystal. He claims when he was a boy younger than my age that he found something inside. He never would say what it was. He only said that because of it he knows the truth about the Pixley secret. That same year the surveyors came, blew up the hole with sticks of dynamite, and hauled away every last piece of crystal."

"So what was Homer like then?"

"He was big and stout like a full-grown country hog. Would have a made a damn fine soldier, except that he had something wrong with his feet. He give me my first swig of whiskey the last night before I went off to the Army. I'll never forget him for that."

Frank reaches under his seat and pulls out a bottle of Old Crow bought earlier in the morning before Davy awoke. He reasons that if a little good, then a lot even better. Although not as good as what Lucy brought him, it holds its own bite.

"Go head take a nip," he says offering the bottle to Davy. "High time you tasted what it means to be a man. When I was almost your age, I was ready to ship off to fight Kraits! Excepting the war ended before I got over there– but by God, I didn't miss Korea! Now with all this talk about Vietnam, I suspect it's just a matter of time before they call you up. So you better start learning how to drink. You don't never tell Lucy a word! Else she'll put us both in the jail house."

Davy promises, gagging on the elixir. He does not tell Uncle Frank this not his first taste of whisky. For nearly a year now, he has been secretly stealing a taste here and there of Lucile's `sleeping medicine' sent over by Homer– just enough so she wouldn't notice– just enough to make him feel good and warm inside.

"Uncle Frank, I've seen the Indian Rock!" He says returning the bottle.

"Don't say?"

"It's up in the cemetery. It's got Indian writing just like the legend says."

"What's it say?"

"It's not really writing, just a bunch of strange symbols. One looks like a giant frog holding a pitchfork with an Indian woman beside him. There was some kind of bird and an animal with a tail like a boat paddle–"

"That be a beaver," interjects Uncle Frank. "I hear tell there used to be hundreds around here before the Aconee River got polluted and moved. They say that now it flows into a reservoir stocked full of trout. That must have been a while back. In over forty years, I never so much as seen a trout, and I hear there ain't nothing to catch except old carp! But go on Toad Face, finish telling me about that rock. Is it as big as they say?"

"It's pretty big Uncle Frank," then adds quickly, observing a familiar pride flash across his uncle's face; "But I bet you could move it with Margrette! It's all white and smooth on one side and must weigh almost a thousand pounds!"

"Back then they didn't have Caterpillars, so I guess it must have taken something mighty strong to move it way up there." Frank concedes with a defiant nod of his head.

"I'd go down there and get it, except I'm not allowed to take Margrette on paved roads anymore. And I'm not about to trust crossing that swamp ditch."

Frank finishes the last swig and tosses the bottle into the bright gleaming red hole.

"Maybe one of these days I'll go get it anyhow!"

"What do you think it really means?" Davy ventures after a brief silence.

"It don't mean nothing. Just like me calling you Toad Face don't mean nothing." His eyes gleam affectionately. "I always figured it to be some kind of joke. Maybe that rock was took up there by a bunch of them plantation slaves in a strong Buckboard. I reckon ten, maybe fifteen men could lift a rock that big. As for the pictures, I've seen some on other rocks down by the river. It don't make no sense at all. Maybe it just tells the location of good fishing holes. You know Indians weren't very particular about things besides hunting and fishing. Be like me marking a good spot so as I could find it again. And it don't take no genius to figure that out!"

When you came right down to it, Uncle Frank has a rather logical mind. What he says makes more sense than anything else does that Davy has heard. Therefore, he accepts without further question this to be the only reasonable conclusion; and at least in the moment decides to put the matter out of his mind.

Frank swings back up into the familiar recess of a throne placed high above limits of mortal men. The diesel clunks and clatters, explodes into a bedlam of noise made all the louder by canyon echo. The hydraulics hiss and squawk to the crunching clawing motion of the enormous steel treads, rooting everything in its path like some terrible animal destructively determined.

Louise is sitting on the back porch darning a pair of Uncle Frank's winter socks. She refuses even to look up as the monstrous thing trembles to a halt. It is all so familiar to her now. This was her lot in life. The only life she can imagine. Louise accepts it, just as she accepts the yellow and red devil that possesses her husband from morning until night.

That evening, as always when he stays over alone, Davy asks his uncle about his father. Frank only grunts and rubs his rough unshaven chin.

"Your daddy was just a man about like any other," he replies after a while. "It don't really matter now. One day I guess you will know everything there is to know. Just like that Indian Rock you seen. It comes a time when everything gets clear. I made a promise to Lucy years ago that she would be the one to tell you when the time comes. But for now, boy, just let it rest."

"But every time I ask Lucile anything about my father all she will say is he was a hard worker. I never even saw a picture! Nothing... nothing Uncle Frank..."

There are tears in the boy's eyes. Frank has seen his nephew cry before, but never like this. These are the tears of human struggle, the lonely weeping of a boy nearly a man suffering silent torment. Without saying a word, he gets up, walks into an adjacent room, and returns with a family Bible.

"Here take this, Davy. It belongs to you. The only thing worth keeping that didn't burn."

Trembling, Davy opens the book to find taped on the inside cover a yellowed photograph of a young man and woman standing together. The faces are not very clear because the light too bright the day the picture taken. Davy recognizes his mother Lori immediately. The man beside her is a complete stranger to him. Yet, there is something about the man. Something that sets him apart, making him different from any other. He has exceptionally broad shoulders and stands straight as an arrow, a full head taller than the shy unhappy woman at his side. One distinctive characteristic even the poor image unable to conceal is the mean squint of his eyes, seeming to project out of the celluloid dimension.

"Don't you ever tell Lucy that I give this to you," Frank commands in a voice almost tender compared to his usual gruff growl. "It's all I got boy, but you at least ought to have that. Now you get on to bed so that I can drive you back early in the morning."

"Thanks Uncle Frank," Davy says before his Uncle turns out the lights. "I... I really appreciate it."

"See you come morning, Toad Face."

Frank refuses to stay even for coffee when he drops off Davy, saying nervously that he has a few errands to run, and wants to make sure that he is ready for work next day. Davy feels better than he has ever felt before. He feels more peaceful in possession of a yellowed photograph hidden inside a shoeshine box at the bottom of his clothes closet. However, this peace ends upon overhearing a telephone conversation between Lucile and Miss Mabel.

"You don't mean it? He saw them where– in the cemetery!" Lucile huffs righteously, "and him being a Jew on top of everything else! I always said that Candy Morgan a devil in sweet disguise."

CHAPTER 17

Man from Atlanta

The man from Atlanta arrives in town late one afternoon driving a gleaming new white Cadillac. He reportedly wears a hundred dollar Tweed suit, and tries to get Homer to break a freshly minted fifty-dollar bill for a glass of cheap rye. Homer comes within twenty-one dollars and fifty-two cents to having enough change, and demands how long he plans to be in town.

"I should be here at least a week, maybe two." He announces in an accent altogether unfamiliar.

It did not sound quite Yankee, but neither is it true southern. Homer concludes that he must be one of those foreigners.

"What you here for," Homer asks without pleasantry.

"I was requested to come here in order to take soil samples from the swamp.

Maybe you could be so kind to direct me to the dwellings of Judas Morgan."

"Never heard of him," Homer spits back suspiciously.

"That's the Preacher," shouts someone at the other end of the bar.

Homer just grunts. He might have first pickings, but always there was the competition.

"Can you tell me where your Preacher lives?" The stranger enquires in a polite sweeping tone.

No, he definitely did not sound American, Homer is thinking to himself. A silence follows. A long and uncomfortable silence, a silence that is no different than all the other silences in Homer's mind. The man smiles weakly, clears his throat, and is about to say something.

"You come to the wrong place, Mister," Homer snorts without humor. "Why don't you ask Miss Mabel down at the filling station where you come into town? Mabel goes to church every Sunday!"

"I don't recall seeing a Gas Station when I came into town," the man replies perplexed. "In fact these are the first buildings I've seen since turning off the service road."

"That's probably because you come the wrong way– you foreign folk ought to learn how to read American! Just keep on going straight. Mabel's been there for years, and she ain't going anywhere. Even a rat could find her with his nose tied!"

Everyone laughs– everyone, except the stranger, who only bows apologetically, backs away searching for the door. The Cadillac departs down the narrow street like a battleship in a stream. Homer grunts again his disapproval, as he funnels a shot-glass of rye back into the bottle. He manages to siphon about half of it. Then decides what the hell-- and pours the rest down his throat.

"Damn if they were not taking over," he curses under his breath. "Another few years and America will be paying rent to every `Jack-legged' country in the world!"

Homer is a true patriot at heart. He stands strongly against taxation, but pays taxes when he has no choice. He believes welfare created only for Negroes, and that everyone who lacks a voted opinion a Communist. He would have readily been one of Teddy Roosevelt's Roughriders, only he was not born then. He would have fought the Germans in World War I, only he was too young. He would have marched off to fight Nazis, except someone had to take care of things and keep the bar going for all those poor souls left behind. Alas, Homer would have gladly laid down his life after the bombing of Pearl Harbor were he not too fat and problems with his feet. And of course, Korea never counted much in his patriotic mind. So Homer never went anywhere, never fought a single battle. Nevertheless, he can tell you about almost any place in the world. Knows by memory the name of every major battle fought in recent wars. This is because Homer use to read a lot. He read works by Kipling and Poe, by Mr. Robert Louis Stevenson, and especially stories written by Mark Twain. He even read a book called Marquis De Sade through the urgings of a woman he once dated. He disliked the book and the woman in the beginning– but, alas, how changeable the heart of man! Homer has even read the Holy Bible completely through, often losing many nights sleep in fear of the Second Coming. Homer use to read so much that someday it possible he may have inspired a volume or two of his own. Only he likes tending bar more. Now he just watches television– only the news-- sharing his little wisdom with the soulless creatures that pay him homage. One fact clear in Homer's mind, this man from Atlanta not his usual kind of customer.

Candy curls on the front steps of the church painting her toenails when the white Cadillac pulls up. This is not the first time she has ever seen a Cadillac, but this one sparkles in the afternoon sun beautifully new. Something familiar about the driver, something about his polished smile causes her to remember someone else. Maybe because he looks a little like her father when he was a much younger man, as Candy remembers from old family photographs. Maybe it is the way he slicks his hair back with a part nearly center; or the way his front teeth stick forward a little crooked and unevenly spaced. She places him somewhere in his late twenties to early thirties. One eye reflects hazel, bright and alert; the other dull green and muddled. The contrast between the two makes him look shifty and untrustworthy. He sports a thin out of date mustache that seems to sprout from the nostrils of a nose even longer and thinner than the nose of Mr. Baily, the Jew time-fixer. Putting all this together, Candy has to admit the man rather dashing at that.

"Candy Morgan!" He cries, crawling naturally out of his convertible. "My-- how grown-up you have become!"

Candy only smiles mockingly up at him, continues painting the last two toes of her white feet.

"I guess you don't remember me none. I'm Jasper, your daddy's cousin. I surely remember you though. You and your father stayed at my brother Duke's place in Atlanta a few years back. You were just a little thing. Girl I sure remember you!"

Feeling ignored, Jasper steps to the bottom of the stairs, clears his throat. His small sly eyes move along Candy's feet and legs and to the open door behind. Like all animals of his nature, Jasper Flynn has learned to be cautious.

"Your daddy is somewhere inside, child?"

"He's not here," Candy replies without looking up.

"Red is a right pretty color... goes nice with your hair," Jasper charms.

Candy shrugs her shoulders, makes a final precision dab.

"How do you like them all finished?" She enquires proudly.

"I would say they were pretty enough to eat."

"Only big bad wolves eat little girls," Candy teases sweetly, as only she can.

Candy squints, predatory challenge in her eyes. Jasper Flynn has known many women in his life, has known certain types well. Candy is that type. She is still raw, presently untamed. Nevertheless, Candy has certain promise, and Jasper Flynn sees himself as the man of that promise.

"I guess your daddy is gone for a good spell?" Jasper ventures.

"It sure is hot out here," Candy sighs, looking toward the dove-winged doors. "It's a whole lot cooler inside."

Candy stands up. Light passes through her thin dress. Jasper is further amazed at how shapely she has blossomed– that Candy is altogether a woman now! She is as a rare gem sparkling amid clusters of common stones, beautiful and without under panties. Within the first hour of his arrival in Liberty, Jasper Flynn referred later only as the man from Atlanta, makes love to the Preacher's daughter beneath the altar inside Liberty's First Baptist Church. No one ever suspects that he is the harbinger of Liberty's already decided doom.

Jasper Flynn meets later with his cousin, Judas Morgan, with smiles and laughter. The Preacher never so much as blinks an eye as his favorite cousin strokes Candy's hair affectionately, all the while calling her his `*little Charlotte*', which he says means a true child of the south. After supper, Judas and Jasper enter into the Preacher's private chambers where they talk for more than an hour. Not even Candy knows the nature of their conversation. By the time they finally emerge, it is clear the two men have arrived at some sordid agreement that greatly pleases them both.

Jasper is provided the small, however adequate, guesthouse rear of the church. It affords a view of the cemetery on three sides; the fourth faces open window of Candy's room. Knowing this, Candy teasingly undresses, and remains naked to be certain that Jasper cannot ignore her. Once the Preacher asleep, she slips out the window and steals the short distance to Jasper's open door. Sometimes avoiding bands of frogs crouching in the grass, sometimes with the sticky slime of a slug on her foot, she snuggles into pleasant shadows of his bed.

She did this each night, and each morning she is back in her own bed before the Preacher awakes. It is the first time Candy ever made love with a man in a bed. First time ever she can remember a man like Jasper Flynn. At first neither the bed, nor the man agree well with her. She keeps imagining his face somewhere else. That face different somehow, changed in a way that she cannot say. Something about the face reminds her of a childhood nightmare, a face that continues to haunt her every time she feels lonely or afraid. In time that feeling will go away, as she becomes altogether accustomed to Jasper and the bed, deciding then that she will never go back to young boys in cramped or worrisome places where mice and insects a constant threat. Now Candy is certain where her future lies. She is also certain that Jasper Flynn and his shiny Cadillac the way to get there- the surest way of escape. Many years later, Candy Morgan will remember a sleeping dragon inside a ruined castle lost at the bottom of a great lake; and at least one frog she hoped one day to change into a prince.

It is half past eight o'clock Friday night. The usual faces congregated at Homer's bar. On clear nights the small flickering black and white television erected on a pedestal over the bar got fairly good reception. Except tonight for some unexplained reason, the signal keeps fading in and out. All day there have been flash bulletins showing actual footage of escalating violence in an obscure little country somewhere in the Far East called Vietnam. It seems to all that the spectral hand of Communism has reached out and touched the world once again. Only Homer really interested, and only because he still has not fully recovered from a hangover caused by drinking the previous night. The front door flies suddenly open. In staggers Jasper Flynn looking-- some say-- pale as a ghost.

"Gentlemen... I have seen the monster!" He announces shaken.

Everyone within hearing immediately recoil, as though they fear that mere contact with his clothes might bring swift and certain destruction upon themselves.

"What do you mean you seen the monster?" Homer braves.

"First I need a drink."

Homer remembers the rye. He has a good memory when it comes to men and their drinks– and especially money!

"You changed that fifty, ain't you?

Flynn reaches into his shirt pocket and tosses a five-dollar bill on the counter.

"Keep the change bartender," he reports loudly. "Money is not so important when you almost lose your life."

He then downs the rye with one gulp, his eyes turning glassy.

"Well what about that monster you seen?" Homer still not impressed, at least not yet.

Sufficiently sizing up his audience, Flynn clears his throat, as though he means to sing a soprano piece, his hatchet gaze sweeping searchingly through the intent congregation.

"I was down in the old river bed near the swamp making a survey. You all know how quiet it is down there." He pauses, giving a few moments for reflection. "The sun had no sooner set than it was darker than the night of a new moon. I was anxious to get out of there fast. Except I got turned around coming back, and every way looked the same. Then I heard a terrifying sound more frightening than anything I've ever heard in all my life. A horrible murderous wail sheared through the oppressive air, boiling right up out of the black mire of the swamp floor. The ghastly sound seemed to be in motion, carried first in one direction, then in another. That is when the harbinger appeared, swooping down from upper darkness. A thing resurrected straight out of a nightmare-- a thing like none on record! Gentlemen it was the Liberty monster. I can't say it wasn't human, only that neither was it altogether an animal. Gray misshapen wings jutted from its back like a leathery cloak, pale on the underside, and flagellated with swollen purple veins. Its face flat and bat-like, with long twisted yellow fangs carved in a pumpkin sized head attached to a deformed body sweating red slime. Landing upright at the base of a fallen cypress, its demon red eyes peer into the darkness. I remain crouch in a nearby shadow only a few feet away, petrified, and daring not to even breathe. The monster stood in excess of fifteen feet tall, with appendages that hung past the knees, and feet like those of a goat."

"It weren't named Baily?" Someone shouts from end of the bar.

Everyone begins to laugh nervously. Flynn only shakes his head, makes a weak attempt to smile, and motions Homer to pour him another drink.

"Like I was saying," he continues, restoring order for the benefit of his listeners. "Those screams I heard were made by a full grown bull wedged tightly beneath one of the monstrous wings like a puppy under the arm of a man. Upon landing, it drops the bull into a pool of stagnant mud. I believe the dumb beast thought it was being set free, but before the animal can run away, a clawed scythe-shaped hand reaches under its soft belly, ripping open the stomach. The bull looks dazed, innards hanging out, and then crumples into pool of its own blood. The monster begins devouring everything. First, it eats the still steaming heart, then the carcass including even the bones. It eats everything, even the head. Before consuming last of the carcass, the creature pauses, looks around, searching the darkness for anything that moved. For a terrifying moment, I thought it saw me. Then with a great swoop of its wings, the fiendish thing is gone!"

There were those like Homer, who remain skeptical about most everything heard inside a bar– unless it is in print! Everyone in Liberty has heard about the monster, but no one really believes in it, at least not as something incarnate. Jasper Flynn is determined to change all that. He goes to the trunk of his Cadillac and immediately returns with a sagging burlap sack dripping black mud.

"What the hell fella'–"Homer shouts, overly concerned that these added stains might not mingle well with those already present.

Flynn slowly peels open the sack. Even Homer gasps surprise. Out plops a human skull with a smooth intent brow, the remains of a living ancestor never recorded in the Liberty chronicles.

"I found this stuck in a cave down by the old riverbed, like a deep funnel gouged into the bowels of the earth– maybe a passage all the way to Hell! Except this skull too big to pass through a blockage of jumbled of bones."

Flynn pauses, steadfastly eyes of those mesmerized. He then boldly turns and faces Liberty's resident patron.

"I tell you there is more than one monster down there and a lot of victims no one knows anything about!"

Homer nervously pours Flynn another glass of rye, pours another for himself as well. Homer will keep the skull. He will first carefully clean away the mud, polish the prominent brow, and buff out the pronounced cheekbones. Homer intends one day to place it inside a glass case in the corner of his bar for all to see so that no one might ever again doubt that Liberty's monster real. He had been sure all along, but it is good to have reminder of things from time to time.

The following Monday Jasper Flynn, the man from Atlanta, drives down main street in his shiny new white Cadillac, not to be seen in Liberty Town again. Beside him sits Candy Morgan smearing a vile of new red lipstick across her mouth. Many years will pass before she runs into her father again. No longer would he live in Liberty; no longer will he be a preacher. By then he lives in a new county named Aconee, and owns most of the land surrounding the manmade Aconee Lake.

"There's more money in real-estate than ever there was in preaching," he will say with a sad smile. "I've heard a lot of dirty rumors, but I know you will tell me the truth."

Candy will know the smile false; will have learned many things about men over the years. Candy tells him lies, as always he knew she would.

BOOK FOUR

Revelations Begin

CHAPTER 18

Dreams of Tigers

Lucile awakes suddenly, and as usual unable to sleep again. She has had another dream about Tigers—dreams them often. In these dreams she sees their suffer eyes eclipsed in shadows of rotting corpses, black quivering lips dripping blood in a Monsoon night. The dreams first started after the evening news broadcast began running specials about the ongoing conflict in Vietnam. They should not run things like that on TV news! Now there is a draft going on in America; and they have started to call up boys Davy's age. Lately this demon torments her body and soul from sundown to sunrise– and there is only one remedy.

"David, I need you to go to Homer's for me this evening," she says coming out of the kitchen, an empty whisky bottle in her hand.

Lucile only calls him David when she is out of sorts, and tonight her patience particularly thin. As for Davy, he has been moping around ever since that afternoon with Candy in the cemetery. Maybe it is a combination of the heat, which has lasted longer than usual this year. There is also that something in the pit of his stomach that lurches violently every time he thinks about Candy; those thoughts now all the time! Always she is a taunting spirit in his imagination. Always she is with someone else! Lucile knows he has problems, but embraces the philosophy that each must learn their own way to deal with pain and deceitfulness of this world.

"Self thought leads to wisdom." She often says when he is a bad boy, as boys sometimes are growing up.

This usually means to bed early without supper. Davy may very well have starved had Lucile not a forgiving nature. Being a practical woman, she probably decided the wiser course is to keep him strong for her errands.

Homer's den crowded as usual-- as it is always on Friday nights. The bar and liquor store, narrow and long, the walls on either side devoted exclusively for shelving Jack Bean, Old Granddad, T.W. Samuels– or any other cheap poison imaginable. A slender slab made of two pieces of oak joined together run down the center, leaving the rest of the room for drunken patrons.

`Badger-of-the-Hill' Homer serves from perch of his throne on the opposite side, uncontested king of this place. It is Lucy first proclaims him title Badger-of-the-Hill shortly after they met. She states he is spitting image of an animal character in a book she once read. That must have been some while ago, because to Davy's recollection his aunt never reads anything except the Sears Catalogue.

"That's not the first time somebody ever called me a vermin!" Homer swore with a good-natured smile adapted over the years serving his patrons, then his eyes narrow cruelly. "I ain't like that now, but once was a time..."

The title, nevertheless, seems somehow fitting. Before long, Homer gains the nickname Badger for short. Only his closest acquaintances, and usually only those of many years, dare call him this to his face.

"How you been, Dave?" He shouts as Davy enters. "I see Lucy send you over here for some more sleeping medicine."

Homer likes better the sound of Lucy than Lucile, but the way he says it is almost triumph, proclamation to everyone within hearing, living proof that he has conquered the affection of at least one woman. He pivots around and begins searching the wall of bottles for a particular label. It is actually amazing that Homer manages the way he does without breaking something. Because he is a big man, enormously thick around the middle, with short fat fingers and sagging robust arms, one would think him incapable to maneuver in a place this compact. As a matter of observation, Homer is so fat around the middle that he looks clumsy. Only he is not clumsy, and performs as agilely behind the cramped bar as a skating bear at the circus.

"Got it," he shouts victoriously, slamming a pint bottle of Old Crow on the bar beside a drunken patron already too oblivious to even take notice. "Tell Lucy that I'll be dropping by tomorrow about three."

This added comment nearly inaudible; the sound of his voice rising barely perceptible above a sudden influx of noise making the walls shudder, causing the many precious bottles of elixir to rattle on shelves stacked against the back wall. It is after all Friday night, and God knows these men need at least one night of riot.

"I'll tell her." Davy promises, stuffing the bottle in his back pocket.

"Dave," Homer begins, eyes bright with revelation, "you graduate next week, ain't that right?"

Davy nods his head.

"Then why don't you stick around for awhile and have yourself a drink or two on the house for celebration;" Homer then lowers his voice. "Hell-- that Jew-Boy's been here since early this afternoon, and he's been buying his self drinks, too!"

Bubba Baily here-- for reasons Davy unable to explain, he feels a sudden flush of excitement by this news. Where was he? Not at the bar, and there are few other places in this narrow oblong chamber he could be. Then a familiar rattle, followed by clanging bells, a sound rarely heard in the liquor den; because none of the regulars can stand sober enough or confident enough to waste a quarter on the pinball machine crouched in an obscure corner at the back.

Bubba hunches over the machine, red, blue, and green lights flashing weirdly over his face. Davy watches on without saying a word. The whiskey shot Homer has given him already beginning to have an effect. Already the pain in his gut nearly gone, changing into a warm good feeling. It is an amazing miracle healing found only in Homer's bar.

Homer first installed the pinball machine in the darkest recess of his store some seventeen years ago. Above it is crooked frame of an expired liquor license hung beside a faded picture of the bartender and another man taken many years earlier. Dust and film of cigarette smoke have nearly erased both features in the photograph. Distinctive Homer still looks almost the same physically, the other a complete stranger.

As for the pinball machine, it has never worked properly. Oh, it receives the loose change the kids put in it on their way home from school before proper bar hours, always tilting after the first ball. Homer keeps promising to have it fixed. Perhaps he even believes that someday he really will. Most of those kids now grown, feeding their money into another escape, while their children continue to deposit dimes and nickels into a machine impossible to beat.

Yet, here is Bubba Baily with a touch like Davy has never seen before. Ball after ball and still the machine lets him play. He is in perfect tune with the mechanism, or else the mechanism in tune with him. The flippers respond as fingers to his touch, launching the heavy shiny ball always to the proper place.

"Did that giant goon ever bother you again?" Bubba demands, pausing to take a sip of his drink, appearing confidently prepared for anything.

"Abraham's not so bad really," Davy replies. "He's just touched in the head, that's all. Mrs. Smith said that Old Abraham has never been known to hurt anyone."

Bubba only sneers; downs the rest of his drink with one gulp; and shoots another ball into the sparkling electric maze.

"But I'm really glad that you came along!" Davy adds quickly. "You never know what those people might do next."

Bubba seems not to be interested in further conversation. He sees something, something inside the machine that means more to him than anyone could ever possibly mean. There are those who would later say that was Bubba Baily's problem all along. He never gave a damn about anyone left alive.

It is only eight o'clock and already the crowded bar has begun thinning out. At half past nine, some distraught wives burst through the door. Each locate a familiar whimpering lump of flesh, and drags it away without much commotion. These are indeed the neglected children of providence: generation after generation, who sweat away their lives in the bright belly of the cotton mill, who eventually become blind to all that is beautiful and true in the waking world. Their eyes grown accustom to dark soulless places. Their flesh carnage to creatures sealed in darkness with them; demons of their own making that feed upon ignorance and bitter bigotry. The mill both their god and their earthly taskmaster: a nightmare chimera pandering to their need, while draining their essence, only to cast the mummified spindles of what little is left into fire. This is their inescapable fate. Only the gaping gate of a sagging edifice known to the worm of their existence as Homer's Bar and Liquor Store promises a Tantalus taste of relief.

By a quarter past ten, only five standing patrons left, including Bubba and Davy. The remaining three huddled at the opposite end of the store whispering secretly, with old Homer leaning attentive over the bar like a corpulent grinning beast giving his approval.

"I'm tired of hearing that damned pinball machine!" One of the men swears, his white head rearing above the rest. "In fact I'm tired of that bloodsucking Jew hanging around here all the time!"

Bubba says nothing at all, but continues rattling the machine, as though he hears him not, the score escalating ever higher at incredible speed.

"Did you hear what I said – *Jew Boy*!"

Whitey Miller, or Cotton Mouth, so named because of his violent nature, is a large legendary man with an ageless appearance. Cursed from birth with the eyes of a snake, he is, in fact, a near albino; his flesh raw and featureless; drained entirely of pigment like a creature existing for unknown centuries in a black sunless pit. Whitey's face narrows, appearing almost flat, with a narrow sloping brow and ears tiny in proportion to his head. Cotton Mouth always wears his silver white hair razed short, which bristles as a glistening hood prepared to strike.

"I guess he don't hear so good Cotton Mouth," Homer taunts.

As for Davy, he does not know what to do. He likes Bubba, but fears Cotton Mouth even more, who is as dangerous as his name-- and when drunk, altogether unpredictable!

Cotton Mouth hates things without reason. He hates blacks, hates Jews, hates the rich, and especially the poor. He hates the Cotton Mill, as restless as his hate, hating the silence of his own conscience even more. Most of all Cotton Mouth hates the haunting memory of a young wife, who became beautiful during the first year of marriage. He becomes jealously convinced that she has changed into a whore for everyone in town. One night after work, he stabs her six times in the stomach with a dull box cutter, later acquitted on a legal technicality. Then his hate grows worse. It spreads through his brain like a cancer, until the evil metamorphose complete. There will come a cloudy sunless morning when a headless white serpent found naked at the edge of Liberty swamp, a mystery as indiscernible as his nature. After an eternity of dying, Cotton Mouth will know peace at last. A pitiful swollen torso, with arms and legs, the last buried, quietly, and without notice, in the old cemetery at the edge of town.

"Ah, come on Whitey, those boys don't want no trouble!" Homer rescues, seeing the distress on Davy's face.

"You shut your mouth Badger! I'm going to have me a piece of that *Jew boy*– and there ain't nobody better get in my way!"

Not even Homer dares to openly cross Cotton Mouth, especially when he is drinking. This particularly evening he has been drinking straight Jack Daniel since the end of his three o'clock shift. His eyes puffed bloody slits painful even to look at. Nevertheless, it hurts Homer's pride to be deposed in this way– especially in front of Lucy's boy. At this particular moment, he is probably considering a familiar saw-off he keeps stashed below the cash drawer. This constant companion just beside a coffee can containing the rusted mechanism of an old Spanish revolver, which he eventually realizes stamped with initials *J B*, found near the old riverbed when he was a much younger man .

Cotton Mouth takes a step forward. The machine tilts. Bubba spins around, grabs an empty glass breaking it in the same motion against the edge of the pinball machine. He then kicks Cotton Mouth twice in the groin. It happens so incredibly swift that Cotton Mouth never so much as raises a hand. Bubba swings behind him, smashing his face hard against the solid oak surface of the bar on that end. He lifts the shocked wheezing man bodily against edge of the bloodied oak surface, whipping the shattered glass mercilessly against Cotton Mouth's stiffened ivory neck.

No one has ever seen Cotton Mouth afraid. His eyes change to dying embers tucked inside a fold of white swollen flesh, and are almost mortal now. His lips quiver uncontrollably, a reddish brown bile dribbling down his chin, his yellowed teeth like shattered pieces of brimstone.

"I'm not a bloodsucker– do you hear?" Bubba snarls in a measured tone.

"P-Please boy, don't kill me!" Cotton Mouth is sober now. "I was just joking. Ask Badger, he'll tell you! I-I didn't mean nothing by it... I just been drinking too much."

Homer says nothing at all. He just watches on like a spectator at a bullfight waiting expectantly for a clean slaughter. Bubba releases Cotton Mouth, pushes him aside. He then orders Homer to pour him another drink. Homer says it is on the house. Cotton Mouth rises and slithers quietly away followed by two ghostly appendages that serve only to shadow his presence.

Cotton Mouth stops coming to Homer's after this, preferring instead to travel all the way to Pixley. Local gossip circulates later that he plans to kill Bubba Baily at a time when he least expects it. But no one really takes the gossip serious, especially after what Bubba did to him.

"Thanks for standing by me." Bubba says to Davy's surprise.

He then steps back to the pinball machine, inserts another coin.

"Bubba sure got that pinball machine pegged!" Homer shouts back as he cleans the mess on his bar.

"You're the best I ever saw." Davy agrees.

"I've been playing these things since I was old enough to steal nickels out of a blind man's cup. –And I started street fighting a long time before that!"

Bubba sends a ball flying into the electric maze. Lights begin flashing, bells ringing. Bubba's face emotionless, his eyes blank.

"You sure showed Cotton Mouth a thing or two." Davy wants to penetrate his barrier of concentration. "People around here are going to think twice before they say anything against you."

Bubba only rolls his eyes, as if to say he could give a damn what people around here think. Davy cannot help but respect him. Respect the fact that he is straightforward, unafraid to stand alone and fight the whole world if he has to. Maybe this the reason why Davy feels compelled to know more about him; just to see how far Bubba Baily willing to go; if he is real or something imaginary.

"Bubba, have you heard about the monster that lives down in the swamp"

"Yes." He says simply.

"Do you believe in him— believe that it exists?"

"No. Do you?" There is challenge in his voice.

"I don't know. Sometimes I think I do, most of the time I don't."

"Do you believe in him tonight?"

Davy's throat goes suddenly dry. Just then, Homer yells that he is ready to close.

"Well, do you?" Bubba demands and purposely tilts the machine.

"I... don't think so," Davy hesitates.

"Come on, it's a full moon, why don't you and me walk down to the edge of the swamp tonight and just see if there really is a monster down there."

A challenge made. Davy's mouth changes suddenly dry, a peculiar queasiness in his stomach.

"I should be getting back home. Lucile needs this." Davy says patting his pocket.

"I think you're just chicken," Bubba sneers.

"You boys get a move on!" Homer shouts, and then looks straight at Davy. "You remember to tell Lucy I'll be coming tomorrow."

"I promise, Homer! I'll tell her for sure."

"Well, are you chicken or not?" Bubba persists.

"No, I ain't chicken. Let's go!"

As they are leaving, Bubba sticks his head back in the door to thank Homer for the free drink.

"You can just call me Badger for now on," Homer replies, his eyes twinkling with respect.

This makes Davy a little jealous, even though deep down he has to agree with Homer. Bubba handles himself like a man, deserving all their respect.

The two talk little as they squeeze through rusted string of bobbed wire fencing, step lightly through pastures encompassed by Anderson's prize sleeping bulls, finally to reach the edge of the marsh. Davy will later learn that Bubba Baily no longer believes at all in monsters, at least not in the kind that stalk the swamps surrounding Liberty. The ones he knows more personal. He will show scars on his feet made by rats when he was a baby. He tells Davy that once he found mutilated remains of a street whore stuffed into a garbage can in the alley behind where he lived, and describes the animal cruelty of one city gang against another.

Upon discovering a fallen tree trunk near a mist-laden pool, they make it their council stool. They talk for a long time as the moon climbs higher and higher, sliding in and out of silver-bellied clouds. Their voices gliding over the dreamscape like tattered sails whispered across a gray motionless ocean. They talk about eternity, cold case mysteries decayed inside stagnant pools of urban legend, and about all the excuses Bubba's father gave when he was still too young to question. He never says what those excuses were because Bubba cannot bear to hate his own flesh that way. Talking too much reminds him that his mother and father always fought a lot. Then a month after he turns twelve, she runs off with a black man, who sang soul in cheap bars. Bubba Baily hates being a Jew and thinks his father a liar and a crook that is always cheating people. What Bubba really feels in his heart, no one will ever know with certainty, or even if he still had a heart then. This night, Davy begins to fear that Bubba Baily is greater than all dangers in the world.

"Let's break out that bottle," he coaxes, returning to the here and now.

"I don't know Bubba. Aunt Lucile will get awful mad if I don't bring her sleeping tonic home."

"We'll just take one swig each. She won't know anything."

Davy knows she will, but decides to do it anyway. It is warming, and this enough to justify the condemnation he will receive. With more than half the bottle empty, Bubba replaces the cap and passes it back.

"I know you got something hot for that preacher's daughter," he says looking Davy straight in the eyes. "Take my advice and forget all about her. She's not worth the effort. No girl who babbles about frogs and princes, and who likes making it in graveyards is worth losing any sleep over."

"How do you know that?" Davy chokes.

"I made her a couple of times. I knew what she was the first time I saw her. Every alley in the City has a girl just like her. You can do better in your life than a street whore."

Davy feels suddenly betrayed. He wants to lash out, make Bubba take back his words. He just sits there, instead, staring into the nearly empty bottle in his hand, the tears burning in his eyes.

"Don't take it so hard," Bubba says, slapping him hard on the back. "After all Mary Magdalene was a whore until Jesus came along. Who knows, maybe Candy will find her savior someday, too."

Suddenly there is a loud splash. Choruses of frogs begin singing all around them followed by a series of splashes, this time closer, louder. Then silence.

A locomotive howls in the distance, as it snakes through sable hills. The sky changed to a grizzled canopy obscuring the light of the harvest moon. Then they hear the sound of heavy breathing nearby, followed by a sickening crunching noise, as though something large scratching wet bones out of a grave and eating them.

They both leap up at the same time and start running. Davy rips the seat of his pants, as he scrambles through the barrier of bobbed wire, and Bubba receives a scratch on the back of his neck. They run without stopping, until reaching the lights of town. Feeble as these are, the nearly warm incandescence enough for them to regain courage.

"What do you suppose that was?" Davy asks between breaths.

Bubba only stares angrily into the darkness. He then picks up the biggest stone he can find, and heaves it in the direction from which they ran.

"Someone ought to kill that thing!" He swears angrily.

This is the only time Bubba and Davy will talk as they talked that night. They shake hands and part ways in the direction of home. It will be several days before Davy sees Bubba again. By then there will have been many changes.

Lucile is still awake, nervously pacing the floor when Davy arrives. Sleep never comes easy to her anymore. The boy she has raised as her son all these years should have better appreciation for all the personal sacrifices made.

"You're going to end like everybody else in this town!" She cries bitterly, her hands shaking noticeably, her eyes red and sore.

If only the bottle were not lost, because of a tear in the back pocket of Davy's trousers. --But who in their right mind would dare go back to find it? The next morning Lucile goes into Pixley to do some shopping and stays gone the whole day. Davy never tells his aunt that during her absence Homer dropped by.

CHAPTER 19

Death in the Widow Pond

Candy has been gone for over a month. Nela Smith no longer requires Davy's services– not since that day Homer stopped by. Homer is a man that recognizes opportunity. Nela Smith a golden goose of promise. Lucile stops seeing Homer so often after this. Her eyes always red and almost every night Davy has to bring her home a bottle of sleeping tonic, only it is no longer free. Then Preacher Morgan begins dropping by to console her. He also is in need of consolation since the kidnap of his daughter. Pixley's Sheriff sends a wire to the Atlanta police, but never receives back an answer. He sends a second wire, and still no reply. He stops trying after that. Maybe he decides that since she is of age, Candy Morgan, half-Indian daughter of the town Preacher, maybe better off to have found a way out.

It is the last week of the month, hot and muggy, a late swarm of June Flies buzzing in the air. Davy's job at the mill fell through; and with all the recent layoffs, appears doubtful he will ever get on. Business at Baily and Son watch repair every day slow, so Bubba spends much of his time in Homer's bar drinking and playing pinball. Davy usually joins him just to forget. Those days lost to idleness limited, because both their savings rapidly disappearing. Bubba rarely worries about things to come. Lessons learned from his father, which say somewhere there is always money to find, or at the least the things money can buy. Bubba wins as usual. Davy wonders why he even bothers to compete. No one could have beaten him ever.

Bubba is still on his second ball when the front door squawks open and closes with a loud snap.

"What's the matter, Red Eye? You look like you just seen the devil!" Homer's grinning face leers across the bar like a predator ready to pounce.

No one knows if Red Eye has another name. He is just a poor bum that blew into town one day without anyone's notice, and has remained here ever since. Homer was the first to give Red Eye his name. Why his eyes are so painfully red remains a mystery to all. One fellow, whose father once a train engineer, said the cause from flying cinders riding too many years exposed beneath coal trains. This sounds logical enough for lack of any other acceptable theory.

Red Eye is what you might call the town drunk, although he probably drinks less than the average of men in Liberty. The only difference being that Red Eye makes drinking his career. Nor will you ever find him doing a regular job with steady hours and a paycheck. Not because he is lazy, working perhaps harder than anyone else in two counties. Early on any given morning, including Sundays, he can be seen rummaging from garbage can to garbage can, while pulling a rickety child's red wagon piled with old clothes, bottles, cans, and anything else he thinks still has some value. When heaped to the limit, he takes his load all the way into Pixley and sells it to the junk dealers for cash. There are those that claim Red Eye once a big man in the South. Others believe him presently rich without even knowing it. Just maybe he is. No one will ever know for certain, because one day he will just move on like all the rest.

"Well, spit it out," Homer coaxes in his usual gruff tone.

Red Eye resembles a wheezing scarecrow with rotting rags hung loosely over broken-stick shoulders. He clings desperately to edge of the bar trembling; his eyes bloody saucers.

"I seen it by gosh– down by the Widow Pond!" He manages at last.

"You seen what," demands Homer.

"I seen the monster!"

Homer grunts, glancing at the polished human skull prominently displayed for all to see.

"It's true! I swear it weren't no whiskey dream, Homer. I seen it just as clear as I see you now." Red Eye looks Homer straight in the eyes.

Homer returns the look for a moment, only to turn away. No one could stare long into Red Eye's inflamed vision without experiencing a peculiar sense of pain.

"You saw it sure– and in the daytime? Well, I'll be damned!" Turning to Bubba: "What do you think about that? Old Red Eye here is saying he done seen it, too. Maybe there be more in them swamps than meets the eye."

The red Tilt light flashes on, and Bubba slams his fist hard against the glass top.

"You better be careful not to break that," Homer warns dryly. "It'll take more than loose change to make her work again."

Bubba pivots quickly, squarely faces Red Eye. Bubba refuses to blink; his eyes steady and unfaltering. Finally, it is Red Eye, who drops his head, a rodent searching the floor for a safe shadow.

"What does your monster look like?" Bubba interrogates.

"It weren't like the one that man from Atlanta seen. It looked most like any man, excepting he had this big head that's cocked crooked to one side. At first, by golly, I thought I was seeing things. I said to myself: There can't be no damned frog that big!" Red Eye pauses, begins licking his lips. "Mister Homer, think maybe you could spare me a glass of Jack? I ain't sold no junk today, but I'll rightly pay you soon as I can."

Deep in his crawl, Homer is good-natured. He never likes to admit it, not even to himself. Anyone who knew Homer knows he will always extend a little credit.

"I guess I can spare you one drink, Red Eye, seeing how you seen the monster, and lived to tell it! So it weren't like that other. Looks to me we got ourselves more than one bogyman down there just like that Atlanta fellow said!"

Homer finishes filling a dusty glass. Red Eye turns up the oblation, gulping down the fiery amber elixir in one shot. When it is all gone, his eyes glaze over, becoming for an instant less red, almost human, followed by a tremor of relief that quakes involuntarily through his entire body.

Bubba looks at Davy and snorts. He has his monsters, too, but keeps them locked away inside. It is difficult for him to be the only Jew in town. There is his father, but he counts less in this world of lost dreams. Maybe deep down Bubba is afraid that people might start `witch hunting'. He knows from history what that can lead to. Davy remembers a story Bubba told him once. He said the grandfather of his father stoned to death in Kremlin Square before the third wave of exodus out of Russia. Those citizens condemned him as a devil worshipper based on the testimony of a six-year-old boy, claiming to see the man without his boots on.

"He has only three toes– just like Satan," swears the child.

However, upon removal of the dead man's boots, they realize that the boy mistaken. Nevertheless, the man was a Jew, and a `Christ Killer'! All return to their own houses justified, leaving the body bruised, battered, and without shoes at the stoic feet of Lenin, a bronzed witness against the deeds of his converted children.

"I think it's just an alcoholic trick to get free whiskey!" Bubba accuses with rage in his eyes.

"I know what I seen," insists Red Eye. "He throwed something in the Widow Pond... I think something… alive!"

Homer's brow wrinkles. He worries about most everything. He worries if it rains; worries if it might snow. He worries if the days too hot or too cold, or if his whiskey delivery is even an hour late. This recent news about the monster throwing something alive into the Widow Pond only adds new fuel to his already worrisome nature. He looks first at Bubba, then across at Davy.

"Now that's a mystery sure enough" he says, and begins tapping his fingers thoughtfully on the bar top.

"Where is this Widow Pond?" Bubba demands boldly.

"Way down in Old Liberty, near the edge of the swamp not far from the home of Widow Smith. Dave here can show you."

The glimmer of a smile flashes over Homer's corpulent face, a smile speaking volumes of challenge

"No Bubba, you don't want to go there!" Davy cries alarmed.

"Just why not?"

"The Widow Pond is haunted by ghost, Bubba."

Just the thought of going there is enough to make Davy shiver. There are many tales of horror associated with this historical landmark labeled by local legend *The Widow Pond*.

In the truest sense, this landmark represents to Davy a place of death. Uncle Frank claims it is the most evil location in the world. And if anyone knows about such things, it is him! After all, his uncle has seen all kinds of ghost in the mountain hollows surrounding the Liberty basin. Everything from the ghost of hanged black men, who haunt curves along the lonely dark road running across Hog Back Mountain, to anthropomorphic creatures that lurk under wooden bridges to eat children. What Frank has not seen with his own eyes, he believes through the testimony of others, whose testimony certain and reliable.

Before getting married a second time, he used to drop in and visit a lot after the death of his first wife. She had been a sickly woman, who often mixed insulin and beer, and against the advice of her doctors probably would have lived forever. Except she started going blind and one day stepped off the end of the back porch, breaking her neck. Frank grows distraught by loneliness, dropping in more often to visit his sister and only nephew. Then he meets his next wife to be and stops coming at all. Maybe this is the reason Lucile dislikes Louise so much. The second marriage of her brother feels like losing a man around the house to another woman. Despite his many failings, Frank presents a good father image, always managing to find time for the fatherless boy. A week before going to the county courthouse for a new marriage certificate, Uncle Frank takes Davy turtle hunting in the swamp. By chance, they emerge at the Widow Pond.

"You know where we're at, boy?" He asks, seeing the discomfort in his nephew's face.

"No... Sir," Davy replies.

Uncle Frank always did insist on respect.

"We're at Death's door."

He then reaches into the black pool with his turtle snare, clamps on to something floating just below the surface. It is the bloated remains of a drowned raccoon. The eyes turned completely white, wiggling gray tadpoles leaping out of its mouth. Frank takes his pocketknife and splits open the stomach. Out issues hundreds of the slimy wiggling liquid creatures.

"They be the Widow's children," Uncle Frank says. "You mark my words, boy, the Widow ain't finished her killing yet. Not by a long shot!"

He then proceeds to tell Davy the legend of the Widow Pond: a legend that goes back to a time even before Liberty became a town on the county map. This all before Frank went to war and came back with skill to handle the indomitable *Margrette*.

"But the strangest death here is when that Doctor fellow found floating face-down. Not a mark on his body, as though he had just fallen asleep– and when you sleep here, you ain't ever going to wake up!" Frank concludes with a snap of his burley fingers.

Davy never forgot the terror in his uncle's eyes, a terror marked through the flesh and into his soul. Homer only eyes the boy, as he might any other customer spinning a whiskey dream, then blurts out what is really on his mind.

"I like your Uncle Frank a lot, Dave, but he tends to exaggerate a lot. I've been living here all my life and I have yet to see a ghost– or even the monster! I would go down there myself just to see if what Red Eye says is true, except that it's Friday night, and somebody's got to tend bar."

"I'm not afraid of the Widow, or any monster!" Bubba reports bravely; and then turning to Davy, "Well, Dave, what do you say? Are you going with me, or do I go alone?"

Yet another challenge, Bubba's eyes as sharp daggers piercing his soul. Davy hesitates, reluctantly nods his head. He has no choice but to accompany Liberty's gladiator.

"Good," Homer congratulates. "You boys bring me back what's in that pond, and I'll give you free drinks all night!"

Homer knows the calculated pact into every man's soul.

"Not for all the whiskey in the world would I stick my hand in that water." Red Eye whines just above a whisper as Bubba and Davy disappear out the door.

Homer only crosses his arms like a patient corpulent locust gorged on quick summer days. Too soon winter might come, a shadow of south flying birds descending over his little domain. On that day, Homer and his liquor store will vanish away, as do all empty promises.

The widow Pond lay at the edge of the swamp behind the leaning obelisk of a brick and mortar smoke tower, all that remains of the Old Liberty Mill, and the home of Nela

Smith. The shallow basin actually belongs to a history even older than the mill, even older than Liberty's foundations.

Much of the tale lost. Only the crumbling sarcophagus of a once grand cotton plantation remains, exposed ribs of the labyrinth foundation, a vine covered section of wall with a charred archway, and tumbled mortar columns smashed to rubble. In the midst of this neglect, a fading circumference marked by the shallow barrier of dark moss-covered rocks with yellow-brown cattails clumped in the center. Shadowed depression of this Widow Pond the only thing left.

"Why do they call this the Widow Pond?" Bubba inquires, bracing himself against a rusted cotton gin in order to remove his shoes.

"This is where the Widow was drowned a long, long time ago." Davy whispers so as not to disturb the tenuous peace of this place, a peace that seems to seep out of the shadows disguised in a formidable ancient mist.

"So who was the Widow?"

"Like I said, Bubba, she died here. They say you can still see her ghost when the moon is full like it's going to be tonight."

"Was she pretty? I mean, was she old or young when she died? I don't think I would mind seeing the ghost of a pretty woman."

"I hear she is over a hundred years old. They say she was somewhere in her twenties when she died. The Widow is a ghost now, Bubba... not a living woman anymore."

"As long as she is pretty, I don't think it would matter. I've seen live women ugly enough to scare a ghost. So how did she come to be a ghost?"

"No one knows for sure. They say that after her husband died in battle fighting against the North– you see, Bubba, he was a Confederate Officer during the Civil War– they say, that each night after he died she would take long walks in her garden and sit beside this pond and cry. I suppose it was a place elegant then. There is a painting hanging in Miss Mabel's Garage of the first plantation built here. It was the grandest house of any I've ever seen."

"The first– you mean there is more than one?"

"I don't know how many there were altogether, but the one at the time of the Widow's death was the last. They say it burned down in the final days of the war, leaving no one to rebuild it."

Bubba rolls up his trouser legs and boldly steps into the rotting black water.

"It sure is cold! Maybe the Widow's soul is still down there!" Bubba teases. "So how do they say that she died?"

"Some say it was an accident and that she just slipped and struck her head on a rock. It sounds better than that she committed suicide. My Uncle Frank says he doesn't think it happened that way at all. He used to hang around a lot at Mabel's when he was younger. She told him that her Great Grand Daddy, who was only a little boy at the time of the Civil War, saw everything that happened from his bedroom window. According to Mabel, every night before going to sleep, her ancestor would watch the Widow come to the edge of the pond, sit for hours, and weep. Then one night a man steps out of the shadows and begins talking to her. He was one of the black slaves that worked the fields, big and powerful, with a deep clear voice.

"It is not good to waste so many sweet tears on the dead." He consoles the woman.

He then reaches out and tenderly touches her moist cheeks. The widow shakes with gratitude in shadow of his presence, feeling the weight of grief finally lifted.

"Tears be proof of a living heart," he continues, placing her fingers to his large brown lips.

He then departs quietly, as when first he appeared. Each night after this, he returns at the same hour. They only talk in the beginning and leave separately. The Widow was a beautiful woman, or so the young boy thought. He describes her as having long raven hair reflecting the shine of moonlight. She was delicate, with cool sensitive Irish green eyes. Men from all around courted her daily, but she would have nothing to do with any of them. Then one night the black man takes the Widow in his arms and kisses her. They act differently with each other after this. Sometimes they remain for hours near the pool holding each other tight. Often they disappear on long walks along hidden pathways. That little boy never said a word to anyone about what he saw. I guess, Bubba, you might say he was innocent."

"Innocent?"

"Yes, why not innocent?"

"You mean to tell me that little Peeping Tom couldn't guess what was really happening each night? You know what they say about women who get use to it. I mean, let's face it, Dave, with her husband gone, and all those sweaty hard slaves around her all the time, she would have had to be a Saint not to think about it!"

Twilight of distant stars sift through the evening sky, scarlet and gold seeping into sable hills, trailing the setting sun as it melts on the distant horizon. Two squirrels battle viciously over an obscure territory hidden from view, as the last embers of day squeeze between fleshy pink clouds furrowing into night.

"So go on, what happened next?"

By now, Bubba's feet and ankles are cut-off half way below the knees as he wades into the black stagnate pool. He stands monarch, challenging any creature above or below to dare challenge him back.

"One night the black man and the Widow talk about something that must have been very important. She begins crying. He turns coldly away, but then she says something that really gets him mad. He then slaps her hard, and runs into the night. The Widow remains beside the pond for a long time rocking silently back and forth. The moon shines bright and full, the night clear and beautiful. The boy must have dozed off. Suddenly, a sound startles him awake. The Widow lay face down in the pond, her flowing white dress filling the circumference, as a shimmering reflection just below the surface. Instantly the black man rushes out of a shadow, scoops her up in his arms, lifting the limp body heavenward, like a dark angel of death. They are as contrasting elements of light and shadow sculpted together, a macabre scene captured in a drama of tragedy. Perhaps, they would have remained like this forever, except for the screams of one of the house servants. She had stepped out on the balcony to find relief from the heat. It was all so terrible, an epic ghastly."

Bubba begins moving slowly, cautiously shifting his weight from side to side.

"Did they catch and hang him?"

"No— that man was so scared that he ran off, carrying the Widow's body into the swamp. The next morning, some white men from neighboring farms formed a posse and went out after him using bloodhounds. Before they could get a good start, it began raining, so they abandoned the hunt. By then it little mattered. They knew no one could survive long in the swamp without food and fresh water, especially *'a runaway slave who had never received anything, unless it fell from his Master's table'*. They figured the poor Widow's body left somewhere in the bog to join those souls abandoned to purgatory. That is the greater tragedy, Bubba; the widow denied a decent `Christian burying'. But in those turbulent days of war, many shared the same fate. Mabel's Great Grand Daddy said that he saw the Widow's ghost many times after that. She would come to the edge of the pond, sit and cry, just as she had done when alive. The worse part of it, Bubba, strange things began happening here after that night. All kinds of animals, big and small, horses and cows, rabbits and raccoons, even a man recorded drowned here. That was

Doctor Smith, when I was less than a year old. Not a bruise on him, or sign of any living soul being there since a long time."

Bubba looks skeptical. It is impossible for him to believe in something he cannot see. Deep down he wants to, yet prevented by hardness within. He wades to the center of the murky pool without the slightest hesitation, without flinching even once. From there he motions for Davy to follow.

"You know what I think?" He says analytically. "I think that Negro man made it out of the swamp alive. They have touch skin-- skin that doesn't bleed so easy! He probably made it clear to New Orleans and opened himself a `*House of the Rising Sun*'."

Davy cannot help but admire the way Bubba's mind works. He is like Sherlock Holmes and Mike Hammer put together, determined to see behind the facade of everything, to peel away every mask, to know every truth, no matter what the consequences. Davy has begun feeling like the bumbling assistant, to serve no other purpose in life than to magnify his brilliance.

"Are you afraid the Widow will get you, Dave?"

Bubba's voice sounds like a sledgehammer in his conscience, becoming a challenge of manhood, the opportunity to follow a born leader. By faith, Davy will do it– faith that as long as Bubba Baily near, he is safe even against spirits.

The water is indeed cold, with over an inch of slime on the bottom. Tiny soft skeletons melt under his pressure, generations of creatures formed by an unknown spark to live and to flourish, then perish here in this murky silence. He jumps back, nearly losing his footing because a crawfish scuttles across his feet. Bullfrogs begin bellowing with amusement from ebon caves beneath cracked spotted rocks clawed together in coils of gray cypress roots spreading serpentine from a network of zombie roots belonging to dead giants no longer present.

"In fact I don't think he ever murdered anyone!" Bubba proclaims, considering all other possibilities. "I think he and the Widow just made it look like she drowned. I mean, she was a proper lady, and him being a black slave and all. Besides, there was a war going on! I think they carefully planned it all. You see, Dave, the Widow knew that one of the servants would come looking for her because it was getting so late. They had everything planned perfectly, only they never suspect someone else watching. It is just luck for them that their little spy fell asleep when he did. After the stage, they hide somewhere in the Widow's house, a place special, and known only to herself. When everyone sure the two dead, they take all the valuables and burn down the house– kind of like Sherman burning Atlanta to destroy all the evidence! That way no one would ever get suspicious. Who knows, Dave, maybe the two of them start that ghost story themselves just to add a little immortality to their lives!"

Davy is truly amazed at Bubba's power of imagination. It all seems so logical, that how could it have happened any other way. He wonders why he never thought about it himself. Davy is about to offer his hand in congratulations, when all of a sudden cold slimy hands grab his feet.

"Jesus– something is down there! It's the Widow's ghost! Help me, Bubba! The Widow wants to take me!"

A thing alien has hold of him, refusing to let go, slithering around his feet and ankles, seeking to drag him down into the choking black water. He trips and falls submerged, chocking on the stagnant water. Twice he frees himself, only pulled down again, the numbing hands of the Widow clutching him body and soul into her everlasting embrace.

Then by some miracle, he is back on dry land. Davy's body tingles with a sensation not felt before, a sensation of the dead rising. Bubba is still standing knee deep in the pond, searching the bottom with his hands.

"I found something, feels all slimy like a squirming eel."

"Careful Bubba-- she's down there!"

"Here is your ghost!" He laughs, and raises an olive meshed sack out of the deep. "Not exactly what I expected to find, but things usually aren't."

Tadpoles of varying sizes squirm in the netting. Some escape, returning to the slime to continue their metamorphosis. The rest destined to perish in the crush of jelly bodies. Davy only signs with relief.

"Something else here," Bubba reports, untangling a heavy object form the webbed netting.

The rusted revolver has lain at the bottom beneath the shallow mud for a very long time, perhaps since the days of the Widow. The cocking mechanism caught by happenstance in the mesh when Davy dredged it across the bottom trying to escape. Resurrected here another piece added to the Liberty legends. Also clear, Old Red Eye had been telling the truth after all.

From this moment, Bubba hates the monster. He hates that it reminds him of his fear as a young boy growing up in bad neighborhoods. Hates that Red Eye is right, and there really might be a monster and maybe even some truth to the Widow story.

He says little when they arrive back at Homer's bar. Since Davy soaked to the bone, Homer offers him an old pair of pants and a shirt he finds somewhere in the back storage room for Davy to wear, at least until his clothes become dry. Almost they fit. Being that they are far too slim for Homer, he wonders to whom they had belonged. Bubba starts drinking hard, plays the pinball machine less well than usual, which even then better than anyone else could have.

"W.S.," Homer remarks, reading initials scratched on the handle of the revolver. "Maybe that stands for General William Sherman. By God– that has to be it! Bubba boy, I think you found here a real piece of history."

Homer tries all evening to get Bubba to trade him the revolver, but without success. Bubba is determined not to part with his newfound treasure. His father will tell him later that the revolver a cheap manufacture sometime in the last twenty years. Whoever W.S. was, it could not have been the Civil War General. Bubba will keep the revolver just the same.

"William Sherman," Red Eye proclaims thoughtfully. "Imagine me being part of finding something out of the history books! Mr. Homer, do you think that pistol has anything to do with that human skull over yonder?"

Homer ponders the white skull preserved on a table in corner beside the pinball machine, along with the only photo of him as a younger man and the yellowed certificate of a liquor license he never bothered to renew. Remains of this human cranial proof there are many unsolved mysteries in this world. All his prompt and glory kept in one place. Homer likes to keep things organized in his own way.

"Just could be old timer," Homer agrees. "I surely would like to add that pistol to my collection. Given enough time, maybe I can strike a deal with good O' Bubba boy!"

Bubba says nothing back, but continues to gaze into the flashing red and white lights of a soulless reality reflecting inhumanly across his face. The rage inside him continues to grow silently ever greater.

CHAPTER 20

The Liberty Monster

Whiskey races like fiery currents. Davy has never seen Bubba drunk– not mean drunk! And he is mean tonight. A meanness that festers inside him becomes more dangerous by the minute. There is no one who will stand against him. Not after the way he handled Cotton Mouth.

Bubba is not very tall, nor his countenance particularly menacing. Nevertheless, his upper body ripples with power. Thick muscled biceps, arms veined with webs of protruding blood vessels, and broad fist scarred from numerous battles. In combination with his speed, Bubba is formidable in everyone's mind. Perhaps, there might be one or two capable of giving him a fair challenge, but it is doubtful to think that any soul in Liberty could have taken Bubba in a face-to-face fight.

By six o'clock, only a few have not heard the firsthand account of the afternoon dredge of the Widow Pond. All continue to praise names of the true hero. Around six thirty Davy becomes sick and vomits until he is dry. He should have gone home then, except Homer knows an egg remedy that works to Davy's surprise. By a quarter past eight, he has succeeded in drinking himself sober again. Bubba drinks at least twice as much, and acts twice as sober; everyone else inside Homer's unquestionably drunk.

"These boys are brave sure enough to do what they done," Homer extols, raising a toast.

"They're just lucky that monster weren't around." Red Eye groans bitterly from a lonely corner near the door.

"Now Red Eye that just ain't called for–"
Homer's appeal too late, Bubba has heard.

"I'm not afraid of any monster or ghost in this hick town!"

Red Eye turns up his glass, slurps down the last drop.

"That's easy for you to say now, while you're safe and lots of people round. I got a silver dollar says you won't go down in the swamp at night. That goes for both of you!"

Of course, everyone knows Red Eye is lying about having any money.

"You have yourself a bet old man. Let me see your silver dollar."

Bubba likes to call a bluff. Maybe by doing so he feels superior, somehow better and more of what he considers a man ought to be.

"I'll cover Red Eye's bet, and throw in another dollar of my own." Homer announces quick to see a fresh new opportunity.

Bubba then turns to Davy.

"Well what do you say, Dave? You coming with me, or do I go down there alone?"

Had Davy not been drinking, he probably could have made some good excuse not to go, except he is now whiskey brave. Besides this, the local hero has summoned him once more to service.

"When do we go, Bubba?" Davy slurs, slapping his best friend on the back.

"Tonight—right now;"

They are still cheering back at the bar even after the duo swagger far down the corridor of Main Street. The full moon has just risen, riding upon billowing surfs of dark clouds, lighting the way for Liberty's young champions filled with unquenchable courage. They are soldiers of fortune going hunting, committed to finding the biggest frog there ever was!

They first stop at Bubba's place to get a few things they will need. Bubba instructs Davy to remain by the door. His father lay passed-out in an overstuffed armchair in front of the television. The show Amos and Andy is playing with the King Fish smiling his famous alligator teeth. Bubba steps quietly into an adjacent room. Mr. Baily shifts violently because of a dream he is having. His left arm falls down. There are numerous scars, like razor cuts crisscrossing each other, and a series of numbers tattooed above the wrist. Davy makes a mental note to ask Bubba later what those numbers mean. Moist tobacco odor permeates the air, a nauseating smell that makes Davy want to gag. Pieces and stubs of black cigars litter everywhere: filling every dish, every kind of receptacle, serving as an ashtray overflowing with moldering ashes. Bubba reappears with a bundle in his arms. Davy follows him outside.

The night air charged with energy, a certain uneasiness that continues to grow with the passage of every moment. Streaks of amber lighting flash behind giant warlord mountains, as the elements prepare cutting swords for some great and decisive battle. Bubba has thought of everything. He produces a pair of green Sears & Roebuck leggings for each of them. There is only one flashlight, and one carbon blue steel frog gig with two serrated prongs. It will be enough for their purpose.

"We'll need this, too." He says, and produces an oddly shaped bottle tucked under his arm.

"What is it?"

"Pass Over wine." Quickly adding: "But don't worry, it won't make you a Jew."

They have just stepped into the backyard when the door springs open.

"Benjamin, where do you and your friend go this late?"

Mr. Baily sways menacingly in the doorway. Davy realizes for the first time just how big of a man he really is. Outside of his cluttered watch repair shop, he more resembles a lost movie prop from the set of Godzilla. Davy half expects that any moment a breath of flame will expel from his mouth.

"We're going frog gigging, Papa." Bubba replies affectionately.

"Then be careful of quicksand." Baily warns. "At least I'm glad to see someone with you. In life it is good to have a brother to help us in our hour of need."

Mr. Baily then retreats slowly back inside his lair. There is something surreal about this scene, which will stay in Davy's mind for the rest of his life.

"What do you say we get started on that wine?" Bubba says, leading the way.

Davy cannot make up his mind if the wine sweet, or if it is bitter– or even if he likes it, being different from anything he has ever tasted before. Bubba brags that his father has cases of the stuff.

"He got it cheap just before we left New York. My old man always likes a bargain!"

"Bubba, why did your father call you Benjamin and what are those numbers tattooed on his arm?"

"You mean numbers like these?" He says rolling up his shirtsleeve.

Stamped on his left arm in almost the same place are several numbers marking Bubba's flesh. These are not neat and stenciled like the numbers on Mr. Baily's arm. They appear crude and unevenly spaced.

"This belonged to my Uncle, a gift from the Nazis. I did it myself. It hurt like you can't imagine. But at least I didn't get blood poison."

"But why would you do something like that Bubba?"

"I think my old man would be glad if he knew. At least he would know he's not the only one. My mother left because of those numbers– and you wouldn't believe how many times we had to move. This is the true mark of a Jew."

He then rolls down his sleeve. Davy does not know what to say, so he says nothing at all. When they have emptied the whole contents of the bottle, Bubba smashes it against a rock and begins to swear.

"Let's go hunt us that damned big frog!"

They descend toward the swamp, past the house of Nela Smith, past the edge of the cemetery. They could have cut through Nela's back yard and saved themselves maybe ten minutes, but then they would have had to pass by the Widow Pond again. One goblin is enough.

A lone crow calls auspiciously, concealed in a shivering Ash grove. They both happen to look up at the same time and freeze in mid step. Looming over them and hunched above the shadows of trees with pitchfork in hand, is a hump-backed giant with bright burning feet, silhouetted threateningly against silver gray of approaching thunderheads.

Spontaneously they break into laughter, commenting on their silliness. This monstrous Goliath nothing more than another toothless specter, a freak of black smoke belching out of two fiery-lipped chimneys straddled atop the mill. Then heaven and earth pass away, as they penetrate into the willows of brown cattails, announcing entry into the barrier of true swamp.

The moon, also surrealistic tonight, distant, wanes as the slow pulse of the universe, blinking in and out of existence. The stage now set for a masterpiece performance of eternity. Sudden gusts of wind sweep through misty avenues, then hisses away into dead silence. Tangled strands of gray Spanish moss cascade down, as disease-infested hair of corpses draped over twisted petrified skeletons, all grotesque. All damned to the same damnation. Shadowy legions stand ready in formation, stretching far as the eye can perceive, snared in a hoary web of slow decay; all making Davy feel in his gut even hope abandoned here.

"It sure is spooky, Bubba," Davy whispers in sudden realization of where they are.

The whiskey had made him courageous, the wine foolishly bold. Now the effects of both are starting to pass off. Deep down he wishes to be home in his bed with the covers drawn over his head.

"Bull!" Bubba scoffs, shining his light at a clump of moldering brush balled around constricted roots of a fallen Cypress. "Fear is something put in people's mind to make it easy for others to control them."

"But Bubba, don't you believe in hell, either?"

Davy has his own doubts; those doubts just now fewer.

Bubba only howls with laughter, and then becomes more serious than Davy has ever witnessed.

"So what is Hell, Dave? Can you tell me? Is there anyone living that knows for sure what hell is?"

"Preacher Morgan says Hell is a burning lake. That the souls of evil men will be thrown there to suffer for all eternity..." Davy regrets already having brought up the subject.

Bubba spins around and faces him. Never before has Davy felt such raw fury.

"You want to know what hell is. I'll tell you! Hell is when you want to die and can't. My father told me lots of times about the way his brother died. He was a Jew just like me, Dave. This number on my arm was his number. The Nazis didn't like Jews. So they built Concentration Camps with gas chambers, and then herded people into them like animals. Can you imagine what it must be like being a man, labeled as a cow marked for butchering? It's all history now, Dave; but it really happened. Still it's funny how short human memory! My Uncle was a tailor and lived in a ghetto near the center of Berlin. Then Berlin was only one city, only the ghettos had walls. He was on his way to work one morning. They just grabbed him off the street, shoved him into a packed cattle car. By chance, my father was in the same car. There was no such thing as good luck in those days if you were a Jew. My father was young and strong then, his brother younger and even stronger. His name was Benjamin, same as mine. Only I like Bubba better, a nickname of a hero in a movie I saw when I lived in the Bronx. Papa would have a fit if he knew— and be sure that you don't tell anyone! My father and Uncle Benjamin figured that together they would survive. Nevertheless, they made a vow between them that if one should die, the other would do what he must to carry on the family tradition. Upon arrival at the camp, they again thought themselves lucky because the Nazi doctors chose them both to be medical assistants. Not the kind of assisting you might think, Dave! The Nazis were doing medical experiments. Things that would make your skin crawl off. My father survived because he had a rare blood type. Uncle Benjamin was not so fortunate. The doctors wanted to put some new kind of drops in his eyes. When he resisted, it took four soldiers to restrain him. For this, they surgically remove his manhood, making him eat his pride. Then they put the drops in his eyes anyway. It turned out a bad experiment. Still they wouldn't let him die. My father had to watch his brother stumble for weeks through the corridors. Because of his promise, he could do nothing. Those monsters enjoyed keeping my uncle alive like that, wanted to make an example of him to anyone else who might think to resist in the future. Then one day I guess they got tired of seeing him bump into things. They patted him on the back, told him to go naked into a shower with a bunch of women and children. He went without question, without any hesitation. Uncle Benjamin knew what those showers were for, but he didn't care. He walked in there proud as when he was still a man and had strength. He went because he didn't want to live anymore. When you're dead I don't think it matters rather there is a Hell or not. It's while you're still alive that you got to worry!"

There is nothing for Davy to say. No experience in his short life that could have prepared him for the horror he has just heard. He feels sad for Bubba, forced to live the life of a dead man, and perhaps never know the meaning of his own life. Maybe his father had wanted it that way. He feels sorry that Bubba might never dream his own dreams, and wonders what kind of dreams those might be.

After many minutes, they arrive at the edge of a misty basin, a shifting gaseous lake stretching far away into the nether region. It seems to go on forever, snaked with many dangers.

"We can't go on, Bubba! Beyond here is quicksand. You got to know where the safe places are. Even then..."

Davy's voice trails away and falls like a pebble into the darken ocean, as he remembers tales he has heard about the many lost souls that journeyed past this point, never to return. If the dead rule anywhere on earth, it is here.

"You wait here, Dave," Bubba orders; "I'm going to swing around and see if there's any other way."

"But there's not!"

"It won't hurt anything to try."

"Come on, Bubba, let's go back. We'll tell them that we couldn't find the monster. No one can say that we didn't try. Besides, I'm not feeling so good. Everything about this place gives me the creeps!"

Bubba immediately lashes out, his teeth bared for a kill.

"I think you are a damn coward, Dave! I knew it from the first time I set eyes on you. So don't try and tell me what you think we should do. From now on, you do what I tell you, or you'll be spitting teeth!" Adding determinedly, "You will wait here while I circle around."

Another challenge, but one he will not accept. Bubba is right. Davy is a coward. He always knew it, but hoped no one else would notice. He had always been the biggest boy in his class, able to bluff his way through. He had in fact gotten into only one fight his whole life. That was just after turning fifteen, challenged by a kid one year younger and almost half his size. He was scared even then. One sucker punch, the kid ran away, the fight over. Once again, his bluff had worked. But there is no bluffing this Bubba Baily. Davy knows that if necessary, he will wait here all night for Bubba to return.

To define a swamp is, in a sense, to define the beginning and the end of all creation. It is a mother to every orphan that stumbles into her nest, a hotbed of life, nurturing to the issue of every seed. It is a place benign; a place hostile. An expanse seemingly empty, mixed with fertile promise beyond the deltas to hatch the offspring of future civilizations. To those past dying, already dead, and blind to the hidden truth of genesis, it is a place of terror. To those that have nowhere else to go, it is a refuge of peace, of hope, and a new beginning. Within the bosom of this soul flourishes the truest definition of primeval spirit, untamed and beautiful, resurrecting to memory those truly alive, while casting a snare for ignorant trespassers. Somewhere in this great domain rules the nameless monster that everyone fears in the darkness of every imagination.

Minutes pass like hours. The wind rises, falls, and begins rising again, moaning woefully through this graveyard of rotting timbers. The moon blinks on and off like a distant distress beacon, suspended in a veil of black clouds sweeping across the sky. The swamp has also begun to change, fading into grey indistinct shapes ever more cabalistic. The ocean of fog darkens slowly, funneled through meandering corridors, all leading to a dead-end. Bivouacs of enigmatic shadows emerge instantly from the depths, rising up as corpses in Davy's mind. A fury of heavy familiar splashes nearby, splashes heard at least once before in the swamp.

"Bubba... is that you?" Davy whispers.

Only silence, as the dull throb of blood races to his head followed by loud flapping, the sound of great leathery wings beating the air, a bloodcurdling shriek, the sickening crunch of soft bones!

"Bubba– answer me for Christ sake-- is that you?"

Again splashing, this time more near--so near that the odor of fresh swamp mud permeates the surrounding air, the mist changed to a sieve oppressive. Gripped by irrational desperation, Davy starts to run. If Bubba made those splashes, he certainly would have answered him! Maybe it is Bubba, only now no longer able to say anything! Maybe Bubba has found the monster– or worse-- the monster has found him!

Davy's fear changes to terror, as he imagines what surely must have happened to Bubba. What will surely happen to him next! He runs blindly, the clumsy leggings resisting his momentum. He trips and falls, bouncing instantly back on his feet. He is only vaguely aware of pain from a sharp stick piercing his jaw. Almost he can feel a hot steamy breath on the back of his neck! The terrible heat shot from those demon eyes! The swamp floor opens suddenly and without warning. Davy falls headlong into oblivion, his screams as the lamentation of the tormented. He manages to regain his footing, stumbles again, and tumbles into a pit of everlasting darkness.

Swamp mud oozes into his mouth and nose, the choking bile vomited from the very bowels of the earth. Spongy, moldy hands clutch at his leggings, pulling him down... down into a nauseous hell from whence there is no escape. Already he is beyond the point of no return, too exhausted even to struggle. Suddenly, something incredibly strong grabs the back of his neck, lifting him bodily like a nearly drowned kitten out of the clutches of certain death. He is resurrected whole!

Once again light returns to the swamp. In his panic to escape, Davy has rushed head long into that treacherous pit of bog. Although impossible to imagine– howbeit true-- the monster's hand has saved him.

The night creature stands perched on the decaying pentacle of a shattered Cypress trunk, with arms extended in benevolent victory. It is a giant, more than six feet tall, with enormous arms and legs, and with a head larger than a Halloween pumpkin. The crest of a dark hump ascends above the right shoulder, resembling an impish little demon balanced on his back and whispering into that ear. The semblance of a face, broad and flat, with features not entirely defined, or else nearly erased. It has large round eyes, possibly lidless, giving the impression of two orbiting spheres askew and out of kilter from the observer's point of view. The nose is practically nonexistent, with only a lipless slit sliced below where the mouth should have been. Liberty's monster is completely bald and without ears to speak of. Only tiny wart clusters instead of eyebrows, nor any discernable human features. Along the chin and neck pieces of a jigsaw puzzle composed of pale matted splotches, where the skin has melted, and fused back together. Most strikingly is the fiery scepter of a chrome-plated trident, as long as the devil's pitchfork held high in one hand ready for a fresh kill.

"*Weistbaily*," proclaims the creature, drool spreading down a misshapen chin. "Father say Weistbaily frog. Lady say frog *Xeantee*!" He makes a jabbing motion with his trident. "Weistbaily hunt frog brother-- *Weistbaily Xeantee Prince of Frogs*!"

In Davy's mind, ghastly choking sounds issue from the slit in its face, a horrible crackling noise that ripples sharply through the fabric of this dark principality. It is laughter of the monster! Now Liberty's goblin has both purpose and a name. Weistbaily is name of a self-proclaimed prince, rising regally out of curling mist, as an emissary of the night accompanied by chorus of singing frogs.

What Bubba thought when he saw Davy kneeling before the monster, he never did say. Only it must have seemed strange to him. Maybe it even makes him a little jealous. He swoops out of the mist waving his black frog gig as an angel armed.

He jabs the tenebrous instrument at the whiteness of the creature's throat. Weistbaily looks surprised, fences the blow, leaping from the perch of his throne. Again, Bubba jabs. Weistbaily effortlessly parries the blow, sparks flying around them both. Then Weistbaily tires of this game. With one quick easy movement, he grabs Bubba's gig, jerking it out of his hand, like taking a toy from a child, sending the inferior instrument flying into the misty basin. Bubba, now unarmed, does something Davy will never quite understand.

He pounces on Weistbaily, locks his legs around the monstrous waist and begins bashing him in the face. It has no apparent effect on the creature at all. With one hand, Weistbaily raises Bubba at arm's length and gently lowers him to the ground. Bubba struggles. However, there is no escaping that tremendous grip. A cloud closes once more over the moon, as a giant hand catching a fluttering moth. Splashes recede into the distance, the croaking laughter echoing through the swamp in haunting reminder of the true sovereign of this place.

"Well, Bubba, what do you think about the monster now? You still think you can bully him like you bullied me?"

Bubba says nothing back. He just picks up his flashlight and heads for Homer's bar. Davy trails behind him, maintaining a safe distance. Both their bluffs now called. Weistbaily has proven this night without any doubt who is the better man. Only Red Eye remains and even he is past talking. Homer has just finished wiping out the last glass, placing it carefully on a shelf behind the bar.

"You boys made it back just in time to help me put old Red Eye out," he says with a yawn.

"We saw Weistbaily!" Davy exclaims.

"Who the hell is Weistbaily?" Homer is not amused.

"That's the monster's name," Davy sputters. "He claims to be the Prince of Frogs."

"Never heard of such a thing– you boys are just pulling my leg to get another free drink."

"It's true, Badger! You owe us two dollars," Bubba insists.

"Now how can I know for sure you boys aren't making it all up? Unless, of course, you brought back his head..."

Homer's smile turns into a full grin. They proceed to tell Homer how Weistbaily had appeared out of the mist, standing seven feet tall and wielding a silver pitchfork. They describe him as the monster he is. They leave out the part about how Davy panicked, and how the creature manhandled Bubba, saying only that he seems invincible by mortal standards. Homer only grunts from time to time, keeping an eye on a recently repaired sundial clock hanging above the door.

"Well, boys, that just ain't proof enough for me to shell out two bucks. I tell you what, come on back tomorrow night and we'll talk about it–"

"No!" Bubba protests angrily.

He then takes something heavy out of his Gaiter legging and slaps it hard on the bar counter.

"Is this proof enough for you?"

Homer's face turns blank, his jaw dropping slowly open.

"Where exactly did you find that?"

"After I left Dave I circled around to see if the ground was solid enough to walk on. At one point the under growth became so thick that I had to get down and crawl on all fours. That's when I found it, just lying on a rock as though someone had left it there by mistake. And from the looks of it, I would say it has been there for a long time."

The hand-made Bowie Knife has indeed been there a long time. The blade turned altogether brown with rust, the black wooden handle dry and cracked. Homer just stares at it in pure astonishment.

"Well... seeing as how you brought this back..."

Davy has never seen Homer struggle so much with his words.

"I tell you what, Bubba, give me this old knife, and I'll give you, not just two, but three dollars– and a free drink to boot!"

Just like that, the deal sealed. An hour later, they help prop Red Eye against an empty crate in the alley behind the bar. Bubba ends up spending the three dollars on more drinks. He never offers Davy even one. Maybe he just decides that his part does not deserve anything. Davy will go less often to Homer's after this night. Decides it is best to leave things alone for a while. He knows Bubba Baily determined to the end, the final test still to come.

"I'll get that freak for this!" He swears after Davy, as they part ways. "You know, Dave, that everything I said tonight is true! You don't understand now, but you will one day. One day you will remember that Bubba Baily true to the end!"

That night it rains. Old men rock tediously in their rocking chairs thanking Jesus, animals howl relief in the hills, and red brick dust washes from the sides of the cotton mill mixed with dye. It is still raining late next morning when a rainbow of promise breaks over the swamp. There are floods of complaints to City Hall that all the lower pastures underwater and something terribly wrong about the drainage. This causes a great stir of alarm. Several wires promptly dispatched from Pixley to the State Governor's Mansion expressing local concern and partitioning an investigation. It will be several months before proper reply received.

BOOK FIVE

Seeds of Eden

CHAPTER 21

Where Shadows Lie

It is sunny all day, and would have been perfect, except for the continual threat of rain clouds that hang undecidedly on the far horizon. Nela relishes days like these. Not too warm, not too cold, a pleasant balmy breeze that sweeps through the canyon valley from the distant Atlantic, proclaiming summer's performance near an end.

Days like these, Nela realizes just how much she loves life. How short the seasons, how nearly finished the debut of Nela Smith, as the theater lights dim for the final act. There is a time all must end. These magnificent stage props taken away like so many empty dreams, some used again in other performances, embellishing other plays: some tragic, some comedies, some cathartic– all ultimately burned with fire and changed to shadow.

Once upon a time Nela believed in reality, believed that the world material, a thing desired, and to be handled. Yet, time and time again she is reminded of the truth, as things new wax old in her hands, the mind always searching desperately for some elusive bright element to satisfy the void. This is the sad price of being rich. The knowledge that things are just things and nothing lasts forever, not even secret passages of the heart. All changed to shadow in the end. Nela fears her heart empty since too many years, choosing to exist surrounded by the props. At least these serve a purpose until last curtain fall.

Nela awakens with a chill. Not because of the air, but because of some other presence remembered from seasons past. She has fallen asleep in the white washed swing chair suspended from the big oak in her back yard. Lately she does this more often. Each time a strangeness of feeling overwhelms her senses, a feeling that she is fading into the seasons… into the very fuse of eternity. It is a pleasant feeling; also, a feeling more terrifying each time it happens.

"You sure mighty gentle looking when you be sleeping," speaks a voice from nowhere.

"Abraham! You ought to know better than to sneak up on people! If I had a gun I might have shot you dead."

"If I had enough teeth I'd eat me a good old steak. Been a mighty long time since I had a steak; Lord knows it's been a mighty long time."

Abraham stands positioned in a shadow just in front of the swing. His brown mottled skin blends so well with the surrounding shade that at casual glance, he still remains completely camouflaged.

"You could not afford to buy a real steak even if you had all your teeth!" Nela huffs indignant.

"Sometimes a man can eat rock before he can belly the hardness in some folk's hearts. It don't matter though `cause meats for the belly and the belly for meats' and whatever the good Lord sees fit to put on a man's table is better than the dish of a king."

"Oh, enough of this, silliness," Nela flusters; "so what brings you on my property?"

"'Cause you be a lady that knows things."

"What on earth do you mean?"

"You and me are both getting mighty old," Abraham yawns tiredly.

"Of course we are getting old!" Nela retorts edgily. "Why? You fear I might die first and leave you with no place to live?"

Reference to the little shanty in the swamp remains a subject of contention even after all these years. Like most of the surrounding property between here and the cemetery, it belongs to the Smith estate. William had discovered the shanty shortly after purchasing the old plantation land. At first, by Nela's own insistence, he had desired the Negro to move out. After compassionate consideration, decides to allow him to stay. Abraham was already old even then. It seemed that he could not possibly live much longer. William actually takes a liking to the old black man, preferring to spend many of his free hours on the collapsing shanty porch, smoking a curious weed Abraham calls Rabbit Tobacco, and listen to the sounds of the swamp night. Now William dead, while and old Abraham still looks the same as then. A fact Nela jealously resents.

"No mam... I ain't afraid of that. But there be lots around here that you don't know! Your doctor husband knowed, but he's done passed on; and all these years old Abraham has kept things to his self. But I ain't going to walk much longer in this world."

"What could you possibly know?"

Nela does not even try to conceal her annoyance.

"I know your husband treated me kindly, and I ain't ever going to forget that. It be time you hear things he said. Maybe the good Lord will move in your heart with mercy. 'Cause the way things stand now, he just ain't got much other hope. I knew you when you was just a young girl pulling up my flowers just for spite. But now you be a grown lady, and got to act lady-like."

"I do wish you would make some sense! I am cold, and I do not intend to spend all evening talking about nothing. Besides, you paid more attention to those damn flowers than you did to me! Now if you have something to say, then say it!"

"He was going to tell you himself except he never got the chance. I remember the first time he brought that young girl to my house. She was all beat up and crying. The doctor wanted her to stay with me a few days 'cause she was pregnant and he was a-feared for her. But that poor child was too scared. Her husband worked a mill shift, and he would be expecting her home. I said she could come anytime she wanted. She come all by herself a few times just to talk mostly, just to sit there on the porch and stare out at the swamp. That girl had the saddest green eyes I ever saw, excepting for your eyes, Ms. Pixley. Your eyes always been the saddest I ever saw-- blue as a summer sky-- but always sad."

"You do not call me that unless I give you permission. I am a Smith now! My eyes are the same as they were then. Why did you leave and never come back?"

"Your daddy knew what was in your heart, and so sent me away. It weren't my fault."

"A white man would have at least tried."

"But I ain't white, and sometimes it's better to let white folks be with white folks. But I never forgot you, even after all these years."

"Really, Abraham... is that the truth?"

"I swear by the good book that it be true, Ms. Nela."

"It is nice to hear you call me by my name."

Nela's eyes change glassy. After all these years, it feels good to hear from his own lips that this man of sculpted presence had not rejected after all.

"I am sorry Abraham. I truly am. Please continue with what you came to tell me."

"Yes…Nela," his voice as a soothing breeze to her perished soul. "Sometimes your doctor husband would come, too, just so we could all sit and talk together, or to listen to me play my harmonica. That girl say there was no place else on earth more peaceful. One night when it was storming bad, she come and left something at my door. I knowed plain well it was her. I could feel it sure in my bones. Few days later, I heard she was dead. What that girl left in the night was a baby boy all burned and suffering. Maybe you recall how I come and fetched your doctor husband out of bed."

Nela reflects back to those many years in the past. She does remember that night. Remembers ferocity of the storm, the fitful specter of a dream, and how she and her husband awakened by the old man's desperate pounding on the back door.

"You gotta' come, Doc Smith! You gotta' come now!" Abraham keeps repeating over, and over again.

William stays gone all night. When he arrives home next morning, her husband more troubled than ever she saw him before. William breaks down and weeps telling her that Whitey Miller arrested for the murder of his young wife. He never tells Nela why-- not really-- and some selfish instinct inside her never wanted to know more.

"Do not say any another word," Nela pleas.

"It's got to be said, Nela. There be more at stake here than just your feelings, or mine."

Abraham then motions to someone behind Nela. She spins around, instantly catching her breath.

"Oh my Lord–"

"He won't hurt you none, Nela. He be gentle as a lamb."

"Weistbaily– Prince of Frogs–" mumbles the monster, dribble coming out of the sides of its mouth.

Nela is altogether speechless. At first, she feels fear, which changes to revulsion by sight of the alien creature. Then an emotion of pity frees from the bowels of Nela's being, a pity springing from the poison of her own guilt. Finally, she must look away. What can this thing possibly have to do with her William?

"He ain't got nobody to take care of him exceptin' me," Abraham says softly. "And I ain't got long left. There be a lot of talk lately about there be a monster. But he ain't no monster, no more than a frog be a crocodile."

"I fail see how this has anything to do with me."

"Look real close, Nela. Look with your heart. He be changed sure enough, but it be clear as day. The doc told me how you was there the night he be born."

Nela looks. She does not wish to see, does not wish to know. Never has she beheld a face more disfigured. It only vaguely looks human. Only the vestige of a nose melted from intense heat, a cartoon mouth drawn without lips, and one side of the face completely featureless. A characteristic particularly distinctive is the bulbous hump on his back bulging through a tear in his ragged shirt like wings beginning to sprout. The eyes… something about the azure calm hauntingly familiar... something nearly forgotten, and long ago, a vague impression from some buried memory in her unconscious.

"He was burned something terrible." The older man's voice reminds Nela of other things from long ago. "The doctor come and did what he could. He knowed that baby be dead before morning. But he didn't die– no mam! It was a miracle. He cried all next day, and many days after. Then he stopped, and never cried no more. Your husband, he knowed who that baby belong. He told me he was aiming to make things right."

"It cannot be-- no it is impossible!"

"Yes mam, it be him sure enough. I kept him secret all these years, but I can't keep him no more. Maybe you have no cause to help this boy. Your doctor husband thought different. And in your Christian heart, I know you will do what's right."

Nela's eyes turn instantly to ice.

"You leave– do you hear? I will not have you talk to me this way— do you hear? If you do not get off my property I swear I will call the Sheriff!"

Then her eyes meet those of the creature, and the lash of her anger changes to deep sobbing.

"Forgive me, Abraham," she weeps. "Please just go away for now. I need some time to think."

"Yes, mam, I'll be going. Please, I'm begging you to help this boy afore it be too late."

"One more thing," Nela says engagingly, as the old man rises to leave. "Who in the world named him Weistbaily?"

"He doesn't talk much, Nela, and when he does it don't sometime make much sense. That's what he calls himself, and Lord knows I got no idea why. He's just a boy full of pity, and lonely. It don't matter much what he say, it's what's in the heart that counts. You think about what I said, Nela, but ain't nobody knows how long the good Lord will tarry. When he comes it'll be like a thief in the night."

Nela stiffly watches the old man vanish into the encroaching shadows of the swamp followed by the monster with human eyes. How terribly he must have suffered. Why all the secrets-- why had William not told her? Surely, together, they might have done something. Why condemn an innocent baby to an existence of poverty and pain when there was this huge house with so many empty rooms that might have sheltered him all these years? Then again, she never did understand much of what really happened that long ago.

Through the veil of descending twilight, Nela's mind drifts back to a hot summer day so many years ago. Whitey Miller was such a beautiful man then, strong and hewn, as though an artisan had just recently carved him from a unique piece of white stone. He knocks on the back door looking for a little yard work for pay.

"I just got into town," he says politely. "I ain't got a regular job yet. But I'm a hard worker and you don't need to pay me much."

Nela usually did not allow strangers in her home when William away. Lately they argue over the smallest of matters; their relationship strained with a future now less certain. Sometimes he is gone the whole night, visiting patients that will never be able to pay him. Even when he was home, William often too exhausted to tend to the needs of a wife. Especially long are the nights, when dreams promise more than life can deliver. Then one night they fight about money. Not his money, but about her money-- money that paid the bills and made it possible for him to provide the services of a country doctor without living himself poor. Only this time he leaves her in confused anger. He will be gone for almost a week. Although at the time, it seems longer.

Maybe this reason enough to invite the young man with serpent's eyes into her parlor to have a glass of freshly made lemonade. She cannot help but admire his broad muscled shoulders, the precision way his hand grasps the shivering glass. She has just finished reading a copy of Ovid's Metamorphoses, a favorite classic since she was a sophomore studying literary history. This moment she feels certain this younger man's visitation nothing less than mythical. Indeed, the pigment of his flesh by far too pale to be anything less than mythical, the young Whitey Miller everything she always dreamed possible. The odor of his sweat fills the parlor like incense, his smile slaying her to the heart as decisively as any sword, the blind witness of the Seth Thomas clock on the mantle in the next room ticking the moments quickly away.

Whitey comes often to her after that, always when the good doctor away. Nela in turn gives him money. She dreams as a woman in love. She thinks about a possible future, a future without William, a future sequestered in the strong arms of Whitey Miller. Then one day, without explanation, the charming prince of her dreams stops coming at all. He never did thank Nela. In time, she accepts to expect nothing more than what already received. Later she hears from her husband that the young Miller man got on at the mill and recently married the younger Tracy girl. After days of persistent inquisition from his wife, William tells all she needs to know.

"Yes, Nela, she is very pretty. Like a fresh summer magnolia just starting to bloom. Whitey already had enough money to make a down payment on one of the mill houses."

Then dolefully adds, "They may even find some happiness together."

To Nela's content, this happiness not meant to blossom. A rumor spread around town that Lori Tracy already pregnant by the time she and Whitey married. The rumors suggest Whitey not even the father and that Lori less than faithful while her husband works his shifts. Even though there is no evidence to support any of these accusations, the rumors persisted. In a small town gossip often justified by its own witness. Nela cannot say that she is sorry really. Still she thinks the gossip disturbing. One predictable afternoon less than nine months later, Lucy Tracy summons William to the Miller residence. Lori has gone into labor. It is about half past three Saturday afternoon, Whitey told to go home early before the end of his second shift.

"Nela, this time I need you to come with me," William pleas. "That girl has had a bad term and I'll need someone who knows what to do in case of trouble."

In times past, Nela has assisted her Doctor husband; that just after they moved from Atlanta to the Liberty Peninsula, when his new practice just starting. William had grown weary of big city life, wishing for a more rural environment, where he could help those most in need. He reasons that his service not essential in a big city with hundreds of doctors from which to choose.

"All the money in the world can't buy even a little peace. I want to provide relief to those who most need it. Together, Nela, we can be that difference!"

So they move from the thriving Atlanta suburbs to this rural community where his skills as a healer most needed. At first, they try to have children, but without success. William is convinced the problem lies within him. Like everything else, he willingly accepts the guilt. Nela later wonders why after so many years, on this night particular night he asked her attendance again.

"It's been so long, William... I don't know if I will remember what to do." Nela is terrified at the thought of confronting Whitey Miller again– and in William's presence! Still some part of her that wants to go. But why this time– why is her husband making this demand? Did he suspect all along, wishing only to torment her?

"I know this girl," William confides. "Her pregnancy has been a difficult one from the start, and her husband not a reasonable man. I wouldn't ask you, Nela, unless I felt it important."

The way William gazes into her eyes squashes her fears and her guilt to rubble... such beautiful eyes, calm, capable of pardoning every conceivable mortal sin. Nela will follow him to certain execution if requested.

Lucy, Lori's older sister, meets them at the door. It is just past seven o clock in the evening by the time they arrive. Nela knows just what to do. With Lucy's aid, she replaces the bed linen with clean sheets and puts a cauldron of water on the stove to boil. Whitey stumbles in three hours later smelling of Homer's bar. Whitey makes it no secret that he dislikes Lucy, a feeling that is more than mutual.

"Well, Doc, is it a boy?" Whitey demands without ceremony.

"There is a problem, Mr. Miller. Lori has been in labor for nearly four hours now, and has already lost her water. Something is not right. I think a caesarean is advisable under these circumstances."

"No cutting– I don't want her to have no scars. Lori's going to be just fine! You'll see Doc– she's going to be just fine."

Lori cries out sharply from inside the bedroom. William, Nela, and Lucy rush in to stay at Lori's side, while Whitey stagers to the refrigerator to take a beer. At first there appears to be no change. Then William sees what he thinks is a head trying to emerge. Upon closer examination, however, he realizes it is not a head. He knows immediately what must be done if the mother has any chance to survive.

"Get the forceps from my medical bag– quickly!" He snaps at Nela.

Dousing the instrument with alcohol, he slips the steel tongues into the contracting canal. First, he must find the head. Believing this accomplished, he commits the unborn to providence and pulls with all his might. The head did not separate, as he feared certain it would. The infant slides screaming into Nela's waiting hands, painful blue marks embossed on either temple. Like the Roman legend of Remus clutching the heel of his brother Romulus, a twin brother follows through the birth canal.

Cause of the delivery complication becomes immediately clear. The first infant has a malformed hump on its back. The head abnormally large and the appendages are unusually thick. William has seen at least one similar birth in neighboring Pixley, only that infant died. However, the second twin appears physically normal, with calm blue eyes almost familiar. In fact, one might say he is exceptionally beautiful, almost perfect. There is no predicting the roulette of nature.

"It's a damn freak!" Whitey bellows upon hearing the news, as though his healthy son does not matter at all.

The only thing his mind can comprehend is the bulge of that imperfect hump. He curses that he has heard the rumors, but wanted to believe them untrue. Now he is sure they are true. He begins calling his exhausted wife names, terrible abusive names, and with such fierceness in his eyes, William fears for the young mother's safety.

"Perhaps it would be best if Lori and the babies were to spend the night in our house–"

"Lori ain't going nowhere!" He growls angrily.

"I promise nothing will happen to her, or the babies. It would just be for a day or two. I can take her in our car.

The back seat is big. She can lie down." Turning to Nela, "We would take good care of them– wouldn't we Nela?"

Nela nods automatically, the events of this night altogether horrifying. She suddenly realizes that the man of her romantic illusions is in fact a monster. She is now witness to what he really is and has been all along. Nela awakened from another dream, sees a truth secondary to the turmoil of her emotions. She regrets those days of passion and pleasure spent with this beautiful pale changeling. Yet, for some dark and unknown reason, Whitey still represents the summit of her lust, which also makes her feel in the moment bitterly confused.

Whitey treats this woman of his past with cool detachment, as he may have treated any stranger. Perhaps, it is all an act; or perhaps he really feels nothing at all. Nela will never know, only that Whitey Miller never once so much as ventures a glimpse of recognition into her eyes. Just another feeling of rejection, another dream dashed on the shores of her imagination. Nela has become accustom to this feeling, a feeling she has felt so many times before. Now only hardness grows in her heart, becoming all the more hard and unforgiving, a hardness that will remain a heel of distain against all serpents for as long as she will live. Nela is just that way when it comes to rejection. Like all things bought with money, the pleasure sweet in the mouth, but made bitter in the gut of reality.

"You get the hell out of here!" Whitey demands rudely; and then makes a menacing jester toward Lucy. "And take her with you!"

"I'm not going to leave my sister to the hands of a mad man!"

Lori sits up weakly and promises that everything will be alright until morning. She looks directly into William's eyes, a look so deep that Nela did not altogether miss the meaning, refusing to see it then.

"Please... please go. I'll be just fine. You too, Lucy... please go!"

"B-But one of your babies..." William stammers helplessly.

"It's no one's fault," Lori quickly replies, her eyes speaking into his another message. "Me and Lucy had a cousin that was born hump-backed like him, and he done just fine. He got married, and even had two boys of his own that were born normal. We all got a cross to bear. His won't be any worse than another."

"But I want to help."

"I said we don't need nobody's damn charity!" Whitey curses, pushing William, along with the two women toward the door.

"Okay... Mr. Miller. We are leaving. But I warn you, if anything happens to that girl or her babies, I'll see to it that you go to prison– or go to hell!"

Nela has rarely seen William angry. But when he did get angry, he was like a Pit Bull ready to sink his teeth into the jugular. Whitey's brutish behavior has angered him more than he cares to acknowledge. Nela considers that Whitey could easily smash him like an insect. Only an inbred respect– or maybe it is an irrational fear of the educated harbored in ignorance– that prevents him.

"You do that!" Whitey hisses. "We mill folk know how to care for our own. Don't need charity from no rich people– and don't need law! You come nosing around her again, and I'll forget you are a doctor. That goes for you, too, Lucy Tracy!"

A visit to the police station makes things no better. The next morning William picks up a bottle from Homer's Bar and allows himself to get drunk. It is the first time Nela has ever seen her husband this way. To see him now frightens her.

The local Sheriff's office in the adjacent county, later piece together the sequence of events that follow. This before appointment of Pixley's Indian Sheriff and also is before someone from the north tried unsuccessfully to form a mill union. As one man put it back then, there just is not enough crime or bad pay in the region to go through all the expense of hiring an officer of the law. The murder of Lori Miller will change that.

According to the official police report, it is clearly a case of homicide with all the evidence pointing to Whitey Miller as the only probable suspect. Several witnesses saw Whitey filled to the brim with courage the night before. Some even heard him make violent threats against his *"whoring"* wife. He has somehow heard that Lori plans to leave him, and take the babies with her. A fact later confirmed in a statement given by Lori's sister. The evidence determines that in a fit of rage, Whitey set his own house on fire. Lori must have tried to stop him, and during the ensuing struggle, stabbed seven times in the stomach with a dull box cutter. Forensics confirms that Whitey managed to stumble from the flaming house and pass-out on the front lawn. However, Lori was not dead– at least not yet. She survives long enough to collect her babies and escape into the swamp. Judging by a burned baby blanket found at the scene, the infants must have already been on fire by this time. A trail of footprints shows the woman fleeing straight into the swamp. Two days later a local duck hunter discovers Lori's frail lifeless body near a bog lake. Bodies of the babies never recovered. Whitey immediately arrested and placed on trial. Testimony by his supervisor, Tom Mackey, states that he is a good worker and strong as an ox; and the Mill little likes the idea of losing a good man on the job. Especially at expense of a married woman rumored to have been less than faithful. Therefore, they get him a good lawyer; the charges of willful manslaughter eventually dropped for a lack of sufficient evidence.

"Besides," argues the defense lawyer, "even if my client was guilty, a man should have the right to defend his own.

By testimony of the deceased own sister, his wife had already made plans to leave him. What kind of justice is that to an honest, hard-working man, whose only reward in life is his family? What man here in this courtroom today would do less if he discovered that he was married to a Jezebel? —And let us not forget how she murdered his only two sons!"

The judge agrees with his brother, fines Whitey Miller twenty-five dollars Court fee, and dismisses the case. What no one knew at the time is that both infants were not in the house the night of the fire. Lori had left one of the babies with her sister Lucy. She knew Whitey would never notice since he always came home drunk. She planned to sneak away after he passed out. It would be an easier escape with only one baby. What Lori did not know is that her brother Frank, who happened to drop in on Lucy later that afternoon, would go back and casually tell a man who works at the Pixley County Office that Whitey Miller could not even keep his wife satisfied. This man happens to be a close friend of Tom Macky, the shift supervisor. A telephone call later, and the proverbial cat is out of the bag. To some there even seems a certain poetic justice in the horrible sequence of events.

William Smith is unable to accept the final decision of the court. Even his testimony of Whitey Miller's violent character the night he delivered the babies passed over with only cool interest that to all seems irrelevant to the facts. When it becomes clear that the trial lacks justice, he does something that Nela will forever admire. He forges a new birth certificate, making Lucy Tracy the legal mother of the surviving infant left in her care. There blossoms a bouquet of gossip about town, as to who the father could be. However, in time Liberty falls asleep to this issue, as it did to everything else.

"Nela, a man makes mistakes in this life. Sometimes those mistakes can cost him everything and cause a lot of hurt to those around him. But a man has to do what is best and right." William tells her with tears in his eyes just a day before his accident. "I just want you to know, Nela, I have always loved you. Maybe at times less a husband to your needs; but I do love you. I know a lot more than you think. All is forgiven. It is my hope that you can forgive me; and especially for the thing I must now do."

These are the last words spoken by her husband. She never tried to understand; never wished to know the true meaning sewn within the seed of those words.

Nela retires to the protection of her white plantation house. It is still her house... at least for now. All illusion, all dust spread upon the wind of night after summer has passed and the last harvest reaped. Illusion of who once she thought to be the only present meaning left to her life. Nela's memories, like her dreams, faded tapestry matching the decoration in her living room. This woman of means realizes just how alone she really is. That she has always been alone. That she will remain alone until the day she dies. Who then will mourn her passing? There are so many things to think about. The time for change has come. Maybe there is still a little hope left to her clinging soul.

"I wonder what on earth Weistbaily means?"

Face of the monster is the last thing Nela remembers, as her mind drifts into another night of dreamless slumber, thanks to ingredients in a bottle given to her by Homer.

CHAPTER 22

The Burden of Truth

Davy opens the door surprised to see Nela Smith standing there looking uncommonly common. Lady Smith, as everyone politely refers to her, rarely, if ever, visits any of the poorly kept mill village houses. To see her now, like seeing the somber, almost familiar presence of a lovely prepared corpse stolen from the fragranced chamber of a funeral parlor.

She is wearing a dress blossomed with pink flowers and a hat to match. Nearly all of Nela's hats match her clothes. Something she insists upon every time she commissions Lucile to make a new garment to add to her extensive wardrobe. Lucile often complains bitterly because Nela never wants to pay extra for the hat. She has explained how difficult it is, even has shown Nela the laborious process just sizing the band; but in the end Nela always gets her way and her discount. After all, she is Lucile's best customer, and the only customer, who always pays her cash in advance.

"Is Lucile home?" She inquires looking past Davy.

"She went to pick up something at Mabel's, some material or something that come in the mail. You want to wait inside?"

"No-- but thank you, Davy, I would prefer to sit out here on the porch. Why not join me... what I have to say really concerns you."

Beyond the cultivated boundaries of her plantation estate, Nela looks venerable, ancient and frail like an old piece of cloth patched with new that could possibly disintegrate with a mere touch. The usual sparkle of vitality absent from her eyes, which makes Davy uneasy to see her look so... natural.

"You are such a fine young man," she smiles dreamily. "I always knew you would turn out well. William knew it, too."

Davy mumbles something that sounds like a thank you. He is in fact speechless, also shy. Davy sincerely likes Nela. However, deep down, he thinks of her more as an employer, and less as an acquaintance. In whispers behind her back, Nela always referred resentfully as the cheap widow. All know she is the richest person in two counties; surviving widow of the only Doctor Liberty has ever had, or will ever have. According to the state registry, Nela is direct descendant of Adam Pixley, the famous frontiersman that drifted into the region over two hundred years ago in possession of bags containing pirate gold, making him the richest and most powerful man in the South at the time.

Adam Pixley's second born, Jacob Pixley, becomes baron of the first dynasty of cotton plantations on the Liberty Peninsula. Nathaniel Pixley, great grandson to Jacob, establishes the First Southern Savings and Loan Bank, buys up most of the surrounding land as far as the Georgia border, and leases it to a consortium of northern investors that sets into motion plans to build the first Liberty Cotton Mill. This lays the foundation of future progress and the dream that becomes Liberty Town.

With progress come jobs and a new way of living. Many flock into to the door of this industrial edifice with hopes of better lives for themselves and their families. They become hostages instead. Laboring from twilight to twilight, and from generation to generation, trapped in the belly of a howling beast. Looming presence of a restless taskmaster, which never sleeps, and never gives more, than allowed by shareholder profits. Those that sweat away the pride of their youth rewarded a day's wage and a cheap gold-plated watch at the end of a lifetime in servitude.

If not for Homer's bar, it is a nightmare intolerable and without escape, subject daily to the demonic demands of constant supervision. Taskmasters assigned to watch their every move and to make sure they never exceed the precious minutes of their breaks; always checking diligently the punched time cards of every shift. These men no different than themselves, except for position, whose only trusted interest is to show a saved dollar on a spreadsheet belonging to the portfolio of an elite living far away in luxury.

Even though Nela not directly one of these, she still represents the greater wealth of the world. For her to arrive at his doorstep unannounced is like the appearance of one of Liberty Mill's absent landlords, making Davy feel altogether uncomfortable.

It is not Nela's fault really. It is just that poor people feel less than equal in the presence of someone so far removed from their daily struggle. Her entire life has been a formula of prep schools and particular breeding. How can anyone born a Pixley possibly know what it is like having to work every day just to barely survive? It is like asking an eagle to imagine the struggles of a rodent.

Nela is a good lady, even kind in her own way, but what did she know about mill-life? Beyond the pleasantry of church socials, Nela Smith remains in lonely seclusion, isolated from community affairs, particularly after the tragic death of her husband. All have a pleasant smile for her; but all recognize, as does she, that their smiles only as sincere as the lining in Nela's purse.

Davy did not feel this exactly, nor is he able to see her as a real flesh and blood person. Fixed firmly in his mind is the iconic vision of the older rich woman that lives in the grand estate at the edge of the swamp. No matter how nice she pretends toward him, this image continues to persist as will so many other prejudices learned.

"Have you ever thought what it would be like to have a brother, Davy?" Nela inquires sweetly.

"No mam."

"Of course not," she pauses, a sad twinkle in her eyes. "When I was a little girl growing up my greatest dream was to be like everyone else. How I would have given anything to be able to run and play with other girls my own age. You may find it hard to believe, but it is not always easy being rich. We all have our moments of emptiness-- you do know what I mean, Davy?"

No, Davy did not know what Nela meant– not exactly! He was born poor and knows nothing else, except to be poor. How can he possibly imagine what it is like to be rich? Rich kids are the ones who always get what they want for Christmas. Whose birthdays never an excuse for some practical need, like new school pants, or secondhand shoes to replace the worn-out pair. From Davy's position, rich kids are always happy. Indeed, how can they be anything but happy!

"Yes, I would have given everything to be like other children." Nela continues reflectively.

"But you always had friends," Davy blurts, unable to contain himself.

"Is that what you think? Davy, I have money. I cannot think of a single person– except my William– who ever really liked me for anything except my money. But I hope this not true about you..."

"Of course not Mrs. -- Nela," Davy lies.

"You are such a sweet boy, and so very lucky, too."

"Why am I lucky?"

"Because, dear boy, you have something I am certain you have missed your entire life. You have in this world a brother, a twin brother!"

"A brother– Lucile never–"

"Lucile does not know– no one knows! Everyone was certain he died. It happened such a long time ago, and is part of a story that I think Lucile ought to tell you herself. Just know that many things were kept secret in order to protect you… maybe to protect us all."

"How– how do you know", Davy demands boldly.

For some reason this news provides little comfort to the balance of his wellbeing. Surly Lucile would have said something to him by now. What is this crazy old woman talking about-- how could he have a brother no one ever spoke about?

"I was there the night you and your brother born... and so was Lucile. Then something terrible happened. Everyone, including the police, thought you both dead. For your own protection, William changed your birth certificate to make it seem you were an only child. But he is alive, Davy– your twin brother lives!"

Nela pauses, takes a deep breath. Hosts of rarely seen wrinkles appear suddenly beneath the heavy veneer of her make-up. Her lips thin and translucent, barely covering the skeleton of Nela's mummified mouth.

"But there is something you must know about him," she continues, placing the small ancient petal of her hand over his. "Your brother was born with an unfortunate deformity, a deformity that has unmistakably marked him for life. I still remember William's words: `like a dinosaur egg about to hatch.' Your brother was born hunchbacked. He suffered terrible scars because of the fire, but he is alive. I have seen him with my own eyes. And so have you! You do know who I am talking about?"

Davy's mouth drops slowly open; his eyes large and teary.

"You're wrong!" He shouts in revulsion, moving quickly away. "Weistbaily's not my brother! He's a monster! Everything you said is a lie!"

Davy jumps up and runs into the house. How did she know-- how could she possibly know? Angrily he slams the door, refusing to hear anything more that this crazy old woman has to say.

Nela wants to reach out to him, wishes to calm him in some way; but what is the use? She had to tell him. Someone had to say the truth before it is too late– before a terrible thing happens. One day he will look back and thank her. One day Dave Tracy will be glad that Nela brought him this painfully wonderful news.

Nela did not wait for Lucile to arrive. There is no telling what she might say or do. Especially now, since it no longer a secret that Homer comes by regularly to Nela's grand white house. Nevertheless, Nela believes that everything has a way of working out in time.

At half past nine o'clock, the phone rings, but when Nela answers the caller hangs-up. At ten o'clock Hannibal Smith, the late doctor's brother and Nela's personal finance attorney, calls to schedule an appointment to see him this coming Saturday.

"It is too complicated to talk about over the phone, Nela," Hannibal assures her. "All I will say is that it has to do with your future. A very, very rich future I might add."

"What on this God's earth are you talking about, Hannibal?"

"You'll see. Say around noon?" Quickly adding, "I could send a driver for you if you like."

"You know that won't be necessary. My car is running just fine. I will be there at noon. Besides, there is an item I need to speak to you about as well."

"Whatever it is I'm sure it can be taken care of at the same time. Nela, you just won't believe what wonderful things presently in the works."

Hannibal hangs up. Whatever news he has sounds important. Generally speaking Hannibal is like a cold sardine at a swim party. About the only thing that ever prods his interest is a new market report or a corporate lawsuit. For him to behave so... so (Nela hates herself for even thinking it) so ghoulish, means that it has to be something in his own interest as well. At a quarter past ten, the phone rings again.

"Damn you, Nela! You are a horrible woman!" The voice at the other end of the receiver slurs barely coherent; "You should have at least talked to me first."

"I have tried, Lucile-- as recently as this spring when you delivered my last order. You told me then that it not important that he should know about the other. I did not agree then; but things have come to light since, things too important, especially for Davy."

"Who gives you the right?"

"There is no right or wrong here. You are a good soul to take care of Davy all these years, but please do not keep the truth from him. Have you ever thought what it must be like as a boy growing up and never know your father or that you have a twin brother? That brother is alive, Lucile. I have seen him with my own eyes. Davy has a brother who needs him now, a boy who has suffered more than we can imagine, and it is our Christian duty to help him before it is too late."

There is an uncomfortable silence. Nela can tell by the sound of a distant sloshing that Lucy is drinking heavily.

"What is all this nonsense about Davy's brother being alive?" Lucile's tone grows increasingly unpleasant.

"I have seen him Lucile. He is like a horrible scorched mountain. It is him-- make no mistake– and unless something is done, he is liable to be hurt, maybe even killed. There has been a lot of talk about town, a lot of fear, and a lot of hate. It may not take much to start a witch hunt."

"You're full of it, Nela. I said to Davy that you are just an old woman with too much imagination, and that your mind is going. He didn't believe a word you said."

"You know it is the truth, Lucile. It's just pride and alcohol that will not let you see--"

"Truth-- it's about time somebody told you about truth! And don't think for one minute that I don't know all about you and Homer!"

"It is my impression that Homer is the kind of man who does whatever he likes and sees whoever pleases him most." Nela's voice has a cutting edge sharpened by years of social etiquette and precise in deployment. "Davy will know someday that everything I said is true. It is time he heard it all. He must hear it!"

Lucy remains silent, a silence bred of frustration and years of disillusionment.

"I'll tell you about truth!" She blurts out of control. "Your husband– the good doctor of this town– was not the angel everybody thought. He was a man like any other. You probably don't even remember the time he came here when my mother was sick. After he gave her medicine, Lori showed him out. She said Doctor `Willie'– that's what she called him– screwed her out back behind the pump shed. All those late night-calls he spent with her. Then when she got pregnant, Lori panicked. That was the real reason she married that Miller snake. Who do you think bought her train tickets? He was supposed to meet her somewhere, and then they were going to run off together to California. Live with that truth– if you can, Nela!"

The dial tone is like an empty call to final judgment. Nela remains frozen in time, still holding the receiver, her thoughts as lifeless as the greater than life portrait in her den. After so many years, you would think the shock might have been less toxic. Deep down Nela had suspected, but never wanted to know the details. Surely, there is justice in all of this. Surely, it is all her fault– but the irony!

Whitey had been justified in his jealousy after all. So it was Lori and Bill all along-- no sin without its own reward. Such torment William must have suffered upon realizing there nothing he could do. That nothing found in his medicine bag to relieve the pain that he has caused.

Perhaps, the finality of this responsibility is what destroyed him in the end. Nela always suspected William's accident no accident at all. If only she had known the whole truth earlier! How much easier she might have born the long years of her own guilt. Now she is old, and it no longer matters. Still things might have been so much different.

Tonight Nela has just accepted something new, something that should have been so obvious that it has taken a lifetime to see it. It was Nela all along; she is the one infertile, not William. The curse of the Pixley gold has reached across the centuries and touched her as well. Now Nela Smith knows with certainty the cost of the father's wage of sin. But more importantly, she is finally free at last! For the first time since the death of her husband, Nela will sleep and dream without any more gifts from Homer. Yes, she will dream, and the dreams will be her own! Davy never did come see her again after this.

CHAPTER 23

Family Succession

The end of that August is the hottest ever recorded in the Liberty Basin. Pools of tar melt in the roads, trapping host of never before seen insects that migrate toward cooler regions, many perishing in the black ooze. There are prehistoric grasshoppers, as long as a man's hand, and petrified wood beetles like crossing herds of extinct mastodon. It is so hot that even the usual plague of summer mosquitoes refuse to venture from the steamy swamp interior until very late at night. It also has become disturbingly apparent that an exodus of frogs migrating inland increases daily. More than a month has passed since the last rain. Even so the lower basin remains flooded, a contradiction that to some creates increasing cause for alarm.

Davy's life has slipped into a pattern of utter boredom. He no longer does yard work for Nela Smith. The mill has stopped hiring– even part time. Davy has nothing else to do, except sit in the shade and sip iced tea. Every now and then Lucile will give him money so he can walk to Pixley and buy them both a beer. Davy can tell she is worried now that Nela no longer supplies her with orders. After all, Nela represents over half of her total business– and there are an alarming fewer people left. What hurts Lucile most, she now has to pay Homer for his remedies just like everyone else.

"Davy, I want you to go to Homer's for me again today." She says one morning from behind her newspaper just as Davy is sitting down to breakfast.

He can tell by the dark circles scorched under her eyes that Lucile has passed another sleepless night. Nor is she in a particularly good mood. Davy once made the mistake of lodging a weary complaint about his chores and nearly received a coffee mug to the head. After this incident, he is careful not to arouse her part Irish temper on her father's side, particularly when she is tired and out of Old Crow.

"What are you reading?" Davy tries best he can to sound conversational.

"It's about that war again– gets that a day doesn't pass that there's not something said about it. It's going to turn into another blood bath just like Korea!"

"Someone's got to stand up to Communist," Davy asserts boldly.

"Communist-- What do you know about Communist? You've been listening too much to Frank's beer talk. Davy, war means going out and killing people! That's something you live with the rest of your life. Ask Frank. Ask him about the nightmares he has still to this day. His war didn't change anything more than any of the rest, but that doesn't lessen the burden in his conscience any. Don't think for a minute that the better ones come back alive!"

Lucile refuses even to look at her chosen son, but continues to stare blankly at the newspaper.

"Uncle Frank said that if it weren't for the military he wouldn't have the county job he has today," Davy makes protest"; and look at all the places he's seen in the world. I've never even been past the other side of Hog Back Mountain. Just imagine what it must be like to go to Japan or the city of Hong Kong. I wouldn't care what I had to do, so long as I can get out of Liberty!"

"That's just foolish talk. Things are going to get better around here– wait you'll see. I talked to Mr. Mackey down at the mill. He says that as soon as they start hiring again he'll be sure to give you a job. Then you'll see things different."

"Jerry Tucker is almost the same age as me. His father signed for him to go into the Marine Corps. Now that I am seventeen you could sign for me, too."

"I don't want to talk about it anymore David," Lucile affirms, folding the paper aside.

"If my father–"

"Not another word!" She snaps.

Davy can tell by the crackling finality in her tone that Lucile near one of her crisis. He knows from experience that she will never give her consent. Besides, another six months he will turn eighteen and never need anyone's permission again.

Lucile has a particular prejudice for war and the kind of violent hatred war surfaces in humankind. It has something to do with a fiancée, who marched off to combat at the same time as Uncle Frank. He and Frank were best friends, but only Frank returns alive. Maybe deep down Lucile has always resented him for this, resents the fact that he came back to continue another day, while his best friend interred, cold and nearly forgotten in the crowed V.A. Cemetery outside Pixley. Davy is the closest thing to a son she is ever destined to have– and by God-- as long as she has any say, Uncle Sam will not touch a hair on her nephew's head!

Just after noon, Davy walks down the street to Homer's bar. It is a sunny pleasant day, one of those days when everything renewed just by sheer brilliance. Even the shaggy line of buildings along Main Street stand revived from the dust of neglect. Davy passes Mabel coming out of the time fixer's shop. Without saying a word, she turns and waddles away in the direction of her garage like a fat summer creature preparing for long hibernation. Given enough time, all of Liberty's clocks will be set in order. There is no sign of Bubba, so he decides that maybe it better this way.

Homer looks lazily up as Davy comes in. There is an unusual quiet, even the bell over the door taped silent, at least for this day, as are all the curtains tightly drawn. It is obvious Homer suffers from a particularly bad hangover from the night before.

"I guess Lucy be wanting another bottle of Crow," he says, rubbing his fat hands together.

"She's like a critter needing sugar!" Davy replies glumly, using one of Homer's own expressions.

"She ain't..." Homer hesitates. "Lucy ain't still mad at me is she, Dave?"

"I think she's madder at Nela Smith than anyone else. I can't say as I blame her much. Nela first steals you, and then speaks all those lies. Nela should not have spoke all those things!"

Homer has no idea what Davy is talking about. He has his own demons to wrestle. Lately, he feels a lot of burden on his already heavy-laden conscience. Homer still likes Lucy (even more than he is willing to admit), but his relationship with Nela stronger than feelings, more practical for a man already looking at life near retirement age.

"Well, you ain't mad at me neither, are you, Dave?"

"I feel about the same toward you as my Uncle Frank. I know you and Lucile got your problems, but that don't mean anything between you and me."

"I'm glad to hear you say that, boy. When you get older, you'll understand more how these things work out. Nela's no spring chicken– and I don't think half so pretty as Lucy– but she got something that Lucy ain't got. And that's all there is to it!"

A long silence passes between them, a silence born more out of mutual guilt than of respect. As for Davy, he keeps wondering if maybe things might have turned out different had he not forgotten to tell Lucile that Homer planned to drop by that day she was gone. He knows it is silly to wonder about that now. Nevertheless, he wonders all the same.

"You see Bubba much?" He asks at last, glancing over at the darken corner that embraces the pinball machine.

"Just about every night," Homer beams proudly. "He's gotten to be a regular. Ain't anybody that don't like him— even if he is a Jew!"

Davy shrugs his shoulders. He did not wish to admit that he is jealous, but deep down he is jealous. Bubba represents everything he always wanted to be. He has managed to command the respect of everyone, including Homer. Davy was only twelve when Lucile first started seeing Homer. It seems that no matter how much older he becomes, he remains always twelve in the twinkling eyes of Liberty's only bartender. Now here is Bubba Baily, less than a year older, who has achieved instant manhood.

"Why don't you try a game of pinball on the house," Homer coaxes, sensing the boy's envy. "That Bubba just can't seem to lose."

Davy simply cannot resist the challenge. Even though he has little chance, he will try. Mostly because it appeals to his vanity to compete against something only Bubba Baily can win. He will try, if for no other reason than to prove to Homer that he is no longer that little boy. He pushes in the plug and inserts a coin. The machine flutters to life. Crackle of electricity courses menacingly through an obstacle course of lighted bumpers and spinning wheels. Bells clang; gears whine and groan, until a heavy silver ball drops into the readied firing chamber. Davy plays the first ball surprisingly well– perhaps not as good as Bubba– but better than he has ever played before. A second ball jumps into the chamber without the machine tilting. Again, Davy plays with a skill surpassing his natural ability. It is as though Bubba Baily here– at least in spirit– influencing the electrified alleys with power of his will. Even now, he manipulates the control: Davy's hands, but not his reflexes. By the time the glowing atom of the third ball ricochets through the maze, it seems certain Davy will achieve what only one other person in Liberty ever has– never a score like Bubba Baily– but enough to win!

It is then Davy happens to glance up to see something never noticed before. Through the reflected aura of dancing lights, Davy recognizes the face of someone in a faded photograph against the back wall. Lurching forward involuntarily, his hands tighten against the smooth metal sides, and the Tilt light flashes on. The pinball machine hums triumphant and goes dark.

"Too bad, Dave– for a moment I thought you were a winner!" He hears Homer say.

Davy is no longer interested in winning. Nor is he even consciously aware that the machine has tilted. He reaches up and begins rubbing away the grime of dust from the picture glass. There is Homer many years younger, and beside him another man, tall, and with strikingly handsome features. What shocks Davy most is that this also the same man in the photo given to him by his Uncle Frank.

"Who is that?" Davy asks, continuing to smear away a film of accumulation decades in the making.

"Why that be Whitey and me. It was just after he come back from down around Charleston."

"Cotton Mouth–" Davy can hardly believe the truth.

"He changed a lot sure enough, but that be Whitey all right. Kind of like old Lucifer once being God's most beautiful angel." Homer chuckles.

"What– What do you know about Cotton Mouth?"

Has Homer known all along what he has just recently discovered? Still there is so much more he needs to find out.

"There ain't much I don't know about him— but what's your interest boy?"

"I guess I'm just curious, Homer. Seems most everybody in town either don't like Cotton Mouth, or afraid of him. I guess I just thought you might know why."

It requires effort not to belie too much emotion.

"Well you seen for yourself how mean old Cotton Mouth can be when he's drinking. No wonder he hasn't killed more than a dozen people by now, or that somebody ain't killed him. That Bubba came mighty close, and Cotton Mouth knowed it, too! He ain't been around here since." Homer pauses to pour himself a drink. "He weren't always that mean. Sometimes he could be downright pleasant. Some men just can't handle their whiskey like others. I guess because he has more than a smidgen of Indian blood. Years ago Cotton Mouth and me was real close. Hell, we was like brothers! He lived with me and my Daddy in the hill country for more than five years after his whole family died in a fire." Homer swallows his drink, his eyes reflective. "My Daddy was a good man to do that. We were poor as you can get, but he took that boy in anyway. Give him food and a roof, only..."

Homer shakes his head, continues to stare into his empty whiskey glass. There he sees many ghosts of things past, of things present, and things still to come.

"Then what, Homer," Davy manages to remain calm. "What happened after that?

"There ain't much to tell really. Cotton Mouth went down in Charleston for a few years where he got a job scraping and painting ship hulls. I hear he met a girl there who was the daughter of a Navy Admiral. I heard also she left him and took off to Hawaii with one of them millionaire ship builders. Then he started drinking real bad. Some men are like that, Dave. Taste of liquor when the soul gets empty and they get crazy hooked on that feeling for life. They say one night he got mean drunk and almost killed a boy with a hammer. So he ran off scared and come back here. Course Liberty wasn't like it is today. The new mill just opened, and people come in from all over to get work. That boy was big and strong, like a bull in prime, handsome corn silk hair and light eyes, with just a tint of blue. There weren't a gal in the county that didn't want to marry him. Except, that is, Lori Tracy. Your Aunt Lori was always picture pretty, and smart– sharp as a pin! She told everybody that some day she was going to a big city and get an education in interior design. It wasn't just talk either. She applied to a big school up north somewhere around Washington, and they wrote her back with the offer of a scholarship. Lori's parents– I guess Lucy told you how they both died just a year before you was born when someone drunk run them off the road on Hog Back mountain– they were both set against her leaving. They figured the best way to keep young Lori home was to get her interested in a man. Now Cotton Mouth had been after Lucy for the longest. Lucy might have ended up marrying him herself, except that her mother insisted it urgent that Lori find a man first. Lucy was good as gold even back then. She arranged a date for her sister with Cotton Mouth. But your granddaddy didn't much care for the likes of Whitey marrying his daughter, and made it clear that as long as he was alive there would be no wedding. Now he didn't say anything then, but later Cotton Mouth told me that it hurt his proud real bad that he weren't accepted in the eyes of Lori's father. He says everything works out even in the end. Whitey always did have too much pride, even when he was just a little hedgehopper. What no one knew at the time is that Whitey forced himself on Lori their first date. Rumor is it happened in the old cemetery while walking her home from a barn dance put on by Anderson celebrating the birth of his second son. As I recall they went to Pixley after the death of your grandparents and got married in the Court House."

"Cotton Mouth's wife was Lori Tracy?" Davy interrupts weakly.

"Thought maybe Lucy told you that already-- Damn boy– I hope that don't upset you none," Homer apologizes. "Lucy swore that she would tell you herself someday."

Davy waves for Homer to continue. He needs to hear everything no matter how gruesome the truth.

"Then Lori gave birth to twins." Homer continues, nonchalantly cleaning his shot glass. "Nobody really knows what happened after that. Some say that Whitey killed Lori and the babies. Others, that it was all just a terrible accident. One night she and Whitey got into a fight, and the house caught fire. They found Lori dead in the swamp beside a bog pool where they say she threw the babies. Whitey claims she went plum loco and knocked him on the head, and that during the struggle he must have accidentally stabbed her. Myself, I'm not sure I believe that. Lori just wasn't big enough, unless Whitey was real drunk. Maybe he was, but it still don't add up. At any rate, he got off. Then he just got meaner than ever; and has stayed that way ever since. Yeah, Whitey and me go back real far... maybe too far back."

Homer is so sufficiently lost in his own thoughts that he does not notice Davy nearly collapsed against the pinball machine, his face contorted with horror. Suddenly his whole life has taken on a different perspective. What Nela Smith had said about Weistbaily being his brother true after all! Since one survived, why not both! But who could ever prove it? One thing certain and without any shadow of doubt, Cotton Mouth is Davy's father. Now Davy hates the man in the photograph, hates that he was once young and handsome, and that even then his mouth full of poison. Most of all, he wishes that Bubba had slain the serpent that night he had the chance. That chance he hopes will come again.

The front door snaps open. In steps Mr. Anderson. He looks somehow different from a couple of months ago. Like a dead hollow stump pulled out of the ground to make room for a new crop.

"What the devil brings you in here?" Homer is truly amazed to see this pillar of the community come into his bar.

"Give me a whiskey," Anderson orders, his eyes staring blankly ahead.

Homer gingerly obeys, pouring the glass with genuine respect, and humbly passes it to this man of stern principals. Emptying it with a single gulp, Anderson immediately orders a second shot.

"Raymond will be coming home soon!" He proclaims, raising a toast in the air to no one. "Uncle Sam took both his legs– but by God he's coming home! Reckon I'll be selling out and moving up to Pixley. What's the point having a farm, if you can't get out to plow the fields? A man needs both his legs to plow– don't he, Homer?"

"Why don't you run on and take Lucile her medicine," Homer says to Davy in a tone unrecognizable. "Mr. Anderson and me got some things to talk about."

As Davy leaves, he imagines a tear on the old farmer's cheek. The gullied and scared terrain of a countenance mapped with pain and disappointment thirsty for a deluge at last. Davy did not go home right away. He walks first down to the cemetery and drinks nearly half of Lucile's bottle in the shade of the Indian rock. She might not like it, but Davy no longer gives a damn. Later he will take the picture hidden in his shoeshine box and burn it, determined that no one else should ever know the evil legacy of his family succession.

CHAPTER 24

Nela Remembered

A slight breeze, almost indiscernible, but enough to billow the nearly translucent white curtains fashioned from Nela's wedding dress by Lucile Tracy. The wisp of air touches the reposing woman's wrinkled brow, playful fingers disturbing her rest. The moon, nearly full, a grinning face shining behind the lattice of a Weeping Willow that grows outside the bedroom window. Night shades camp provocatively in the corners of her bedroom, rising as spirits in the air– shadows of those things to come--and always with them shadows from the past. The darker shadows steeped in ancestry. These the ones that plague most her rest, transgressions of acts made immutable.

Nela had driven to Tootersville early that morning and did not return until after dark. In the words of her late husband, the powder-blue Buick matches Nela flawlessly. Equipped with real leather seats, a richly polished wooden steering wheel, and even has the original factory whitewall tires.

Tootersville is just short of twelve miles due south of Pixley. However, three miles of that a negotiated steep climb to the top of the plateau, the remaining distance measured in country miles, empty, except for a farmhouse or two. Occasionally a boarded-up barn decaying by the roadside, a few stray cows, and many memories of abandoned dreams. Nela always enjoys the drive going, but dreads the way back. Today she had not minded because there are many things in her mind to consider.

The Seth Thomas strikes nine o'clock in the drawing room, sending an expectant chill through construction of strong timbers. All quiet, except for the inauspicious sound of a rat gnawing somewhere within the walls, its days less numbered than the strong foundation. Nela has been trying for a week to find it. Maybe she can persuade Homer to help her. He seems to know a lot about that sort of thing. As for the greater problem, it is uncertain anyone can provide much consolation.

Nela decides finally to get up, surrendering to the ghost of restlessness. Slipping into her favorite saffron silk robe to cover her nakedness, she passes through the chambers of her house without turning on the lights. Like Nela herself, the garment she wears changed faded with age, only she does not notice. Nela navigates the corridors with precision, aware of the position of every potential obstacle, comprehensive of every pattern designed within the tapestry of present existence. She smiles respectfully up at her husband's portrait as she passes through the parlor. As always in time of perplexity, Nela takes strength in something that the good Doctor often said.

"Keep your head, and remember always to think things through. It's better to be late to battle, ready and armed, than to be early to the front unprepared."

She always did greatly admire the way Billy thought about things. Not just things about medicine and gentry, but about most all things, especially things that require experience found through wisdom, more than in book sense. He could have easily been comfortable anywhere. Bill Smith the kind of man that would wrestle another man for a can of cheap beer just to prove he can win. Then help him up afterward and treat his bruises with the gentle concern of a saint. He could have been anything: a general, a carpenter, a scientist, a farmer. He reminds Nela so much of her brother Nathaniel, which is probably the main reason she married him. Although, it is uncertain William or Nathaniel might have made very good bartenders. That is a position better filled by a man with another kind of character.

Nevertheless, Bill's sensible philosophy continues to guide her in times of crisis, even these many years after his departure. Through the parlor and into the kitchen, then out onto the back porch. Here Nela pauses, takes a deep breath, and passes into the airy darkness of night. Something on the walk moves! It is only a frog. Nela has grown accustom by now seeing so many of the distasteful creatures around, especially the larger ones that have lately begun to migrate from the deeper swamp. She accepts this as only the beginning.

"So they really think they can get away with it!" She mumbles to herself, meandering blindly along the familiar garden path.

State Legislators have already passed approval on all the plans, have gotten all of the necessary endorsements, and have satisfied the interest of every potential objection. It looks now as though there is nothing to stop them. A secret proposal, a shady quick deal, and just like that--down the drain with people's dreams, their heritage, their memories! All drowned at the bottom of a lake in the shadow of the expensive Aconee Dam Project!

Without so much as a passing thought about the consequence to thousands inhabited hectares of Carolina history, these predator moneymakers have silently conspired to sacrifice the whole region for a Mammon's reward with a few nefarious strokes of a sharpened pen!

Just to make the transaction more inane, a pious pigeon named Judas Morgan has sold everyone down the road by keeping his mouth shut– some man of God! There is not a single slope on the south Piedmont Plateau without his name and the name of his cousin, Jasper Flynn, on the deed.

For the past two years, Jasper Flynn, then a private citizen, has been making anonymous bids through the State Land Assessment Board for the worthless hill country surrounding the Liberty Peninsula. All of the properties have two characteristics in common. There is limited direct access to the elevations, and few resources of surface water. Purchased for pennies, because no one could understand why anyone in their right mind would want it. Making the impropriety worse, Morgan and Flynn conspired together to use congregation money to do it!

This is their fatal error. By the time Nela finishes with them, the smiling Liberty Preacher and his con-artist cousin will be lucky if they only use tar and feather to run both out of the Carolina state!

The greater dilemma, Hannibal Smith, the only surviving brother of her late husband, like usual up to his greedy waist in sin. As always, it is about money and profit. Maybe Hannibal's fault is not altogether his own. Maybe he just lacks the knowledge of another way to be. There had been a third brother born hunchbacked, who would have been the youngest, except he died at an early age with complications of the heart.

The tragic loss of Jesse greatly affects William and Hannibal. Only their choices guide them along different paths. William chooses to sacrifice his life to sickness and infirmity, while Hannibal becomes a big business attorney, quickly gaining ruthless reputation. That reputation often discourages William; makes him feel ashamed. Nevertheless, Hannibal remains his only brother since Jesse's loss. A life bond of survivor's guilt yoking the two brothers together; a yoke they continue to shoulder into adulthood, and all the days of their lives.

For this reason, William always chose to turn a blind eye to the often unscrupulous deeds of his younger brother, believing him better than he truly is. Now only Hannibal left, Lawyer and brother-in-law dedicated to protect the legal interest of the last heir of the Pixley fortune.

After William's death, Nela often feels Hannibal over-reacts to the most insignificant details. For example, the time she arrives at his office without a hat during a `*dog day*' summer. He becomes more excited than a frightened schoolchild, insisting how foolish at her age to take such a chance! This is also the day he convinces her to place all estate assets into a trust granting him the power of attorney in the event that something unexpected should happen to her. Nela thought at the time this to be simply a burden of extreme concern. After all, Hannibal and his deceased brother's widow the only remaining family either of them has left. It seems only good that he would want what is best for her. However, in time she has begun to grow suspicious of deeper motives in his nature.

No, she cannot blame her late husband's brother really! He is, after all, a man of business. As is the nature of most businessmen, Hannibal denies himself the humanity to make judgments not based on profit. He is just another big hungry fish in a little stagnant pond. Now, thanks to his tireless efforts, Tootersville will soon be on the map right across from Pixley. To this finance lawyer, it is not a question of right or wrong. His only true doctrines of this world being monthly interest charges, annual returns, percentile points, amortization, and legal tax loopholes. Because Nela is family, he owes it to another lost brother to give her a chance at "*making a killing.*" It simply never occurs to him that she might object to what he considers the greatest business opportunity of a lifetime.

"So here are the facts, Nela," he begins, seating her comfortably in his office. "Liberty Mill is selling to me all its interest at half what it is worth. The state reimburses me, along with a built-in twenty percent return. The mill has further agreed to purchase back all portable equipment at retail market price."

Hannibal pauses here to light one of his black Cuban cigars. A limited supply destined for depletion, since the recent Cuban missile crisis. Nela feels certain that this habit alone responsible for his chest being narrow and sunken, while Hannibal's waist spreads nearly round as Homer's girth. For reasons of his own, Hannibal never married.

Since he is already nearing sixty, it seems doubtful that he ever will. Maybe because he is too much of a lawyer at heart, because all of his emotions add up to cold facts and calculated figures in the end. He limps slightly, since attacked by a neighbor's dog he tortured as a boy. He has male pattern baldness, which he unsuccessfully tries to conceal with a cheap toupee, and an annoying habit of never looking directly into anyone's eyes. Nela never really felt completely comfortable in the presence of Hannibal Smith. Only today does she truly begin to understand the reason why.

"But that's not all, Nela," Hannibal continues coolly, blowing a puff of gray sot weed smoke into the air. "The state has further agreed to purchase, at absolutely no cost to the mill, another location site comparable to the one they are abandoning. In addition, they have agreed to subsidize the expense of building a new facility, as well as transport all useable equipment to the new location as soon as Liberty Mill closes." A greedy smile flushes wickedly across Hannibal's face. "Nela, they want to buy that worthless acreage outside of town that Bill acquired just before he died– our property!"

Yes, Nela remembers. William had wanted to build a charitable Child's Hospital Clinic for the mountain people living in the vicinity. It was his dream, a dream that could have made a difference in the lives of hundreds of people too poor and too ignorant to accept new ways. At the bequest of his brother, Hannibal found the land and negotiated the deal for its future development. The lower elevations surrounding Tootersville, situated on the opposite ridge from Pixley, prove more accessible to the several farming communities sprouted along the fertile slopes to the south. It is ideal in every way, and Hannibal assures Bill that the investment feasible. He advises placing the holding in a family Trust Fund making all parties executors, including himself for tax purposes. A groundbreaking ceremony scheduled to commensurate the project.

No shovel ever broke the earth or plans for a future foundation after William's death. The land continues to remain barren to this day, the Child Clinic never even begun. Nela could have continued the project with her own money; only who possessed the professorial insight and medical knowledge to see it through completion? All these years Hannibal keeps promising to find someone else with Bill's knowledge. Like all promises, it has come to nothing. At the time, Nela harbored too much resentment in her life to see the true importance of her late husband's vision. Now that her eyes open, she must make Hannibal see also.

"I only need your signature of release, Nela. Once the deed is free from all encumbrances, we will be richer than ever dreamed possible!"

That is it! Of course, profit is the only motivation that Hannibal knows. If money truly is the root of evil; then are all men of business fiery embers of the devil's soul.

Hannibal goes on to explain everything in as much detail as he dares. It all happened as things like this often do. First, there is the election of a new governor three years earlier, the Honorable Mister Duke Flynn, brother to Jasper Flynn, and first cousin of Judas Morgan. Governor Flynn's initial proposal after assuming office is consideration for a second Nuclear Power project. Plans for Lake Keowee project are already underway and now is the best opportunity to capitalize on the prosperity of future dreams by building another one, howbeit smaller. In the confusion, a lot of money made available to pay engineers driven more by appetite, than by vision. Rural South Carolina destined to grow into more than a smattering of small communities dotting the map.

A response of opposition to the proposed plan rings out immediately from both the House of Senators and the State Congress. Nuclear Power plants are expensive. This also means that the state will need to fund another dam project somewhere. Dams cost a lot of tax dollars, an extravagance certain to arouse indignation from local residents. The sheer magnitude of this proposition means procreation of thousands of acres of residential farmland, as well as displacement of "*only God knows*" how many inhabitants.

"True," replies the Governor to his caucus. "But tax payers don't always know what might be best for them. For example if Kennedy had told the American people how much it was costing each one of them just to send one ship to Cuba, or how much it cost them each day for every advisor sent to Vietnam, probably no one would want to pay that either. It is the responsibility of government to look ahead. Gentlemen, I promise you, we who occupy today must make the policies that will determine fate of all our tomorrows."

Duke Flynn proves the Devil's advocate. With these words, members from each house begin seriously considering the inevitable advantages guaranteed by a project of this magnitude. As one by one, they give their silent endorsement.

In fact, they begin lining-up at the trough so eager that hardly is there more than a whisper of opposition when knowledge surfaces that the contractor chosen for the project is Jasper Flynn, the governor's own brother. A common vote decides that this minor detail has little bearing on the facts. Jasper Flynn, licensed by the State, and according to perjured testimony, qualified to build dams. His timely services promise to be good as anyone. Besides-- and perhaps more importantly-- Jasper Flynn just happens to be immediately available.

Many of Jasper Flynn's methods sited somewhat unorthodox, if not unprofessional. For example, the employment of unskilled laborers to perform task usually assigned to highly technical staff and certification of materials rated below standards. Nevertheless, the dam will go up according to schedule. Any imperfections considered minor; and certainly will not show for quite some time.

The project does go so well that Jasper Flynn drives up from Atlanta only on few occasions to conduct brief site inspections of the project during the entire six-year construction period. Usually he simply takes the word of his Foreman, a man with flawed integrity because of several addictions, that everything proceeding in accordance to the plans. With a nod of satisfaction, Jasper crawls back into the plush interior of his new Cadillac and is gone before the next shift-change. Rumor is that on at least one occasion, a much too young girl wearing way too much makeup seated in the front seat beside him smearing on bright red lipstick; but there is no one who will say anything against the Boss.

Of course, there are many geologically favorable reasons for building the dam. First, the natural underground springs in the swamp surrounding the Liberty Peninsula, seep up through traps of quicksand with an immensurable capacity presently wasted on replenishing the outlying drainage. Second, only a few miles to the north-west runs the stretch of the detoured old Aconee River at a constant incline of forty-seven degrees relative to the natural flood plain of Liberty basin. The dam site, chosen nine miles away due east, is ideal in every respect, spanning the adjacent area of the Pixley County Water Reservoir, making the valley ideal with calculably minimum population relocation.

Construction has already begun in the natural canyon between Hog Back Mountain and the Piedmont Plateau, where tributaries slow to a sluggish crawl before reaching the glades filtering into the Atlantic. The final stage of the operation will be the redirection of the resourceful Aconee River back along its original course to accommodate the pumping station for the future nuclear hydroelectric plant. There are even now plans in the works for a public announcement in advance of the first stage of completion. By then it will be already too late to change course.

To those still remaining on Liberty Peninsula (which should be few after permanent shut-down of the cotton mill) will be offered an appropriation fee for their property, along with a carefully calculated relocation allowance. Advanced statistics show this amount significantly low, mostly awarded to producing farmlands, casualties too negligible to cause any media concerns. Nevertheless, a compensation package exists, just in case, providing someone is registered and able to obtain legal representation. Even then this amount based on the principle of present mill village market values, amortized over a ten-year period. Also providing one can find a lending institution willing to carry the principal.

"There will be more legal complications than hairs on a dog," to quote Duke Flynn.

Within a few years, all the surrounding land will be at the bottom of the Aconee Reservoir, a great brimming new lake sparkling with economic possibilities to every investor involved. Then future constructions on resort property can begin, which is where the real money will be. Duke concludes that the secret to every success is a bit like fishing. Reel out the line slowly by degrees. The less people know about the hook, the less they will be able to fight later after it is too late.

Hannibal could not be more pleased with recent events. This is his chance to become truly wealthy, to become more than just another small town lawyer. Yes, he has Nela Pixley, last heir to the famous Pixley family as his client. Only she also keeps the purse strings. Secretly he has always envied the position of this woman of means. Hannibal envies her because she has never been anything except rich. Now is his turn, opportunity of a lifetime finally to break the noose of those strings!

"Just sign this document, and I will take care of the rest."

"I will not sign, Hannibal!" Nela affirms resolutely, her eyes narrowing to sharp daggers belonging distinctly to a Pixley.

"Nela, please be reasonable!" Hannibal pleads waving an ink pen in her face. "What's done is done, and there is nothing anyone can do to change the facts. All we can do is make the best of things. I know how you feel about your house, all the years invested there. It is going to happen all the same; rather they buy the land or acquire it through other means. With that extra money you can purchase ten better houses, and afford to decorate them in real southern plantation style if that's what you want."

"I can already afford to decorate any way I please," she snaps back sharply. "It is not just the money, Hannibal... money cannot buy a clear conscience or peace. William was your brother. Surely, some of what he was must be in you. Ask yourself, Hannibal, what would he have wanted you to do?"

Hannibal sits pensively back in his chair, appearing that moment stricken. Nela's eyes judging daggers disturbing his clouded soul. It did not matter if what she says true. After all– what can possibly be truer than money! Today they are also discussing his money. Money he deserves after all these years.

"Dear Nela, I know what you are concerned about. Rest assured that I have already arranged to have Bill's body exhumed and buried here in Tootersville. You must think now about what he would have wanted for you– for me his only brother!"

Hannibal has now assumed the pleasant manner of an undertaker.

"William wanted to build a Child Clinic! He would never have considered any other purpose. You know the plans he had for that land. William always hoped you would build his clinic if something happened. He believed in you, Hannibal; only you never gave a damn about your brother or his dreams!"

Nela is angry. It was not often that she got angry, but when she did, there can be no reasoning with her.

"That's not fair, Nela," Hannibal croons, his eyes narrow, silvery. "I'm not a doctor. What do I know about hospital clinics and such?"

"As much as I know about crooked deals; I refuse to sign that deed. There will one day be a clinic on that land just as William wanted, or there will be nothing."

The Pixley bloodline surges through her as never it has surged before. Nela knows how to be shrewd, and as tough of a negotiator, as any man bred to the purpose. This is her true nature, the power and the foundation that has made the Pixley bloodline as a strong weed rooted firmly at the edge of a terrestrial precipice, more deeply anchored in a dark place below, impenetrable by mortal apprehension. She determines not be swayed, nor seduced by any glitter, unless it is of her own making. Hannibal knows this, too.

The lawyer's mouth begins twitching on one side. Suddenly he is a man like any other, dangerous, and frighteningly unpredictable. He methodically closes the pen, places it in lapel pocket of the grey vest covering a starched white shirt.

"I'm sorry you choose to take that attitude, Nela," he says calmly, returning the paper deed to his office safe.

"I am sorry, too, Hannibal... but I just feel some principals more costly than money can buy."

"Was there something else you wanted to talk to me about?"

A frightening calm now replaces his earlier enthusiasm, a calm hiding the turbulence of a lifetime building within him.

"Yes, I wish to change my will. I have learned something about William. Something you should know, too, Hannibal."

"Tomorrow, Nela…tomorrow I'll drop by with all the necessary papers and you can tell me everything. Now I have an important matter to attend to at the courthouse. Tomorrow will be time enough."

There is that unusual twitch of his mouth again.

"Hannibal, I hope this does not make us enemies," Nela's tone softer now.

"How could I ever be an enemy to my dear brother's wife? Goodbye Nela."

There is such finality in Hannibal's voice that she becomes speechless. Without further conversation, Nela rises and is out of the door before her mind can grasp the greater meaning of their conversation. Once inside the privacy of her car, she begins to cry. The world is indeed the many plans of mice and men! The mice, it seems, will always drown in the end, simply because they are unaware of the boat's condition. While men busily make provisions to preserve their own bones against nature-- a nature, they can little control.

"But what a Pixley Hannibal would have made!" Nela thinks admiringly on the drive home.

As much as she hates everything her brother in law represents, a part of her impressed by the genius of his plans. It is as the echo of her father's voice, and his father before him, going all the way back to the original Pixley.

Nela expends remainder of the day meandering along narrow deserted country roads. If only the good doctor were here, he would know what to do. If only her brother Nathaniel were still alive. Nela, one of three children born to the wealthy Pixley family, is the last of the family line. A heritage going back as far as Adam Pixley, the famous frontiersman, who helped settle this region.

Her youngest sister dies of a rare blood disorder when Nela twelve; and her twin brother, only minutes older, perished on an island in the Pacific, during one of the worse battles against the Japanese during the Second World War. Death permeates Nela's younger years, extravagant funerals with black curtains drawn for mourning. It seems no generation ever escapes tragedy of the Pixley curse.

Nela loved Nathaniel most. He was the kind brother every girl dreams of having. Tall, handsome, and strong, yet gentle and humble, blessed with blond wavy hair circled around striking Nordic blue eyes. She cannot remember Nathaniel ever being cross during all the years they grew up together. When Anna fell ill, he tended her like a nurse, often waking in the middle of the night to bring his little sister a glass of cold water to keep her comfortable.

Like many in his generation, he resisted getting involved in a war far from the shores of home, but finally volunteers for service, choosing to become a medic. Maybe Anna's long-suffering impressed him with a purpose; made Nathaniel realize life more precious than glory or fortune.

During the first years of the European war, Nathaniel works as Assistant Vice President in one of the family's holding companies. When another specter of threat rears its head from across the seas with the Japanese bombing of Pearl Harbor, he can no longer remain safe on the sidelines. He first wanted to be a Navy Corpsman, but lacked the needed credentials. A month before turning twenty-five, Nathaniel enlists in the United States Marine Corps. Her brother returns home for two weeks after Boot Camp at nearby Paris Island, then to North Carolina, insisting on receiving First Aid field training. Nathaniel Pixley ships-off the following month to the Pacific Iles, where he will die in the battle for Iwo Jima.

"You must not go!" Nela pleads the night he packs his bags before departing. "You are needed here at home. I need you!"

Nathaniel looks compassionately upon his only remaining sister, a woman now. He always hoped to meet someone as pretty as Nela, someone as loyal and devoted. Engaged to a girl he met in Charleston for two years, he thought her the right one, but disappointed in the end.

"The family businesses will do just fine without me, Nelly. I have a higher duty. All those young men shipping off and dying in the defense of America– can I just sit here and do nothing? A major conflict is going on; leaving thousands wounded or killed every day. I must do my part in this war to end all wars."

Nathaniel Pixley departs next morning on a train car filled with other men in military uniform. How impeccably handsome he looks in his Marine Corps greens, Nela remembers thinking to herself as he boards the platform at the Pixley station. Her brother is only a Private First Class, but to Nela he commands the presence of a General off to save the day.

Three months later, a notice from the War Department arrives by special courier. The war ended only days after his unfortunate death, accidentally killed by friendly fire from the ricochet of a stray bullet.

Amelia Pixley, devastated by the loss of her only son, turns to the refuge of alcohol. Realizing that not even her family fortune can change the termination of life, she becomes a recluse, desiring to see or talk to no one, not even her only living daughter. She prays daily for strength, prays that Nela will one day forgive her because of the terrible cruelty in the world of men. One rainy Sunday in late March, Amelia Pixley hangs herself in the basement of the family mansion, without so much as a goodbye to Nela. By chance, the kitchen maid discovers the gruesome body before Nela knows. Believing the door to the cellar always locked, the housemaid grew curious when it opens easily from gentle pressure. Her screams of horror heard clear down into the Liberty basin. It will be many years before Nela ventures into this keep alone.

Nela, now the last remaining Pixley, finds herself caretaker of a grand estate. For many months, she avoids to venture into the basement. It was always the one place off limits her entire life, barred by a narrow locked door. The Coroner's office removes the door so that the Undertaker might retrieve the body of her overweight mother, and never places it back. Even then, Nela continues to avoid the basement, even when her adopted black cat disappears below, refusing to come back up for nearly a day.

Upon marrying the dashing doctor from Tootersville, they decide together to purchase another house located on the Liberty Peninsula. It is time to put to rest all ghost. Now there are no servants, the grand mansion vacant since many months. Nela spends several days going from room to room gathering the things she most wants to keep and designating the rest for an estate sale. Now she feels strong enough to exercise final dominion over the mysterious realms of this inherited principality and explore the crypt of her shrouded ancestral past.

She finds many disturbing histories, things dead and not dead; things better left in obscurity. Those things most revealing she will keep hidden from the world, even from her husband. This is the day she discovers the secret truth of the Pixley gold and a diary written in the hand of the ancient patriarch to her family name.

The city council of Pixley County agrees to buy her estate and all its furnishing to dedicate as a heritage museum and cultural center. Nela will never return to the place of her nativity. She hopes the move to another home made with the love and charity will plant roots of a better future sewn with better values of her new husband. She hopes this might be enough to cleanse the Pixley legacy of past transgressions. These are dreams only, now already so long ago... all so long ago.

By time Nela finally did get around to reading the diary of Adam Pixley, many things will have changed. Now she lives alone, her husband dead since many years. Her hands tremble uncontrollably, as the truth sinks into her mind and gnaws into the pit of her stomach. Revelation her dead ancestor a monster more than Nela can endure. Adam Pixley was no hero, but a man driven by the worse kind of passions: by cowardice, betrayal, murder, and even infanticide. The final entry jabs into her conscience like a javelin forged by the flames of impending judgment.

"The Spanish gold eats into my soul like a canker worm. Since all these years, a day does not pass I wish I had never found that first coin. The Aconee children called me a fallen angel. Now I know it to be true. Their grave silent now, but the monster never allows me rest. It was the monster that murdered my brother—murdered my son! I know who he is now! He is one that can never know the meaning of *Shelecheyanu*. He is coming! I thought he was dead. I thought that by killing them all, my secret might die with them! No man or angel can kill the Prince of Xeantee! I see his eyes each night as quicksilver burning into my brain. I know he is even now near! One night the frogs will sing his name-- Prince of Frogs-- Prince of the Night-- *The Xeantee Aconee*!"

Adam Pixley never set foot onto the Liberty Peninsula again for as long as he lived, believing the Indian spirits still present, believing in the hour of his just retribution. In time, he would retrieve the rest of his gold and place it in a secret coiffure for all future generations of his name to pillage as needed.

Now nearly all the gold gone; and of all the Pixleys that went before, only Nela remains to read the truth of what really happened. Only she inherits the few remaining pieces of the fabled Pixley treasure, like golden hooks in her soul. Only Nela left to bear the burden of sin. She will seal these dark confessions and remaining coins in an airtight box, along with the talisman given by her husband and hide them within a secret crevice of her stone fireplace. Here they will shelter safely until fallen angel of Adam Pixley rises from the pit.

Nela thinks she sees the shadow of someone crouching beside a chrysanthemum bush. –But no, she is mistaken. Nela leaves her neatly trimmed garden path to follow a little used trail dominated by weeds and other varieties of undergrowth. She steps on a snail, feels the ooze between her toes. A shriek cries from the tree directly over her head, followed by a heavy flapping of wings. Nela neither looks up, nor slackens her pace. No longer do noises in the night fret her imagination with expectancy. Things known are horrifying enough.

Life grows short, becomes shorter all the time. Nela's only remaining desire is to feel as much carnal sensation as she can in the time left. The Widow Pond remains unchanged, still and black, smooth as polished marble.

Nela always comes here when troubled. The first time was on the night after William's funeral. By then she little cares if the legends about the pond true. She hopes a little that they are true. All she knows is that her William gone and that this Widow Pond has taken him. Instead of death, it imparts spiritual peace. She returns often after this. In the beginning, she remembers hearing a sound like the crying of a baby in the swamp. Sometimes the crying lasted for hours without end. Then the crying stops. Nela never did know what made the sound... not until now. Yet, here in this place the peace remains. Tonight Nela needs the peace of the Widow Pond like never before.

The moon lost in an eclipse of shadows, the night breathing darkness. Nela seats herself on a smooth stone near the pool's edge. She wishes to see her own reflection, but the waters absorb all light, releasing nothing, only her dark shadow outlined on the surface. Liberty's fate is not the only thing on her mind. She has heard the rumors about the Time Fixer's son, about encounters with the monster that lives in the swamp. Mostly, Homer gives her the news. He is the local chronicler when it comes to Liberty's latest gossip. It is enough to make Nela realize that Abraham's fears justified. That it is up to her to do something.

Therefore, she will do the only thing she can. With renewed determination, Nela Smith will resurrect vision of her late husband's Child Clinic and arrange care for the less fortunate twin. She will also make sure of Davy's future, but her heart reaches out most to Weistbaily-- such an unusual name!

She knew. As soon as she looked into the creature's eyes, she knew. Nela instantly convinced of the kindness trapped there. She sees eyes of kindness, eyes that belong to none other than William. Only her mind refused to see it then.

Maybe Abraham has seen all along. A truth she has never wanted to see. Now nothing from the past matters, only in future can things be different! Nela has decided within herself to undo all past sins-- to erase the evil committed by Adam Pixley! There remains, however, one small obstacle. The excitingly brash and bigoted nature of Homer, who has a way of making Nela feel young again.

Nela likes Homer. Maybe she is even a little fonder of him than she cares to admit, but she also knows what kind of man he really is. Knows he is only an over inflated bag of wind: a man that just naturally stretches the truth and with a mind calculating the prospects of a comfortable retirement. A retirement her money will provide particularly well. It is not the first time the affections of a man purchased for a morsel of meat and a warm place to sleep. Nela does not care so long as he can be house-trained. Homer will be sorely disappointed in the end.

"Weistbaily," Nela again speaks to no one, "such a strange name for him to choose on his own."

She must know the source of such an unusual name. From where did he learn it? A name clouding her soul, a name not of Abraham; not born of the sons of men; but a name chosen from the simple clarity of the creature's own thoughts. It seems there should be a meaning; only that meaning presently escapes her reason.

What disturbs Nela most, the hideous mask of a face with human eyes that continue to haunt her even now. Behind the horror of this visage is her William: a kind clear soul that neither judges, nor condemns– his heart good to the end. Tomorrow she will take Hannibal to see Weistbaily face to face. Then he will understand. He will help her build that clinic. He will surely change just as Dickens's Scrooge character changes upon seeing the spirits of past, present, and future. Then Hannibal, only surviving brother to William Smith, will exercise his legal knowledge to put a stop to all of these crooked proceedings!

There is a noise. Something-- no, someone watches her from the shadows. He has followed her; has waited a long time. Nela thinks to run; only where might she flee? Is there any place to save her now?

Nela smiles as she gazes into the mirror blackness of the Widow Pond. How near to William she is just now. She thinks of Davy with all his beautiful life before him. Thinks it sad she will never see him again.

The sound of footsteps in the grass behind her, heavy-- an all too familiar limp: odor of cigar smoke fills the air. It not intended that she escape.

"You should have signed the papers, Nela," he says looming over her.

His shadow reflects as the presence of a dark angel in the pool. Then, as if on cue, frogs begin to sing, a melody that almost she understands. Nela knows Liberty's monster has found her at last.

She feels the shock of incredibly strong hands around her neck; feels the terror, as he pushes her head steadily down. She opens her mouth to scream– no sound! Cold dead water quickly rushes in, filling her lungs with pain.

A peculiar snap heard in back of her neck; the pain gone, a feeling of peace, as her body slips limply away like a lost garment in an irresistible flow. Her mind fading into the slime... the silence... forever... and Nela Pixley, last heir of Adam Pixley, sinks into the dead waters of the Widow Pond.

L. A. Espriux

BOOK SIX

Prince of Frogs

CHAPTER 25

Ode to Father Abraham

Abraham steps out on the sagging porch of a house built even before he was born. He grew up under the shelter of these bowed posts, remembers well the squabbling loyalties between brothers and sisters. Watched his mother die of a disease that made her chin swell to the size of a watermelon. He went away for a time; had gone far. Lived fancy in fancy cities and fancy women. Cities built by white men and for white men. In the end, this broken down old shanty glitters most in his thoughts.

The sun slices into the horizon, setting ablaze the sentry of trees bivouacked against the western sky. Clouds part in the east, a sea of lapis lazuli emptying into the nethermost regions of the swamp. Somewhere in this nether region reins a Prince with his Lady, surrounded by hosts of subjects invisible to the light of men.

Abraham lowers stiffly into his favorite rocking chair. It groans bitterly. The wood brittle and decayed, shudders beneath the weight of his mortifying flesh. A lone dying bee drifts over his shoulder and lands in the palm of his hand. How easily he might crush out the life; how easily it might sting. Then a gentle breeze timed just right, and the bee is gone. The old man smiles as he considers the division of days that separate all societies and nations of men. In the end, nothing new, nothing changed. The peace of twilight fashioned the same to all. The fruit of bountifulness distributed without measure in season to the great and to the humble, to the wise and to the fool. All things provided by providence in fullness of time, to the newly born; also to the dying. The evening breeze blows without judgment, giving relief to sparrows inhabiting uppermost branches, soothing even to rodents that dwell within the darkest root passages. It is all so simple, so extraordinarily simple. So simple in fact that it has taken him a lifetime to realize it: so plain to see, the choice in the seeing. Now he understands the mystery that separates all creatures. Sees clearly the miracle of meaning supplied to his reason these past seventeen years.

Abraham will always remember the night Liberty's monster came to the swamp. Indeed how is it possible to forget? He reckons it to be just before midnight, night a terrible tempest brewed in the Atlantic. Later recorded the worst hurricane to hit the Carolina coast in recent history, it moves inland, hissing through channels of lowland passages hurling destruction in its way. It is a night uncannily dark, possessed of tempest wind, forked lightning, and hailstones that drop from the sky big as summer apples. The barrage of ice projectiles pound the tin roof of the small shanty like legions of angry demons trying to get in.

All this causes Abraham to think about another storm he witnessed while living down around Charleston. The frothing waves churning up shell-encrusted stones, pieces of shipwrecks, or whatever else the depths might release. What Abraham sees most in his mind is the body of a dead black man later washed-up on the beach with rope burns around his neck. No one even tried to know name of the man, or who hanged him and why. The police said it could just as easily have been a white man, because a storm knows no color. Nevertheless, this man not white; nor the first Negro lynched in the south.

This event forces Abraham to realize with renewed clarity the tremendous force harbored beneath the surface of apparent calm. Apparently, the motions of the currents tame, all seemingly peaceful on the surface, as wave upon wave of change lick the boundaries of altered coastlines. It is more a feeling than knowledge; and to feel something in time is to prepare… and to endure. So he returns to the only home he has ever known, hoping to find the peace remembered from childhood.

Perhaps, he had expected to rediscover a little of that past security here. By then the house empty, swept clean since many years. Nearby rest the unkempt graves of his mother and father, and smaller grave of an infant dead of cholera when Abraham only six years old. A rush of cattails has claimed that ground since a very long time. Only silent memories left to keep him company.

A few years after his return, someone buys the nearby large plantation-style house built after turn of the century and begins making renovations. It has sat empty through days of the Great Depression, even before Abraham departed on his odyssey to see the world. Still it has managed to weather time, preserved in haunting splendor. More than one boy has lost a dare to spend an entire night near its ghostly boundaries.

However, at least one of the Smith couple recognizes immediately this to be the fulfillment of dream. A new coat of white wash, a few rotting boards replaced, and the house is immediately born again. Abraham never considered that his little shanty also included in the deed to their property. All that he knows is generations of his family have lived here going back to the early plantation days.

Only crumbling sarcophagus of the host plantation left, slabs of imported stone and a shallow frog-infested pond remain a fading epitaph of those grand bygone days. This splendid age, once representing the idyllic dreams of this world abandoned to shadow.

Recollections handed-down through woeful songs sung by slaves sitting at night on the porches of wooden shanties continue to haunt Abraham's vision of his ancestral past.

Only this history of blood and sweat echoed from now vanished cotton fields greater than his desire in the present. The melody sewn into fallow earth, much like the epitaph of a man, once his soul finally departed.

Abraham finds himself the last living testament to inhabit these walls. Once he is gone, as always the swamp will prevail, swallowing-whole an age that once was, and better forgotten. There exists a myth in Liberty that all men created equal. However, that little applies in his lifetime.

If the woman had her way, he would have been cast-out on the spot, the rotting timbers of his home burned to the ground. He still recognizes Nela even after all these years and wonders if she might still bear a grudge against him. He first saw the young girl when she was barely a teen. Hired to do gardening work on the Pixley estate, Abraham wishes only to do his job. He has witnessed how white men can be when it comes to their white women, and he wants none of that kind of trouble. They were both so young then. She comes to Abraham almost every day to tease him, even goes so far as to pull up the fresh flowers just planted.

"Why are you so cruel, Ms. Pixley?" He demands finally.

"I am most certainly not cruel," Nela replies without apology. "I just cannot help wondering why a big black man like you spends his time planting flowers and trimming shrubs."

"'Cause we all ain't born with money and live in a big house," he replies tactfully. "Your daddy hired me to do a job, and I intend to do it the best I can. You are pretty as a picture, Ms. Pixley, but I weren't hired to gab when there's still work to be done."

"Nela," she corrects, looking longingly into his large brown eyes. "Call me Nela. A woman likes to hear her named spoken by a man."

Therefore, Abraham calls her Nela after this. She comes each day for the few summer weeks he is there. Sometimes she comes to talk, sometimes just to sit on the grass nearby and watch him work. Mr. Pixley wisely perceives his young daughter's interest in the newly employed black man. One morning the head gardener calls Abraham to the gardening shed, pays him his daily wages, and tells him not to come back. Nela Pixley will be a grown woman before he sees her again. It will be many years after the death of her husband before they actually talk face to face.

William Smith is a practical man, rational to a fault and merciful by nature. Mostly he is too good to force a man out into the elements. He arrives fearlessly at the door of his shanty and faces the old black man alone, faces him as a man to a man. Abraham will always respect him for this. Together they talk as men, reason as equals. In the end, they share a pipe of rabbit tobacco beneath the shade of the shanty porch and have a conversation as men until the sun goes down.

William Smith comes to visit often after that. Sometimes to talk, sometimes just to sit and to listen to the sound of the swamp. Abraham is always glad when he comes. He neither judges, nor does he ask questions; not even when he brought that young girl. Abraham knows what is going on. He has seen that look in her green pretty eyes before, the longing of a young girl in love. That is another dream from long ago-- and no business of his anyhow!

Then arrives the night of the storm, a night when many things changed. There is a scratching sound outside his front door, a sound like wood beetles gnawing into the bone of his spine. He thinks it just the wind moving the heavy branches of a large Milk Wood tree whose roots have pushed beneath the porch foundations since many years, causing one side to tilt sharply. He knows it is not that really, but already he has grown old and past caring.

Flinging open the door, he imagines a figure running into the swamp, a skeletal apparition glimpsed for an instant only in a flash of rogue lighting. It appears hunched low to the ground, crazed, like an animal in pain, vanishing as a ghost into the night. Almost Abraham did not see the soaking lump of material deposited at the edge of his porch. Perhaps it would have been better had he left it there and gone back to bed. He reaches down and it moves. Startled, he pulls back his hand, imagining a snake prepared to strike him dead.

"Old man you are getting a-feared!" He scolds. "Whatever be in there is sent of the Lord– and he ain't sent you no sting, exceptin' it be good."

Peeling back the course material of a Navy grey woolen blanket singed and with burn holes, Abraham shocked by what he sees. The old man begins to weep.

Who could do such a thing? Why is it even still alive? Only the eyes human, pale blue, like an autumn sky; eyes pitiful, trapped in a mass of burnt tissue. There remains only a siliceous crimson patch where the lips and mouth ought to be. The ears completely shriveled away, with only an ashen ridge where should be a nose. The thing refuses to cry, as though this ability the first agony destroyed. Only the silence of acceptance remains, the eyes staring calmly up at the looming presence, helpless and without expectancy. Abraham paralyzed in the moment, just stands there and gazes into the humanity of those eyes, timeless, an image from the past rushing into his mind, something terrible that happened when he is only a boy– *Lord that long time ago!*

A brush fire set on purpose by the landowner, in order to make room for a new crop field. It is a hot August day, a Dog Day of late summer. A day made that much hotter by the red and amber flames, licking sweat from brows of those hired to keep the dragon under control. A rabbit leaps suddenly out of the smoldering inferno. It hops around in a circle, stopping finally in front of Abraham and remains perfectly still. Its hair and ears singed away, the front and hind paws roasted and bleeding. It just sits there wiggling its nose and looking up at him. There is no suggestion of malice, no protest, no fear. The creature's eyes shine clear and forever-- near freedom at last! Then a tall white man with big black boots grows tired of seeing it that way steps forward and kicks the suffering animal back into the flames. Abraham has altogether forgotten about the incident, until just now.

Abraham removes a worn pocketknife from under the pillow of his bed. He knows in his soul the merciful thing to do. More than once, he has ended the suffering of some hapless creature mutilated by the steel jaws of a trap, or the careless aim from a hunting gun. Those were animals without condemnation of an everlasting soul, incapable of the knowledge of good and evil. Only a man possesses a mind darkened by thoughts and deeds from the heart altogether unspeakable. An animal kills because of instinct. Only the human imagination is capable of exacting brutality for the sake of brutality. Generations of birds will migrate to the same garden year after year for as long as there is a pleasant wind and food to find. Yet, only the wingless spirit of a man born with potential to soar someday into heaven transformed, or tumble from on high into a pit of everlasting fire.

Abraham lunges forward, his mind made up. As he bends down, those eyes just continue to stare, filling his soul with innocence no longer remembered. He gently cuts away pieces of the harsh cloth tangled around the infant's neck and slips them away from a peculiar hump formed upon the infant's back. A strip of burnt flesh comes off with it. The blue eyes stare off into the distance without tears, without even blinking.

Abraham next goes to a cupboard and pulls out a darkened bed sheet with more than a decade of embedded stains. This the only extra linen he has, but at least it is clean.

"What do men need with more than one sheet anyway?"

He proceeds to tear the material into several strips. Then boils some water, adding a recipe of salt and local swamp herbs his mother instructed as good for healing. Into this solution, he soaks the strips of rags. These will act as bandages. After applying a salve of cooking lard, and then the wrappings, he goes to the cellar. The unruly goat did not particularly like to be disturbed at this hour, giving its milk reluctantly. Dipping one end of a clean rag into the warm goat's milk, he squeezes drops into what remains of the hungry infant's mouth. Those calm blue eyes just look at him; seeing clearly into his soul, until the old man breaks down and sobs.

Abraham bangs on the door of the big white house at the edge of the swamp for what seems like an eternity before rousing the doctor and his wife from their sleep. It is a wonder that they heard him at all, considering the storm's increased ferocity.

"You gotta come! You gotta come– quick!" He pleads when finally the door opens.

William Smith grabs his bag and an overcoat without protest or question, following Abraham into the stormy night. The services of a doctor needed; there can be nothing else more important.

"William, at least put on some boots." Nela appeals to him, glancing suspiciously at the old black man dripping water on her clean rug.

A look like Abraham has seen before. The look of anger, mixed with bigotry and mild disgust, as one might have for an unclean creature brought into her freshly garnished home. It is a small human failing easy to forgive. Nela is a pretty woman, a sad woman, made all the more sad by the knowledge that her fresh youthful beauty already beginning to fade. In the wink of an eye, she will be gone. Only the fading image of a worldly dynastic dream to remain, a regal fable fixed in a dissolving tapestry of lost elegance. In future course, what might become of Nela Smith? What abyss then might remain fixed between them?

William Smith weeps bitterly when he sees the horrible tragedy of this night. He tells Abraham that he has done well. That even with his medical experience, he could not have done better under the circumstances. No facilities exist– ot even in Pixley– that can handle a burn victim this severe. There might be in Atlanta, but it is certain the infant will not survive the trip.

"He'll probably be dead before the night is done," the doctor pronounces sadly. "The best we can do is keep him comfortable and let nature take her course."

He then tells Abraham that he recognizes this to be one of the twins born to Lori Tracy, the young girl who he brought here in months past. He is concerned for her safety, and for the safety of the other baby. However, there is nothing to do until morning.

When morning finally does come, the truth is more terrible than even the doctor could have imagined. The Miller place a scene of smoldering ruins; Lori and her two babies missing. At first Whitey pleads ignorance, until later a hunter finds the young woman's body in the swamp with stab wounds matching those of Whitey's box cutter.

Abraham hears that there is a trial; hears the verdict shocks nearly everyone. Abraham is not everyone, nor is he all that much surprised. He has witnessed white man justice before, knows from experience that courtrooms are the market chambers of moneychangers and taskmasters. William Smith comes often to his home bringing fresh linen, salves, and store-bought milk in cans. He is as much perplexed as the old man that the infant continues to survive, and even seems to be getting stronger.

"Must be the high salt content," he says on one such visit.

"Salt– I hasn't been giving him any salt, excepting what's in the bandages."

"The bandages are important for the external healing, but I bet odds ten to one that the goat milk you've been feeding him is loaded with salt. I've watched her licking the lime on the stones out front. At first, I could not figure why. Then it struck me that she wants the salt. Salt helps prevent osmosis of the blood and burn poisoning from setting in."

"If that don't beat all!" Abraham grins with proud satisfaction. "The Lord's providence surely take care of his own."

William Smith does not reply. The usual eloquent wit of his speech has succumbed into an obscurity of simple utterance. Gone also, his customary smile; that smile now replaced with pursed lips and brooding deep lines that make his countenance severe and wearisome. His eyes grow dark and empty from sleepless tormented nights. He is no longer at all like the man Abraham has grown to admire and respect. It is as though bitterness has crept into his soul, a bitterness that clouds daily his once so clear reflection.

"They let Whitey Miller out this morning," he announces, a hint of anger in his tone. "He's over at Homer's bar right now bragging."

"Don't you worry none, Doc Smith," Abraham consoles"; the good Lord, he knows how to reserve the evil for judgment."

A silence passes between them, a long empty silence born of mutual friendship. William Smith's eyes squint painfully, his face weathered marble.

"In a week or two I'll be taking the baby to Atlanta." He says finally. "There is a special clinic there to handle cases like his. But first I have something that only I must do."

Several nights later Abraham hears the voices of two men nearby, or from deep within the swamp. It is difficult to be certain. The first sounds very much like William Smith; the other growling hisses made by only one man in

Liberty. Then a single gunshot rings out followed by silence. Abraham searches, but can find nothing. Next morning Nela Smith discovers the body of her dead husband floating face down in the Widow Pond. Mysteriously, there is not a mark on his body, nor is there any gun. Nevertheless, Abraham is certain in his heart that Whitey Miller responsible. Knows, also, he can never prove it in a white man's court. All this he keeps in the integrity of his soul these many years. Now he hears news that someone has found a revolver with the initials W.S. in the Widow Pond. Sooner or later, the Widow Pond surrenders all her secrets.

Abraham listens carefully. Almost it is hem of a melody hummed by his father on the porch at night as young Abraham drifts in and out of sleep. He has forgotten that tune... until just now. He has forgotten the stench of sweat, which always clung to his father's quiet presence ever since Abraham old enough to remember. How calmly and at peace that man accepts death in the end.

Abraham hears in the wind that melody not heard since a long time. He knows that tonight frogs are singing to their promised sovereign. Almost he understands the meaning to their song. The constellation clock set to strike precisely. His hour come at last!

It is as another promise made long ago that presently fills him with sadness and with joy. Abraham believes that his father hears also, the music playing eternally through time without time. A song prepared in honor of a prince sent to restore all things.

Abraham watches the monster change year after year, the pockmarks on his face waning, like characteristics in the full visage of an autumn moon. Sometimes there appears a difference of expression on this terrible canvass, a variation ever so slight, as the whisper of a breeze across face of a still pond. He never fully comprehends what that difference means. It is as though this creature hears something, something tuned only to his hearing, something that imparts comfort. However, never the utterance of a word issues from his mouth.

In the beginning, even after the burns nearly healed, the infant cries every night into exhausted sleep. Then the crying stops. It happens suddenly, Abraham recalls. Just one night silence, and the droning of frogs return to the Liberty Swamp.

Often Abraham awakened by violent groans as the growing child slumbers in fitful dream, panting like a wild beast as he twists and claws at the hump on his back. During the worse of these episodes, Abraham plays his harmonica or reads over him passages from the Holy Bible. This always seems to do some good. After a while, he learns to make a deep-throated croak to indicate he wants something, a sound as inhuman as might be made by a rabid dog or a trapped raccoon. This as near to speech ever he utters, convincing his guardian this evidence of mental defect.

Yet Abraham cannot deny the haunting divinity in the boy's eyes, inspired by light that shines from deep within, as though clear passages into a vastness that touches every moment of every hour of every day. A vastness filled with solitude, overflowing into every spiritual meaning conceived through elemental existence. A reflection so vast that even the swamp impatient and short lived. Then one day that spark of the infinite passes away. His eyes changed dark and natural, as his own. This is the day Abraham first becomes apprehensive of the reason the creature born and made to suffer.

Abraham is himself a large portly man– once stronger than a spring bear! This a dream from the past only fondly remembered. It is clear even in the early days that one has come, who will exceed him both in stature and in strength.

His legs swell firm and taunt, like cypress trunks, his arms as the mightiest limbs of a Carolina White Oak. At the age of fifteen, he can support one end of the front porch single-handed, while Abraham adds stones to the foundation. The hump does not change so much, except it grows larger, protruding over his left shoulder as the dark side of a mountain at sunset. Curiously, many of the blisters on his face never completely go away, becoming hard globules just under the skin, clustered together with colonies of tiny warts around the eyes. On what remains of the outer cortex surrounding the ears, only leathery petals. Nor do his lips reform fully. Fortunately, enough un-melted flesh remains to make his face appear almost human; the uneven slit edged with just enough volume to prevent the teeth and jaw from being hideously exposed.

Areas where the fire burned most intense, heals finally after many months, becoming motley patches of pale scar tissue. Nor does his hair ever grow back completely. The few strands that do remain turn completely white and corpselike, reminding Abraham of a slave legend about a beautiful woman, whose hair changes completely gray one night because of a dream. She could not remember the dream; nor can anyone provide explanation. It is just another cocooning of nature, happening without apparent reason.

Abraham never knew what to call him. He thinks of many names, but none seems to fit. Therefore, he calls him Tadpole in the beginning, until the right name should come along. It never does, and in time, Tadpole sticks. Until one day in the swamp, the boy proclaims his own name.

It is spring, the swamp born again after a long and cold winter. Of all the changes undergone by this nether region, transformation into spring the old man's favorite. Marshland blossoms in a way that is different from the dry places. It happens suddenly, and all at once. One day dead and stagnant, the next regenerated, but never really safe. Stalks of green cattails shoot up everywhere. Wild flowers hang as garlands along faint trails of safe passage, while dry lily beds deceptively camouflage treacherous quicksand holes on either side.

"If death is indeed a Lady," Abraham muses, "her beauty most beautiful during this time of year."

The morning of change comes unexpectedly. Abraham and Tadpole leave early to hunt small game. He does not enjoy killing– killing for pleasure is to those desiring trophies! He kills that he might eat and blesses the unfortunate creature that surely must fall his prey. He sees this as an act of reverence given to a fellow being, a chosen sacrifice of life for life. Each morsel of meat is as the flesh of sacrifice to restore his strength and his spirit, all mortal days numbered by this cycle of death into life. It is always sufficient to his needs: miracle of benevolence to the poor and to the rich alike.

Abraham sees this as natural attrition through mystery of faith, a temporal adjustment of need provided to every creature in the course of time. The matrix of this present veil limited, concealing a condition of grander design, conceived to translate all things carnally designed through a passage opening into infinity beyond. Only a blessed few permitted to glimpse this meaning, as an abiding testament of revelation for edification to others.

It is already well past noon, and still nothing sent to cross their path. Abraham does not care really, not this day. He knows that eventually something will come. Always it does. He grows tired more quickly of late. His feet cold and wet, because of cracks in his rubber boots, the old man's body not as strong as it used to be. His silent ward wears a pair of high top green gaiters Abraham fished out of a rubbish pile. There was a small rend in one leg mended good as new with an orange bicycle patch. However, no amount of mending able to change countenance of his adopted son.

"Well, Tadpole, what do you say we stop and rest our bones on that couch yonder in the sun?"

Abraham refers to a fallen cypress tree. Piles of gray Spanish moss pad the wide breath of the rotting bark. At one end of the couch climbs a barrier of twisting roots to form a perfect backrest. Hung above is a crown of swamp flowers, forming a chandelier of green vines.

The swamp filled with furnishings such as these, if one has imagination to see them. He reclines back on the soft wood bench and closes his eyes. The sun feels good on his face, penetrating, as the warmth seeps deep into the worm of his being. He recalls other days like this, while days remaining less certain and fading. He is nearly nodding into a lazy dream, when the log lurches suddenly, nearly upsetting him from his precarious perch. The first thing Abraham sees upon opening his eyes is the boy knelling like an Apostle in prayer.

"What devils got into you, Tadpole?" He manages, recovering his balance.

The boy does not look up, as is his usual habit when the old man speaks. He is watching something, something crouching in a hollow beneath the fallen tree. His face begins twitching spasmodically; his eyes roll back until only white shows. Then both his arms shoot forward with the speed of a loaded trap.

"Father no sleep now!" He growls in an almost human voice, sending the Abraham tumbling from his armrest and landing at the boy's feet.

The creature appears to be laughing. At least it is as close to laughter as Abraham has ever witnessed. Clutched in both hands and raised high over his head is a king size bullfrog.

The swamp suddenly begins cheering. A chorus of frogs that seem to be singing praise to a revered presence, a resounding echo that sends chills up and down the old man's spine. His eyes now open to something new and not seen before. Abraham will soon realize the Liberty monster has greater meaning and definition of purpose to those that know him not.

"By Jehovah, Tadpole, you be able to speak!" Abraham cries joyfully. "Why didn't you ever say something before now?"

The boy sits down on the fallen tree, the Bullfrog hanging limply at his side. He appears changed somehow, his countenance somehow sadder, wiser, as one who has just discovered a destiny.

"Come on Tadpole– say something else!" Abraham coaxes.

He will not speak again. The miracle of words, after a lifetime of hearing, bears no more significance to him, than the obvious statement itself. Abraham persistently tries to make him speak again, to say something—to say anything at all! Until finally, he throws up his hands frustrated.

"You be the strangest critter I ever know!" He concedes good-naturedly. "But one thing sure; you ain't no dummy! –And you got the sharpest eyes and fastest arms I ever did see! That gives me an idea sure enough."

Early next morning Abraham excavates a small leather pouch hidden in the secret recess beneath loose stones at the foot of his hearth. He then walks east toward the old riverbed, passes the cemetery, and skirts around the outer circumference of the red brick mill belching scarlet clouds into the clear blue morning sky like a restless dragon awakened from sleep. Crossing the access bridge connecting the Liberty Peninsula to Pixley County, he heads toward higher elevation where the air less humid.

He meets Red Eye coming the opposite way. The white man only hangs his head and crosses quickly to the other side, the rusted child's red wagon squealing obscenities as he scurries quickly away.

It is past noon by the time Abraham reaches Anderson Brothers Farm Equipment and Feed Store. The storefront actually a renovated barn once used to raise market pigs, swept clean and transformed from the inside out. The twin brothers, owners of this iconic establishment, good old boys of the south, embodying the narrow-minded pleasantry of country pass times.

"There's a poor old black fellow just come in," whispers one of the owners to his clerk. "Go see what he wants, and then get rid of him!"

Oscar is little more than a corpulent boy with pink puffy cheeks. The clerk, many years his senior, nods obsequiously, and happy to obey without question.

"What can I do for you?" The clerk demands with a not so pleasant smile.

"I want me a frog gig," Abraham replies, his eyes roaming the shelves.

"A frog gig... well, we don't carry anything like that here. You'll want to go down to Buster's Sporting Goods. Yep, I think he carries things like that."

The clerk removes his handkerchief, covering his nose and mouth.

"I know you got it! I seen it here not so long ago. It's about yea long, bright, like it come straight out the furnace."

Abraham makes a wide jester with his arms. To the little clerk he looks like a terrible ogre ready to devour him. The Anderson boy must have thought so too. He whistles to his brother Arnold, and the two come running over.

"What kind of trouble you making here, Boy?" He demands approaching with caution.

The other brother appears from behind a John Deere carrying a crowbar. The two identical in every way: both stocky, both wearing the same kind of clownish pin striped overalls; and both filled with the same kind of fear that manifests into the same kind of prejudice.

"There ain't any trouble," Abraham replies softly, slowly lowering his arms.

He knows from a lifetime of experience what can happen if he moves the wrong way. Taking a slow breath, he continues.

"You got a king size frog gig somewhere in here, and I aim to buy it."

The first brother sizes up Abraham looking a bit stupefied.

"I heard Nelson here tell you we don't carry things like that. We're too busy to have a dumb nig–"

"Hold on, Oscar," interrupts Arnold, still holding up the crowbar. "I bet he means that blubber iron the advertising company from Atlanta give us while we was selling them Howard Johnson Outboards."

"By Jesus, Arnold, I think you're right! That long trident-thing all chromed like a car bumper." He turns to Abraham, his countenance almost intelligent. "I know you people like things that shine. But you got to learn that first you got to have something that shines of your own."

Oscar looks over at his brother and winks, and then at the clerk, who only smiles nervously back, handkerchief still in hand. Without saying another word, Abraham steps over to the sales counter, opens the dusty pouch, emptying out several silver dollar coins. All in mint condition, all dating back to the time of President Grant.

"Get this gentleman his frog gig!" Snap the two brothers in unison to the clerk. "And will there be anything else, Sir?"

Abraham has what he came for. He tucks the brightly chromed instrument under his arm, snorts a blast of bad breath in the clerks face, and departs the way he came.

Next, he makes a stop at Nat and Sons headstone cutters. He has in his pocket a flat white stone picked up down by the old riverbed that he wants cut into a special shape and polished.

"I want you to chisel the words Prince of Frogs just like you do on them gravestones."

He runs into similar opposition here as well. Once again, a few pieces of silver achieve what flesh and blood has failed through more than a century of trying. Still, they wonder at the meaning of the words he has them inscribe into the face.

The sun is just setting when Abraham pushes through the last thicket that shelters his little shanty from judgment of the world. The boy is sitting in his favorite spot under a Weeping Willow at the edge of a flooded glade. By midsummer, the flesh of water will recede, exposing rotting roots and black pungent swamp mud. For the present, at least, it is as beautiful as any fairy tale, a dark silky surface reflecting an enchanted kingdom found only in the marsh.

"Tadpole, I got something for you," Abraham says without ceremony. "You did me real proud yesterday. I'm sorry I got mad after you the way I did. I know you ain't got anyone to call mama and daddy. Lord knows, I ain't been much of either, but I raised you best I could. Now I know you be no idiot. I wrestled all night, and then it come clear to me. This here is for you, Tadpole."

He raises the trident out of a burlap sack at his side.

"There ain't another frog gig like this anywhere in this county. Just like there be only one Prince of Frogs!"

The boy takes the shimmering trident without any hesitation. Never has he seen anything like it before. A glint of sunray catches in his eyes like silver slithers shed by the chromed instrument itself. He raises the sharpened tips toward the sky, grinning ghoulishly.

Miraculously, he changes again before the old man's eyes. A sprinkling of gold and green mantles his shoulders, as the last rays of evening light dissolve weakly through the trees, igniting the bright tip of the trident into a staff of pure incandescence. He is no longer that creature made of shadow, no longer is he deformed. This moment suddenly transfigured into a reigning monarch, he is a prince with authority to subdue all darkness. Old Abraham wonders

within himself at what surely must be the end of these things.

Abraham presents him the white stone with a written declaration of his coronation, along with a green mesh sack. Reverently taking the polished white stone, he begins tracing the chiseled letters with his fingers, the meaning clear.

After sunset, they again descend together into the swamp. The old man shows the boy how to use his new scepter; shows him how to take careful aim and when to strike. He learns with only a little instruction. An arm tensioned like a slingshot, the aim true; his release as a flash of lighting! He is without any doubt born monarch of this place.

The full moon high in the night sky by the time they return to the shelter concealed behind a barrier of cattails. The green mesh sack bulging full with a bloody brood, the boy happier than Abraham has ever seen him. Next night the Prince goes alone. This will be his habit every night after. Often not to return until morning, sometimes gone for days; always he is satisfied by his newfound purpose.

Abraham never persists to know where he goes or what he does. Always he brings back plenty of frogs– so many, in fact, that Abraham begins peddling them about town. He is not by nature a sociable man. Truth is that he prefers more the company of frogs! But since most everyone else in Liberty likes the taste of frog-legs-- with maybe one or two exceptions painfully recalled– this adds up to a fair amount of change every day for store-bought provisions. Not that he has any desires to become rich. It just amazes him that folks so eager to pay for something they can easily go get themselves.

He knows also the real reason why no one dares venture into the swamp at night. Because of the ghost stories and legends of monsters told by fathers to their children from generation to generation, they live in fear of darkness, encroached in lairs of false security. He knows none remember where these stories come from, each new progeny falling victim to secret past deeds further removed from the truth, until only fear and darkness remains.

Second time the creature speaks; it is his name. How he came by this name, the old man has no idea, nor knows what it means. Only it is a name that suits him somehow, a name clear as the Milky Way slicing across the night sky, as certain as foundations of the deep.

"*Weistbaily—Weistbaily*-- the creature states emphatically one evening returning early from the swamp.

"What on earth are you talking about Tadpole?"

"Weistbaily Prince of Frogs," proclaims the boy, raising his trident into the night.

It is a name never heard in living memory; name of Liberty's monster. A name of promise destined to live eternal.

Abraham would never know when the white stone vanished from the cellar where the boy sleeps during the day. Nor is he aware that it is now the enigmatic possession of another. Even if he had known, nothing would have happened any differently.

Every day Abraham grows weaker, more tired than the day before. A fact he beholds clearly reflected within the nebulous depths of those eyes grown more ancient than his own reflected in dark pools of swamp water.

It is one thing to realize that the element of strength fading. Another altogether humbling to accept that even weakness into even greater weakness diminishes. To be aware that the fragile connection binding body and soul continues to dwindle, with only a rotting thread left, frayed beyond mortal ability. Then what-- what is to become of Weistbaily when he is gone? He has partitioned the aid of Lady Smith. Did really she hear?

Weistbaily must have sensed the old man's fear. Yes, he has begun to learn much about fears that exist beyond his realm. He finds the old man napping in his rocking chair on the sagging porch. He says something in his father's ear. It is as a voice from far away. A voice heard often, as though spoken from within a dream.

"It is time," the voice says soothingly"; Father sleep– Lady sleep! Frogs say Weistbaily come soon. Weistbaily Prince of Frogs promise peace... promises forever."

By the time Abraham struggles back to consciousness, he is alone. Then wonders if perhaps all of life just a dream. Still, the old man waits just the same, and is glad that his time grows short. His bones old and decayed like the chair that cracks under his weight, like the weather-rotted porch that has shaded generations since the days of slavery forgotten in the shadows of brilliant white houses that continue to reflect in the light of imagination. All destined to shadow in the end.

He is the last remnant of those days, the last stone cast down in condition to something new... something not necessarily better, just not the same.

The air grows moist. With the twilight come swarms of mosquitoes that relentlessly gnaw the parchment of his flesh. He knows their hours of torment near end! It no longer matters. Soon Abraham changed stronger than the elements.

An ocean of mist appears in the nether world. Another gibbous Indian moon watches in silence through a net of swamp groves, slipping sensuously from shade to shade. A sudden chill touches the old man to the core. The mist crawling and slithering, devouring all that it touches, the frogs as children singing far away.

Then Abraham sees her. She is pale, dressed in moonlight– beautiful, as always he knew she would be. She moves light as air– as light itself! Her eyes approach ever more near; her lips as fruit of future promise filling his soul with warmth.

"I'm afraid," he sobs weakly just before the end.

Liberty Epic of Shadows

Now she kneels beside him, a presence clear, and forever. The old man touched by true peace at last. Father Abraham dies quietly in his rocking chair remembered only by his adopted son. This marks revelation of another sign heralding approach of other shadows still to come.

CHAPTER 26

Chime of Liberty Bell

The Liberty Bell, donated to the First Baptist Church by a sympathetic practitioner even before laying of the foundation stone, represents the symbol of Liberty's pride.

It is an exact replica of the original Liberty Bell in Philadelphia, reduced in scale to accommodate the separately constructed steeple. It measures five feet in circumference around the lip, stands four feet from lip to crown, and weighs over three hundred pounds. Like the original, it is composed of seventy percent copper, twenty-five percent tin, and trace amounts of other metals, including gold and silver.

They say that once it was shiny and bright, like burnished brass, when initially raised into position. However, like all things new, it has grown tarnished over time, turning dark, with pale green fractures. Nevertheless, each Sunday it still rings faithfully clear after so many years, calling the devout and the curious to the edifice of Liberty's chapel.

It rings even now in the distance calling all to morning service, as Davy crosses the land bridge and circles around to the dry riverbed. Surely, Lucile is already on her way to Sunday school, taking special pride in never being late. But not Davy, not this Sunday; he has gotten up extra early just for this occasion. Has studied carefully the forbidden topography using a map his Uncle Frank keeps in his house stolen from the land survey office. He is ready for Jasper Flynn's monster, or anything else that might be down there.

After news of Nela Smith's unexpected death and for other reasons not altogether clear, Davy has decided to hike into the Devil's Den. Like everyone else in Liberty, he has always been afraid of this landmark place. Maybe, it is partly because of the name, but mostly because no one from town ever comes here, and never alone. Bubba might dare; but he would do anything, which somehow counted less.

A longtime ago, the place called Devil's Canyon, later renamed the waterfall mouth of Devil Skull. That when there still ran a fledging river, and long before construction of the reservoir to the north. Now the place just called Devils Den.

The only safe way to get there is to pass along the swamp perimeter, hike around the basin, and skirt along the southern base below the Pixley Museum. Another access shorter, but requires negotiating a treacherous stretch of swamp to the northeast side of the peninsula. Davy shutters, considering this prospect altogether out of the question.

The ridge above marks the beginning of Pixley County, home of the founding father. On a separate ridge nearby nests the shabby habitation of Uncle Frank, his timid wife, and her personal nemesis, the invincible Margrette. The rump of Hog Back Mountain curls sharply from the north, then turns southeast, until the tail almost butts into Piedmont Plateau, where perches the town of Tootersville on the upper slopes overlooking deeper valley.

The two acclivities jut parallel to each other continuing to travel in a southeasterly direction on opposite sides of the Liberty basin to create a bottleneck passage, where marsh water drains into the lower delta. These are not true mountains, at least not the elevations found in the northern part of the state, where the mighty Appalachians melt into the Blue Ridge foothills. They are, nevertheless, respectable altitudes, with conditions ideal to certain projects provided enough money and will available.
It is already early noon by the time Davy reaches the extended jaw at the bottom of Devils Den. The dry mouth

below is now only a gaping hole with twisted teeth of grotesque rock formations worn smooth. It gives Davy an eerie feeling to step through this carved valley of calcified rocks worn smooth by a nonexistent river. He imagines himself one of the children of Israel passing on dry land through the midst of the Red Sea. Only there is no crushing wall of water to fear, no sign of an Egyptian army bearing down on him. In places, it is only as deep as his waist, and then drops suddenly several feet over his head. There are distinct cavities, once spawning holes for strong river bass caught by his Uncle Frank and Homer when they were both younger men.

To Davy it is like stepping into the past, a past before he was even a desire in his father's loins. When he– whomever he is– surely walked these same riverbanks and perhaps went skinny-dipping in the very spot he now stands. Nothing except an occasional shrub grows in the dry rocky bed, marked by some inaccessible crevices that serve as habitation to families of badgers and chipmunks.

He arrives at the base of a boulder approximately thirty feet in diameter, geometrically flat at the top, perhaps shaved away by an ancient glacier. Here the riverbank particularly steep, so he hauls himself up with the aid of hanging Ivy Vines. This giant table makes an idyllic place to stop and rest. Closer examination reveals evidence of severe erosion caused by centuries of rushing water cutting sharply into the out-cropping lip. Carved into the smooth top are several barely decipherable Indian pictographs similar to the ones Davy saw on the rock in the Liberty Cemetery. One is Candy's distinctive Frog Prince holding a giant pitchfork, along with etchings of assorted animals and fish. A familiar triangle appears, sheared away at the peak, and another with three sides, sliced in half by the corrosive elements of time.

Davy still is no closer to know what any of these images mean. However, for some peculiar reason he feels that something terrible happened here, something long ago, and without any evidence.

As he sits down, a soft breeze begins to blow. Just above a whisper, he can almost hear the audible sound of someone saying the word *'brother'*. He turns quickly around, looks in all directions. Again, he hears, or thinks he hears in the swaying branches of a nearby tree the word *'brother'*.

"Who said that?" He shouts.

The breeze dyes down, only silence. Davy decides it just his imagination. Who would be calling him brother anyway? He leaves the rock and continues along the upper bank. Several yards further down he finds a gaping hole gouged out of a wall of sandstone about twenty feet high, along with pieces of shattered quartz. The hole confirms Uncle Frank's account of the dynamite destruction. Scattered about, slices of ironstone with traces of crystal embedded on one side, jagged remains testifying to the violent explosion. Picking-up one of the fragments, he examines closely the grey discolored crystalline shard.

Davy has seen this type of formation during a school science field trip to a cave in North Carolina. This also the day he first sets eyes on Candy Morgan sitting in a seat just in front of him. He fantasized the entire bus trip to be beside her. How wonderful the thought of touching softness of her flesh and to press his lips deliciously against hers. In reality, they never so much as speak the way there or on the way back. Still, it was a nice daydream.

On this trip, Davy learns about stalactites and stalagmites. More interestingly, he learns the existence and definition of a Geode. Volcanic droplets composed mostly of ironstone on the outside with an inner core of crystal caused by mineralization of certain elements combined with condensed hot gases trapped within. They usually range in size from a few inches in diameter to a few feet.

The one described by Uncle Frank would have had to be enormous. Yet, here is the evidence. This manmade hole confirming the dimensions of his Uncle's description of how greedy curio hunters blinded by glitter of profit willfully destroyed this ancient relic of nature. Only remnants of shattered fragments remain. The rest transported away and sold to souvenir shops, embellishing the inventory of rock collectors oblivious to potential meaning of the geologic phenomenon.

Although Davy is no expert, he feels the loss of something important, something that might have shed some light on the genesis of existence. However, the greater enormity of tragedy escapes even his understanding, so he simply tosses the fractured shard aside.

Stepping into the center of the open hollow, the hair on his arms and head begin to stand up. A chill passes through him and into his bones. Yet, there exist no feeling of malevolence; rather, a strange peace exudes from this place. It is as though a spirit remains here that time or chaos unable to dispel. Davy begins to shake, as his eyes fill with tears. He quickly climbs out of the depression, struggling for several minutes to shrug off the effects of this sudden inexplicable rush of excitation.

Finding a suitable spot some distance away, he sits down, retrieves his hastily packed lunch consisting of soda crackers and a tin of sardines marinated in mustard. He eats quickly, unceremoniously washing all down with a swig from one of Aunt Lucile's empty whiskey bottles filled from the water faucet. Davy continues to explore the dry river basin, finding what appears to be a graveyard of stones bearing Indian pictographs describing events that resurrect within him latent memory. Not his memories exactly, but memories of someone else remembered from long ago. As though awakening from a trance, Davy becomes aware of present time again.

Judging by position of the sun nearing the rim of the Piedmont Plateau, it must already be well past four o'clock. Davy wonders if perhaps he should turn back now. Night comes early to the Liberty Peninsula, being a geographic depression located between the two elevations. Besides, what more is there to discover here? Once again, he hears a barely audible, almost familiar voice whisper '*brother*'.

"Who's there?" He shouts leaping to his feet, and looks around defensively.

No reply, only a moist breeze rises from the swamp barrier on the other side of the extinct riverbed. Then he sees something he did not see before. The pictograph rocks arranged according to some design, spreading out from the central location where he now stands. The berry paste used to emphasize the outlines faded, nearly eroded away in places, changes incandescent, suddenly clear.
All these pictographs made by the same hand and through eyes of the same intelligence: all testifying to things that Davy's conditioned mind has difficulty to accept. Here mystery of another epic, not yet understood.

Is it possible Candy right after all? Is it possible there really is a Frog Prince and that he has been here in the Liberty Basin all along? Maybe Candy Morgan is also right about believing through faith in absence of flesh and blood reasoning.

Davy has seen enough to impress his young mind for life. Evening shadows have begun to grow over the valley, shadows that slip sinisterly into other shadows, as he turns back toward home. He sees an Indian holding a sling watching him from behind a boulder– the apparition as suddenly gone! He spies another shadow crouched beside a bush, only to vanish in movement of a light breeze.

Hastening his pace, Davy longs for light and comfort of civilization. Arriving at location of the shattered rock, he trips and falls because of a snare of vines prepared in the way. Jumping angrily up, he begins cursing nature for the happenstance of this trap. Then his eyes catch a gleaming object shimmering atop one of the larger pieces of broken geode, as though intentionally placed here for him to find.

The white rock stands out different from all the rest, polished smooth like tombstone granite, and hewn into the definite shape of a dove's wing. Chiseled on one side are the crisp bold letters that read "Prince of Frogs." On the opposite side, the name "*Weistbaily*," crudely scratched into the face. It is name of the monster!

Although he does not understand meaning of this trophy, he slips it into his lunch sack for later scrutiny. Another moist breeze rises from the swamp basin and again the word '*brother*' carried upon the twilight air. This time clearly articulated. Davy clearly makes out two silver eyes on the opposite shore of the dry riverbed watching him through a camouflage of foliage.

His heart begins to pound, his mouth dry with irrational terror. He sprints into a full gait, jumping over every potential obstacle, acutely aware that a siliceous serpent of evening mist has risen from the swamp valley, now flowing into this extinct basin like a ghost river at his heels. He imagines demons in the air joining packs of wild animals. As he passes the gaping jaws of Devils Den, he can feel many hot breaths licking the back of his neck. Even these Furies are no match to the adrenaline of his terror.

Davy is across the access bridge and back on the Liberty Peninsula, by the time he slows to a quick pace, struggling to catch his breath. He has escaped the thing he saw possessed of those burning eyes. At least he hopes that he has. In days to come Davy will better understand the importance of these events and the prized gift now in his possession. He will ponder the meaning of Prince of Frogs; but most he will wonder why name of the monster appears.

Just then, the Liberty bell starts chiming, calling the faithful to evening worship. Davy decides to join the congregation in prayer. Not because Candy might be there–

not because of Aunt Lucile's insistent coaxing. He goes because he wants to go. He takes a place in the last pew and begins weeping for no reason. He hears nothing that the preacher says, but feels the spirit of the Lord all the same. He finds peace in his soul for the first time. Davy did not have his terrible nightmare that night; nor will he ever dream it again.

CHAPTER 27

Weistbaily Prince of Frogs

One does not know name of the monster that haunts Liberty Swamp. He is in all minds a shadow slipping into shadow, hiding by day, prince of the night. He learns to altogether shun the outside world of men, their treacherous machines, and particularly the cruelty of their imaginations. He is a figment only, existing darkly in a landscape unreal.

He does not judge, because he does not comprehend worldly indoctrination of right from wrong. He knows no hate, because he does not recognize outward difference between the skins of men. He neither hopes, nor despairs; or lusts after the proud things held dear by that world beyond.

Only here matters. Here he is regal and beautiful. Here he is lord of a secret and vast principality existing beyond the fringe of things living and not living. The swamp realm of another kingdom; the frogs his loyal subjects inhabiting alleys of grand cypress halls.

The Lady of the swamp has appeared to him since those early days, while suckling goat's milk in his father's house. She became his mother and his teacher. From beginning, she has revealed to his awareness many secrets, teaching him to discern between quicksand and solid ground by scent only. She showed him how to handle serpents without dying, and how to see without the eye of light. She imparts to his comprehension respect for creatures made different. Those born on wings above and those hatched from mud below. All things made lovely in season, all part of a symbiotic whole.

She manifests other things as well. Things special, and altogether hidden, made of even smaller things, becoming everything seen and handled. Even now he continues to grow daily in her wisdom and her strength. He is the true heir apparent; and the frogs know him by his chosen name.

Father Abraham has never seen the Lady. He has lived all his life in her shadow, without glimpsing even once her presence. Yet, the old man's heart true, as a smooth river stone purified by years of erosion. He believes all things possible, even if he is unable see them with his eyes. Like a child, his father hopes continually for all things. Nor is he is anything like the others. Those who exist beyond and separate, who purposely isolate themselves in dark illusion, blinded by greater brightness they cannot see. Most they fear the shadowy demons that lurk in the darkness of their own consciences.

Before the face of Father Abraham, there is only a bright void— then vague half-life memories consumed in tongues of flame, and the pain. That terrible nightmare of fire never completely extinguished. His soul made calm each time Father Abraham reads to him from a black book always near. Each night sound of the old man's voice quenches the torment in a deep soothing baritone drone that binds the shadows.

In the beginning, he hears only noise, distant intonations meaningless. In course, he begins to comprehend that the sounds form a pattern; and that these patterns are words with meaning. The meaning of those words start to paint pictures, and soon the pictures change into stories. Stories about people and places not animated through deeds of the flesh alone. Events that speak about angels, some fallen, and others in the presence of an everlasting thrown.

Night after night Father Abraham sits as a protectorate presence reading to him by light of a flickering candle, quieting the bedlam of screams within. Until he begins to know by heart the genesis of Adam, beginning with firstborn Cain, who murders his brother Abel. Enoch, a man translated from the earth; and Methuselah, the ancient, whose life and death marks end and beginning in the days of his grandson Noah.

Noah, the eighth person, instructed to build a vessel saving the remnant of humankind after release of a great flood upon the earth. Only Noah, his sons and their wives spared, along with two of every animal in a great vessel called an Ark.

By memory, he can count the generations after the flood and the nations that follow. He sees mighty Nimrod in his mind, born a predator, which stands against the God of creation. Inspired by fear and rebellion, this mortal man divides the world of men by constructing a magnified tower in an attempt to touch heaven. This project brought down instead, through pride of confusion. Afterwards God's spirit speaks to another man named Abraham in a dream, instructing him to depart into wilderness and making a covenant of promise that he will be father of future Messiah.

He observes strictly in his heart the commandments of Moses, delivered after the days of bondage to the Pharaohs of Egypt. He feels within himself the consuming judgment of Samson against the Philistines, armed only with the jawbone of an ass. He learns the meaning of mercy, as revealed to stubborn Jonah that even the wickedness of Nineveh forgiven through repentance, spared from divine retribution.

The Psalms of David sing special meaning to his soul, as he shares the lamenting heart of this simple Sheppard boy made King. Most he understands in this man's life the joy and sadness of divine destiny, as innocence changes to bloody shadow.

From ashes of deepest despair, this King of an earthly principality sees the hope of salvation to every generation provided by the Lord of his Lord and submits in the end to peace.

Each night Abraham reads, his young mind opens to such wonder of excitement established through ordinances immutable, becoming commandments of greater constitution and greater promise inscribed in a heaven beyond this universe of mortal passing. This and more contained within the worn pages of this book read by his father. As all the while, the Lady whispers to his heart these words true; and then something else miraculously happens.

Just one night the one Father Abraham tenderly calls Tadpole is silently born again, his spirit bearing witness to a greater spirit. It happens quietly in presence of a full moon. Upon watching the graceful presence march geometrically across arcade of a starry night sky, he suddenly begins to weep, raising his hands to the architect of wondrous vision. Earlier father Abraham had read to him chapters from the book of Mathew about a man named Jesus born in Bethlehem, a city of Judaea. Now he knows God's chosen Messiah, who he is, why he came, and the truest measure of sacrifice. This night he also receives revelation of his own destiny.

Always he keeps these things to himself. He neither speaks nor indicates that he understands. Nevertheless, he in time is able to imitate the sounds he hears. However, he will do this only in audience of the Lady. Until one day, in the fullness of time, she gives him utterance in presence of his Father Abraham.

This particular day, visage of the swamp radiant as a queen adorned. This is just one of her many faces, just another chimera glimpsed in season. A day like this as a puddle splashed in time after a deluge lasting many generations; and yet secretly mixed in the miry mud is residue of kings fallen, and kingdoms still to fall through ebb of centuries. Only presence of this moment appears in time divided by time, with eternity gaping at both ends.

Ascending above every principality is shadow of the Lady, planting and reaping the seasons.

The king bullfrog crouches in a shallow beneath a fallen log. Before actually seeing it, he feels its presence; a feeling part the Lady, part his own. He knows how much it will please Father Abraham. Knows there is nothing the old man likes better than fried frog legs. It is as the matrix of all living things fashioned in quickness of time.

He perceives the creature as a continuance of existence beyond his own, symbiotic, ever changing and ever patient, as the bog pits that snare those lost great and small. This instance, he is one with the frog, one with the bog, and one with the Lady. He becomes catharsis of action, a motion absent of locality, a being altogether timeless, without future and without past. Strange that what Abraham thinks to hear as speech, not so much language, but manifest groaning expressing joyful apprehension of purpose.

He is confused why this offering causes confusion in the old man's eyes. His gift meant to bring joy, not anger. He thinks it curious the next day when he awakes to find Father Abraham gone. This is the first time he has ever left without saying something. He waits all day at the water's edge, thinking he has committed some grievous wrong. Then how wonderful to see his father break through the barrier of cattails bearing gifts, his face made pure by the revived smile in his eyes

Never has the boy received anything more wonderful. It is a thing pleasant to see, a thing pleasant to hold. It is cold and warm, fearful and exciting, all at the same time. Lifting the remarkable fashioned instrument toward the evening sky, a most amazing thing happens. It begins to burn with a strange fire; burn as the morning star born by brazen elements in mix of twilight shadows.

Words engraved on the tablet of a white stone at first puzzling. In time, he will understand– just as Father

Abraham intends he should understand. This also a promise fulfilled by the Lady since beginning.

That night Father Abraham takes him into the swamp, and shows him what he already knows by instinct. He is a mighty hunter with sword of justice in his hand. His kingdom not realized through weaker substance found in worldly confusion.

He is Prince of Frogs! His kingdom, gray and hidden, stretches into eternity. He is the proclaimed sovereign of many subjects demanding justice, his strength the arm of judgment to slay giants, and the wisdom of a king divining truth among shades of mortal dispensation. His greatest hour is still to come.

Not a soul in all of Liberty he does not know. He watches them in their windows talking and laughing, reverently attached to a flickering kaleidoscope box flashing images made of shadow and light. He watches as they change shifts at edifice of a restless beast and stumble home. Nearly always, they first spend a few hours in the den of one called Homer. Their names unimportant to him, but the face of each he knows memorial. In the simplicity of his mind, they are no different from all other creatures that inhabit the swamp.

The corpulent man that serves potions from berth of his greedy perch and the one that slithers in the night like a pale serpent, he beholds with particular distain without knowing why. They are both made of the same clay; both cursed with eyes empty; both pandering fear to ensnare weaker souls.

He learns to pity the one with burning red eyes that cries like a child at night, and sleeps until morning in the ruins of a gutted smoke tower. He has known the visage of the young, who change old; and the forgotten, whose eyes have grown dim, past seeing, past hoping.

There is one new among them, one who does not belong. This one unique from all the rest, he alone has no fear. And one among them is his brother.

Because he sees, he knows. Because of what he knows, no one sees him back, except through terror of imagination. To them he is the monster of their nightmares, a myth only to keep children in bed, a shadow of things forgotten that haunts dark places in their minds. He alone is aware of true purpose.

Knowledge of his name comes to him one evening without expectation. Father Abraham arrives home shaken and angry. Never has he witnessed anger in the old man before. At first, he does not know what to do. It hurts him to see Father Abraham this way. Hurts him as a son to see the kind eyes of his father made red with humiliation.

"Me hunt frog!"

"No, Tadpole let it be," Father Abraham says in his soothing way. "That boy's got nowhere near your strength–but he ain't all bad, just filled with pain, and blind sure enough. Lord if he ain't got the anger of demons, and meanness to match! He just don't know better. Remember, he is your brother, Tadpole, and my brother, too. Don't we never forget that. We all be the same under the skin; and just as the good book say: we all ought to pray for faith how to love our brother."

Not long after this, he hears two voices talking in the swamp. They sit in the dark drinking from the same bottle. Their conversation loud and boastful, their eyes glistened with reflection. They are as frogs crouched in moon light. One familiar; the other he knows hurt his father.

The one tall and blonde he has watched often, cutting grass for the pretty woman that lives in the big white house near the swamp's edge. The other, short and dark, hunched down low to the ground, a wild animal readied to spring. The tone of their conversation grows more somber, until he hears only the croaking of their voices. Therefore, he decides to play a joke on them.

Leaping from the perch of a fallen tree, he lands hard with both feet in a shallow pool. He then makes several jumping strides toward the two, careful to remain in the deeper shadows. Frogs begin singing, announcing his coming. Finding body of a rotted cypress truck, he heaves the dead roots out of black mud and tosses the carcass in their direction.

They are up and running even before the loud splash. He follows them into town. The shorter dark one throws something heavy into the night, shouting *"monster."* He continues to follow this one, even after the other separates and enters a familiar shabby white house with a green porch and green shutters hanging askew.

The dark one must have sensed his presence, because every so often he spins around with clenched fist, peering menacingly into the night. Upon arriving at the last of a string of old unkempt buildings spread along the deserted avenue in similar disrepair, he pauses and stares intently in his direction, the sparkle of animal eyes searching the fold of every shadow.

"I'll get you!" He yells belligerently and disappears through the arch of a door.

This particular building is different from all the rest. Poised prominently above the front facade shines a newly lettered sign lit up by two cones of light. The letters read, **WEIS T BAILY AND SON**. Approaching more near, now exposed, he spells carefully "W-E-I-S-T-B-A-I-L-Y." The door flies suddenly open, a beam of light slices a hole into the darkness just beside his head. Without so much as a rustle, he is gone, vanished into a pocket of even deeper night.

"Whoever you are out there I swear I will get you and you will wish you never heard the name of Bubba Baily!" Shouts the dark one, and violently slams shut the door.

He continues in his mind to see the letters on that sign even long after he is back in the protection of his swamp. They change somehow in his imagination, growing into a solitary word. From the word, an idea begins to manifest with meaning, becoming a name that he recognizes, a name the Lady of the swamp confers upon him immutable.

He begins pondering his new name, as he might ponder the sullen change of the marshland at different seasons of the year, as in each season, the Lady kneels by his side.

She is the blossoming fragrance of spring, the lush fuse of summer, the nakedness of autumn, the frozen hibernation of winter. Ever since the beginning, she has guided him through halls of the quick, revealing to him places of things dead and forgotten. She has known always the burning in his heart, and knows his moment near.

She is beauty of the swamp, mediator of this place, unveiled naked upon the earth. He is her chosen vessel, now reborn with a name uniquely his own, written indelibly upon the rock of foundation.

That night he takes the smooth white stone given to him by Father Abraham to a special place deep in the swamp. The Lady steps before him, a pale shimmering reflection of light to guide his way. She brings him to a place secret, a place undisturbed and alien, a place that appears altogether different in the night. It is as an obscure crater hidden on the dark face of the moon. Here beats the ever-present heart of the swamp, a bubbling black lake, stretching listless into a misty basin.

In the center of this vision, an ancient cypress trunk climbing high above the mist and mounted with a throne prepared in a cloven cleft. Sometime during its prime, lighting split this tree, allowing two separate appendages of equal stature to grow, as a forked tongue out of the living root.

Now only this dead stump remains, worn smooth and petrified, preserved regal through the waiting ages. Where the fused halves continued to grow are companion armrests, and at the center a prepared seat, slightly concave in waiting anticipation. Hung above the natural chair, a richly embroidered reef made from creeping laurels of thistle laced with wild swamp flowers in full blossom. This princely crown needs only to be broken from this mother vine to anoint the head of the *Prince of Frogs*.

The Lady does not speak in words. Her meaning whispered from a realm beyond the thoughts of men. Her presence made transcendent through elemental change. She is the truth in all things: that which moves, and that which does not. Things made alive and things that are not-- these only beginning statues of her wisdom. She has shown him how to pass over bubbling waters without sinking, and how to see without the eye of light. She is his mother and mentor, all that presently exists, and all that might ever be. She is the mind and soul of one *Xeantee Aconee*!

Mounting the prepared rest, he places the waiting crown upon his own head instantly transformed. No longer deformed or hunchbacked, he is as the glory of man now made perfect. Frogs groan in delirium, chanting over and over his new name. The name becomes song in harmonized beauty, praising in ascending escalation the presence of the Lady and her chosen heir apparent. In his glorified hand shines a gleaming scepter of death and life. He is the unchallenged monarch of this place– the resurrected *Prince of Xeantee*!

Then silence. He takes the white stone from his pocket, and using a tip of his trident, scratches the letters of his new name just as he hears the frogs speak it. *Weistbaily*– a name he has known always— *Weistbaily*– one born of the flesh of his flesh, now the bone of his bone! The name *Weistbaily* magnified through the constellations, as sure as the course of countless galaxies spun enigmatic: myriad rings of burning suns flung into distant universe. It is a name above every name, written boldly from end to beginning, and meaning of something altogether transformed new. It is his name clearly proclaimed at last.

"***Weistbaily--***" announce his many subjects, thronging the throne of their restored prince.

In one hand, he bears judgment of his name written upon a white tablet, his shining trident poised and ready to strike. A sudden flash of light parts the black waters unmistakably true, followed by eternity of silence.

The late August moon climbs full above the lattice of nature's handiwork, the northern sky furrowed with shimmering umbra. Mist rises portentous, slithering around this crowned Lord, a golden king bullfrog withering on the raised tip of his burnished trident.

"***Weistbaily Prince of Frogs-- Prince Xeantee,***" they sing again from within folds of dividing mist.

Their awaited sovereign sits back down on his seat profoundly regal, the Lady knelling passionately at his side. All quiet, except for an occasional– croak— croak– an errant splash here and there– only sound of his heart beating to resonating heavenly spheres. The purpose of his hour fully realized.

Weistbaily finds the old man, as though he is only napping in his chair. This is the second coming of death. Obedient to his promise, the son lifts his father and carries him through the grand halls of his ordered kingdom. As promised, the Lady receives him lovingly into her bosom, receives him as a mother receives one of her lost children.

The black waters ebb slowly over his face, covering the peace of Father Abraham forever. In course, Weistbaily, Prince of Frogs, will mark on the white stone below declaration of his new name, the word *"brother."* A testament made of future promise.

CHAPTER 28

Killing of a Brother

"And the Lord said, '*If any man thirst let him come unto me and drink. He that believeth on me, so say the scripture, out of his belly shall flow rivers of living water.*' Let us all bow our heads and silently pray for the soul of our departed sister."

Preacher Morgan closes his Bible. The afternoon has turned slightly overcast; the sun, a red burning disc smoldering in a haze. The Preacher prays to himself that few last minute mourners arrive. He has some personal business to attend to later in the day.

Nela Smith lay dead six days before Red Eye finds her floating face down in the Widow Pond. By then the body already badly decomposed, rotting tadpoles caught in the net of her hair, her eyes drained of color. The undertakers did what they could. After all, this is not the usual cheap Mill funeral. Hannibal Smith, the late Dr. Smith's brother, insists no expense spared, finally agreeing that a closed casket in the best interest of everyone. Most disturbing, however, the whispers around town that Nela murdered.

According to the coroner's report from Pixley, the victim apparently died of strangulation, not from drowning. In further support of this theory are the massive contusions around the neck and shoulders, with flesh under her fingernails indicating struggle. Although, the supposition frightening, the widow's unfortunate demise will remain on the police record unsolved, until many years later a DNA match confirms what no one ever suspected.

Homer becomes particularly solemn after this. He had found in Nela the perfect soul mate, someone to whom he could almost bare his true self to, someone who understood and accepted his facade anyway. Now she is departed from his life, never to return.

Lucile stands opposite Homer at the graveside, drilling him with fatal glances, which he makes an uneasy effort to avoid. There are others present, wealthily dressed that no one knows. They all leave together without saying a word to any of the local residences. These are acquaintances from Nela's world, a world far removed. The last to pay respects announces himself as Nela Smith's late brother-in-law, arriving in a new model chauffeur driven limousine. He wears an inappropriately warm dark gray wool business suit with a pink carnation over his heart, attached to the lapel by an enamel pin stamped with a physician's cross of two snakes entwined around a blood-red staff.

"She so much wanted to be buried with Bill. Now together they can forever rest in peace," he says, placing the pink carnation on the eloquent mahogany casket special ordered for the occasion.

Then, adds something about Nela being a remarkably stubborn woman, whose greatest failing is that she cared too much. Hannibal always was one for short speeches that add up to nothing.

"My name's Homer. I knew Nela... you might say real good." Homer says somberly, extending his hand.

The other man only looks him over for an embarrassing long time, as he may have reviewed a poorly prepared financial statement. With an arrogant smirk on his face, he turns toward Preacher Morgan.

"Nela's favorite Bible verse is the Sermon on the Mount," he says, saluting Judas Morgan as a comrade reminded of higher responsibilities.

He then departs with the same irreverence as when he arrived. The harried nature of this last minute attendee ushers an abrupt end to the Preacher's well-rehearsed eulogy.

In a way, Bubba Baily is there, too. He remains on a nearby hill beneath a twisted dogwood tree throughout the entire ceremony. What could he be thinking, or why has Bubba bothered to come at all? He must surely know that all the devout women in town will only murmur against him the same. Nevertheless, Bubba watches over them from a distance, brave and alone, as an archangel prepared for an approaching last battle.

Lucile manages somehow to bump into Homer after the funeral. Or was it the other way around? They end up departing together. The rest of the graveside mourners resemble a horde of black birds flocked together, following a stronger scent elsewhere.

Bubba remains where he is. He and Davy have not talked to each other since that last night together in the swamp. Rumor is that he spends a lot of time hanging around Homer's– that Bubba *gets drunk* a lot. Davy guesses it is true, but deep inside he hopes it is not.

"How have you been, Bubba?" Davy asks, reaching the shade of the dogwood.

Bubba raises a dark heavy eyebrow and grins.

"I joined, Dave!" He reports proudly. "My dad was fit to be tied when I told him, but there's not a damn thing he can do about it! Nothing anyone can do about it now!"

"Joined... you joined what?"

"The Marines– The first on the hill– Toughest outfit in the world– Devil Dogs! Dave I'm a United States Marine now! Or at least I will be after I finish Boot Training. I leave for the Island next week."

Davy has never seen Bubba so enthusiastic. He is like a young studding animal in first heat.

"Why did you go do something like that?"

Knowing Bubba he should not be surprised; but like everything he did, it is so sudden, so extreme-- yet, natural somehow, natural for him. That is it! Bubba Baily makes everything seem so natural.

"Didn't you know, boy, there's a war going on? The communists are going to take over the world if we don't do something to stop them. My father knows that, but he would rather let somebody else do the fighting– well not me!" He smiles and reaches into his back pocket. "Besides in the military at least they pay you to drink!"

He hands Davy a full pint of Old Crow, minus a swig or two. His acceptance is automatic, or maybe just a well-rehearsed habit that makes him reach for the nearly full bottle without thinking. Maybe, too, it is because Bubba makes it seem necessary; therefore right, and somehow inevitable.

"I think I'd rather wait until they draft me," Davy heaves, choking down the after taste. "Lucile says the war doesn't make any sense. I've heard a lot of people say that."

"They don't know what in the hell they're talking about! If you don't think communists are real, then look at our economy. Dave did you know that over a third of every tax dollar goes toward defense spending? The communists are real all right! I read where China has so many people that the only thing holding them back is the Great Wall, like a Dam ready to crack open. Unless we make a stand in Southeast Asia now, they will be flooding into our cities next Then how safe are you going to be?"

Bubba has apparently learned a lot during his indoctrination briefing. Davy has never really considered the balance of powers in the world, certainly never this way. He imagines Bubba, along with thousands like him, all rushing together against the base of a great leaking dam and plugging live munitions into the cracks. It seems only a question of time before the walls crumble altogether. Nevertheless, they are determined to blow it themselves, rather than let it fall naturally. At least this inevitable end predictable, as long as there is someone left to push the button. Again, Davy turns up the bottle before passing it to Bubba.

"Have you heard what people are saying about the way Nela died? Davy asks, hoping to change the subject.

Bubba's eyes narrow, his body physically recoiled like a rattler ready to strike.

"I heard."

It looks as though the sun might break through the haze, but already too near the horizon to restore any brilliance to the umber sky. In a matter of minutes, the simmering ball begins melting into the swamp, spreading into a nadir of darkness. Two black men carrying shovels approach the open grave. They sit down, talk and laugh, smoke a cigarette or two, then begin sealing the hole. It is all somehow unreal, somehow sad and irrevocable, attesting to the fact that Nela Smith dead and gone. Just another carcass unnaturally preserved in a wood casket and buried in a hole beneath mounds of earth, until the last trump of eternity sounds.

This moment, Davy sees in Bubba his own reflection. He no longer cares, so long as there is enough whisky to deaden the reality of things. There will be a time when Bubba will suffer. A time when Bubba Baily will experience the worst kind of pain possibly imagined. Maybe this the true reason he came to Liberty in the first place, as a hungry lion prepared against days of famine.

It is business as usual that night at Homer's bar. Not everyone knew Nela. A few hear that a rich woman died, but not more than this. These are the silent children of witness working graveyard shifts, who sweat all night in artificial brightness, and remain in dark rooms with black curtains drawn during the day. They are only half-aware, trapped in a bedlam of constantly humming machinery further dulling the power of their natural senses. In a moment quick and irreversible, the roaring hungry beast might reach-out and grab a man's arm or even devour his life. It is enough for them to know no escape from purgatory. What is the death of an old rich woman to these, a woman that never offered them anything, except a downward glance?

Homer's heart just is not here tonight. The funeral has left him feeling empty, emptier than a glass of his best-selling whiskey. He has felt this way ever since hearing news of Nela's tragedy. He knew something wrong when she did not answer her door. He even thought about reporting her absence to the Sheriff. Now it seems strange to him that he never did.

"It wouldn't have made any difference even if you had," Lucy consoles after the funeral. "Nothing you could have done would have made any difference at all."

As always Lucy is-- by God-- he is lucky to have a good friend like her near to his swollen heart! Perhaps he had even been a little hasty to believe that Nela anything more than a passing fancy. Nela was a special woman, no doubting that, but Lucy is here and now. Actually, he would have preferred to be with her tonight. Except this is Friday, and Homer just cannot bring himself to disappoint so many good paying customers.

It begins as any other Friday night. The usual patrons flocked around the bar. Homer on the other side pouring drinks as fast as his fat fingers can ring them up on the cash register. The same faces, the same drinks, the same meaningless conversations-- little ever really changes in Liberty Town. It would actually be cheaper to buy by the bottle and take it home. Here a single shot costs a dollar– but then there is the wife. She might find the bottle; the rest would just be a waste down the drain.

Tonight there is also another difference. The pinball machine Bubba is always playing partially covered by an apron in a dark corner noticeably silent. It appears someone accidentally spilled a drink and shorted the works. Homer offered a week's supply of whisky to anyone that could tell him who did it. No one ever came forward. Now the machine idle, destined to forever occupy an unkempt corner congested by dusty cobwebs, a final high score frozen on the counter, as lasting testament to its defeat. Davy decides perhaps this also the reason Bubba so quiet tonight. Sometimes he talks about nothing particular, even cracks a smile from time to time at a drunkard joke, but none of it real. Davy should have suspected then what really on his mind.

At half past nine, there are only twelve souls left, not one sober enough to be trusted. Bubba and Davy are sitting on two up-turned crates nearest the front window. Davy has begun rehearsing one of Frank's fish stories: the time his uncle brags about hooking a hundred pound catfish in the swamp lake south of the peninsula. Of course, as in all of his Uncle's tales, the monster manages to get away. Bubba only stares disinterestedly out a small window facing in the direction of the swamp, on occasion nodding his head through a fog of vacant contemplation. Then he unexpectedly makes his move.

"Cowards–" he shouts so everyone can hear. "You're a bunch of yellow belly civilians!"

All becomes quiet, so still that Davy fears they might all rush upon him at once. Bubba smiles; he likes the odds.

"What you mean, Bubba boy? You got no cause to say something like that."

Homer has a lot of pride and begins easing his hand under the counter. Bubba jumps to his feet, looks Homer coldly in the eyes.

"Well, are you?"

"I don't rightly know what you're talking about..."

Homer relaxes from any further movement. He knows from experience that there is more than one way to shoot a critter.

"That murdering monster is still out there! -And all that you brave men can do is sit around here getting drunk like nothing happened-- when every one of us ought to be out there now hunting him down!"

Bubba begins pacing around like a caged tiger hungry for blood.

"We don't know for sure who killed Mrs. Smith," Davy interjects weakly.

"Sure you do, Dave. We all know. If it wasn't for me, he probably would have killed you, too, that night we saw him. I knew then what to do, but he got away. Now look at what has happened."

It is so obvious, which is probably the reason they are all stunned by this revelation. No one even suspected– but of course-- it has to be Weistbaily! There is no one else it can be!

"I say we go down there tonight and get him!" Bubba commands. "Else tomorrow maybe we'll be burying somebody else's loved one."

"By God, Bubba, you're right!" Homer suddenly swears bitterly, hot tears running down his cheeks.

Homer's sanction sends the mob into a frenzy of blood lust. It is as though a needed spark instantly ignites alcoholic rivers in their veins, consuming the mob in hate. Bubba has made everything so perfectly clear. How the monster stalked into Nela's home as she slept. How he must have immediately broken her neck, and then dropped her limp rag-doll body into the Widow Pool just as he has other things in the past. Bubba makes them realize that Weistbaily is actually challenging them all, daring anyone to come after him. Now it is their turn-- hour of vengeance here at last!

There are those that refuse to go for one reason or another. Homer, who has taken another kind of oath long before tonight, decides it his duty to remain behind.

"Bubba, here, take this," Homer says, tossing him his trusty sawed-off single barrel. "Blow a hole in that murdering monster just for me!"

"I will Badger!" Bubba promises, and begins clumsily manhandling the weapon.

No one dares laugh at him.

Face of a gibbous moon grins heinously down at them through veil of meandering mist sent to guide the mob. Horace Bacon, one of those unable to go because his work shift starts at ten, donates several good flashlights to the purpose. Homer provides a stock of warming whisky just in case. They are ready to the man, ready to face every monster hell unleashes.

The beams supporting the tin-roofed porch sag tiredly, a dwelling abandoned by the living. The windows mostly boarded-up; the front door ajar, patched and badly weathered, a place testifying of once living presence.

"This be house of the Negro fella that sells them frog legs," someone in the company volunteers.

Bubba demands some matches, kicks down the door, and steps boldly inside pointing the shotgun like a Hollywood soldier. He reappears a moment later, fire licking the shadows around him. He next grabs a battered rocking chair poised near the entrance and flings it into the burning passage.

"Even a damn vagrant ought to learn how to live decently!" He swears bitterly, slinging the shotgun over his shoulder.

The inflamed shack burns brightly, becoming a torch to light their way. A ghastly red glow spreads around them. Shadows fold and unfold, to create yawning passages that altogether swallows the waning brilliance. Scales of mist coil along surreptitious avenues, as the ghost of a giant slithering reptile. The drawn sabers of flashlight beams prove ineffectual to penetrate more than a few feet into the thick armor of encroaching darkness. It is so terribly quiet that each soldier secretly fears that something unnatural afoot.

Bubba leads the way without once wavering from his objective. He is Ares, god of war, holding his drawn sword. Obsessed, as was Captain Ahab, provided a fresh charge of zealous souls to spend upon his vengeance. They arrive at the edge of a smooth black lake, where the fog parts serendipitously, swirling around what appears to be two tree stumps in the center. Instantly choruses of frogs begin signing around them, piercing shrilly the humid night air.

Weistbaily does not comprehend why so many men from the outer world have ventured into his domain. He has never seen a frog gig like the one Bubba now carries; but remembers this presence from before. Yes, at least two frogs he knows. The Lady said he would come, has made a promise to his name. He is Weistbaily, the only Prince of Frogs! He is brother to them all! But why so much fear? He will make them to finally understand.

Weistbaily remembers the pretty lady that floated free in the pond, and in his heart made glad her days of waiting ended at last. Glad, too, for Father Abraham now released into the bosom of the swamp. So many now— why have they come? Without knowing why, the Liberty monster senses something wonderful almost to happen.

"Weistbaily," he proclaims, landing out of nowhere.

"Monster–" Bubba cries, stepping back, shinning light into the disfigured face.

The posse freezes motionless, suspended in terror, as the hunchbacked monster ascends out of the swirling gray. He is to all a winged apparition rising from the rotting depths of a black lake. Here stands the monster always they have feared. The monster within each one of them manifested at arm's-length from their brave leader.

Weistbaily is a giant greater than Davy remembers, more grotesque than any could have imagined. He begins mumbling something that makes no sense, saliva dribbling from rift slashed across his misshapen face. In everyone's mind, it is a fiend out of the deepest pit of hell. The tormented voice of an abomination already damned. Bubba aims the shotgun, pulls the trigger, followed by a loud click– a dud! Bubba opens the chamber, fumbles for a second shell. Homer has provided him with only three.

The creature still does not perceive the imminent danger, only aware of an instinct growing stronger and stronger within his being. Why have they come to his special place? Do they not comprehend the honor? Why this escalation of fear—why can they not see? The thing in Bubba's hand is what perplexes him most.

A sound at his feet; he sees what no normal eye could have seen. With one free hand, he reaches lightning-fast into the invisible water, raising a serpent into the air. It is the largest Water Moccasin anyone has ever witnessed or ever heard recorded, pale and withering in the monster's strong grip. The giant serpent measures not less than twelve feet long, and at least as large in diameter as Homer's girth. It is perhaps as ancient as the swamp, sliding through centuries of moon light, avoiding presence of every man, never glimpsed or caught until now.

The poisonous snake tries to bite its captor. However, before it can sink the deadly fangs, Weistbaily snaps it away like flexing a powerful whip. He begins whirling the vile serpent around his head, careful to keep his arm always extended. The water snake whips and snaps, rippling and flailing in the mist. The hooded head wrenches back, the sharp teeth in its bleached venom-filled mouth distended; only prevented by gravity from doing harm.

Bubba continues to fumble with the second shell, shoves it finally into the empty chamber. This second shell is also a dud, the loud click like the sharp sound of a trap triggered in his soul. Now better experienced, Bubba empties the chamber and rams into the barrel his last round. This is when the monster says something.

As before, none understand, none except Davy, the word and the meaning this time altogether unmistakable!

Now he clearly comprehends what the creature has been saying all along.

"Bubba no, don't do it!" He cries.

The blast shatters the swamp to silence. The Goliath's knees buckle, the snake slips from his grip, hurling harmlessly away. Weistbaily is not dead– not yet. He manages to lift himself up again. The buckshot has ripped a terrible wound in the stomach and lower part of his chest. This is not all. Sticking in the creature's left side, just below his hump, is the bright silver trident, reason why he did not fall over completely. Bubba desperately searches his pockets for another load, but finds none. The monster extends his arms toward Davy and says again unmistakably clear the word "***Brother***"; then stumbles backward into the lake.

"No–" Davy cries, rushing forward to save him.

Bubba grabs Davy around the neck and holds him back. In everyone's mind it seems certain that Weistbaily already dead even before the black waters close around him, swallowing the monster of Liberty Swamp whole.

Davy glimpses something like a beautiful angel chained and fluttering deep in his eyes. Then fade into an abyss, as invisible arms pull the creature gently down. This is the way of the swamp; the way she cares for her own. Multitudes of amphibious creatures surround the stunned party invisible, and begin chanting mysteriously in a way not usual for frogs. In Davy's ears, it is as the song of angels singing. They sing a name he knows, has known always… the name of his lost brother.

The next morning notices appear around town announcing that the mill closing for good. The Pixley Daily News later confirms this to be true. Also disturbing, the loss of a prominent citizen in the local region found dead in his office late the night before, after apparently choking to death while smoking a Cuban cigar. Hannibal Smith buried in a plot far from his brother after the fashion of all moneychangers. A few days later, the time fixer's son marches off to the Marine Corps Boot Camp training facility on Parris Island. No doubt in anyone's mind Bubba Baily is a natural born killer.

CHAPTER 29

The Exodus

Red Eye and the Preacher are the first to leave Liberty. The church doors carefully removed from the hinges, the polished wood interior mostly gutted, along with the pulpit and the pews. The Liberty Bell that awakened the faithful every Sunday morning remains abandoned in the tower. The workers conclude that the wooden beams of the higher steeple supporting the edifice far too rotten for safe extraction. Any other procedure more costly than the bell is worth.

Another crew from Pixley come after the closure and guts the Liberty Mill. Entire walls demolished to allow removal of large hulks of equipment originally constructed piece by piece from inside. The dye vaults emptied, the generators dismantled, fixtures ripped out, rupturing pipelines, and exposing hemorrhaged masses of electrical wiring. In barely a few weeks, the site little more than a mutilated hollow corpse, except for several hundred sealed barrels purposely forgotten in the basement. Soon the only remaining memory of Liberty Mill will be the location of a good fishing hole, a maze of silent catacombs haunted by treacherous currents to tangle lines, and caution buoys to recreational boaters, marking position of the two submerged smoke stacks that might pose hazard to some of the larger vessels.

Homer mans his bar like every day. The morning paper has come late. Sometimes it does not come at all. The headlines read, "A beloved President Assassinated in Dallas." He merely yawns, folds the newspaper, and pushes it aside. It seems the whole world gone *"plum loco."*

Liberty Epic of Shadows

He reminisces on better days–days seen through eyes of his father, describing what the world like before Homer came along. That also before rise and fall of the first mill built on extreme end of the appendix-shaped Liberty Island, known then only as a secret hunting ground marked by a grove of cottonwood trees. It is here that his father brought him as a boy to shoot Turkey in the fall, deer and quail after Christmas. Those memories so clear just now; so clear that Homer wonders why he has not remembered sooner.

How regal his father wearing oilskin gaiters, fingerless wool gloves, and a red stocking cap. He knew the call of practically every animal in the forest. His sense of smell keener than the prey he stalks. Homer loved his father, the familiar animal odor of his breath, the almost pleasant smell of fresh meat always on his hands. Then one night a few weeks before Homer turns eighteen, his father goes hunting in the Liberty Swamp never to return.

There is a distinctive snap, followed by a dull flopping noise in the back storage area. Homer smiles triumphant, the sign he has been waiting for.

"At last--" He shouts to no one, rubbing his fat fingers together.

The rat has been evading his attempts to catch it for weeks. This time is no different. The trap lies balanced on its side, the bait untouched. Homer shivers. That is twice since last night. Either it is big as a dog, *or--* Homer immediately banishes this thought from his mind!

Homer has never actually seen the rodent, but evidence of its presence undeniable. First, the bags of chips scattered over the counter. Then a wad of twenties Homer keeps stashed inside the wall, gnawed beyond recognition. The greatest loss, disappearance of a gold coin he has kept since many years, discovered in a cave along the Aconee River. This memory lived by a man inspired through greater hope of past expectations, just now so clear in his mind.

Morning of his thirty-third birthday, Homer decides to go bass fishing just before sunrise. The New Deal passed by Franklin D. Roosevelt in its second year promises to make things better-- not just for the south-- but for everyone! Maybe not in time to save the dreams of all, but just might make way to a better future.

Homer always did like to go fishing along the Aconee River. It just makes him feel as a young man should feel in prime-- and always the possibility that one day he just might run across the big one! At this junction of his life, he lives on the Pixley side of the river, lives alone and in isolation. Homer never did have many friends. The ones he did have mostly just drinking buddies. He has had a few romances, but none that ever lasted long enough. It has already been more than a decade since his father vanished without a trace in the Liberty swamp. In less time than that, location of the first Liberty Mill lost in groves of Cattails, even as a new one built. Whitey Miller still somewhere down along the coast.

"No news good news," Homer grunts to himself.

The Liberty Peninsula remains still mostly deserted, except for a few decaying shanties, some poor farms, and a few makeshift living quarters for the demolition crews. The only thing left of several elegant plantation homes that once existed here are mostly barren foundations, dissolving into Cypress foliage since the abolition of slavery. A necklace of smaller dwellings strung along a gravel and asphalt road, begins at a wooden access bridge crossing over to the island peninsula, and coils into a tight circle around what will one day be Main Street of Liberty Town. These last remnants of a failed second dynastic vision surround the obelisk of a gutted smoke chimney abandoned during the Great Depression, while future completion of the new Cotton Mill promises to change all that.

Homer climbs along the banks of the Aconee River casting his fly upstream and allowing the swift current do the work for him. He suddenly snares the behemoth of his imagination since so many years, the rod bent double from the force. He follows the fighting leviathan downstream, careful to keep his rod always elevated, leaning as far over the edge as he dares without falling in.

The strong river bass leaps out of the water, twisting and turning, angry at the capture. Homer is using a '*Meek*' number five reel, spooled with a new medium-strength silk line; the polished cane rod handed down from his father's, father's generation, strong and solid, with just enough flex so as not to break. After a fight lasting nearly twenty minutes, the aquatic animal lays exhausted on its side, submitting to final conquest. Almost he pities the gasping creature. Except it is a beauty Big Mouth weighing no less than seven pounds!

Homer steps to a small waterfall on the Pixley side of a canyon wall, trickling from a source above. He guts the fish, washes his hands and face as a disquieted Pontus Pilot after pronouncing final judgment. The sun has already begun to creep from behind the eastern extent of the Piedmont Plateau, splashing into the river valley, igniting the north wall into a golden fleece. This rock face is composed mostly of pyrite, which under the right circumstance of light reflects brassy yellow, molten gold to all but the experienced eye.

"Fools Gold," Homer muses to himself. "The fabled Pixley's gold!"

Only a few actually believe in the legend of Pixley's gold. Some stories report that he discovered a mine with nuggets as large as a man's fist just lying on the floor. Other accounts say that it the stash of a Pirate's Dead Man Chest. Still others suggest that Pixley made a league with the devil, and received cursed power to change this worthless pyrite into gold coins. These are stories only, told to keep small children in their beds at night: stories that conjure images of an old troll-like creature that still lurks under bridges or in branches of trees to snatch away the disobedient and overly curious. Then something catches his eye lying at the base of a large rock.

The barrel and cocking mechanism, although decayed by many scores of years exposed to the elements, unmistakably the rusted remains of a flintlock pistol like the kind used in the fifteenth or sixteenth century. Homer knows this because he once had an association with a pawnshop operator originally from Charlotte that showed him a collection of old guns and knives. This encounter provides Homer with some education about the history of ballistic evolution. Even a weapon from this long ago still deadly placed in the right hand. This particular pistol most favored by notorious bloodthirsty pirates, a hand weapon similar-- if not identical-- to the one held by the famous frontiersman in a larger than life portrait that hangs in City Hall. The handle turned to dust since many decades; and lodged in the barrel is an unfired led ball. Nevertheless, this is the grandest prize Homer could ever have imagined. He loves guns old and new, and this is the oldest gun he has ever held as his own. This useless relic will remain in his mind the best of all his earthly treasures, until one day another comes along nearer to the emptiness in his heart.

As Homer prepares to turn away, something else catches his eye. No, more than a dim reflection behind the falling water, an unnatural glow that looks at first glance like a shimmering ghost. Braving to peer behind the cascade, he sees a narrow opening streaming a bright aura. Being portly even then, Homer is barely able to squeeze through. Once inside, he stands amazed and takes a deep breath.

The interior shimmers as a crystal cage and is nothing he has ever seen before. Pointed clusters of stalagmites and stalactites climb along the inside walls menacingly sharp. Light filters down from somewhere above, fracturing the shards with luminescence reflected through an exposed quartz window above, positioned just right to catch the sun's rays in early morning.

Homer suddenly feels the jolt of a benevolent energy passing through his body. Momentarily shaken by the experience, he quickly resists, wanting no part of anything spiritual, be it good or evil. He is just that way about things unnatural, preferring to remain grounded to the solid understanding of the earth for as long as he can. This is why he never goes to church and often takes a drink or two alone. The reason he may decide to make selling whiskey his future living, to watch ghost bury their ghosts, without ever wishing to get personally involved.

He is just about to leave the empty chamber, when something else grabs his attention. Something that has lain undisturbed for many generations wedged in the crevice of a rock, waiting for a special eye to discover it. Using his pocketknife, Homer extracts the gold doubloon. It is as a bright spark igniting the greed of his imagination, spreading through his mortal veins as rivers of fiery elixir. Gold— *Pixley's gold–* not just fable after all! This must be the legendary pirate cave of Adam Pixley— and all this time, it has been right here under the nose everyone!

Homer will keep this discovery to himself, just as he does everything else that might be important. He carefully hides the pirate pistol in a coffee can, and then wraps the gold coin in a napkin safely concealed from the knowledge of men. No need to take chances where gold is concerned-- especially when it is his gold!

This happened decades ago, and Homer has managed to keep his treasures secret all this time. Now one of those treasures missing. He knows in his heart that no mortal hand stole his doubloon. Nor does he think to see it ever again. As consolation to his loss, he reaches under the bar and touches the stash of a rusted coffee can. The enigma pirate's pistol, black and dirty from a preservative of old engine oil, retains the touch of certainty in Homer's mind. At least no rodent or hobgoblin can take this from him.

Loss of his gold doubloon surely the worse sign of all. He had kept it through good times and through bad, resisted the temptation to spend it even when he needed a loan to buy inventory for his bar. As long as he possesses a piece of Pixley's gold, Homer feels rich, somehow better than his fellow Libertarians that never see more than the sum of their weekly paychecks. Now with that wealth gone, he has become like everyone else. Only Homer will never admit it! He will never admit that like his patrons, he was once an employee of a soulless monster.

Excavation for the new Liberty Cotton Mill continues on schedule with only a few hitches after the first mill went bankrupt prior to the Second World War. This larger and more modern facility creates renewed optimism to those living in the poor south. Promise of new jobs advertised to infuse life into empty shells of lost souls, and guaranteed employment for their offspring. Prosperity will surely prevail atop the bones of bygone generations. Along with a few new homes to shelter the rich, the wooden bridge replaced by a land access road, changing the name to Liberty Peninsula, and a business district with paved streets, this modern technological achievement will introduce *state of the art* machinery to the stagnating region. Already Homer sees himself as part of this new era.

Homer is one of the lucky ones. He accepts a job burning spent cotton thread spools. After promotion to Dye Foreman, a retirement career looks promising. He probably would have stayed on were he not struck down by an illness. "*Sclerosis of the liver*" the doctor calls it. What they call it matters little to Homer. It means he can no longer drink; and if Homer cannot drink, he cannot endure the hell trapped inside a mindless cast of raging machinery every day for the rest of his life. He, therefore, chooses to do the thing he likes best instead.

Taking all of his savings, he converts one of the abandoned construction offices into a bar and liquor store. Maybe Homer no longer can drink, but by God, he will be around those who need it most! He continues to cheat from time to time with grave consequences. The same doctor pronounced it doubtful Homer will survive past fifty. Now that doctor dead, Homer still alive and selling poison.

Homer has been witness to many changes since then. He has seen wars come and go; witnessed the dream that was Liberty Town rise up in a cloud of prosperity; now only a wispy ghost town. He has watched young men grow old before his eyes; old men that simply stop coming on Friday night. He knows all the faces since the beginning. Always the faces change. Faces that keep coming and going, until now there are hardly any faces left at all.

Another snap; followed by an unnatural silence; and again nothing. It is getting close to evening, the shadows grown longer, the smashed pinball machine crouched in the corner under his expired Liquor License like all the other dead demons in his past. This further reminder of many strange things happening around town since the mill closed down. The strangest being the night the door to his back storage room busted open and his most cherished whiskeys wasted. Pixley's Sheriff called it a senseless act of vandalism.

"Ain't been burning no crosses have you, Homer?" The Sheriff jokes.

"I don't got any enemies…at least none that's still living." Homer reflects half to himself.

"Well, that might be so, Homer. But I would say somebody don't know that." His voice changes more serious, "and you best hope they don't come back sometime when you're home."

This happened several weeks after the funeral of Nela Smith and after the dispatch of Liberty's monster. Homer takes a weekend off to accompany Lucy on a visit to her brother's place. He and Frank go back far, maybe too far, and so end up drinking too much. They both pay hell the next day with the worse kind of hangover! It is the first time in over twenty years that Homer closes on a Friday night, and the only time someone robs him blind. There is an odd discrepancy between what the Sheriff says, and the way the report reads. It states that sometime around midnight someone or something broke down the front door after twisting off the lock. Nearly every whisky bottle in the place smashed. The pinball machine in the back rolled upside down, mangled as though attacked with a sledgehammer. Mr. Baily, who lives just down the block, claims he never heard anything, even though his windows open. The only item missing by Homer's own account is a cash box of money he cannot verify.

However, the bleached human skull in his possession causes some legal controversy. Homer learns that it is against the law to display human remains in a public domain. Therefore, the bartender cited on suspicion, until his story verified as to how he came by this ghastly souvenir from a patron named Jasper Flynn. The human cranium sent down to Atlanta for forensic testing and determined to be the same skull that went missing some months earlier from the antiquities lab. A warrant issued for Flynn's arrest, even if he *is related* to the state governor!

"The monster come back to take his own!" Homer mumbles half under his breath.

"What do you mean by that, Homer?"

"Nothing, exceptin' he'll be coming for us all one day." Homer exhales with conviction. "Maybe even for you Sheriff. Indian, Jew, Negro– even us white folks– there ain't nobody going to be safe!"

The Sheriff only shakes his head bewildered. The elements in this crime just do not add up in his mind. If the object theft, then why should anyone destroy bottles of valuable whiskey, but not take a few dollars in the cash box? Certainly, no one left in town that might wish to vandalize their only watering hole; nor is it likely Homer has any insurance. Therefore, Sheriff Taylors decides there is more to the crime than meets the eye. Homer may not be talking, but it is certain he knows more than he is willing to say.

The greater mystery is not just the vandalism and theft, but what the intruder has left behind. Putrid black swamp mud oozes everywhere, down the walls, tracked and smeared from one end of the bar to the other. In some places it is as much as an inch thick, unlikely the result of just being tracked in. It takes Homer, with Lucy's help, three whole days of steady cleaning to get it all. Even then, the odor continues to linger, an occasional whiff like a dead mouse in the bottom of a trash barrel. Homer gets use to it after awhile. He never restocks his shelves like before. Why should he bother since there are so few patrons left? Those that still do remain have little or no money. The loss of the white skull especially saddens Homer. Now who will ever believe?

Homer bends stiffly down and resets the rattrap. He thinks a good mouser might be more practical– but a rat this big... he is not so sure! The front door squawks prodigiously open and then closes, like the spring of another kind of trap, followed by a rapid succession of clattering knocks. Homer rises to his feet and smiles. He knows Lucy Tracy's footsteps anywhere.

"Hi, Lucy," Homer says, stepping out of the back room. "You wouldn't happen to know anybody with a mountain lion I could borrow?"

Lucy's face breaks into a smile. It happens naturally, happens every time she remembers the way Homer looked when they first met each other. It is a Sunday Morning, Lucy on her way home from church service. Homer squats in the middle of the sidewalk tying his shoelace, his large fingers intent to make a fine knot. He reminds her of a little boy, dressed, but far from neat.

"That is a fine way for a lady to meet a gentleman," she remarks with a humorous sweetness in her voice.

"What–" Homer nearly curses, but thinks better of it; then snorts to his feet. "Excuse me, Miss... my name be Homer. I'm the owner of that bar in town none of you Christian women like." Quickly adding: "There ain't no more sin there, than anywhere else!"

Homer never did like long introductions, only short pleasures.

"Yes, I know," Lucy replies, and smiles her smile. "My name is Lucy Tracy. Of course, since you are such an independent gentleman I should be on my way."

Lucy is a slender woman, a little too narrow in the hips, and with a head maybe a little too large for her body. This defect compensated by her smile, combined with the fortune of nature that she has good teeth and an upper lip that curls only slightly up. She has the propitious habit of wearing her hair in a bun, giving effect of being matronly. To all except Homer-- that is-- a bit old fashion in taste, more than a little attracted to this passing woman on the street.

Lucy's real charm in her eyes– witches eyes to her mother-- but to her father the eyes of an angel. Indeed, they are special, like portals into a timeless blue-green ocean, darkly beautiful, sad, and frighteningly deep. Lucy has loved only once before, swearing never to love again. There are many who dared to court her, miserably stricken down by the cold severity of past pain, which she stabs as a stake pulled from her own heart. Then along comes Homer into her life–her `***Badger on the Hill***'– as she playfully refers to him after moments of special intimacy. Unexpectedly, Lucy's heart becomes full again, her life a belated blossom that has managed to survive lovely, even past the spring of her years, waiting to bloom in Homer's embrace. Alas, this simple man born and raised in the Carolina hills unaccustomed to emotions and thoughts more pressing than the resupply of his bar, realizes almost too late the true honor that is his.

"Lucy, that rat must be one big critter," Homer says, leaning across the bar toward her.

Lucy presence always causes Homer to feel a bit boyish. Yes, this is what he likes most about Lucy. She makes him feel young again.

"Maybe you're not using the right kind of trap." Lucy knows a thing or two about catching rats.

"There ain't any bigger! I say there is something plum spooky about it."

Lucy's smile goes away. It happens so suddenly that it is as if the light of the sun gone out.

"What's the matter Lucy?" Homer consoles and steps out from behind the counter. "Don't shake your head. I know something be bothering you."

This the one thing Lucy loves most about Homer. True- - Homer bit of a boaster. True– he often skirts around the facts. Nevertheless, beneath this selfishly corpulent exterior shines the most sensitive mind Lucy has ever known.

"David is home," she sighs, tears gathering in her eyes. "He arrived late last night. Something is wrong. He won't tell me what, but something... I can feel it."

Lucy is trembling. Homer cannot ever remember seeing her tremble. For her to do it now is unsettling.

"Dave is grown-up," Homer says in an attempt to strengthen her. "You got to let him go. He's a fine young man, and you did a good job raising him. Maybe now the time you told him what you told me."

Lucy's eyes narrow; her body instinctively stiffens. Then relaxes; her softness returns. Homer is right. The time has come, but easier said than done.

"I told him to drop by and see you later." Lucy's eyes drop to the floor, as she begins gathering one side of her skirt. "He promised that he would." She begins to shiver. "I just don't know... he seems so changed now. If he does, would you... I mean..."

"I'll do what's got to be done, Lucy." Homer feels his throat dry, a sudden craving not known since a long time.

Immediately Lucy brightens.

"My `**Badger on the Hill**' –thank you!"

Homer reads in Lucy's eyes the unquenchable sadness. The emotion all mothers feel when letting go of a son. There have always been tigers in her mind, and this the worse of them all.

"He leaves again tomorrow morning. David said that the only reason he came back was to see Liberty one last time the way it is. I felt that at the same time he was saying goodbye to me, too. I keep thinking about that Baily boy, and what happened to him. Davy is not like him... is he Homer?"

This time it is Homer's turn to tremble. Bubba Baily, even his name sounds as a ghost now. Homer recalls that last night when he and Davy came back from the swamp, recalls the look of madness in Bubba's eyes, and the stench of gunpowder that clung to his flesh along with greasy sweat.

Homer has since received two letters from Bubba. The first while he is still in Boot Camp; the other four months later postmarked FMF WESPAC, Republic of Vietnam. The first letter as you might expect to hear from a young man away from home, about his new life in the military, about discipline, weapons, the absence of girls. The second letter reads like an excerpt from a chronicle in Dante's Inferno.

"It's another black monsoon night," Bubba writes. "I'm back on line again. Hell– it's better than being out in the field! At least here, I can find a dry smoke. Last night two Zappers tried coming through the wire. You should have seen them, Homer. There wasn't much left after a belt of

M-60 rounds torn them apart. Still they don't give up. Kill a hundred today and tomorrow two hundred take their place. Like rats– Zappers come only at night! Usually they're rigged with plastics or grenades, and otherwise naked, except for a black cloth covering the groin. They're so full of Opium that you just about have to blow their own booby traps to stop them. You can't fight rats! They come– and they come– and sooner or later, the rats are going to win! It's gotten that I don't want to sleep anymore. I take a lot of Obesitol– that's something like Gook liquid speed we get through the Black Market. They say it's mixed with Water Buffalo piss. They say it makes you hallucinate after a while. I don't care, so long as I don't sleep. When I sleep, I dream. Always the same dream! It is night. I am crouching in shadows, water up to my chin. I think maybe it's a rice patty, but I'm not sure. I am waiting– always I am waiting! Then I hear a voice say 'It is time'. Time for what-- no one tells me anything around here! Frogs begin singing around me. They sing his name over, and over. It is a name I heard once, only I don't remember when or where. Then a shadow ascends suddenly over me, flash of lighting in his hand. It's him! He is coming Homer! He is coming back for us all! You'll see– Weistbaily will be coming for you, too!"

This is the last time Homer will hear from Bubba Baily. Weeks later, a *Missing in Action* notice marked Special Delivery from the War Department hand-delivered to the watchmaker's shop. Bubba's body never found. Not long after that Weis T. Baily packs up all of his clocks and moves away. This will mark the beginning of the second wave of exodus.

"No, Lucy, Dave's not anything like him," Homer reassures at last, hoping this to be true.

He then reaches behind the bar, slips a bottle into a brown paper bag, and hands it to Lucy.

"You go on home now and let the old Badger handle things."

Lucy sighs deeply, as she deposits the bottle into her handbag.

"Tell him... tell Davy that I always loved him as much as Lori ever could. He'll believe more coming from you, Homer. Tell him why... you will tell him why!"

Her eyes sparkle with respect, searching his face inquiringly. Homer just winks and then grins ghoulishly at her from behind the bar. He does this to all his patrons sooner, or later. As always Homer will do what needs doing. Will say what Lucy has wanted to say for eighteen years, but never able to find the right opportunity. Then again, maybe opportunity has little to do with it. Maybe it is just fear that old Cotton Mouth might find out. It is certain this will never happen now. Homer has seen to this personally. He smiles to himself. Justice comes to all in course of time.

Lucy Tracy leaves not once mentioning that the United States President has been gunned down like a dog in a south Texas street. Maybe she is tired of rumors carried on the wind and accepts the only thing left to do is for the dead to bury their dead. Homer might have made mention of it himself were it not for the mysterious rodent in the storeroom that continues to gnaw his insides.

At half past seven, Tommy Grover, the ex-superintendent from the mill, drops in for a couple of drinks and a game of checkers. His body is long and thin, with flesh moldy and bleached-out from too many years in the dark. He is nearly bald, with an ostrich neck that moves cautiously up and down when he talks. He has been an employee at Liberty Mill for forty-one years. Like everyone else, laid-off permanently and without benefits. Grover, however, refuses to be bitter. Bitterness is for old men, and men who have lost their faith. This man sees himself as neither old, nor forsaken. He has been witness to more things than he wishes to remember during his stewardship as taskmaster inside the boiling belly of Liberty Mill.

Grover has the reputation of being one of the *good guys*, a man whose first loyalty was always on the side of the man under his charge.

"So what in the name of Jesus are you going to do in Florida?" Homer inquires conversationally over a game of checkers in response to the news that Grover is moving there in a few days.

"My wife has a brother who manages a motel right on the beach. Maybe something like that... besides, Homer, I hear that the surf fishing is real good down there!"

"Tommy, I never knew you to like fishing," Homer says, making a double leap across the checkerboard.

"That's because I never had time, Homer, never had any time for anything except work," he replies dryly. "For now on, I'm going to have time for everything I want to do!"

The game ends with Homer making a double triple leap with one of his kings. This is not at all surprising, since it remains common knowledge that Homer is the crowned checker champion of Liberty. Grover finishes his drink and stands up to leave.

"You hear that, Tommy?" Homer insists, turning suddenly toward the back storage room.

"Hear what, Homer?"

"Like something bumping and scratching around back there."

"No, I didn't hear anything, but maybe you ought to go and take a look see."

"Nay... probably just a rat– got me a big one somewhere, Tommy– but he ain't going to be here for long!"

They both laugh. Tommy Grover is still laughing as the door closes behind him, leaving Homer all alone. A solitary laugh now, a sound somehow tragic, filled with expectation and dread. This is how it is when all his customers gone. When Homer alone with Homer.

CHAPTER 30

Ancestry

Homer is napping when Dave arrives. He lies propped in his high-backed chair custom made to support his weight. His feet rest on a narrow ledge beneath the bar; his fat fingers locked tightly together. He looks as though he has been here for a long time. Like all the other dusty cobwebs clinging in dark corners, refusing to let go. His body grown old and pathetic, reminds Davy of a sickly bloated animal without long to live.

"Hi Homer," Davy's voice rings clear and deep, altogether trained in the tone of war.

"Da–Dave-!" Homer manages through a peculiar gurgling sound in his throat.

He instantly staggers to his feet and begins clearing the counter, embarrassed at being caught sleeping– and during bar hours!

"You look a little pale, Homer."

"Damn this weather!" Homer curses, and automatically pours them both a drink.

"All the changes around here are enough to test the mettle of any man. I watched them extract last of the turbines down at the mill. They just blasted a hole in one of the walls and hauled it away. Yes, Liberty has changed a lot since I went away."

Homer can see clearly in Dave's eyes what he really means. It is like looking into the bottom of a freshly emptied glass and seeing a trapped tiny being there, the reflection all too familiar, elusive, and soon forgotten.

"I received my orders, Homer."

"Lucy said she thought something was going on."

Homer tries to sound natural.

"I didn't want to have to tell her myself. You know how she feels about war... she just doesn't understand about the spread of communism and things like that. J.F.K. knew, but they finally got him! Now it's all left up to us."

Homer shakes his head thoughtfully. Dave is no longer a boy to receive instruction. He has come into his own at last, a warrior, young and full of vengeance.

"I know what you mean, Dave," he agrees; "women got their own kind of logic alright."

"You have a good way with words, Homer. I've heard her say that you have a devil's tongue... and she likes you a lot."

Now Homer is indeed a double-headed dragon. He looks across at the young man through puffed eyes. How much older he suddenly appears. A lot like Bubba– hell fire and brimstone– they are just alike! A loud popping snap interrupts from the storage room, followed by a sickening flopping like a large fish inside a rubber suit. Homer's eyes brighten as he rushes into the back triumph.

"Damn critter!" He swears, returning with the empty sprung trap. "That makes three times in a day. Hell– I just never saw anything like it!"

A slimy white chunk of cheese skewered in the center remains untouched; the bait still securely attached to a large instrument much resembling a spring-loaded guillotine. Homer believes in homemade remedies and back yard solutions to handle all problems. He has custom designed this trap for a very large rodent indeed. It is an execution device capable of severing the spine of the biggest Tom Cat or break bones in a man's hand if one should be clumsy. Either this rodent is extraordinarily cunning, or else no rodent at all. Whatever the species, it seems determined to remain a mystery.

"You heard it didn't you, Dave? What kind of damned rat makes a sound like that?"

Davy only shrugs his shoulders in acquiescence. There are other things on his mind more important than the feats of a Houdini rat. Homer wipes his mouth and places the trap under the bar where it will remain.

"I heard that somebody killed Cotton Mouth," Davy says in a detached tone.

Homer looks apprehensively toward the darkened corner with shattered remains of the Pinball machine. Only a pale shadow where had hung the picture of Homer and Whitey Miller together. That all past now, dead and buried, a past of broken dreams and twisted fears too long ago to remember with any clarity.

"Cotton Mouth was a mean man at times. Maybe he wasn't always like that, but when he turned mean, he turned plum mean! A man like that sometimes makes himself a lot of enemies."

"I guess he does at that. In the end I guess we all get what we deserve."

Silence... time for the truth has come. Homer's promise to Lucy; something owed to Dave. Unpleasant duties seem always to befall Homer. This is his lot in life, his pound of flesh to bear.

"Dave... I got something to tell you... something Lucy wants that you should know before you go away again."

Homer begins shifting his weight uncomfortably from side to side. He takes several deep breaths, tries to look Davy in the eye, then wanders down to their two empty glasses.

"What is it you want to say, Homer? That Cotton Mouth was my father." Dave's eyes are as blue steel taken fresh out of the furnace and then dipped in cold water.

"Cotton Mouth– Hell no boy— I guess he could've been maybe, but he weren't the one."

"But the picture– you said– Uncle Frank told me!"

"Most everyone thought it was Cotton Mouth because he and Lori were married. Even your Uncle thought so. The truth is she was having an affair with that Doctor fellow all along. Maybe if she weren't so young she never would've chosen Cotton Mouth being the kind of man he was. Since Whitey forced himself on her their first date, she reckoned it as a kind of revenge." Homer looks away, relieved to be done with it. "Lucy suspected the truth as you got older. But it was Nela who finally let the cat out of the bag. I swear I didn't know a thing about it!"

Homer concludes the confession by pouring them both a drink of his best whiskey. This is what men do when face-to-face ready to bare truth of every lie. At least this is what Homer believes in the labyrinth of his heart.

"That day I asked you about the man in the picture-- why?"

"I didn't know myself, Dave– so help me! I always thought you were Lucy's own. She told me only after you went away. I knew Lori had twins, but like everybody else, I thought she drowned them in quicksand. I swear I always thought you to be Lucy's boy."

Homer did not say that the other twin a monster. Maybe he thinks it better this way, or maybe he just refuses to believe them spawned from the same flesh and blood.

"Damn her!" Davy curses bitterly. "She could have at least told me herself. All these years she lied to me!"

"Lucy knew that if Cotton Mouth ever found out that you were still alive, he would sooner or later finish what he begun. He was a dangerous man– and being part Cherokee got plum loco when drunk! Maybe Whitey was crazy, or maybe he was just plain evil. Dave, Lucy done what she done for your own good. He'd have killed you boy– that you can rest sure of. If Lucy had known you weren't his, I'm sure things might have been different."

"So... Nela was right about everything."

Homer glumly shrugs his shoulders. It pangs him to think about Nela. Of the few women he has known intimately, she remains the one he most regrets having lost.

"I reckon she did, but never said anything about it to
me. I first got to know Nela just after... well after your real
Daddy found drowned in the Widow Pond. She took to
drinking Gin for a while, so I ordered a whole case just for
her. You could say we got to be good friends. Nela was a
Lady and wouldn't dare be seen coming to the bar
regularly, so I delivered a bottle every Sunday night for
nearly a year. Never saw a woman take to Gin like that. She
told me once that she didn't think her husband's death an
accident, but there was never any proof. She said she heard
a gunshot that night. Since no bullet marks found and
without proof of a gun, William Smith's death officially
closed as an unfortunate accident. Then Nela got social
conscious and didn't want that I bring her any more Gin, so
we just stopped seeing each other. Now I ain't got anything
against society! But me stop tending bar and becoming
more proper? I just never was ready for that. Me and Nela
sort of drifted apart then. But by God— I know it would
have worked this time!"

"What made Nela suspect it wasn't just an accident?"

"I reckon it was just something she felt, and the fact that
that her dead husband's revolver was missing. I didn't think
about it again, until you and Bubba found that old rusted
gun in the Widow Pond. Remember, we thought maybe it
might have belonged to General Sherman. Then I got to
thinking later how Whitey, just after he got out of jail, went
about town bragging that he'd taken care of the man who
mongered his wife. I also remembered a wound on the side
of his face just above his left temple that looked a lot like a
powder burn. At the time, it didn't mean anything. After
you and Bubba brought me back that gun, I got to thinking.
W.S. would also stand for William Smith. Now it all sort of
fits together and makes sense. Your Daddy was real upset
over Lori's death. I remember how he personally attended
the trial and testified against Whitey. When they handed
down the verdict, he just shook his head and walked out of

the courtroom. As I see it, he decided to make his own justice. He probably told Whitey to meet him at the Widow Pond. Only your Daddy weren't a killer! Whitey was probably so full of whiskey that he just didn't care. The rest... well, we can only guess what must have happened."

"I'm glad that snake is dead, Homer! I wish... I wish I had been the one. He took everything– everything... my whole life!"

"Old Cotton Mouth's days of killing are over for sure," Homer consoles.

"Maybe he killed Nela, too. She told me that she knew Weistbaily wasn't a monster. She said she was sure he would never harm anyone."

"What else did Nela say?" Homer wants to know.

"She said that Weistbaily... was my twin brother. Do you think she was right about that?"

"Hell, boy– how could you be akin to that monster? Besides, he's dead now. You ain't got no living brother, and it's best to let it go at that!"

"Why did Lucile lie to me for all those years? I feel, Homer, as though I was just born. My whole life has been nothing but a lie. She could have at least told me herself. At least Lucile could have told me the truth herself!"

Davy's speech has begun to slur from the effects of too much un-watered whiskey.

"It don't matter none now–"

"It matters to me, Homer! It will always matter!"

There is sudden murderous rage in Dave's eyes. Homer steps back instinctively. He knows all too well what drink can do to a man's soul, knows from lifetime experience that the best way to avoid a whiskey fight is to pour another glass.

"Sure it matters, Dave," he agrees. Homer always finds a way to agree with everyone. "That's not what I wanted to say. Here, have another on me. I just meant that Lucy done the best she knew how raising you. I say she done it pretty good judging by the way you come out."

Dave downs the drink in silence. He does not need to look into Homer's fat grinning face to know what he is thinking. His hand reached naturally under the bar, touching something familiar. Dave knows that Homer always near to the cold steel barrel of his sawed-off shotgun. The same one Bubba used on the night of the murder. Old habits bear no loyalties, and no friends.

His gaze stares past Homer and into a small oblong mirror placed sideways on a shelf, nearly obscured by empty bottles of rare tonics. Of course, he should have known it all along. How could everyone have been so blind? He has the same flax in his hair, the same brow, and the same hands. Even their eyes the same shade of blue. The face may be different, but that only because of what happened. Perhaps the pallor of their skin slightly different in the day, but all the bones, even the tone of their voice the same. The monster spoke the truth, only no one could hear. He could not hear!

Why did Nela never say anything before? Those many afternoons cutting her lawn, trimming her hedges, sipping lemonade in her parlor, why in all that time did she never say anything? A stranger would have seen the resemblance immediately. Nela had to have known– surely, she saw! She knew them both from birth, but never said anything about how much alike they look... until too late. How darkly Liberty keeps its secrets.

"Hell, Homer, I used to think that maybe you was my real daddy!"

"Me! –Damn, Dave, if I was to have a boy like you I'd be real proud! You're a good old boy, always been, too! Why I remember..."

Homer feels suddenly flush, feels a peculiar lightness of being. There is an odd ringing hiss, as blood rushes to his head and drains slowly into his legs. Dave's voice hollow and long ago. The hiss changes to a loud beating sound like the unsteady strike of a sledgehammer pounding inside the cave of his heart. Then Homer's vision blurs and he is somewhere else.

He squats in black mud up to his chin. It is night, the darkness long and endless. He hears nearby the sound of frogs, a weird, unearthly chorus singing a name over and over again. A name he remembers hearing more than once in his dreams, ***Weistbaily-- Weistbaily!***

"Homer... Homer... you okay?"

Dave fades into focus like an apparition from another time. He is a big boy, familiar, almost a man in the Marine green dress uniform. Always they send strong boys with clear eyes and young dreams to fight wars for dying old men, who have stopped dreaming since a long time. It seems somehow not right that it should always be this way. Alas, the chosen many always the naive and the foolish-- only the gung-ho young can be counted on not to surrender for the sake of peace.

Homer sighs deeply and exhales a breath of relief. He is glad at least to be alive. His eyes will perhaps see another sunset and hopefully another sunrise. He may again feel the cold. Maybe even know the warmth of a woman's touch, if for only a few more hours. It is not Homer's fault that there will always be names to fill the cemeteries and plentitude of bones for rats to gnaw.

"Just the whiskey," Homer manages, shaking his head. "Use to be that I could down a whole bottle without as much as a headache. Now... now I got to be more careful."

Davy gives a nod of understanding. Yes, he knows all he needs to know now. It is well past dark by the time Dave Tracy leaves Homer's bar. He is last seen stumbling along Paul Revere Road by the old cemetery at the edge of town. The next morning Lucile finds in his bed a dead bullfrog and a bouquet of wilted flowers plucked from a grave in the cemetery. Homer never tells Lucy the conversation between him and Dave. There are some things better left man to man. It will be more than two years before Lucile sees her sister's son again. He will have changed more than ever she could have dreamed possible.

BOOK SEVEN

Promise of the Here After

CHAPTER 31

Homer's Iliad

It is as a black sea that crept out of the lower valley and surrounded the doomed little town over night. Frogs are everywhere: on sidewalks, in cellars, even perched on rooftops.

"Now how the devil can a frog get on top a house?" Homer muses to himself.

It little surprises him that they are capable of squeezing under the door and through cracks where the baseboards buckle from the floor. Still it is certain that frogs lack ability to fly. Equally sure they cannot climb up vertical walls, nesting like bats in the steeple of the Liberty bell tower!

"No–someone must have thrown them up there... someone– no, but that couldn't be."

Homer feels another shiver coming on. He steps to the back of the bar, pours himself another drink, and sits back down upon the throne of his existence. Once was a time when he did not need to drink alone. Once was a time– *damn that noise*! He downs the double Rye with one gulp, turns, and courageously faces the window. Soon Liberty and its monster will be only a lost legend-- Homer's Bar and Liquor Store, a rotting lair for catfish.

Between the cornerstones of these walls, Homer has counted begotten generations divided by sickness and death, has heard rumors of wars to end all wars, and wars that never seem to end. The only thing still standing in Liberty older than the liquor store is Homer himself, unless the ghosts counted. Homer chuckles. There certainly are enough ghosts– *and of course the monster*!

Just then, the building shakes, as though something large and sluggish brushes the outer wall. Homer quickly pours himself another drink— not much longer now!

Homer only a boy when first he heard about the monster. That about the time when the northerner mill people arrived to survey the land track populated by abandoned plantation ruins, and before the First Baptist Church erected at edge of what would become a consecrated cemetery.

He and his father live together in a raw timber house on the lower south ridge of Hog Back Mountain. Homer never knew his mother. She died shortly after giving him birth, and Homer's father never wants to talk much. When he did talk, it is most always the incoherent mumbling of mountain shine. Homer's earliest childhood memories are vague, mostly dark and shadowy visions glimpsed only in dream. Some seem less real-- others altogether too real!

However, he will never forget one particularly hot summer night. He crouches in the shadow of a Chinaberry tree, seeing the moon struggle in a tangle of upper branches. His father and a neighbor pass a bottle of home-brewed corn whiskey between them and share stories about Coon hunting. A sudden shriek pierces the night from the swamp below. Homer hops automatically to his father's side, nestling near a cold Winchester rifle, the lifeblood of their mountain existence.

"The monster sure enough," exclaims the neighbor.

Homer's father stiffens and takes another swig of the pure elixir.

"Your papa, here, he told you about the monster... ain't he boy?" His eyes bloody sockets; his pale face drained by the slow poison of too much alcohol.

"What kind of monster?" Young Homer braves to ask.

"It come straight out of the Devils Triangle one night– the worst storm I ever seen! My own brother lost his life in that storm. He was on one of them big company cargo ships. They never found nothing, not even a life jacket! That night the monster crawled up into the swamp yonder like some kind of prehistoric fish. Then it growed legs and arms and started hunting folks just like your papa and me hunt Coons. I hear tell that the frogs start singing when it comes– singing just like God's own angels!" He winks at Homer's father, reaches up, and makes a feeble grasp for the moon. "One of these nights that monster's going to snatch us all away!"

There is a ring of truth to the drunkard tale. That vision in the old man's mind Homer unable to shake off– even for the rest of his life. He never forgets those glaring red moonshine eyes that seem to glow in the dark. The moon, an agonized skeleton snared in a net of China Berries, desperate to escape the twisted grasp. To this day, he still remembers the hot whiskey breath that contaminated his flesh to the bone, through the bone, and into his soul.

The fall of that same year tragedy strikes the Miller place further down the valley. A fire begins mysteriously in the middle of the night. All perish, roasted alive, all except for Miller's youngest boy, who survives by a miracle. In all appearance, the boy had taken a trip to the Out-House where he falls asleep. Young Whitey is bewildered at first why the night so bright, or why so many neighbors present. All stand helplessly by while the house burns to the ground with his whole family inside. When finally he does know, Whitey Miller never sheds a tear, never talks about it to anyone, as though memory of the incident died with the dying of the flames at dawn. His only inheritance a Bowie Knife made by hand and with a six-inch blade. The wooden handle, though badly charred, retains a grip, the kindled steel bright as new.

Homer's father, being a good-hearted man, takes in the orphan. There are no living relatives known to anyone. Like most poor families inhabiting in the surrounding hills, the Millers wandered in from parts unknown. Everyone else on the mountain already with more mouths than they can feed, and one more mouth only means that much less for the rest.

Whitey grows fast, grows to be big and strong like mountain boys do sometimes. Homer is a year older, and strong as a bear. Whitey quickly surpasses him in stature. Maybe because Whitey is part Cherokee, a bloodline inherited from his mother born in the upper Appalachians, he has tendency as a youngster to throw terrible temper tantrums over the smallest of things. In the beginning, it is almost humorous; more the reaction of a spoiled child denied. As he grows older, a truly violent nature begins to emerge, a murderous rage pure and without challenge, a rage that grows more dangerous with each passing year. Add to this, the pale, almost albino pallor of his skin and eyes, cursed with some random gene rarely seen in nature, he often looks and acts possessed. In later years, even Homer tremors when Whitey Miller pitches one of his fits of anger, especially terrifying when he is drinking.

Something else Homer and his father learn, Whitey sometimes likes to kill things just for the fun of it. Usually it is a small animal like a squirrel or a field rat. Then he kills something big, something that belongs to someone else.

It is just after suppertime a man named Anderson, who works a farm down near the swamp valley, knocks at the door accusing Whitey of shooting one of his siring pigs. Whitey grabs his small caliber gun determined to shoot the farmer as well, only Homer's father home to stop him.

"Did you do it, boy?" He demands sternly, looking Whitey squarely in the eyes.

The boy, almost a man, searches the ground for some place to hide his guilt. He knows from experience that there is no escaping that piercing stare. Then his eyes narrow to burning slits and he runs off humiliated. Homer's father just shakes his head gravely, promises to pay Anderson twelve dollars in sweat for the pig to let the matter drop. The farmer is not altogether satisfied. Still, without a legal confession, even the promise of a little money better than no compensation at all. Besides, as Homer's father wisely points out to Anderson, he can always butcher the pig for next winter's meat; his twelve dollars lost just to feed a fire of meanness.

It is not long after this Homer's father vanishes in the Liberty swamp, vanishes without a trace. Excavation for the second, more modern cotton mill has been going on for several weeks on the island-peninsula. Homer asks the Work Foreman if he can spare a few men to help find his missing father.

"I met your daddy a few times. He even lent us a hand a while back to roll a big rock up that hill yonder. By the Lord's own grace, we'll find your daddy if it takes a month of Sundays!"

Three days later, and not so much as a paw print of his Coon dog. The Foreman despairingly abandons the search having received severe reprimand from a Supervisor sent out by investors of the future mill.

"I'm sorry, boy, but your Daddy must be gone for good," the Foreman apologizes. "The mill folks are giving me hell. –And you know how people with too much money are! They'd rather spend a million to build a place for their own bones, than waste one dime to save a man's life who don't count!"

That night Homer goes home and cries, until finally he sleeps. The next morning he deposits all of his father's things into the back tanning shed, locks the door, and swears never to go inside there again.

Toward evening Whitey comes home mad as the devil over something.

"Damn– I know it's got to be around here somewhere!" He curses and begins turning everything upside down.

"What are you looking for?" Homer demands.

"You seen somewhere my knife, Homer?"

"No, I ain't. Still that don't give you the right to tear up the place. Daddy's gone. Now it's just you and me left. Your knife will show sooner or later."

Whitey begins pacing nervously. He washes his hands several times, continuously wiping them on his britches. Homer can see by the expression on his face, that Whitey thinks his knife also gone for good.

"The monster got him!" Homer blurts near tears.

"There ain't no monster, Homer," Whitey sneers back. "Your Papa probably got drunk and wandered off into a bog pit. You know that dog of his never had no sense. He probably jumped right in after him!"

"Shut up, Whitey– you got no right to talk like that!"

"I'll talk any way I want, and you can't do nothing to stop me!"

Then Homer realizes that Whitey is full of corn whiskey– his father's whiskey! No longer able to endure injury, he hits Whitey square between his pale serpent eyes. It is like striking the trunk of a tree. Instantly those eyes change red and narrow. He starts to growl, lashing out as a demon embodied with evil force. He lifts Homer over his head and throws him against a wall, splitting the baseboards. Homer is truly angry for the first time in his life, filled with a rage that nearly matches that of Whitey himself. He continues to attack, kicking, biting, and clawing. Both covered in blood by now, as two colossuses spawned of the same force. It seems only a matter of time before one, or both, collapse dead. Finally, when he becomes too exhausted to continue, Homer finds opportunity to retrieve a single barrel saw-off hidden behind the wood stove.

"I'll blow your snake head right off– so help me!" He screams between breaths, his finger already squeezed on the trigger.

"There ain't no need for that!"

Whitey is dead sober now.

"I think it's time you clear out of here." Homer threatens, motioning toward the door with the gun barrel.

Whitey does not say another word. He backs slowly away, turns, and slithers out, as was his habit. Later Homer hears word that Whitey seen jumping a freight train heading for the coast. It will be several years before he hears from Whitey Miller again.

Homer never did get over the loss of his father. It was the monster, and he knows it. The man with the red eyes had been right about everything. It is only a matter of time.

Before building of his bar, Homer takes up residency inside the abandoned temporary construction office at the junction of two intersecting dirt roads and begins selling whiskey that the waiting might last a little easier. He waits through good times, and through bad. After so many years, Homer is still waiting for the monster to come. Only now, he waits alone... waits and listens.

Toward the end, nearly everyone departed– everyone except Homer– perhaps the last living soul in Liberty. The waters have already risen to the edge of East Main Street. Another two weeks– maybe three– and you will need a rowboat just to go to the end of town. It remains a mystery how many frogs there are everywhere, particularly for this time of year. Homer never knew there were this many frogs in the whole damned swamp! Homer concedes there is a lot about frogs he does not know.

Just another Friday night and Homer sits alone in his chair dozing behind the bar. There has not been a customer for more than a month, nor does he expect one tonight. The bar is his home– for a little while longer at lease. Besides, old habits, like old men, rarely die easy. Homer never did catch his unusual rat. So finally, he just stops trying. Neither he, nor the rodent will inherit in the end.

All day it has been cold and overcast: one of those days when it is best to start putting calking around the windows and doors. The kerosene heater next to him knocks most of the chill, but occasionally an icy finger touches the back of his neck. Lucy Tracy now lives with her brother out in the country. She had asked Homer to buy a house somewhere so that they can live together. Homer refuses, saying that his money is his, and will remain in his own pockets! Why should he waste his life-savings just so she can live in one of those fancy Pixley houses!

After Dave stops writing her, Lucy moves in with her brother, since Frank's wife ran away with a passing stranger. It is now going on three months, and he has not seen or heard from her since. Just as well, since it only confirms to Homer something he already knows. All women want the same thing– and want men to give it to them! –But by God, he misses her! Maybe next week he might drop by and see how she and Frank are getting along.

Lately he has been thinking a lot about Bubba. Homer admits that he never particularly liked Jews much. He cannot say why really, only that the feeling always seemed natural. It is just the way of things; the way they have always been. That Bubba Baily, Jew or not, Homer liked him! He was one of a kind! What a full-grown man he would have made! Homer certain he had fought the good fight in the end, and died boldly for ideals not really his own. He can just see him now, weapon in hand, holding his position in that strange and foreign land– Bubba fearless to the last! In a way, Homer wishes he had deserted and is hiding out somewhere-- but knows Bubba would never do that—because he is too much a patriot; too much loyal to his own conscience.

Homer's greatest past regret is that he never actually saw Weistbaily for himself. Just now, he would surrender everything just for one glimpse of Liberty's monster. It is that night Bubba killed Weistbaily in the Liberty swamp, which occupies much of his thoughts these days.

Homer is still waiting when they arrive. The two boys stagger in looking sickly pale. The rest of the mob must have returned to their homes to wait and see what might come next. Homer knows then that something extraordinary has happened.

"You boys look like you could use a drink," Homer says from behind the bar.

"There's no amount of drinking that will change what happened tonight!" Davy shouts tearfully. "We murdered Weistbaily!"

"Murdered...?"

For the first time in his life, Homer finds himself truly lost for words.

"We killed a monster!" Bubba shouts back.

"Where is the... body?"

This one souvenir Homer does not want.

"He sank into a bog pit. Maybe I could have saved him, but Bubba wouldn't let me!"

Dave has become altogether hysterical. After a moment of deeper reflection, Homer takes back the saw-off, wipes it clean, and stashes it back under his bar.

"You boys ain't got nothing to worry about. Some of those bogs got no bottom. Nobody around here is going to say anything. It's about time someone had nerve to kill that monster."

Bubba tosses up his glass, downing the freshly poured shot of whiskey all at once. Homer remarks that he is already starting to drink like a man.

"I don't think Weistbaily was a monster," Davy insists angrily, grabbing Bubba's arm. "You wanted to kill him all along– and we both know why!"

Bubba's rage shoots out like judgment itself. He spins around, grabs Dave by the throat, pinning him helpless against the wood counter.

"You murdered him Bubba!" Davy chocks.

"No, Dave, we murdered him– don't you forget that!"

Homer sees right away in Bubba's eyes that what Dave says is true. Bubba is a murderer, and will murder again if he needs to.

"Ah Dave won't tell anyone," Homer intercedes, pouring Bubba another whiskey. "He's just tired, and maybe a little sick from all this. I know that boy like a son. He would never say anything against you, Bubba."

"See that you don't," Bubba commands, his eyes dark and cruel.

Davy nods his head in obeisance. Bubba releases his hold, empties the second shot of whiskey as the first. After getting his wind, Davy starts moving toward the door.

"Where are you going," Bubba demands without turning around.

"Home... just home."

"Remember what I said, Dave. You tell a soul– I swear I'll come after you!"

"I won't tell anyone, Bubba. It wouldn't change anything even if I did. Besides, you are right. We murdered him. Weistbaily was innocent, and we killed him anyway. And we're going to have to live with that for the rest of our lives."

"You know Dave– you are wrong about everything! You think you know why– well you are wrong! God chose us as an example for all the rest of you. We suffer persecution, just so you can find peace. We kill the innocent, just so you can know salvation! What do you know about love? You believe Weistbaily dead, but I know different. I know he will rise again! That is truth learned from my father! That's what it means to be a Jew."

Davy is already gone. Homer has no idea what Bubba is saying. He stays for more than an hour pouring down drink after drink. It is likely he would have tried to drink the place dry, if Homer did not stop him.

"Weistbaily was a monster– wasn't he Homer?" Bubba slurs in a drunken stupor.

"Why sure he was Bubba boy. Ever since I was knee high to a grasshopper that monster has been scaring daylight out of people. Of course you know what that man from Atlanta saw!"

"He wasn't anything at all like that. Why Weistbaily-- why that name? I don't know, Homer... I just don't know why..."

"Weistbaily is sure enough a peculiar name for a monster," Homer agrees.

"He called me brother... why me?"

"It don't matter now. The best thing you can do is just forget all about it."

"I didn't really want to kill him. Someone had to! Someone had to be the one. You believe me, don't you, Homer?"

"Sure I do, Bubba."

"I really didn't want to kill him..." Bubba keeps repeating, even as Homer ushers him out the door.

It has begun to rain. It makes no difference. Nothing makes any difference now that he has killed the Liberty monster. What more can nature do against him!

Homer watches Bubba stumble down the empty street. Once he steps off the curb and falls. He is instantly back on his feet again, kicks an empty garbage can clear to the other side, and then disappears into an alley between two darkened buildings. What a man he might make someday, Homer thinks admiringly. This is the last time he will ever see Bubba Baily. Now it looks as though all of Liberty's monsters dead. At least Homer hopes they are all dead. Of only one can he be personally certain.

Homer always knew that Whitey Miller was bad. Even as a young boy, there was just something about Whitey stuck in the pit of most people's stomach like rotten fruit. However, he never knew just what evil his adopted brother capable of until the night Bubba found Whitey's lost Bowie knife in the swamp. Then it all became perfectly clear in his mind. Whitey had killed Homer's father. That is why he was so agitated that day many years ago when unable to find his knife. He must have suspected then that he had lost it in the swamp. Knowing how superstitious he can be, Whitey would not have ventured back to look for it. Even if to do so meant saving his skin! This probably the reason he so quickly jumped that train for Charleston. Year after year, the swamp had preserved the evidence, through change after change, the knife remaining undisturbed on the rock where Whitey mistakenly left it. Here it waits for Bubba Baily to find and bring to Homer.

Homer spends one whole Sunday scrapping away the rust with one of Nela's kitchen sharpening stones. She sits patiently in an opposite chair watching him as though she is observing just another natural event that occurs often in vicinity of her garden patio.

"As the Good Doctor always said, 'a measure of oil and a pound of perseverance will restore life to the worse of metals'," she quotes inspiringly.

"He said that, did he?" Homer grunts his lack of interest.

"I swear, Homer, I have never seen you so determined about anything."

"This is the work of a lifetime," Homer replies bitterly. "There's a white snake around that needs killing."

"Let Ahab beware of Ahab!" Nela warns with another annoying quote.

"What do you mean by that?"

Nela smiles triumphantly.

"Oh, it is just a line from Moby Dick. What you said just now about killing a white snake reminds me of what Captain Ahab said about killing the White Whale."

Homer has never read Melville. Now that his eyes are starting to go, likely he never will. Weeks pass. During the passage, many things happen. Nela found in the Widow Pond mysteriously drowned. The night Weistbaily hunted down in Liberty Swamp. Bubba has shipped off to South East Asia, Dave now at Paris Island for Boot Training. Then one evening Homer feels the time for justice arrived-- feels it time to set things right.

He knows Whitey's habits, as well as he knows his own. Knows that on every Friday night he goes into Pixley to drink, ever since that night when he pushed Bubba too far. Homer takes a bottle of his finest whiskey and waits at the junction of Paul Revere where it joins the access road. A cold breeze whines through the bottleneck of Devils Den, proclaiming the approach of another Atlantic winter. The night sky clearer than ever he can remember; the two Liberty Mill smoke stacks straddled menacing above the somber terrain belching a malevolent body, standing as a hunter stalking prey. Nevertheless, the sky of autumn night prevails, compassed by a myriad of winking stars, each point of light representing but a single heartbeat of eternity, a heartbeat that will out-endure the brief history of the entire human race.

Homer feels small just now, feels the futility in his lust for vengeance. A few minutes longer, and maybe Homer would have abandoned his plan and returned to the familiar comfort of his burrow. Just then, a ghost appears slithering toward him out of the shadows. Even at a distance, there is a distinctive presence about Whitey Miller, a pale pallor unequaled by any other living thing.

"You want something to drink, Cotton Mouth?" Homer's voice rings out when Whitey is past him.

Whitey whips around, his squinting pink eyes searching the darkness.

"Badger... what brings you out here?"

Whitey is too drunk to sense his imminent peril.

"I come to finish something from a long time back. But here, first take a swig of this," Homer replies, passing Whitey the bottle.

Whitey's eyes brighten greedily as he gulps down the offered whiskey. It never occurs to him that this is his last– that his torment almost to end.

"You never did find that knife, did you, Whitey?" Homer says reflectively.

"What knife you talking about?"

"This knife," Homer sighs, producing the razor-sharp instrument from under his coat. "The one you used to murder my Daddy before drinking his whiskey."

Whitey is just now beginning to understand.

"I don't know what you're talking about, Badger! I-I best be getting on home."

"I think you know exactly what I'm saying. I think you killed my Daddy and his dog. Then I think you buried them in a bog hole. Only you forgot your knife. Now that knife has come back to kill you. My Daddy always said there is a justice reserved to every wicked act. I waited a long time for this night!"

"No, Homer– you're the only family I got!" Whitey pleads.

"Why, Whitey? Daddy took you in and reared you like you was his own son. There were even times when I felt he took more stock in you than in me!"

"You don't understand, Homer. He caught me stealing his bottle and beat me good with a stick. That night I followed him hunting. I just wanted to scare him a little, make him think that maybe there really was a monster in the swamp. Only that damn dog sniffed me out real quick and tried to bite me! I always said that dog didn't have a lick of sense! When your Daddy saw that I'd gone and killed his dog, he started cursing and swinging his possum gun. He said a lot of hurtful mean things. Said he always figured it me that set fire to the house while my family slept. His eyes were plum crazy, Homer. He wanted to kill me, and I knew it--"

"So you killed him first!" Homer interrupts.

"We're like... brothers, Homer."

Whitey's eyes blur with tears, his neck turning stiff.

Homer feels a weakness of compassion come over him. Whitey is right. They are like brothers. Whitey remains the only living testament to the passing of all that he is and all that he will ever be. Surely a devil, but even a devil can be a source of comfort when that all there is.

Whitey strikes faster than most men capable being sober. Only he is getting old; his reflexes dulled. Besides, Homer expected just such a move. With one effortless motion-- no more than a flash of reflected starlight in the night-- and Whitey drops to his knees chocking on his own blood. He tries to speak, but no sound. His eyes glaze over. For a fleeting moment, he looks pitiful like a forsaken orphan. Then Whitey Miller slumps over and falls face down upon cold cracked earth. Liberty's monster dead at last.

What Homer does next, even he cannot explain; not even later to himself. He strips the corpse naked, cuts off the white serpent head and wraps it in Whitey's own clothes. Only a taste of whiskey remains; which Homer promptly swallows. He next heads straight into the swamp, walking for the better part of an hour. He should have worn Gaiters, but that has never been Homer's way. Times when the icy water climbs above girth of his waist-- sometimes he can barely see more than a few feet ahead because of thick pockets of mist. Homer no longer cares. He no longer cares that his next step might be a quicksand hole. There is still one thing more left to do.

Homer knows when he arrives. How he knows remains a mystery, only here the resting place of his father– the place where Weistbaily descended. It is a place of silences: a place where life and death one and the same. Using the bowie knife as a weight, Homer heaves the bundled head of Whitey Miller into the misty basin. Now at last the memory of his father can rest forever in peace. His grave finally marked. Homer will never forget how the frogs begin croaking in a way never heard before. It sounds to him like a name almost he knows, a name he has heard before... maybe in a dream.

Homer must be dreaming now. He is vaguely aware of everything around him. The cracked window that he cannot remember how it got that way. The large hole in the plaster made when he took a blind shot with his sawed-off shotgun, hoping to surprise his invisible adversary. In the distance, he hears the Liberty bell knelling for no one. It did this sometimes; lately it happens more often. Then Homer hears in the distance something else, a sound clear as the memories and the thoughts of his childhood

"Lord! –They are singing!" Homer marvels, as his empty whiskey glass slips from his hand.

Homer feels keenly the oak wood bar under his feet, the kerosene heater like a smiling demon squatting beside him. Something is happening– something Homer unable to grasp through reason.

Tentacles of gray ugly matter have begun growing over everything, twining and flowing, like a cancer out of control. Homer tries to rouse himself, but his body refuses to respond, paralyzed by peculiar numbness, as his heart and organs sink into a hole at the bottom of his spine. Then he clearly recognizes corpse of his terror– comprehends the meaning of Xeantee for the first time in his life! Now that his existence at the end, he understands everything!

Homer hears the sluggish thing as it slithers and crawls across the floor out of the storage room. It is the ripping of tight flesh, the sound of wet bones chewed in a cemetery. The air grows suddenly moist and sticky, made stagnant by the stench of many centuries trapped in shadows. The empty bar as a wine press filling with the blood of all those lost souls perished here.

He is the monster Homer always feared might be. A destroyer with a bright and terrible sword– an angel without mercy raised out of darkest pit! His eyes flame– his mouth a consuming furnace!

"Jesus, spare me--" He cries feebly, lifted bodily into a blistered withering sky.

Feels less the pierce in his heart-- then feels nothing at all. So Homer takes his place among many shadows… forever to sing his name.

They never did find old Homer's body. His death destined to remain as anonymous as his birth. It is only fitting that he should sleep with Liberty, since here the only landmark of a man named Homer, and his few days on earth.

CHAPTER 32

Legends of Heroes Forgotten

A President of the people long buried and remembered by a flame. The Vietnam War lasted and lasted, until no one thought it would ever end. One day it finally does end. By then, too few left that remember why we were over there in the first place.

The rural south has truly begun to prosper, attracting tourist and new residents from all over the country. Many miles east of the state, spirals two steel and concrete edifices above the horizon, much like giant cotton spool cylinders, representing one of the South's first Nuclear Power Plants built in part by the Army Corps of Engineers. Now preparation underway for a second nuclear installation meant to rival its predecessor.

The gleaming white face of the extended Aconee Dam project, erected between bluffs of a narrow canyon where two ridges nearly meet, is a testament to wondrous achievement. A new Aconee Reservoir made brimming full from the shores of Hog Back Ridge to the lip of the Piedmont Plateau, stretches from the banks of Pixley's new country club and golf resort and into the bottleneck of what used to be the brim of Devils Den. The shores opposite now littered with rich condo-estates and imported white sand beaches along the shores of Tootersville. Already forgotten, the Liberty ghost town drowned at the bottom of this grand lake. Yes, these are prosperous times indeed, a time when all past sins forgotten.

However, a few still do remember. They remember how the frogs kept migrating by the thousands from the lower swamp like a plague unleashed. They say that old Homer remained the longest, barricaded inside his bar, and even threatens Pixley's Sheriff once with a saw-off through the window. They remember that the bell steeple atop Liberty's First Baptist Church broke off, somehow floating for days like a disembodied spirit wandering through the waves; and how the bell begins knelling mysteriously before vanishing into the deep. Most everyone agrees that a piece of underwater debris tangled in the rope. Nothing more superstitious than this-- just something caught in the current below. Then one morning it is gone. Liberty's bell never rings among the living again.

Ten years later a soldier boy comes to town. He limps a little because of a piece of hot shrapnel that nearly took off his leg. There are those that think he looks familiar, only they cannot place him. Then again, maybe he is just one of those bums from the Pixley V.A. Hospital that lives off the charity of taxpayers.

He later gets married to a woman that wants nothing more in life than to live close to her roots. At least they share this in common. The only thing in common they do have. Nevertheless, Beth Ann makes him a good mill wife. She is used to the drinking, used to being all the time poor. She even seems to want a beating from time to time, so he obliges her when the whiskey burns hot enough in his veins.

The cotton mill is exactly as he remembers. It could not be more exact were the old edifice dismantled, brick by brick, and rebuilt here. The mill refuses to hire him on in the beginning because of his bum leg.

"A gimp ex-soldier boy ain't good for much!" The Super says.

Dave Tracy proves him wrong. Proves what a man can do, even if a piece of hot shrapnel the size of a man's fist nearly torn off his leg. He shows them all– *by God*! His leg might be dead, but he is still alive and in need of a job! His leg might be dead, but he can still work a full shift even if it means lower pay!

They decide to put him on graveyard burning empty spindles. After a while, some of the fellows start calling him names behind his back. They often make reference to his red eyes, which makes them uncomfortable. He stopped caring long ago about what people say, so long as he has enough to drink. God knows how much he needs to drink! Beth Ann wisely begins hiding his government pension money every month so they will have enough to live on. It is not much. It never is. Still it is better than what he brings home from his job at the mill after stopping at the local bar. She knows ways of making it stretch-out all right. Beth Ann is just naturally born to mill village life.

Lucile continues to live with her brother Frank a few miles outside of town. Frank is retired now, and ever since his wife ran off with that "*hippy biker*," he has just stopped going anywhere. At least brother and sister have each other. Lucile got old after Homer vanished, and still waits for him to come back. Frank has told her that Homer must be dead; but she continues to insist he is alive and that one day he will come back to her. She does not even recognize Davy when he comes home. No one she ever loved comes back the same.

It is early spring when the waters show signs of trouble. It seems unimportant at the time. An annoyance only, just something emptied from the grave that will go away as suddenly as it began. Red pools belch to the surface and spread crimson through the lake like blood. At first state officials try to keep it quiet, denying any possibility of danger. Even when two members of the Country Club die mysteriously, and others fall seriously ill. Still no one wishes to believe that the cause might be the water. Soon all the fish begin dying. The imported white sand beaches change rust-red, resembling the dry bloodstained bones of a recently dead animal, stinks, and becomes infested with swarms of biting black flies.

By end of summer, someone from Washington sent down to do testing on the water. A prominent local citizen named Judas Morgan meets the man at the train station. According to his indictment, Morgan offers the agent a sizable bribe to go back and just forget about the testing. No one knows what the agent says back, except that he looks none too happy, with Morgan rushing hurriedly away looking even worse. After only a day of samples, the Country Club beach closed, a public health hazard sign posted.

"There are chemicals in there that could eat off a man's flesh if given the right concentration," warns the Washington official. "I am recommending an immediate Federal Investigation to determine those parties at fault here!"

However, there is no investigation. The Country Club closes voluntarily. The condominiums boarded up and abandoned. A Class Action lawsuit soon follows, launched against the State and Morgan Realities. Before the case can go to trial, Morgan will hang himself from the bell tower of Pixley's Second Baptist Church. The courts rule in the end there is insufficient testimony to prosecute anyone else still living.

Davy runs into Candy at her father's funeral. She now goes by the name of Candice Taylors. Her husband, brother to Pixley's Sheriff Taylors, is a Pentecost Preacher with a congregation in Macon, who Davy takes to be one of those `*holy roller*' types. Candy still looks good, even after three kids, but the thing he finds most remarkable is her peace. A peace he has not known or seen before– at least not among the living.

"Poor father," she says, when he comes to offer his condolences. "He handled the keys of life in his hands for all those years. He opened the door for so many others, but he himself would not go inside."

Davy only nods his head. Candy still sounds like a preacher's daughter in his mind.

"Do you remember that day in the cemetery?" He braves to ask after a long and uncomfortable silence. "The day you told me about the Prince of Frogs… the day we—"

"Yes… and no," she interrupts; then her eyes smile compassionately. "But there are a lot of things I don't remember completely from the past. Sometimes I think I was another person then. I know I was lost. How about you, Davy... did you ever find your faith?"

"I spent a year in Nam. Now I'm married and got a job. I guess you might say there's a certain amount of faith in that. You must know by now, Candy, that none of it is real anyway. Nam taught me this. It's all just a question of luck. That day you say you don't remember, I loved you, and I continued to love you in my mind for a long while after. In time, Nam took even that away. Do not think I didn't pray over there. I prayed every day that it would be someone else. Until one day, I no longer cared if I lived or if I died. Now I'm just waiting my turn along with everyone else. If that's what you mean by faith, then I have enough to last eternity."

"You still don't understand," she says without blinking, without judgment. "But you will, Davy– I promise you will!"

"I stopped dreaming like that a long time ago. Dreams are for women and boys. When you go to war something happens, Candy. Something you can't explain. Just suddenly you're a man, and don't know how or why."

Just then, a small girl with striking auburn hair comes up and starts tugging on a fold of her mother's long dress. She is maybe nine years old, very much resembling Candy as remembered by Davy, especially the way her locks fall across the face.

"Mommy I want to go home."

"This is my youngest, named Shelenna. Shelenna, this is Dave Tracy, a friend from a long time ago. Say hello to Mr. Tracy."

"Hi," Davy says awkwardly, knelling down and trying to sound friendly.

The little girl shrinks instinctively into the plaid material of Candy's dress, distrusting of this stranger with painful red eyes. It makes little difference to Davy. He no longer believes in human connection. Just another tragedy of the battle scares he carries within.

"Shelenna is an unusual name."

"My husband says it means *"Reflection from Above,"* based on a word very old in Native tradition. My mother often spoke a word like it, only I did not fully understand the significance at the time. Now that I am a mother, I understand more the meaning of *Shelecheyanu.* I have learned many things about the world and myself since then. I am no longer ashamed of my mother. No longer am I ashamed of my Indian blood. Shelenna is my blessing of peace now. Also constant reminder of things lost in the past."

Candy begins affectionately stroking her daughter's head, looking to Davy as mothers everywhere in the world, even those forgotten, or never known.

"Do you also remember Raymond Anderson?"

"I remember," Davy says reflectively. "I heard what happened to him even before I left. I always supposed he went back to Liberty, and now living somewhere else with his father. Or maybe he married that girlfriend of his."

"I guess you didn't hear that Mr. Anderson died of a heart attack just a few weeks after Raymond came back. In the beginning, after settling of the estate, he went to work in his two brother's farm equipment store. Unfortunately, that didn't last long because he was always drunk and rude to the customers. He's been in and out of the hospital over at the V.A. ever since."

"How do you know all this Candy?"

"Because our church goes there once a month to minister to those poor men-- some such a terrible mess that at times I ask the good Lord why it his will that they survived. Davy, I would like you to go in there sometime and just talk to Raymond. I think it would do you both some good."

Davy says he will think about it. He and Candy talk about other things as well. About school days and good old days that were not so good, except in retrospect. Maybe this is what makes them seem good now. They are past, toothless of mystery and of pain.

"There are some dreams that are real, if only you will allow yourself to believe." Candy says just before leaving. "I used to look for a Prince to come and save me; but once I saw what men could be like, I stopped hoping in fairy tales. Then one day I realize he has been knocking on the door of my heart all along just waiting for me to let him in. Now I have found my Prince– and he will never leave me!"

Tears of joy well in her eyes, pure as light. Davy wants to say she is crazy, but he knows that she is not crazy. Candy has found something. Something real that he wishes he could find, but fears too unworthy to receive. Nevertheless, his meeting with Candy that day makes Davy feel good. For the first time in many years, he does not go to the little bar across the street from the main entrance to the V.A. Hospital.

Just when it seems the worse already past, the final deathblow comes. It is too bad about the Country Club, too bad about the lakeside condominium development. Tainted water makes little difference to thirsty cooling coils of a Nuclear Reactor. Only there has to be water.

Like everyone else, Davy hopes it is a good thing that plans for another future new Nuclear Power Plant already in the works, earmarked for completion in just a few years, promising to bring greater prosperity to the southern region.

Not the rich south, but the poor south, as modern innovation can also mean better paying jobs. All agree that the best days of cotton mills coming to end. These dinosaurs destined to die out and disappear in the footprints of progress and global trade. It is doubtful his generation will be the ones to get those new jobs. Maybe the next might have a chance... just maybe. What did he know about radiation poisoning, birth defects, or the possibility of a meltdown someday? All he cares about is a place to work and a future for his children. Then the truly bad news hits like a meteor rock falling out of the sky, shattering the dreams of all, and sending the deacons of society scurrying to and fro in panicked derision.

It is as the red veins in a wino's temple seeping through fractures in the dam wall, dripping portentously along the white face: Aconee Dam cracking like an eggshell!

Still the worse sign is to come. Overnight appearance of a widening scarlet fracture slashed across the southeast wall resembling a cankered bleeding wound. This is indisputable evidence of criminal negligence, because of too many cost corners shaved and the many pockets lined at the expense of safety inspections allowing for improper construction.

The concrete proves to be of the lowest grade, the steel reinforcement too little, and mostly substituted with pig iron. The experts all agree that the structure's failure imminent. As a measure for public protection, the Aconee Dam must come down. In less than a week, the Army Corps of Engineers load up all their equipment and setup a command site somewhere near the Georgia border. Moreover, the N.R.C. files a report writing-off the entire future power plant project, calling it an economic disaster without equal.

Later in the news, a playboy executive named Jasper Flynn indicted by the F.B.I. surrenders to authorities on charges of Income Tax evasion, willful fraud, and a variety of other charges. In a plea bargain arranged by his lawyer,

Jasper agrees to turn state evidence implicating several high-ranking government officials. His older brother, State Congressman Duke Flynn, also included in the indictments, proclaims complete innocence, quoted to say:

"God as my witness, there are elements of greater importance and greater consequence than meets the layman's eye. Get this investigation over with so that I can go about State business. Tomorrow waits for no man! Future prosperity belongs to those who take the golden horns in their own hands!"

Duke Flynn is still as slick-tongued as ever, and many continue to feel he will make the best governor in South Carolina's history, providing he can survive the fallout. It looks like this is going to be the biggest corruption case to plow through the South in years. In the end, however, it will only help those with money. Like everyone else, Davy is little surprised.

CHAPTER 33

Reckoning

Three days before the scheduled controlled demolition of the Aconee Dam, Davy goes for a last row across the magnificent man-made reservoir. The floodgates partially opened to allow the water to bleed-out slowly; holes drilled and ready for prepared strategic dynamite charges at the base. The Army Corps of Engineers are able to bring something down, as well as build it up, except the latter accomplished in only a day.

This particular day is Thanksgiving, a hint of approaching winter already in the air. At least the cold helps to sting him sober. He has passed another bad night; awakened early in a sweat and with dry heaves. A drink would have been better, except all the bars and Liquor Stores close on holidays. Beth Ann found his secret stash and poured it down the sink. She took her licks like a good mill wife. He thinks she even enjoyed it. Damn that woman has a way to dig under a man's flesh! He never can understand why everything closes on holidays. His nightmares never stop– not even on the day of Thanksgiving. Not even after so many years since he ate cold turkey from a can.

He remembers still the smell of rot; leeches and buffalo shit packed together in his jungle boots! That the day he almost died– the day before he was supposed to go home. Just a peculiar ringing in his ear, time laboring against the pounding of his own heart, an acrid sweet odor like a slaughterhouse in early spring; his life changed forever. But by God— he is one of the lucky ones!

For the first time, Davy realizes just how big the white face of Aconee Dam. It must be a quarter of a mile wide at top water level, a concrete wall wedged between the two reinforced sides of a solid rock canyon. In the bright morning sun, it is a titan sculpture reminding Davy of the Biblical Samson mightily braced between two brazen pillars. This grand edifice destined to fall the next day without ceremony.

He hopes the bobbing bottle might have even a taste of whiskey. It pains his bad leg to have to reach so far. What is a little suffering compared to a man's thirst? Especially a man already so many years drowned in refreshment; and still his thirst not satisfied. Instead of whisky, Davy finds that the corked bottle contains something else. The scrolled piece of paper, tainted brown and brittle, preserved in the sour-sweet smell of Gin. With it is a crumpled business card from a University in Atlanta that reads Jeremiah Wake, Professor of Anthropology.

Davy recognizes the bottle to be a brand Homer use to pedal. Like so many other of his "slow moving" elixirs (which Homer himself usually ended up drinking because no one else in Liberty able to afford it), this one is old, and so rare that it belongs in a museum of ancient concoctions. Almost he throws the scroll away in a fit of bitter frustration. Then realizes there handwriting on it. Usually he did not care to read, especially not when hung-over! However, this particular morning Davy does read. As he reads the words written on this piece of rolled paper, his body begins to tremble, a spring of stinging tears well up, overflowing from the dry desert of his red eyes.

His star wondrous appears in heaven bright
Shadows awake from ancient sleep
Prince Aconee borne upon wings of night
Frogs congregate children at his feet
Peace made in Valley Xeantee

Face in a canyon grins sepulcher white
Place Fallen Eagle makes his nest
And walks still an Indian spirit blind of sight
His soul stripped naked without rest
Bones forgotten in Valley Xeantee

Blood weeping at first morning light
Recalling sin of the father's shame
Summer flies consume his flesh into twilight
The beaver proclaims treachery of his name
Violence remembered in Valley Xeantee

Xeantee Aconee where fountains meet
Frogs singing his chorus tonight
Souls rise from graves buried deep
Legions resurrected into hoary flight
Days restored in Valley Xeantee

Davy just sits in that boat drifting aimlessly with the current until sunset. Times he starts weeping for no apparent reason. Just as suddenly, his sobs change to laughter. Now he knows what Candy has been saying all along. Knows the terrible secret Nela kept to her grave. Not Weistbaily born the monster! It is Davy all along. Yes, he is the true monster.

To Bubba Baily the name Weistbaily mockery to the tribulations of his people and to the tormented memory of an Uncle made to suffer death in a Nazi concentration camp even before he takes his first breath. Branded with the name of a dead man, hung as an albatross of guilt around young Bubba's neck without choice, or ever really knowing why. That name tattooed in his soul like mark of a crucifix bearing witness against worldly sin.

Bubba, therefore, renames himself, demanding acceptance-- not as a Jew-- but just as a man. And what a man he became! Bubba and Davy forged by alliance of guilt through shared emptiness, becoming a brotherhood bound by proud mission to slay the common monster of their fear, a blood oath of defiance handed down from father to son. The true cost measured weight of their immortal souls. Bubba the arm, but the iron forged by Davy's own pain.

Yes, he is guilty, as surely as if he the one to pull the trigger. The name Weistbaily made forever greater than all their apprehensions, signed by promise of innocent blood written through Milky Way of the universe. It is the name of his... *brother*. Not only is Weistbaily Davy's brother, but the brother of Bubba, of Homer, and of Abraham. All blind by the same blindness, and they knew not his hour. In death, Weistbaily has redeemed them all, a mighty hand sent to raise them up in time divided. He is song of *Prince of Xeantee*-- as one resurrected forever in a realm not of this world!

Davy recalls again the white tablet scribbled with promise, a special rock mixed in the dry riverbed of the Aconee River those many years earlier. He remembers the whispers that frightened him so. Why could he not hear then? He begins again to weep for the lost brother he has murdered; the brother rejected and recognized too late. He still has that rock somewhere, only he cannot remember where. In time, it will come to him, as do all things in course.

It takes a week and a day for the waters to drain off completely after the floodgates opened fully and a hole blown in the base of the Aconee Dam. More than six months pass before dry land completely restored and for the birds and the animals to begin migration back to the Liberty Peninsula. The outer walls and steeple of Liberty's First

Baptist Church remain somehow intact, except the bell tower detached, and swept away.

Only the razed foundations, consisting of a few brick partitions, mark location of the buildings that once lined Main Street. All that is left of the Liberty Mill are dungeons of two smoke towers haunted by bats and a most sickening smell. An odor that will linger on for generations to come and will house many legends of ghost and headless monsters.

The cemetery, except for mysterious disappearance of the white Indian Rock, remains the same. It is funny how no one ever thought about those sleeping generations during the prosperous days of Lake Aconee Resorts.

Beth Ann leaves Davy a short time after he stops drinking for a drunkard piano musician that plays in a small bar outside of Easley. She says the reason being that she no longer feels loved. That at least when Davy drank he acted like a man. Last time he saw his wife, she had a freshly bruised lip. Nevertheless, the woman seems happy– as happy as Beth Ann will ever allow herself.

Davy is the first to return to Liberty. He takes up residence in the church cellar. It requires weeks of sweat and hard work to make it livable again. Time is all he has left– too much time and too many memories to forget!

Every last Friday of the month, Davy walks four miles to Pixley and picks up his Government check from the Post Office. Pixley has changed much since the waters resided. The V.A. Hospital now in the process of closing down, all the patients soon to be transferred to a larger facility in Charleston. The Post Office, reduced to half-staff, also prepares to move to a different location. Word is that the mill has begun laying-off in record numbers, with plans soon to close altogether. Seems to Davy he has heard it all before.

Then one Friday he finds something in his Post Office mailbox that shocks him as surely were the letter sent from the grave. In a way, it is just that, a letter written by the hand of a dead man.

A dispatch from Bubba Baily postmarked FMF WESPAC, Vietnam. The envelope crumpled and soiled from years of collecting dust in a crack between two letter bins. The date stamped even before Davy began his boot training. The same month Bubba Baily vanished without a trace. The tone dark, deeply disturbing, a warning sent from hell.

"The nights are long, Dave. You wait, you wait, and nothing happens. Fear is the worse. It's like a cancer– like the jungle rot in my boots killing slowly the soul. In the beginning, I thought the stars here an inspiration of the universe at night. No city lights to fade their glory– no mortal instrument that can dull the effect of this alien hemisphere! Then one night the sky changes dark. It starts to rain. Rain, and more rain– God, it never ends! Even the mosquitoes are a relief from this incessant drizzle. Pounding and the pounding inside my head— the sound never stops-- things in my mind that refuse to die! I have witnessed stunning things, Dave– amazing things! Things that would make your flesh crawl. There are no heroes, only cowards– only butchers! They come unarmed like shadows to die in the wire just so the Viet Cong soldiers can cross over on their flesh and bones. We kill shadows all night. Kill and kill– until machine gun barrels begin to melt! Then a Cobra swoops down and finishes the job. Ten rounds a second, and every tenth round a red tracer, a stream of scarlet pouring in the rain like hot blood. Then all is quiet until morning. We see the shadows for the first time. Young pretty girls slaughtered in the dawn as scattered flowers. Young pretty girls as fallen angels wrapped in morning mist. Mothers crawl near the gates at night rigged with grenades. But their children are the worst enemy, bringing death in candy bags. Fathers snipe us from behind water buffalo while planting their rice patties. What kind of people are they? Don't they know why we are here! Why we have come at all? This is no war– it's judgment! It seems that every day someone dies. Someone I knew. Now I don't care anymore. I don't care if tomorrow it's my turn. I don't care that I'm never going home. I don't care! Still I will never forget one night, Dave; the night we hunted us a big frog. The frogs here are almost that big. Almost they hunt you back! We killed one for the record– didn't we, Dave? We had to do it– someone had to! We did it for everyone else! We are the ones who going to suffer… but it had to be done. Someone must always pay..."

"Someone always must pay..." Davy whispers solemnly to himself.

Why should Bubba be the only one?

The next morning Davy decides to go over to the V.A. Hospital and look up Raymond Patterson. He did not know what he would say really. Maybe there is nothing to say. Still he wants to see Raymond– if only once without his legs. There is no feeling of victory or remorse, only curiosity in the knowledge that it could just as easily been him.

Raymond is sleeping when Davy arrives. The nurse, a crude black woman with fat arms, might have awakened him first, but this not the V.A. way. In her eyes Raymond just a bed number, who ought to be paying rent like everyone else. Davy is unprepared to see Raymond sprawled naked on his bed, his two amputated stubs tucked up into a quivering jelly of beer flesh. He looks very much like a dead tadpole floating belly-up in a stagnant gray pool.

"Who the hell are you?" He shouts, jerking suddenly awake.

"Raymond Patterson?" Davy's tone is without emotion.

"Yea, I guess you could say I'm Raymond."

"You probably don't remember me, but my name's Dave Tracy. I used to live in Liberty–"

"A village boy–" Raymond spits.

He fumbles with the corner of his sheet and pulls it over him so only the upper torso visible. Instantly he appears a man again. A man– although a little wasted from lack of a descent diet and exercise– whole and present as Davy once remembers him.

"I was in Nam, too," Davy continues. "I know a little of what you went through."

"How could you know?" Raymond scoffs angrily. "Yea, I remember you. You are the mill-boy that bumped against my girlfriend the night of the party before I left. You're lucky my old man stopped me. I was ready to tear you apart."

"You probably could have then," Davy replies matter-of-factly.

"But that was then, wasn't it mill-boy. You were lucky that night, and looks like you were lucky in the Nam, too. I got it the second month in country. One minute I am scouting for booby traps, the next I am lying face down in mud with loud ringing in my ears." Raymond snorts a weak attempt at laughter. "I didn't even know those were my legs. Both blown clean off, and I thought they belonged to some other fool. Look at you– not a scratch!"

"I was a lot luckier." Davy concedes. "A piece of shrapnel blew off my knee cap. They had to weld all the bones together so I can never bend it. But at least... it's there."

Raymond's mood begins to change somewhat. He is not exactly more friendly, but less on the defense. Maybe he has just grown sick and tired of being kicked around, finding it easier not to care at all. He and Davy end up talking for an hour. They talk about what it was like to squat all night in leech infested rice patties, unable even to swat a mosquito because Charlie somewhere near. They remember the silence and the pitch black of long monsoon nights, filling their lungs slowly with water... slowly drowning. They remember the dance of Cobras above the clouds spraying death, like the steady hand of a drafter etching a cage of red death from the air. Then for no apparent reason their conversation turns toward Liberty. What it was like growing up from a different point of view. Raymond never believed in monsters– at least not then. He says that later he would change his mind. That today he knows what real monsters made of.

"You still visiting–" the nurse demands crossly, bursting unceremoniously through the curtains and swinging her fat arms tiredly. "Time he get fed. Everybody that don't belong has got to get out right now!" Then turning to Raymond: "Look at you– not even dressed. Lord Mercy– if what's left of you ain't more trouble than it's worth!"

She then mumbles something about being glad when "*they all get transferred out.*" Davy turns to leave not wishing to cause Raymond any further embarrassment. He promises to come back again sometime. Promises he and Raymond will again remember things they both prefer to forget.

"You think I look bad," Raymond grunts, as he crawls like an almost human worm from his bed and into a waiting wheelchair. "You ought to go see this guy on "*New C Ward.*" Napalm– or maybe it was an incineration grenade– friendly fire just the same. I think it was probably Napalm. You know how many bad calls there were. Anyway, his mind is completely gone. No one knows who he is, or even why he ended up here– a living *John Doe*. All he does is ramble through the halls repeating the same word over and over again. Sounds like a name. Maybe it's his name. So that's what we call him, *Weistbaily*."

"Did you say, Weistbaily?"

"Why, mill-boy, you think maybe you know him?"

Davy makes no reply. He knows Raymond will not care. That he is beyond caring about anything now. At least he is still a man, whole when the covers drawn, which is better than many.

"*New C Ward*" is actually part of an acronym for the wing of a new long-term convalescent ward added back during the last days of the Korean War in anticipation to larger numbers of casualties. The planners were not disappointed. It is in truth little more modern in design than the rest of the hospital, except better heated in winter because of electrical base elements, instead of steam radiators; and installed air conditioning for hotter months.

However, the air conditioning remains off during the summer; in winter, the heat maintained always to a minimum. The name "*New C Ward*" has hung on just the same, becoming more or less a symbol of hope to the thousands of passing shades that once wandered these halls. The belief that somewhere is a place of promise to heal the reality of their injuries. Today the corridors empty, the lights dimmed to save electricity, and a skeleton staff thinly spread to attend only the basic needs of those forgotten in this nearly abandoned hulk haunted by only a few lingering ghost.

Davy finds the monster of "*New C Ward*" sitting in a dimly lit room beside a barred window that looks out at a grove of ash trees. Looming above these, the sarcophagus ruin of the eastern rim of what is left of the Aconee Dam barely visible.

"Bubba, is that you?" Davy asks softly. "It's me, Dave Tracy from Liberty."

He does not turn or say anything, but continues to stare out the window intently watching something in the distance altogether invisible to mortal gaze. Davy understands immediately what Raymond meant. He has never before seen a man so disfigured– perhaps once– but that was a long time ago.

Both ears have been singed-away, the nose little more than a lump of white melted flesh. There is evidence that plastic surgery tried to restore the partial semblance of a mouth and functional eyelids. Instead of creating a more human effigy, it only grimly emphasizes the unreal visage of a Halloween mask. Except for a sparse corpse-like patch of long hair on the right side of his head, he is altogether bald, the surrounding flesh slick and matted like melted ice cream. No beard or mustache that Bubba surely would have had by now, the eyebrows erased, nor are there any discernible eyelashes.

"Weistbaily..." he growls in a deep grating voice without even looking up.

No, this cannot be Bubba Baily. The voice all wrong, nothing about him even vaguely familiar. Surely, Bubba is dead and this only someone he knew– someone to whom he told the grisly story about Liberty's monster.

"Weistbaily–" he says again, turning his head and looking straight into Davy's eyes.

Then Davy knows. Still he must be sure. Taking the monster's left arm, he peels back the sleeve of the light blue hospital garment. Here all the proof he will ever need, the only proof that could have truly convinced him. The number of his lost uncle incinerated at Auschwitz long before Bubba conceived and branded with his name. Numbers made by Bubba himself, crudely cut into his flesh with a sharpened knife. Like the postmarked letter, Bubba Baily somehow lost in the clutter of administrative shuffle.

Bubba's mind completely gone; or so it seems to Davy. The only intelligible human utterance being the name of Weistbaily, the name of a monster they both know. At times Davy thinks he glimpses a glimmer of recognition in Bubba's eyes. Then his face changes completely blank, as he again repeats the name '*Weistbaily*'.

The V.A. is all too happy to release Bubba Baily to Davy's care. Maybe they believe the story. Maybe they are just glad to have one less patient to deal with. At any rate, they stamp the name of Weistbaily on the release form, saying only that it makes the paper work simpler.

Davy tries for months to locate Bubba's father, but without success. He knows that wherever the time fixer today, there lives a clock named *Weistmeister* with the shadow of love and death looming forever near. That he will always remember his son– just as he will always remember his brother– just as he remembers all those buried dead and those not buried.

Bubba Baily now hunts frogs in the Liberty Swamp with a chromed frog gig Davy has custom-made for him. Usually he hunts alone; more often hunts by night. No one sees him much, and those who have swear that it cannot be anything human. Some of the old timers that still remember say the monster has returned to Liberty Swamp. Still no one will ever dare venture there alone to find out. Bubba keeps to himself, shunning strangers that on rare occasion wander accidentally onto the Liberty Peninsula. Bubba always was a loner.

Davy keeps track of time for both of them. He knows that time is all they have left. He knows of a place in the swamp, a place where there is a bell half buried in the mud that once rang clear from the steeple of Old Liberty's First Baptist Church. This where Weistbaily descended and continues even now. A kingdom of shadows Bubba goes every night to hunt frogs.

He is Nimrod descending into the nether regions with mighty sword drawn. Always the frogs begin to sing at his coming, chanting the name of their resurrected prince. It is a name everlasting inscribed clearly in stunning heaven: *once a son of man– now son of God— Prince of Frogs!*

BOOK EIGHT

The Past Remembered

CHAPTER 34

The Reconstruction

Jeremiah Wake is a man of fragile disposition. He cannot hold his liquor, so he rarely drinks; his stomach cannot tolerate rich foods, therefore he eats a bland diet. He dislikes traveling very far from home, and does so only when deemed necessary. However, what he lacks in social graces, Wake more than compensates for in determination. He might have been clinically classified autistic, at a time when no clear diagnosis existed. Not even his wife and only daughter will ever fully understand the intricate nature of his work. However, a brilliance Jeremiah Wake possesses above all others is his analytical mind, a mind capable of seeing a collage of meaning, where others see only a jumble of disorder.

Now at last Jeremiah Wake thinks he has pieced together much of the story surrounding the Liberty Basin mysteries. After the analysis of information accumulated over a lifetime, the histories of many disassociated events begin to fall into place. It is the job of an archeologist to reassemble what time has dispersed. Of course, there will always be a few pieces missing, but enough for a beginning, middle, and an end. Jeremiah likes solving puzzles– in fact he is a man driven until he does.

This particular puzzle begins with his father, who participated in excavation for the new Liberty Cotton Mill prior to the Second Great War. Traumatized by the unearthing of a mass-murder grave while draining portions of swampland for the foundation, never again does he find peace. He tells young Jeremiah often about a smooth white rock, flat on one side and with a basin, marked by unusual Indian pictograph symbols. In order to preserve the evidence, he and his men roll this boulder to the top of hill as a memorial to those many lost souls.

His father finds something else as well, something he thinks meaningful. A charred alligator tooth drilled through with a hole and engraved with pictograph symbols similar to larger drawings etched on the larger rock.

"I think this belonged to someone special." He says, placing this recovered artifact on the fireplace mantle. "This is the reason we will always keep it special. One day, Jeremiah, you will be the one to find out the truth. And there is a truth here to be unearthed that no one wants to talk about! Something so dark I can no longer sleep well at night. Their blood cries out to me, son; and you are the one to set things right."

Jeremiah often studies the pictographs engraved on that alligator tooth, but has little comprehension of what the symbols mean. One is the profile of an eagle's head, the other stick-shoulders of a scarecrow body draped with a long overcoat. Between these is a nearly erased two-dimensional pyramid his father mistakenly thinks to be an Indian Tepee with flames shooting out of the top. What possible meaning could these symbols have, other than indication that the engraver knew something about ornithology and agriculture? After the passing of his father, Jeremiah tries unsuccessfully to find the described Indian Rock. However, he does find other artifacts, which only deepens the mystery.

Along the shallow rapids of the Old Aconee River are several rocks of variable size with pictographic engravings that match the style of those on the Alligator tooth. The patterns put together seem to be telling a story, a story that Jeremiah only partially understands. A common motif is the stature of a larger than life figure pointing benevolently toward the sky. On many, he holds a three-pronged spear; and on another, the trident changes to what could be described as a Christian cross. Some depict presence of one reminding Jeremiah of a faithful Moses extending a beacon toward an island geographically similar in shape to the now Liberty Peninsula. Engraved on other rocks, stands a monstrous creature draped in animal skins breathing fire from its mouth and with lighting shooting from its eyes.

On still other series, the same creature changed reverent, as one extolling blessing upon a multitude. Common motifs are pictograph drawings that express judgment. One exemplifies a frog-like being lifting skyward a withering king Bull Frog at point of a pitchfork, an instrument similar to frog-gigs sold at local sporting goods stores. Another depicts the pierced head of giant prehistoric water snake hanging limply from the tips.

What Wake logically concludes to be final representation in the series is a sequence showing a revered chieftain falling asleep, surrounded by mourners. Above the congregation are, in all appearance, angelic presences seated upon celestial thrones, dissimilar to the animism often embraced by most indigenous North and South American cultures. Clearly, these representations span scores of years.

However, a reoccurring theme is the insertion of a pyramid shape almost identical to one barely recognizable on the badly charred talisman. In Jeremiah's mind, the significance of the polyhedron constructions bears little relevance to his anthropological and archeological investigation. His prime interest centered on deciphering the pictograph inscriptions, with only vague comprehension of their truer meaning.

The first real breakthrough comes when the Smith couple invites him to the famous Pixley Estate before converted into a heritage museum. Doctor William Smith is an acquaintance of Wake's father, first introduced by Smith's lawyer brother, Hannibal Smith, whose practice resides in a small adjacent town named Tootersville. It is Wake's third year working at the forensic lab of the Atlanta

Investigative Crime Center. As a favor to his father, Wake drives an assigned vehicle one hundred and thirty miles beyond the border of his comfort zone to examine what will turn out to be a treasure trove of unrecorded history.

Before relinquishing the home of her ancestry, Nela Smith, the good Doctor's newly espoused wife, and last of the Pixley heirs, has discovered several unusual relics while sorting through centuries of family heirlooms. He likes the pleasant nature of William Smith immediately, feeling within this man a compassionate nature also shared by his father. There is something predatory about the wealthy former Pixley lady, which makes Jeremiah uneasy. Her presence arrogant and possessed by an air of superior challenge, causing the educated professor to stammer slightly, a nervous habit when speaking to the female gender leftover from his childhood.

"I think this could be Basque," confidently proclaims the Doctor's wife, handing him a leather-bound volume.

Even then, Wake's reputation as a linguistic scholar unparalleled in the south, being proficient in several languages– even languages considered dead when compared to the modern vernacular. The woman is right in her deduction that some of the personal commentaries added to the Spanish Ship's Log contain Castilian conjugations unique to the Euskara speaking populations.

These hardy inhabitants are synonymous with the highest peaks of the Pyrenees Mountains, an ancient geographical divide separating Spain and France throughout early European histories. Yet, it is very different from modern day Basque, further bastardized by Spanish influence during the domination of the Habsburg Empire of the middle seventeenth century. A history of cultural infusion further validated by consistency of many log entries made by a one Jacob Belasko, last Captain of the Spanish Galleon, Libertad.

"Y-Yes, you are right Ms. P-Pixley," Wake stammers, after a quick glance at the ledgers.

"You may call me Nela Smith now," corrects the lady, glancing affectionately at her husband. "William and I are starting a new life together."

Wake only nods pleasantly as he continues to sort through the contents of this treasure trove. The Latin Bible obviously a personal possession of one of the Mission Priest that ventured to spread the Gospel into the new Americas after the early Conquistadors establish an entrenched Spanish presence.

The greater mystery, however, is the parchment scroll. Jeremiah recognizes immediately the script to be original Hebrew taken from the Book of Prophets. To be exact it is the seventh chapter of Isaiah, which details the expected birth of the Jewish Messiah. Jeremiah wonders what connection there could be between this scroll and the captain of a Spanish Navy Galleon in service to the House of Hapsburg. More perplexing, why would a man representing the revived Holy Roman Empire be in possession of this kind of Jewish artifact, usually reserved to Rabbis only?

Wake will later discover that the greater find is a white rock entwined with red hair of a human scalp. The few small engravings etched on the surface suggest only a rudimentary meaning at the time. What strikes him most is symbol of an eagle's head identical to the one on the gator tooth talisman still on the mantle of his father's house, confirming that this stone and the inscriptions originate from the same source. These further linked to those found in the old riverbed, making the historical connection unquestionable. Carefully cataloging the contents, followed by another brief exchange of pleasantries, Jeremiah takes the trunk contents with him back to Atlanta for further scientific scrutiny.

After many months of research, he is able to discover the identity of the Libertad's captain. He also traces the lost ancestry and name of Friar Miguel from a manifest entry. By digging into buried achieves requested from Spain and Portugal, Wake is able to piece together a general history of the events that lead to a shipwreck off the Carolina coast.

In the year 1640, a Spanish Galleon, commanded by a native Basque seaman named Jacob Belasko, departs Central America loaded with a full cargo of gold. Harboring briefly in a Portugal port of Brazil, it boards a demon-possessed Inca Shaman Priest, and then sails up to the coast of North America, making a stop at the Spanish port of La Florida Mission. Here a Franciscan Friar named Miguel comes aboard officially representing a displaced company of fifteen Indians, described by Captain Belasko, as having strange characteristics uncommon to the indigenous populations. After departing Florida, the Libertad caught in a storm and subsequently stranded in the Sargasso Sea of the Bermuda Triangle. During this time, there are threats of mutiny spurred on by the First Mate challenging the Captain's maritime authority. The situation becomes even more precarious, when Belasko orders half the gold cargo dumped overboard in order to lighten the ship.

"Were it not for fear of my two pistols given to me by my father, I think the day of my command would have been lost to these Spaniards, whose courage rest in their bellies! I look forward to the day when the Basque free from tyranny that breeds men such as these!" Captain Belasko writes in his personal log following the incident.

After many tense days, another storm frees the Libertad. Because of the storms intensity and because of a damaged rudder, the Captain makes the decision to run the ship aground. All the crew abandons ship, except for three sailors, Captain Belasko, Friar Miguel, and the fifteen Indians, consisting of three men and twelve women.

Also joining the roster of survivors is the formerly possessed South American Shaman. In a previous personal entry, Jacob Belasko skeptically describes in some detail a secondhand account of an exorcism that takes place prior to the storm that frees the imprisoned Libertad from the Sargasso Sea. By an act of bold faith, Friar Miguel faces the demon with only a cross and his Latin Bible. The giant from the Amazonian jungles changes from a wild beast to a man restored to his right mind, now peaceful and benevolent, freed from spiritual bondage. Captain Belasko records the event *"supernatural"* and altogether *"miraculous,"* as he personally struggles to reconcile this occurrence with the pragmatism of his experience.

These twenty-one souls manage to make it ashore using wreckage from the ship as it breaks apart. The three sailors have salvaged a bag of gold each, which they secure inside wooden water barrels prior to the exodus. The survivors trek inland, hoping to find a more commodious location. Because of his unique knowledge of swampland, the South American eventually appointed guide to the exhausted party. Following the extraordinary rescue of an Indian woman, and subsequent events, the native group bestows upon the strange giant from another continent the title of *Xeantee Aconee.* This again is particularly perplexing to the sensible mind of Captain Belasko, but even he starts referring to him as the Xeantee Aconee in his future journal entries.

Upon discovering an island of dry land surrounded in the heart of a swamp, the Indians decide to stay and make this place their new home. However, not all wish to remain here. The three sailors want to find a European settlement, where their salvaged gold will mean something. Friar Miguel simply wants to go home. Captain Belasko is now in love with an Indian woman named Amadahy, and no longer plans a return to Europe.

Nevertheless, he is compelled to accompany the Friar and remaining crew beyond the perils of this swamp. The one referred to as Xeantee Aconee accepts to guide them through the dangerous terrain. The decision to leave the love he has found particularly difficult for Captain Belasko.

"I see in the eyes of Amadahy that she does not want me to go. Tonight she calls me Emanuel, name given by my Jewish mother." The Captain writes in his journal on eve prior to the excursion. *"She says that my name, like our love, means a word in her language she calls 'Shelecheyanu'. The sound awakens within me something spiritual, a word somehow familiar, a word once I knew from long ago. So many things awakened by this native woman. If only I might remember. These Indians are an unusual lot, like no Indian I have ever seen. According to Miguel, ancestors of these people once had intimate contact with a group referred to as the 'Dragon Clan. He thinks these were early Vikings, which would explain the color of their hair and eyes. I, too, must agree their general appearance in some ways similar to those encountered in the northern straits near Terranova. Maybe Amadahy is right to be apprehensive. But for me to fail in my responsibility to men still under my charge would remain a stain on my conscience and bring shame to the memory of my father. If at all possible I must see to it that they reach a trail of solid ground."*

The remaining log entries are more pragmatic, describing building tensions, mostly having to do with the First Mate, a man named Luis-Fernando. Along the way, one of the sailors lost, bitten by a giant Water Moccasin that only adds greater anticipation to the expedition. The last record tells of the remaining five reaching banks of a raging river below an inaccessible canyon.

Animosity between the First Mate and Captain Belasko only intensifies. Miguel has taken ill, his feverish body placed into a quartz chamber along with the three bags of gold coins. Jacob makes his final notation referencing his personal struggle of faith in a God he does not know, secretly envying apparent peace of the South American and Friar Miguel. Here the entries abruptly end.

Jeremiah can only presume the continuation of an untold story. At least some of the mystery reasonably solved. He now knows that Jacob Belasko has maternal Jewish ancestry, his mother giving him the surname Jacob Emmanuel. This explains in part the origin of the Hebrew scroll. Because of the religious climate at the time, it stands to reason why he would omit the name Emmanuel in his official capacity. Nor are there any collaborative references contained in the nautical registries retrieved from European archives. It is only vaguely clear how the Ship's Log and the Latin Bible manage somehow to survive whatever happened to the expedition.

The linguistic root of the word *Shelecheyanu* presents particular challenge, a variant unlike any found among the indigenous populations inhabiting the continents of South and North America. This will require greater future examination.

An even more perplexing question in Jeremiah's mind is how did Nela's early ancestor come in possession of these artifacts, especially a functional flintlock pistol belonging to Captain Belasko, nearly fourteen decades later? Somewhere there must be a missing forensic link.

After this meeting with the Smiths, Jeremiah returns to his native Atlanta, where he will devote years studying the artifacts now in his possession. Investing some free time and few resources into this European connection, he only scratches the surface of what really happened or why. Upon receiving tenor at the University of Georgia a few years after the death of his father, Jeremiah on occasion brings his anthropology students to the Liberty Basin for a day trip to search for clues along the dwindling Aconee River that runs through it. This once raging tributary now reduced to a trickle, because of ever increasing commercial demands taxed on the regional waters. Soon there is no water at all, only a dry riverbed.

Many new pieces of the puzzle only further confirm the ledger entries provided by the Captain of the Libertad. It is now certain that the Libertad shipwreck seeds a unique non-indigenous population sewn on a swamp island known today as the Liberty Peninsula. Yet nothing conclusive enough to qualify as concrete evidence of their cultural existence, or provide explanation of what happed to them.

Through persistent examination, Wake's prevailing theory is that one special individual in each generation anointed *"the one chosen"* in accordance to maternal ancestry, assigned task of safeguarding certain artifacts ritualistically important. Upon reaching maturity, this coronate chieftain must make holy pilgrimage to the shores of the *"Sacred River."* Upon completion of this rite of passage, the participant deposits among the unique white rocks particular to this region an engraved testimonial of that generation, along with fragments of another history seemingly even much older. Only Wake remains unclear as to the greater meaning within context.

When put together, the disjointed pieces construct a pictograph record of vagabond immigrants surviving many disasters and eventually finding refuge on an island through leadership of a revered Shaman. As Wake has already surmised, there is consistency of theme personifying an anthropomorphized protectorate armed with supernatural ability. However, through many constructed references, it becomes evident that this Messiah subservient to an even greater power. Although the physical records disjointed, recurring motifs remind Wake of the Biblical battles waged between angelic forces.

More disturbingly, this trained anthropologist begins to suspect there stronger indictment of Adam Pixley's involvement in the inscrutable disappearance of this historically unrecorded Indian tribe. This partly in relation to the trove of artifacts contained in the trunk of the Pixley Estate, but more it is just a gut feeling. Still, there is nothing here to suggest genocide. The evidence only forensically confirms there once an Indian tribe living on the Liberty Peninsula with more than a vague idea of their origin. The consuming question in Wake's analytical mind is what really happened to them, and why?

In all this time, Jeremiah Wake is unable to piece enough together to concretely resolve the mysterious disappearance of the lost Aconee tribe. Then one night, he hears an announcement that will resurrect the enigmatic Indian Rock.

It is a fall evening many years later, Jeremiah in his wood workshop participating in a new hobby. His wife has convinced him that he will need something to keep his active mind occupied after next year's impending retirement. He has discovered a passion for the wood he carves, the feel of the grain in his hands, each different, each with a unique touch that seems to blend into the fiber of his flesh, and mix with the eternal composition of his soul. It is as close as he can ever be to the embodiment of living history. If he had his life to make over, Jeremiah would choose to be a carpenter.

A late night radio talk show fills the emptiness with background noise. He rarely consciously listens, tonight being no different. Then he hears something about the Liberty Peninsula, so he sets aside his wood crafting tools to pay closer attention.

A man named Jasper Flynn makes the extraordinary claim that he has seen a living monster in the Liberty Basin north of the Georgia state line. What interests Wake most is the supporting statement made by a girl with him named Candy Morgan.

"I lived many years in Liberty at the feet of my daddy Pastor," Candy says with practiced sincerity. "The monster that Jasper describes is just like the one drawn on the Indian Rock in the cemetery. I think the monster has lived in Liberty Swamp long before the first white man ever set foot there."

The next day Jeremiah Wake calls the radio station and acquires the address of the two guest speakers.

"I-I am sorry to disturb you y-young lady," Jeremiah says hesitantly when the door opens.

"If you are here to see Jasper, he's still sleeping and don't want to be disturbed."

"I am actually looking for a Ms. C-Candy Morgan."

"I'm Candy, sugar," Candy replies in her own seductive way. "What can I possibly do for you?"

"Y-You– are you the girl on the radio station last night?"

"I surely am!"

It is not as much what she says, but the way she says it that makes the academic professor uncomfortable. Candy not much older than Wake's own daughter, when once she attended public school; except this girl wears too much makeup he thinks inappropriate to her age. Nevertheless, Jeremiah reminds himself that he is here on business, not to cast stones of judgment.

"I-I heard you say that you know the location of the I-Indian Rock in Liberty. I have been s--searching for that r-rock for as long as I can remember. W-Would you be able to tell me the pre-precise location?"

Candy hesitates, then again smiles sweetly.

"I can draw you a map if you give me five dollars. I can even tell you where Jasper saw the monster."

"That will not be n-necessary. Just a map to the location of the I-Indian Rock will be more than s-sufficient."

The negotiation complete, Jeremiah Wake returns to the Liberty Peninsula several months later and finds the rock just where Candy Morgan said it would be. After a few days taking pictures and deciphering the hieroglyphic meaning, Wake attempts to share some of his preliminary findings with a gruff bartender named Homer, acclaimed by all to be a local authority. This a puzzle of another kind altogether unsolvable, so Wake leaves in Homer's corpulent hand a copy of what he believes to be a translated keynote decipher of a canto he hopes will unlock the lost Indian language.

Without further waste of time, Wake returns to his faculty office at the university and begins the laborious task of assembling the anthropological conjunctions of meaning spanning scores of years. With this decipher key, he now has the necessary tools to make the Aconee language live again, spoken from the mouths of Aconee Indian ancestry.

As Wake has always suspected, and the evidence already shows, these are unquestionably the descendants of those fifteen Indians, passengers of a ship, which foundered on the Carolina shores in 1640.

Friar Miguel referred to as the *Holy One*, with power to cast out demons, becomes their self-appointed intercessor, making possible passage to the European continent aboard a Spanish Galleon bearing the ship registry Libertad. This fated voyage destined to fall victim to more than one maritime disaster.

After shipwreck of the Libertad, all fifteen of the Indians survive, referring to themselves as '*The Water Clan*'. The Captain and his crew described as the '*Out-Clan*', except for the South American, simple called the *Aconee*. In a later translation the name Aconee, changes to Xeantee Aconee. Within context, this seems more to express a title of elevation. Wake suspects the use transient to something else, only he is presently unable to discern logic of the connection.

The Captain of the Libertad becomes romantically involved with one of the Indian women named Amadahy, whose name translates, *"Soul of Water"*. She will later bare him a child, and call his name "Qualetaga-Tahmoh," interpreted as *"Angel of the Father,"* constructed with an unknown variant. Dialectically this name, like Aconee, also seems descriptive of a title or position, always expressed in the superlative. Jeremiah is never completely certain of this translation.

Aconee serves as guide to the small party of Europeans, leading them to banks of the Great River. Here a serpent of greed usurps its head, setting in motion a series of unfortunate events. All on the expedition perishes, all except for Aconee. Although receiving a deadly wound to the head by the serpent's sting, he miraculously survives.

Referred to here as *The Xeantee Aconee*, he returns to the tribe and reveals the final resting place of Friar Miguel, relating in detail how the Captain sacrifices his life by dragging the demon into the raging waters never to resurface. Amadahy is grief stricken by the news, because the one she calls her beloved Emmanuel fails to return as promised. Subsequent records repeat how *"Soul of Water"* continues to mourn this loss until the day her body received into the waiting arms of the swamp.

This Xeantee Aconee represented more in terms of a spiritual leader, than just the position of a tribal chief. He is an emissary sent by the Great Spirit to the *"Water Clan."* Jeremiah begins to understand the name Xeantee Aconee, when used alone can connote "*The Prince*," but can also mean simply "*the frog*" when applied with another variant of dialectical inflection. Again, he is less than certain of this translation. Nevertheless, after comparing all the text, Wake becomes convinced that when the two names used in conjunction with the word *Shelecheyanu*, it changes to the superlative, elevating the meaning to *"Salvation by Water'*.

Qualetaga-Tahmoh, son of the one named Emmanuel and of Amadahy, grows into manhood instructed at the feet of Xeantee Aconee. In the course of his life, Tahmoh makes several pilgrimages to the banks of the Great River to pay homage to his father and to the shrine of Friar

Miguel. It seems that in later generations, the name Tahmoh translates as a spiritually appointed title and position by design of *Shelecheyanu.*

As much as Wake can make out, this chieftain, often depicted as a larger than life presence covered under mantle of animal skins, stands armed, sometimes with a sling, sometimes holding a javelin spiked with three spearheads. Nearly always the raised cross of Friar Miguel held in the other hand, like a beacon of light extended toward heaven.

This coronate Tahmoh must journey at least once in a lifetime to shores of the *Sacred River* and deposit continued testament to the Xeantee Aconee among the white river stones, a record spanning more than a century before ending abruptly.

Wake is now certain without a doubt that some of these chronologies express events, which happened in an even more ancient past. In these series appear references to a large oblong square lodge with an open door resting diagonally on side of a mountain. In some stands the larger than life figure of a man holding a staff toward a radiant sun. Another shows the same structure surrounded by a variety of animals herding together.

Another series depicts hunting parties, armed with spears and draped in animal skins, following giant migrating Bison through frozen tundra.

If Jeremiah's suppositions correct, these pictographs produce strong evidence of the ***Bearing Land Theory*** predicted by Fray Jose Acosta, Spanish Missionary, who proposed that all mankind and animals seeded from the European Continent. It seems to Jeremiah that these Aconee Indians retained historical witness of this event, perhaps passed down through oral tradition. Organizing the pictograph drawings into a template, a gradual topographical change occurs, becoming free-flowing rivers, lakes, and tree-covered mountains. Remarkably, the superficial appearance of the people changes little, suggesting that this migration period brief in terms of anthropological and geological time. The suggestive meaning of this quandary continues to rage even now among earth theorist.

Later images describe contact with fierce invaders called the "*Dragon Clan,*" resulting in a truce and interaction of peace. This is no doubt when the Vikings arrive and intermarry with the natives, as reasoned by Friar Miguel.

Although Jeremiah has never considered himself particularly religious, he has begun in later years to discover a spiritual value to present being, thanks in part to these enigmatic records left behind by a lost tribe. Wake will continue to struggle for decades deciphering the greater significance of these meanings. What does become clear at the time is another repetitive theme illustrating a constant struggle between principalities of light and darkness.

In the simple Aconee way of thinking, there are many spirits occupying positions in the physical and non-physical world. These create the spectrum of differences in human nature, properly classified as the *"soul"* of each individual. However, in course this soul energy presented with a directional choice, which ultimately determines an eternal condition.

It is through this interpretation that Jeremiah Wake begins to comprehend more fully the meaning of *Shelecheyanu.* In nearly all contexts, the word *Shelecheyanu* is a life force that properly translates as *"Spiritual Blessing"* or *"Gift from Above."* Something either is in *Shelecheyanu,* or is not. Put more simply, the elevated concept of *Shelecheyanu* infused with more than normative interpretation. Rather, it represents value of an ascribed state, dividing things alive from things not alive. However, in transient usage *Shelecheyanu* literally means continuity, or "*Everlasting Life*"; whereas, anything not in *Shelecheyanu, defined as* inert, or *"Everlasting Death."*

The real breakthrough for the Professor of language is the prophetic narrative expressed by Qualetaga-Tahmoh made in his later years etched onto the backside of the white ceremonial rock with the shallow basin discovered in Liberty cemetery.

On this boulder of unusual geology, character symbols of a coded written testament made in the future tense. It is this prophecy that provides Wake with the linguistic key to unlock both the language, as well as to fill-in many of the missing congregations. Even though this narrative constructed with a similar vernacular, it describes an apocalyptic future. Using this, in conjunction with other sources, Wake begins to piece together a meaning that has evaded him since so many years.

Here depiction of a bird-like creature that falls from the sky (*Wake believes this to be an Eagle)*. This fallen Eagle allowed presence and position, becoming a peaceful member of the tribe. Then something happens and this "*Wingless One*," which also can translate as a "*Fallen Seraph*," commits the worse kind of betrayal by murdering the heir apparent that ultimately leads to apocalyptic genocide. This singular obscure canto left on the backside of a ceremonial rock supportive of inflective meanings also referenced elsewhere. It supplies graphic detail to a future resurrection, following the destruction of a monumental effigy described as the "*White Face*" suspended over a valley.

Although the meaning within context not completely clear at the time, it provides enough information to allow Jeremiah to use it as a cipher tool proving that an Indian tribe called Aconee once inhabited and thrived on the Liberty Peninsula. There is further evidence that genocide did happen here, but still without confession or enough physical proof. Nevertheless, this information Jeremiah

Wake freely shares with Liberty's gruff bartender for the benefit of all. The enigmatic Indian Rock once again lost among headstones. At the time, not even Jeremiah fully comprehends the ultimate meaning of the prophetic judgment yet to come.

All this and more Jeremiah Wake is able to discern after paying Candy Morgan five dollars for a map to the Indian Rock camouflaged in the Liberty Cemetery before the waters flooded the region after announcement of the Aconee Dam Project. One thing Candy says to him before closing the door leaves Wake particularly perplexed.

"He is coming back!" She says with eyes wide open. "The frog will change into a Prince, joined by his Lady, and stand upon the footstool of the world forever. That is what unconditional love means, Mr. Wake. It means to keep a promise always!"

This is the last time Jeremiah Wake speaks with Candy Morgan, daughter of Preacher Morgan, minister of the Liberty First Baptist Church. No one else in Liberty at the time having even the slightest interest to know their days already numbered.

Much of the mystery now solved, except for the ominous reference carved into the Alligator talisman, concerning the one called *"Angeni-Cuauhtemoc."* Jeremiah is reasonably sure he understands this to mean literally *"Angel of Fallen Eagle,"* but cannot determine the greater significance of its meaning.

Chapter 35

Epilogue of Jeremiah Wake

It is Dave Tracy, who finally helps Jeremiah Wake fit in place the last piece. Tracy is a patriot to the region, a man born and raised on the Liberty Peninsula with roots going back generations. He was here before any talk about the future dam project and subsequent drowning of the Liberty Basin. For some reason he returns after the resurrection and is again a permanent resident.

Wake meets Dave many years after the scandal of corruption and forced demolition of the second most expensive nuclear project in the state. There is another facility approximately a hundred and fifty miles southeast near the Georgia border, financed by Duke Energy and advertised to provide cheap electricity to the region. Christened the Oconee Nuclear Station, located near Seneca South Carolina on Lake Keowee, it represents a modern marvel of turbine-powered infrastructure.

The failed Piedmont District Project has since acquired the notoriety of being an economic disaster propagated by greed in high places. Many nefarious deals made involving a corrupt state politician, a local preacher, and a lawyer representing investment assets of the wealthy Pixley Estate. Without any living estate heirs to prosecute, both the lawyer and the preacher now dead, the state tries to launch an investigation into the business activities of the state governor. This like opening a can of intertwining worms climbing up the food chain all the way to Washington. The motion squashed under mountains of contradictory testimonies and conflicting paperwork.

Dave is well in his forties by now, looking older than his years, which makes Wake feel ancient in comparison.

Although born with less opportunity and with little formal education, Jeremiah cannot help but admire the raw exuberance of the man that meets him at the Pixley Train Station. Maybe because Dave is an ex-Marine Corps Veteran, or because of the claim that he no longer drinks alcohol after experiencing some personal epiphany, Wake feels a rare kinship, not easily defined by words.

Dave Tracy moved back to the Liberty Peninsula after the waters subside and return to their normal course. He now lives with another Vietnam War Veteran named Bubba Baily. This Baily fellow is badly disfigured, rarely saying anything coherent, usually just ramblings about 'gooks', about mosquitoes, and killing frogs. Often he speaks the name Weistbaily, in context of someone he refers to as a *Prince of Frogs*. But Dave knows how to handle him. They are, after all, survivors of the same war-- and that has to count for something!

Dave tells Wake how he watched the reservoir drain from the shores of the Piedmont Plateau. First to rise out of the depths, appears the intact two smoke stacks of Liberty Mill, then lower steeple roof of the Liberty Baptist Church, absent of the bell tower. Last to emerge are catacomb walls of the Cotton Mill, along with skeletal ribs of what was once a town, like exhumed foundations of a lost civilization.

It takes a full year after the controlled demolition for everything to dry up and for seeds of life to break through the earth and thrive as before. Dave and Bubba are unofficially the first to return, taking occupancy in the gutted church basement.

"I first heard about you from this." Dave retrieves from his shirt pocket a piece of paper stained with old gin. "I'm not much of a reader, but what you wrote there made me think about many things. Made me realize that there is a lot of history right here in Liberty I never knew anything about."

"Yes, Mr. Tracy, I remember very well the day I gave this to a bartender named Homer. Then I though it likely that he would just throw it away. I'm glad to see that I was wrong. At the time I did not understand the full meaning of the curse."

"You weren't that wrong, Mr. Wake. I found it corked inside one of Homer's whisky bottles. I doubt anyone else ever saw it. Homer was just that way when it came to secrets. He always kept them in places secret to him."

Dave never could shake the feeling that old Homer still walks the earth. Just something about that man will always remain immortal.

"That was all such a long time ago, Mr. Tracy. However, in the life of archaeology, even a thousand years only a blink of the eye. The Indian Rock was the most important find of all. It provided me with the decipher key I needed to understand inflective meaning to the Aconee language. That is how I was able to unlock the prophecy. I have published many more details on the subject if ever you wish to read them."

"Thank you, Mr. Wake; maybe I will and maybe I won't. The day I found that bottle floating in the water near the base of the dam I knew. It all became so clear. The red dye bleeding through the cracks the way it did. I knew then it was retribution. But also, Mr. Wake, on that day I accepted forgiveness. Of course, I didn't know about the rest, until I heard you on the news down at the VA Hospital. Now I think I understand a lot more. All I know for sure is that day I found peace with God."

"I am glad to know at least one person truly appreciates my efforts." Wake says, passing back the shriveled paper. "But I am sure you did not call me here just to show me this."

"I also found something in the ruins of the Smith house."

Dave hands Wake a waterproof box containing pages of a diary and a charred turquoise piece of jewelry. He will leave out the part about also finding a few pieces of gold doubloons. These he keeps safely hidden for him and Bubba in preparation of a future rainy day. If the Vietnam War taught him anything, it is to take care of yourself-- because no one else will give a damn!

"It's hard to believe that nothing survived. Her house was so grand and eloquent to me when I was a boy. Now only the lower part of the chimney left– this where I found these in a box hidden behind one of the loose rocks."

Wake immediately recognizes this to be the same costume ornament worn by Nela the day he first met the newlywed couple at the Pixley Estate those many years earlier. Still considering the trinket of little value because of damaged appearance, he pays it little interest.

"You mean the old rich woman that owned a good portion of the land sold to the state at inflated prices before official announcement of the Aconee Dam Project?"

"I knew Nela Smith personally." Dave corrects. "She would not have had anything to do with that kind of corruption. I just feel in my heart that she was innocent. You know she died over a year before the official announcement came down about the water redirection?"

"No, I did not know. Still, the transactions all made in the name of her estate holdings. She surely must have known something about what was going on."

Dave only shrugs his shoulders impartial to the accepted records. What was the point of arguing those facts now? Nela, like everyone else in Liberty, gone since many years- - all now only ghost in his mind. Only walking spirits and unkempt graves resurrected testament of what really happened here.

"The diary is written in longhand, which I find hard to read, but clearly signed Adam Pixley. Something about him being a British soldier and living with Indians... and something he writes about his brother. I'm sure that with your experience, you will be able to better make it out."

"Thank you, Mr. Tracy. I will endeavor to do so. If you like, I can send you a translation describing in detail the beliefs and spiritual practices of the local Aconee Indians that once flourished here. It is time everyone knows the truth about this lost tribe."

"Don't bother. Bubba and me know all we need to know about the past. Some things better left dead and buried. As for truth, it's all relative. Men live and die-- there is no truth greater in the here and now. Also, everyone around here just calls me Dave. I'm not college educated like you, and somehow mister just sounds too formal."

"Of course Dave… as concerning the artifacts, I am certain the museum in Atlanta will gladly pay you for them."

"Again no, Mr. Wake, these things never belonged to me. To accept money would just make me feel like a grave robber. Mrs. Smith was a good lady no matter what her family did or what people say."

Jeremiah Wake thanks Dave Tracy and returns to Atlanta. At last, he holds in his hands the final piece to the linguistic riddle. He spends two full weeks, laboring day and night over the handwritten diary composed by a man unlearned in good penmanship. It is a record obviously made in later years of Adam Pixley's life, more of a confession, than anything meant for historical prosperity. It is personal admission of mass murder spoken from the grave.

Adam Pixley, a man born and raised in the Irish countryside, joins the ranks of the British Imperial Army and later dispatched to the New America to fight against the Colonist. He tells how his entire platoon massacred in an ambush. Briefly knocked unconscious by a bullet graze to the head, only he escapes, deserting into a nearby swamp. Adam would have surely died of exposure in this hostile region were not for some terrible apparition, which he calls the *Prince of Xeantee*, a grotesque giant that lifts him out of a bog pit and carries him to safety. After this miracle, a local tribe of Indians calling themselves Aconee, nurse him back to health, eventually accepting him as one of their own. He befriends one particular Indian named Tahmoh, who he calls Jack. Jack also becomes in his mind the brother with whom he never bonded.

Adam will marry an Indian woman, and together they conceive a child. The man might have remained content had his wife not taken ill and die. He becomes bitter, rejecting the peace he has found among these Indians. He begins to hate Jack, who he is convinced somehow responsible for his lost happiness. Mostly, he begins to hate the existence of his only son that reminds Adam continuously the face of his dead wife. Driven mad with paranoia, he begins hearing voices. These voices speak to him through a Spanish coin found those many years earlier during his original trek in this lost swamp region. Finally, he discovers way of escape from the isolated island he now refers to as his prison.

Early one morning Adam stealthily follows his Indian friend, one familiar with the ways of the swamp, through a maze of marshland. He has already stolen certain preserved relics from the other man's tent that the Aconee regard as spiritual talismans. Adam stalks Jack to the banks of a raging river and sees him enter into a cave hidden behind a waterfall, then reemerge holding a silver object. Once he believes the Indian gone, he enters the cave himself. Here Adam Pixley becomes possessed, discovering inside mounds of Spanish gold doubloons glittering upon the floor of this strangely lit chamber. He also finds what he thinks is a pirate's pistol, suited to a recovered lead ball he saw fall out of Jack's pouch months earlier. Upon stepping outside to test his new weapon, he faces his Indian brother waiting for him.

Adam laments how he regrets killing Tahmoh. Describes in detail how he desecrates the body, and how demonic ghost torment him that first night alone in the cave. The demons continue to haunt him, refusing to allow his soul peace for the rest of his days.

Taking as much gold as he can carry, Adam hikes into the Carolina highlands. Less than a day's journey, he finds a colonial settlement and joins himself to the local population. They readily accept their eccentric new citizen and the golden coins he spends. Adam Pixley is in their minds, a man of the frontier and a *"gentleman of wealth"* sent by providence to enrich their lives.

Scores of months later, Adam Pixley will return to the newly christened Liberty Swamp with a band of paid henchmen and a few Mohawk warriors, ordering massacre of the Indian inhabitants. He demands the scalp of every child, unsatisfied until presented one particular skin with long Viking red hair. Convinced that this trophy the hair of his first begotten Indian son, Adam Pixley believes all past sins buried. He later lays claim to a parcel of land at the edge of a cliff overlooking the Aconee River Valley and miles of swampland beyond. Here he will build the prominent fortress of his famous estate.

The last page of the diary is torn-out, as though something written here someone else does not want published. Nevertheless, Wake thinks that along with other sources of collaborating records, he has enough information to finish the tale.

Adam Pixley purchases all the land from beyond the river canyon to the end of the Liberty Peninsula, which includes the cave where he found the gold fortune located just below his mansion dwelling. It is his belief that the quartz crystal of this place able to ward off the demons of his nightmares. According to many accounts, he waited through the long years for the monster of Xeantee to come. When finally death comes, it is a thief in the night.

In accordance to his instructions, Adam Pixley buried in a prepared mausoleum on the Liberty Peninsula with this inscription chiseled into the stone face: *"Until The King Shall Come."*

A town will spring up named Pixley in his honor, as his heirs continue to flourish richly into golden ages from his pirated prosperity. The barons of the Pixley Family Estate destined to reign supreme from generation to generation, through slavery and emancipation, through wars and rumors of war, remaining rich even during the days of the Great Depression. As with all royal dynasties, they begin to dwindle in numbers over time. Some commit suicide, some become fruitless, and others simply drift away, never to return.

The last Pixley recorded in the official documents is a woman named Nela, wife to the good Doctor William Smith. This the woman Jeremiah met those many years ago, before she donated her grand estate to the county as a heritage museum. Many say all that happened in this part of the state mostly her fault. At least the Pixley name is easiest to blame. It is common knowledge that all rich folk the same in the end. Always the moneychangers are eager for new opportunity to increase their personal fortunes, regardless of cost to others.

After a lifetime of research, Jeremiah Wake now believes he sees the complete picture. Not that it will make any difference to the past; but another piece fit into the ever-changing collage of the present world puzzle. Wake sends a sample of the scalp with red hair to a new DNA testing lab in Virginia. A month later, the report comes back revealing that the donor female with recombinant markers of Scandinavian, indigenous people of North America, and populations inhabiting regions of the Southern Levant in the Middle East. Even Wake almost misses magnitude of the revelation.

This same DNA evidence reveals something else even less expected. Later samples obtained from the local inhabitants living around the vicinity of the resurrected region, reveals unmistakable genetic markers. The first sample taken from the badly decomposed head of a male found in the Liberty Swamp tied into a bundle of cotton tissue consistent with clothing worn by mill workers, along with the rusted blade of a Bowie Knife. Although predominately Mohawk, this man's DNA also contains helixes of genome code found exclusively in the unique Aconee Indian samples already on record, thanks to the documented efforts of cultural historian Jeremiah Wake.

This discovery further prompts Wake to set out on a personal campaign to gather as many DNA samples as possible from willing donors. Sometimes voluntary, often requiring discreet offer of a small financial incentive, generations of DNA samples acquired for purposes of scientific research. He finds that nearly all the original inhabitants contain recessive recombinants consistent with the dead Aconee.

Although, Candy Morgan, wife of an evangelical preacher, has passed on while giving birth to a third child, her husband kindly provides Wake with strands from her hairbrush. Even more interesting, a later sample acquired from Dave Tracy reveals that he and Candy share gene sequences consistent with siblings, although many generations removed.

Wake never obtained any of old Homer's DNA, which is not surprising, since this gruff bartender remains in his mind an enigma of unparalleled genesis. By this accumulated evidence, it becomes clear that the unique Aconee tribe never lost after all, but has managed to survive dormant for nearly two centuries.

Davy only exhales deeply upon hearing the news of Candy's death. Just another gravestone in his past, just another memory buried and better forgotten. Jeremiah will never see Dave Tracy after this, deciding that the dead must bury their dead, each in their own way at the end.

Without really knowing why, Jeremiah turns his attention again to Nela Smith's charred piece of costume jewelry charitably given to him by Dave Tracy. Cleaning away years of accumulated grime, he discovers the pendant not a fake after all!

This is without doubt a *Scarabaeus saucer* originating from ancient Egypt. The turquoise blue color, not paint, as Jeremiah originally suspected; rather a basalt quartz mineral composition made by a heat-infusion process called *Faience* to imitate real turquoise typically worn by wealthy class citizens when Egyptian society still flourished at its peak roughly around 1200 BCE.

Modeled after the dung beetle, the scarab represented to the general population symbol of rebirth and afterlife protection in connection with the sun god *Khepri*. Although common then, few have survived through history. Nor is this one just an amulet. Someone has used the scarab face of a stone amulet to create a locket composed of brass and copper.

Because of exposure to intense heat, the metal has fused and melted together, making the case appear impenetrable. Wake driven by more than just curiosity, spends several days meticulously cutting and prying open the locket. His efforts at last rewarded with the two halves separating. What he finds is stunning revelation, further adding complexity to many mysteries.

Reexamination of his many notes made through the years, Wake realizes that this locket also fits description of the heirloom given to Captain Belasko by his mother, which he in turn passes on to his Indian wife Amadahy the morning of his departure never to return. If his suspicions prove right, this could contain forensic evidence of vast importance.

Inside is a preserved strand of coarse black hair. Engraved on the inner lid are ancient Hebrew letters of *Masoretic* text. These letters spell the word *Shekhinah, which* means *"presence of God in the world"*.

Comparing the DNA of these hairs to those of the recovered skull stolen from the Atlanta Forensics lab and later found in Homer's Bar, the match is irrefutable. This means that the late Doctor Smith, husband to Nela Pixley, actually of Basque, Ashkenazi Jew, and North American Indian ancestry. More specifically William Smith is a direct bloodline descendent of Jacob Emmauel Belasko and Amadahy.

Most importantly, this finding provides validity to claim made by many Rabbi Scholars that certain genealogies trace back to the Biblical patriarch Abraham. According to scripture, Abraham sired Isaac, and from Isaac came Jacob, renamed Israel (father of the twelve tribes of Israel). Thanks to Joseph, a brother rejected, these twelve tribes dwelled in Egypt for 400 years, until Moses raised-up by the hand of God to lead these Israelites to a promised land.

Wake conjectures that this particular scarab accompanied one of the children of Israel during the Exodus. In later Hebrew religious practice, the winged scarabs become symbol of strength and greatness of *Yahweh* over other Israelite deities such as the Assyrian *Baal*. As for the word *Shekhinah,* Jeremiah will reserve for linguistic comparison only at the end.

Many of the anthropological facts unearthed during his years of painstaking research, makes Jeremiah begin to doubt unquestionable theories of scientific and historical acceptance. Revelations discovered quite by accident, destined to create ripples of dissension throughout the intellectual, as well as religious communities.

Suggestion of ideas so radical in implication, the world of academia turns upside down and ultimately threatens Wake's professional credibility. Theories considered outlandish-- even labeled ridiculous-- by daring to challenge the institutional acceptance of *Uniformitarian* logic and theological beliefs.

One evening while sitting in his study, Wake accidentally spills coffee on some of his notes, including a black and white picture taken of the Indian Rock in the Old Liberty Cemetery. Hanging the picture on the shade of his Tiffany desk lamp, he sees something never noticed before. Shape of the flat surface of the rock resembles a landscape. Not just any topography, but a survey map of the Liberty Peninsula before construction of a connecting bridge, when it was still considered a swamp-island. Wake knows this because he has done extensive historical research of the Liberty Basin area since evacuation of the floodwaters that drowned the area. But this is not all. Something about the shape of both the island and the rock face familiar.

Racing to his library, the Professor of Archeology retrieves a translated book written by German meteorologist, Alfred Wegener, titled *The Origin of Continents and Oceans.* In this volume, Wegener postulates that once the earth a vast super-continent, he calls *"Pangea,"* which in translation means *"all lands."* His famous *"continental drift"* theory proposes that because of some cataclysm in the distant past, this super-continent fragmented into drifting plates that have been moving apart ever since. Turning hastily to a page containing a postulated map of the original *Pangea* landmass, Wake compares it to the flat surface on the Indian Rock. The similarity is striking!

Quickly searching his documented materials, Jeremiah pulls from his notes another photo of a pictograph taken years earlier during an excavation field trip with his students to the nearly dry Aconee riverbed. Here again is the same geological shape, except that on this map rests a rectangular structure surrounded by several triangular pyramids.

Using the Indian Rock as a template, Wake surmises that, except for difference in scale, the geophysical similarity between the pictograph drawing, surface area of the Indian Rock, and the Liberty Island almost identical. Even more astounding, the cartography of all three corresponds to Wegener's theoretical mapped area of *Pangea*. More must be in play here than mere coincidence!

Retrieval of the talisman found by his father, Jeremiah further confirms that it, too, has the same distinctive shape. How could these Indians have acquired insight to principals profoundly debated by contemporary science as only controversial theoretical possibility? Is it conceivable that they retain genetic reference to collective cultural memories denied through present comprehension?

This new evidence suggests that these Aconee Indians spring from roots going back to the genesis of human existence, bearing integral witness of prehistory events found fragmented in nearly every world culture, and specifically mentioned in Biblical text considered myth in the minds of many.

Taking this astounding revelation into account, Wake begins to suspect more going on here than just mere diary entries of tribal generations, or cultural cross-contamination by early Viking explorers, as he had first thought. Some of the narratives relate definitely to events of a historical record even much older than the Vikings. Motifs describing a global deluge repeated in annuals of folklore found throughout many regions of the earth.

Wake begins to comprehend a context of greater meaning to the seemingly simple representations engraved on associated rocks that shows several varieties of beast herding passively together into a valley. Often in the distance stands a figure at the mouth of a large rectangular vessel. On one boulder, the same vessel from a different angle resembling an oblong box gripped in the midst of stormy elements. Then another pictograph is again this same vessel floating solitary upon a calm sea, distinctive arch of a rainbow overhead. Last of the series shows the craft on a landmass with what appears to be a bird flying above it with a tree leaf in its mouth.

This is an impeccable narrative of Noah's Ark preserved by a North American Indian tribe for hundreds of centuries before the first foreigners stepped foot on their shores!

The more often Jeremiah studies these images, he begins to realize that mixed within the jumble of generational records detailing localized events, lie submerged elements of a more profound story. These latent memories reaching very far back into time, describes conditions of the human experience even before the Ark of Noah. Wake had always dismissed symbol of two-dimensional pyramids to be inconsequential to the value of his research, even though they appear often.

It is only after the drowning and subsequent resurrection of the Liberty Peninsula that he returns to the old Aconee riverbed. Now water flows freely through the channel, restoring the tributary to its former size and strength. Wake follows the course to the mouth of Devils Jaw, where the tooth of an outcropping rock formation divides the waterfall. Here he sees something not recognized before, even though he has hiked here often alone, sometimes with his students when he taught at the university. But never has he seen this geology restored with the wash of water.

Plainly visible upon the tooth appears the distinctive proportional vertex of a tetrahedron, with a radiating quartz aperture suspended above the peak. Having recently finished a marathon of personal investigation into symbolic meaning of "*Eye of Providence*" and its links to the secret occultist society of Free Masonry, Wake is astonished how similar this representation in comparison to so many others stitched within fabric of the earth's chronology.

Gathered from several current data sources, ranging from anthropological reconstructions using 3-D satellite technology to modern theoretical Quantum Mechanics, Wake has surmised that the many fragmented records accumulated from archives of the distant past describe a *Terra firma* very different from the present conclusions of Uniformitarian Science.

There is much corresponding proof that the astronomical position and design of the numerous ancient tetrahedron structures discovered in different quadrants of planet earth represent potential sources of power helixes capable of amplifying indefinable energy signatures from a region of space within space, termed *"subspace."* There is even suggestion that they could potentially be transmission beacons corresponding to mega forces, which construct sympathetic resonances on a vast scale.

This would redefine everything humankind thinks to know about governing principals believed deterministic quadrants of organized mathematical models to describe time and space. Even the slightest alteration on the sub-molecular level would potentially change the fabric of everything, equivalent to a drop of water disturbing the surface tension of a still lake, or the flap of a butterfly wing in motionless air.

In other words, concept of reality more a baseline interpretation, conditional to static observation of non-static quantum forces organizing existing structures through atomic excitation. A concept far too revolutionary, considered outlandishly theoretical for any serious acceptance.

All along, these Aconee Indians have been referencing genesis of antediluvian and post-diluvium earth, where spiritual positions, although abstract in substance, describe conditions of motive force. A time when angelic beings moved openly among humankind in physical form, imbued with power to corrupt the mortal soul through unbridled passion, thus creating an alliance of rebellion against the God of creation. A rebellion so determined, that it brought about the geologic disaster known as the *Great Flood of Noah*, described in the Book of Genesis, and verified through other text found in roots of nearly every human society.

To these Aconee sign of the pyramid, not a burial chamber to enshrine remains of mortal internment, but evidence of dormant genetic memories to describe process of channeled energy through a focal point aperture that connects many unseen warring spiritual principalities.

This connection intended to create a portal of translation from eternal potential to temporal position, making possible manifestation in physical form. The tetrahedron geometry of this particular structure designed with capacity to amplify unquantifiable raw force through a matrix, which ultimately manifests into a directive of choice defined as good or evil, deterministic by source code of inception.

Through a medium, they call *Xeantee Aconee Shelecheyanu,* a reunification occurs, instantly transforming dissociated energy on the subatomic level, thus rewriting or reversing a corrupted code that modern science refers to as entropy.

While going through accumulated volumes of linguistic dictionaries, Jeremiah runs across yet another tantalizing element of contention, which will provide unanticipated answers to several questions.

The Hebrew word "*Shehecheyanu*," found in the Talmud, has the meaning, "*extol of blessing or thankfulness for everything.*" It cannot be accident that the word and interpretive value so similar to the Indian expression *Shelecheyanu.* Is it possible that distant ancestry of these North American Indians originates from the so-called *Lost Tribes of Israel?* Or perhaps the Lost Tribes are metaphor of something else that happened in a prehistoric world, signifying cosmic events radically changing heaven and earth. A word that describes beginning and end of angelic battles raged in a celestial arena, with post-diluvium human history only the entropic conclusion of that war. To the survivors, *Shelecheyanu* represents reprieve or stay of execution by measure of benevolent mercy. In its simplest translation, *Shelecheyanu* means *'spared by grace'*.

In support of this potential link is archaic use of the word *Shekhinah* engraved inside the locket given to Jacob Emmauel Belasko by his mother. By base interpretation, *Shekhinah* expresses intercession between spiritual and mortal condition. In effect, it represents mediation by one sent on divine mission.

To the professor of linguistics, and renowned cultural expert, this sounds very much like the prophecy of Messiah found in the Judaic Book of the Prophets and New Testament accounts of the resurrected Christ. Yet, how can such a radical idea find acceptance of proof in the rational arena of academia?

This, too, will remain theory only, but enough corresponding evidence to create reasonable doubt in the minds of present, as well as future forensic archeologists, such as himself.

Gazing into the darkness of the Georgia wetlands that touches the perimeter of his Atlanta home, Jeremiah thinks about his father, a simple man who just wanted to know. He thinks about the future of his children and grandchildren, whose destinies already designed through Jeremiah's own past.

He thinks about Candy Morgan, a girl lovely, as a wounded Seraph remaining faithful to the end that one day a prince would save her. He thinks about Dave Tracy made bitter by truth discovered too late; and about Bubba Baily, who never had a chance to believe through his own experience. He thinks about a bartender that waited through many years like a ferryman promising forgetfulness to all entering his establishment. Only to be forgotten in the end. Most of all, Jeremiah Wake thinks about one *Xeantee Aconee*, who Bubba calls *Weistbaily*, a name to live forever in heaven eternal.

Even as he closes his journal, Wake cannot help but question if the epic of Liberty can ever truly rest. He knows there will always be those that will say somewhere hidden deep in the Liberty Swamp is a pirate's chest filled with gold coins. A place known only to Adam Pixley, a place haunted by demons and living monsters, a place of ancient curse.

In this solitary location remains the gold of the gods, once custody of the Aztecs, the Mayans, and the Incas. Pillaged treasure houses laced with hidden catacomb mazes designed within ancient pyramids made in worship to the sun and the moon. These desecrated idols of *fallen angels* with twisted images and tarnished crowns bestowed upon servile monarchs: all melted together into bright bullion.

Gold forged into shining coins stamped with the imperial crest of another empire already consumed by brightness so bright, as to blind spirits. It is the curse of Spanish gold first envisioned by Cortes in the grand halls of a foreign temple in presence of a ruling demon rising above every earthly principality.

This prize so greatly coveted by greedy Conquistadors and fortune hunters. Treasures from the New Americas trickling along the steppes of the Andes, through jungles ruled by evil force, and into even darker rivers flowing irresistibly, as molten blood into the bellies of Spanish Galleons that wait daily to transport unchained Mammon across the world's oceans. It is a trail of dazzling destruction spanning the burning ages of violent civilization reserved to final judgment. It is of this world, a fortune so great that a man may even sacrifice his eternal soul.

The last voyage of the Libertad gives final testament to an end and a beginning. A Portuguese Friar known only as Miguel, a South American Shaman Priest converted by power of the Holy Spirit, a Basque sea Captain, surnamed

Emmanuel by his Jewish mother, along with fifteen unique Indigenous folk of mixed genetics from a shrouded past again displaced by tragedy. All brought together through a shipwreck on the Carolina coast, sparking combination of unforeseeable events, ultimately leading to even greater tragedy, meant to inspire resurrection of greater promise.

However, is this testament any more tragic, when compared under the lens of progressive world history? Are not the innocent of this earth slaughtered daily out of existential necessity? Is there mortal difference between practical need and hungry illusion of desire? And is material gluttony the only balance against obsessive fear of the unknown?

Always promise of some better estate sanctified to things already dead, than provision for the thriving multitudes presently alive. Lavish crypts constructed to entomb bones of the wealthy, yet never enough resources to shelter those dispossessed. Perhaps, the term sacrifice the only true measure to define reverence toward God. For without sacrifice, can there be any definition of bounty, or hope beyond carnal satisfaction?

Jeremiah Wake has spent his entire life wanting to understand. Only now realizes he knows nothing, as once he thought. So much changed to shadows now... all shades from days past, making Jeremiah think of verses taken from the Holy Bible in the last chapter of the *First Book of Chronicles*.

After the siege and occupation of the Canaanite city *Jebus*, renamed *Jerusalem*, King David calls to order the Twelve Tribes of Israel in the twilight of his earthly reign. He knows his human course fulfilled, his youngest son Solomon heir apparent to the throne. Solomon will become one of the richest kings on earth, instructed to build the first Temple to enshrine the *Ark of Covenant*. This first covenant a shadow of Messiah to come, breaking down the middle partition between mortal substance and eternal promise.

David, a man of humble countenance in the sight of God, contritely bows his head with the congregation of Israel and extols blessing of thanksgiving to the Lord of providence.

"Both riches and honor come of thee, and thou reigns over all; and in your hand is power and might; and in your hand it is to make great, and to give strength unto all. Now therefore, our God, we thank thee, and praise thy glorious name. But who am I, and what is my people, that we should be able to offer so willingly after this sort? For all things come from you, and of your own have we given thee. For we are strangers before thee, and sojourners, as were all our fathers: our days on the earth are as a shadow, and there is none abiding."

"Yes, all made of shadow passing into shadows," the historian whispers to himself.

All things received in season from above, and nothing a man may inherit or declare as his own. In this final reflection, Jeremiah Wake turns out the light of his Study and sleeps, as do all men in the irresistible course of time.